Promise Me a Rainbow

FIVE STAR

Promise Me a Rainbow

CHERYL REAVIS

Five Star
Unity, Maine

Five Star Romance Series
Published in conjunction with Maureen Moran Agency.

November 1999

Five Star Standard Print Romance Series.

The text of this edition is unabridged.

Set in 11 pt. Plantin by Al Chase.

Printed in the United States on permanent paper.

Library of Congress Cataloging-in-Publication Data

Reavis, Cheryl.
    Promise me a rainbow / Cheryl Reavis.
        p.   cm.
    ISBN 0-7862-2200-X (hc : alk. paper)
    1. Large type books.   I. Title.
PS3568.E2695 P76   1999

99-41966

To Richard, for making me believe

Special acknowledgment to
Dr. Thomas F. Clark of Davidson, North Carolina,
creator of the real "Daisy and Eric"

1

Near Riverfront Park, Catherine Holben stopped to buy a gnome, telling herself that she merely wanted to get in out of the rain but also knowing that it was the sculpture in the window that drew her inside. She passed the shop every weekday afternoon on her way to the bus stop, and while she had often looked into the artfully cluttered window, until now she'd had no real inclination to buy.

According to the small hand-lettered sign that rested at her feet, the gnome was called Daisy, and it cradled a gnome-child named Eric against its breast. Gently smiling Daisy and almost sleeping Eric, amid the jumble of collectible Hummel figures and David Winter cottages and Emmett Kelly clowns. DAISY AND ERIC in a carefully executed calligraphy on the sign. And below that, the word RETIRED.

She stepped up to the door, reading the embellished goldleaf lettering on the glass: THE PURPLE BOX. And below that, CURIOS. The shop seemed to be empty, and she expected a bell over the door to jangle when she entered. Indeed there was a curling bracket for just such a bell above her head, but the bell itself was gone.

She took a moment to allow her eyes to grow accustomed to the dim light. She was wet with rain, and she was immediately enveloped by a wonderful texture of smells: bayberry candles and rose-petal potpourri; chocolate; and ancient, oiled wood flooring that squeaked when she walked on it. The place reminded her of something, and she frowned with the effort to remember. Something in her childhood, perhaps, because the display cases appeared to be the original ones, made of heavy wood-framed glass. It was difficult to tell precisely what line of merchandise the owner sold here; there was such a conglomeration of things. She could see crocheted lace collars and rows of silver spoons and brightly colored silk scarves in the display case nearest to her. And purses. Black and gold and silver-sequined evening bags. And for the most part the entire store was subtly lit by what looked like Tiffany-style lamps, each with a small white price tag dangling from the shade. She looked upward. Two overhead lights hung from the high ceiling, but they were too far away to be of much use to a browsing customer.

But she wasn't browsing; she knew exactly what she wanted and why she wanted it, for all of her rationalization about inclement weather. She looked around her for a clerk, hesitant to call out for someone who might be standing nearby in this shadowed Victorian attic of a place.

"Hello?" she said after a moment.

An elderly woman promptly came in from the back of the shop. "There you are," she said, as if she'd been expecting her. The woman wore rimless spectacles and a large amber brooch centered on her formidable but tailored bosom. She was neat and stout, exuding a confidence reminiscent of matronly first-grade school teachers who always have everything well in hand. "I've wondered if you'd come inside. I've seen you looking in the window. Is there something I can show you?"

"The sculpture. I think they're gnomes—Daisy and Eric." Catherine felt herself prattling. There was only the one gnome sculpture, and there was no reason why she shouldn't look at it if she wanted. She waited while the woman went to the window to get it, feeling guilty and sly. If she was still married to Jonathan, he would see it as a morbid self-indulgence, as some kind of primitive throwback to fertility icons, a preoccupation with her inability to conceive. Jonathan was not given to preoccupations. He cut his losses and moved on.

She took a deep breath as the woman set the gnomes gently on the display case.

"Do you collect these?" the woman asked.

"No. This is the first one I've seen." She reached out to touch the gnomes, noting again the pleasant feeling that looking at them gave her. There was a small foreign coin embedded among the daisies and leaves in the base.

"You'll find it a bit expensive, then. This mold has been retired. I should warn you, there's no such thing as owning *one* of these works. Once you've bought one, you're hooked."

She gave the woman a token smile and inspected the gnomes more closely, turning the sculpture around to see the back. She read the price tags, feeling the woman's eyes on her. It was more than "a bit" expensive.

"The coin there is a 1945 British threepence—so it's one of the early castings," the woman went on. "The ones cast later have a coin from Holland."

"The coin . . . is it for good luck?"

"I'm not sure. Perhaps. As I understand it, one never knows with these creations. I seem to recall one of the gentlemen gnomes having a coin early on, and then he didn't in later castings—because the rascal had spent it!"

Catherine let herself smile genuinely this time, pleased that she hadn't grown too bitter to appreciate a bit of whimsy. In the past three years she had seen herself as being nearly consumed by the obsession to have a child, an obsession that fed on each cyclic failure, month after month. Now she would have believed herself resigned to her childless state—if she weren't standing here trying not to buy this particular sculpture.

"They're modeled after real people, you know," the woman said. "Most of the collection is; I think that's why buyers are so drawn to them. Of course, you'd have to go to an authorized dealer to see the current pieces. I'm selling this one for a friend."

"The price is firm?"

"Oh, yes, I'm afraid so. As I said, the mold has been re-tired. The value of the piece will appreciate. In the long run it'll be worth more than you pay now."

Catherine looked at the sculpture again. The woman was right. One did feel drawn to it, or at least she felt drawn to this one. It had been a long time since she'd simply wanted something, something that was within her grasp, something with but one redeeming quality—that it gave her pleasure.

"Do you need to think about it for a while? I could hold it for . . ." The woman shrugged. "Twenty-four hours?"

"No," Catherine said. She never had been one not to be able to make up her mind, and she wasn't married to Jona-than anymore. Self-indulgent or not, she wanted the piece. "That is, if you'll take a charge card."

The woman beamed. "My dear, we aren't as old-fashioned as we look. We'll take anything you've got, as long as it isn't revoked or expired. But there's one thing I'd like to do. I'd like to keep your name and address on file here if it's all right—in case the owner should want to buy it back from you. I believe he's only parting with it because he needs the money. Would that be all right?"

Catherine didn't answer. She followed the woman along to the cash register, her mind filled with the sudden image of some sad, elderly man mourning the loss of his gnomes.

"He hasn't asked me to," the woman added quickly. "It's just something I thought I'd do for him—just in case. One has to be so careful with men. I could have bought it myself, but it would have made things awkward for him. He's very proud. Would it be all right to keep your name and address here? I wouldn't give it out to anyone else."

"Yes, all right," Catherine said.

"Oh, good. Thank you, my dear. He's such a nice man when you get to know him. He's a widower. He did all the glass lamp shades here in the shop. That's where I met him— in a stained-glass workshop. Both our children thought we needed a hobby. He was wonderful at it—such patience for a man his age. I was terrible. I broke everything I touched. He called me Crash. I don't suppose you'd be interested in one of the lamps?"

"Not for some time," Catherine answered, and the woman laughed.

"But you must come in again, anyway—just to browse. I'm close to the bus stop, so I get a lot of browsers. Now, if you'd just sign your name there—and put your address and telephone number along the bottom."

Catherine wrote quickly. She'd indulged her whim; now she was anxious to get away. She watched while the woman wrapped the gnomes in newspaper and placed them in a purple box—very subtle advertising on her part, Catherine thought.

She ran her fingers restlessly along the smooth wooden edge of the display case while she waited, and she suddenly remembered a place from her childhood. A "smart" children's shop with display cases like these. A small family business that sold blue velvet dresses and black patent-leather shoes and white rabbit-fur coats. A place where her mother had never been able to buy her anything but where they had always gone inside to look.

Catherine felt a twinge of guilt. By her mother's example, she had been well taught to postpone her own personal gratification, and subsequently she had never gotten blue velvet, patent leather, or white fur. But then, her mother never had had to deal with the temptation created by a plastic charge card.

She had to run to catch her bus, and it was still raining. She sat by the window near the back, holding the conspicuous purple box and staring out wet glass at the familiar streets. She had always liked the downtown section of Wilmington. It was old but rapidly becoming refurbished, a fact that she'd somehow missed until just recently. It was as if she had been seriously ill, too ill to note the changes in her environment, and yet she'd supposedly participated in the business of everyday living. She'd functioned. She'd gone to work, done her job, come home again. But her thoughts had all been turned inward.

She was barren. How appropriate the word was. *Barren*. It called to mind everything she felt about her own body, that it was dried up, hostile, useless. She was thirty-two years old and no longer married to the man she had loved. It would have been easier if she hadn't believed that he'd once loved her in return, perhaps still did. But he had wanted children— not adopted children and not borrowed children. *His* children. He had loved her, and he had left her in spite of it.

At first she had thought she would die from the overwhelming sense of betrayal. Her body had betrayed her, and, subsequently, her husband. For a time she deliberately let herself suffer for something for which she was not to blame. According to the infertility specialist, neither of them had been at fault; it was just one of those things. There was no physical or hormonal defect in either of them, and she believed that Jonathan had tried very hard to accept that fact— intellectually. But what he had communicated to her on an emotional level was something else again. She had sensed, rightly or wrongly, that it wasn't merely that he felt she'd failed him, but more—that he felt she had somehow done it deliberately, as if her ability to conceive was something she withheld from him for reasons of her own. They'd been told to get on with their lives, to relax, to stop *thinking* about it. But Jonathan couldn't accept any alternative way for her to experience rearing a child. What he'd wanted was for her to be realistic.

She had tried to understand, did understand, as well as a woman who needed to nurture something could. For Jonathan the child *had* to be his own. She had kept thinking about Charlotte Duffy, a woman she'd met at the gynecologist's office. They had been admitted to the hospital at the same time, Charlotte for what their mothers would have euphemistically described as "female trouble," and she for another round of infertility testing. Charlotte had three children of her own, and she and her husband had just adopted a child from some impoverished Central American country. Charlotte had shown her picture after picture of her newest, a dark-skinned little girl, and later, as they lay in the restless, artificial darkness of their hospital room waiting for some semblance of sleep, Charlotte had confessed what she believed to be a shameful, yet wonderful, sin. She, Charlotte Duffy, had brought this child, not from the safe cocoon of her own body but from the horrors of war and hunger and disease. She loved her adopted child best.

Jonathan had listened politely to the story of Charlotte and her adoption, but Catherine believed that he had seen her willingness to adopt a child like Charlotte's as some sort of mental aberration, brought on by the desperation of her infertility.

In the end he had been realistic enough for the both of them. Time was running out. He had wanted his own child, and he hadn't waited to see if his marriage to her would bring that about. He had already wasted three years, and regardless of Charlotte Duffy's confession or the success stories they'd heard about other childless couples who'd adopted, then had children of their own, he'd wanted out.

Their uncoupling had been agony for them both, her incredulity compounding his guilt. He had been her best friend, and it had taken her a long time to believe that he had done to her what she never would have done to him, no matter how badly she'd wanted a child. He had left the marriage.

She still saw him from time to time—at his instigation and out of his sense of responsibility toward her. They had been friends first, then lovers, then marriage partners, and she thought he missed her. She thought, too, that he wanted—needed—to salvage some working part of their relationship, something among the ashes of what once was a marriage so that he could say, "See? I haven't destroyed everything."

But he *had* destroyed everything. She had failed at the most basic validation of her womanhood, and his abandonment had made the failure a thousand times worse. But, abandoned or not, passive in her failure or not, she did not want to live on the fringes of his life now. She was clearly a survivor, though she took no credit for it, and she hadn't pulled herself up by her own bootstraps. Her survival was simply something that *was,* like her inability to conceive.

She took it as a sign of her recovery when, eighteen months after the divorce, she suddenly noticed that some of the 1950s aluminum facades had been taken off the downtown storefronts to reveal the old two-over-two windows, and that the layers of paint and neglect had been sandblasted down to the original brick. More and more businesses were moving into the old-fashioned stores, small, nondescript places with catchy names like The Purple Box. Concrete sections of the sidewalks were torn up and replaced with brick, and there were benches and flowers and newly planted trees. Through traffic was kept to a minimum, and the old downtown had suddenly become a place for pedestrians. She began to enjoy that, the freedom to crisscross the street from store to store, and she began to realize that she wanted to be in the company of people again. Not necessarily to talk to them, though she did sometimes indulge in conversations with strangers, but just to watch and to wonder about them. She had lost her insatiable curiosity about the people and things around her for a time, but somehow she suddenly had rediscovered it. She had always known that about herself—that she was innately curious—and perhaps that had been the key to her survival. Whatever the cause, every day she was getting better.

The rain had lessened by the time she reached her stop, ten blocks away. She lived alone in a yellow-brick, three-story apartment house called the Mayfair, which had a green terracotta roof. The bricks were dingy with soot and time, and there was no central air-conditioning, but it had two huge oak trees in its minuscule yard, and the rent was relatively cheap. The front and side entrances were all French doors, three panes of beveled glass across and five down, so that security was probably nonexistent. Most all of the tenants were long-time residents who considered the building "theirs," a good thing if one wanted one's comings and goings to be under constant surveillance, not such a good thing if one put a high price on privacy. Thus far she hadn't minded their scrutiny. She had no illicit lovers she needed to hide; she had no lovers at all.

She entered, expecting Mrs. Donovan to give her a report on the mail delivery and the daily comings and goings. Mrs.

Donovan had a bird's-eye view of the front door, the mail-boxes, and the foot of the stairs. She was the sister of the woman who owned the apartment house, and she had the remarkable luxury of having both a wooden and a screen door to her apartment. The screen was ostensibly because Mrs. Donovan preferred a draft to a window-unit air conditioner. In actuality it was because, in the summer at least, Mrs. Donovan was the unofficial keeper of the Mayfair gates. Sometimes, when the draft in the front hall was strong, one could smell the cigarette smoke wafting in from Mrs. Donovan's apartment, not because she was a smoker but because she sometimes lit Lucky Strikes and blew the smoke around her living room to remind herself of her dead husband. Mr. Donovan had been gone for more than thirty years, but for Mrs. Donovan, with the help of a Lucky Strike and a nostalgic mind-set, he had only just left the room.

The wooden door was closed today.

Catherine checked her mailbox in the quiet downstairs foyer, tossing everything but the bills into a flowered trash can that was kept close by. The stairs to the upper floors were wooden, layered in coat after coat of brown enamel paint and impossible to climb without making a racket. It occurred to her that unless a burglar confined himself to the ground floor, there was no need for the Mayfair to have any security. She climbed the stairs quickly, appreciating the stamina she'd acquired from living three flights up. When she'd first moved here, she'd had to rest at every landing. If one could believe clichés, she supposed that every cloud did have its silver lining and that her now strong legs and lungs were the direct benefit of having been forced to move to a cheaper place—that and the serenity she had gained from living at treetop level. She liked that about her apartment: that it was in the front and that the windows looked out onto the tops of the oak trees.

"Catherine," someone said as she climbed the last flight the sound a bit distorted by the echo off the bare wood of the stairs.

She looked upward. Jonathan sat on the top step. He never wore a raincoat or carried an umbrella, and he'd left a trail of wet footprints and rain droplets up the stairs.

"You're late," he said, getting up. "I thought you got home a little after five."

"I don't keep a schedule, Jonathan." She shifted the purple box to her other arm so she could unlock the door, resisting for a moment when he took it from her.

"No, I didn't mean to imply that you did," he said carefully. "What's in the box?"

"None of your business," she said, because it was the only answer that might keep him from looking.

He smiled, the smile boyish and winsome. She had always liked his smile, and a memory immediately surfaced, one of her lying in his arms on a rainy Sunday afternoon.

She pushed the memory aside. "What do you want, Jonathan?"

"I just wanted to see how you're doing."

"I'm fine." She opened the door and he followed her inside.

"Are you?" he asked, and she glanced at him, suspecting that he came to see about her so often now because she really was fine and that he was willing to offer her the comfort of his presence now that he knew she was strong enough not to need it.

She took the box out of his hands and set it on the table by the front door before she turned to meet his eyes. "Yes," she said evenly.

"I'm glad," he answered, but he looked away. There was no mistaking his relief, his anxiousness to accept what she said as the truth. He gave a soft sigh, as if he were bracing himself for something.

"Catherine—"

"Jonathan, what is it?" she said sharply. She had known him long enough to know when he was filled with purpose, and she was still too emotionally battered to play guessing games.

He smiled again. "I'm not keeping you from anything, am I? Are you going out with someone or something?"

She felt her irritation rise, suspecting, too, that Jonathan, regardless of his need for her to be independent, still wanted her to be alone and unattached.

She picked up the box and took it into the living room for no other reason than to have something to do. She knew divorced women who found new men almost immediately, but she was still coping with her internal shortcomings. Intellectually she believed that she was attractive enough, trim enough, educated enough to be sought after again, but somehow it hadn't helped.

"Sorry," Jonathan said as she set the box down on yet another table. "I shouldn't ask that, should I? So tell me. How's the new job?"

"How did you know I had a new job?"

"Word travels."

"Whose word?"

"Mrs. Donovan downstairs."

"Oh, fine," she said. "Then suppose *you* tell *me*. How am I doing? Do I like it or not?"

"She's not sure. She's not even sure what it is you do exactly—or if she is, I don't think she considers it a fit subject for mixed company."

Catherine smiled. "No, actually I don't think she does. I believe she finds it a bit . . . inappropriate."

"Well, now you've really piqued my interest. We can still

talk, can't we? You could even give me some coffee. I'd really like to hear, Catherine."

She almost believed him—even if she had become the formal-sounding stranger, Catherine, the one with whom he couldn't live any longer but with whom he wanted to talk about her job—when he was standing here in a jacket much too wet to have left on. Clearly he wasn't planning on having this take long.

It was raining again, the wind driving it against the front windows.

"How about it? Some coffee and conversation before I brave the storm?" he said, cajoling her.

She gave a little gesture of acquiescence and walked toward the kitchen. "Well, come on," she said when he didn't follow. "This isn't a restaurant."

He smiled that smile again—the winsome, charming one—as he followed behind her.

"Do you like this place?" he asked, looking up at the high ceilings in the kitchen. Her apartment was a far cry from the restored Victorian town house they'd shared in a quaint, shady neighborhood of two-car young professionals. Now she didn't own a car at all, and the Mayfair was like a once beautiful, aging woman, whose beauty existed only for those who remembered it.

"I like it. It's quiet. It's got a lot of character—French doors, wrought-iron flower boxes on the front windows."

"That bad, huh? I can't get over you living here with all these old people."

"They're nice, and I can afford it," she said as she set the kettle on the burner to heat. She looked up at him, and his eyes shifted away. He didn't want to talk about the decline in her standard of living. He sat down at the kitchen table.

"So tell me about the job."

19

She leaned against the sink, her arms folded protectively over her breasts because he was looking at her so intently. She still found him attractive, much to her dismay, and probably always would. "It's with the city school system. Technically I'm working as a medical-careers instructor, but actually I'm more of a special-needs teacher."

"For handicapped children, you mean?"

"Not handicapped. Pregnant." She moved to the cupboard to get down the cups and a jar of instant coffee. "I've got five at the moment. One is barely thirteen years old. They didn't want to put a child that young into a regular classroom, and they wanted something more cost-effective than homebound tutoring. So as long as they were setting up a project to handle her, they decided to throw in the rest of them. They expect thirty or more by the end of the school year."

"Have you got the credentials to teach them the three R's?"

"They don't want me to teach them the three R's. Pat Bauer is going to do that. Believe it or not, they want me to teach them what they really need to know—how to take care of themselves while they're pregnant and how to take care of their babies." She could do that whether she had one of her own or not.

She turned away as the kettle whistled sharply, lifting it off the burner and handing him the jar of coffee and a cup and spoon. There was a time when she would have fixed the coffee for him herself.

"Pat's going to come in half days for the academics. The rest of the time I'm going to do prenatal nutrition, early childhood development, how to read a thermometer and buy baby food, and anything else I can think of that might help—" She stopped because he was again staring at her. "I like it and I'm good at it, Jonathan." She didn't tell him that she'd taken a major pay cut to get the job, or that she'd worked as a volunteer for nearly a month with no pay at all until the program for pregnant students had been funded.

"I know you are. I know how involved you get. It's one of the things I always liked about you. Pour the hot water, will you? Who held your hand every time you were burned out?"

You did, she thought, but she didn't say it; she poured. It was true. He had held her hand all the times when she couldn't deal firsthand with death and dying and disease anymore. It was only when she hadn't been able to give him a child that he wasn't there for her.

"I thought Pat was still too sick to work," he said.

"She's managing the half days all right."

"Are you . . . sure this is the right thing for you to be doing?" he asked when she sat down at the table.

"The right thing? Because I couldn't have a child of my own?"

He seemed not to mind her candor. "It's bound to remind you."

"Jonathan, everything reminds me."

Especially you. She didn't say that, either. "Or it did," she qualified, because she didn't want to go through the guilt and the remorse again, not when she had no inkling who should forgive whom and for what. She got up from the table. She was tired of being civil, and whatever his visit was about, she had had enough of it. She wanted him to go.

"Catherine, you know I'll always care about you, don't you? You know that if you ever need anything, you can ask me." He reached toward her and would have touched her if she hadn't stepped away.

She looked into his eyes, thinking only of Pat Bauer, who was seriously ill and forced to depend upon an estranged husband for help, a husband who had made it clear that he was in love with another woman. She had no intention of becoming another Pat Bauer.

"What's wrong?" she said.

"Nothing's wrong. I just wanted to make sure you know that you can count on me if you ever needed . . . things."

"Why would you want me to know that? What sort of things?"

"Catherine, you really know how to take a man's goodwill and shove it down his throat, don't you? I just want things settled between us. I just want—I have to go," he said abruptly. He got up from the table, leaving the coffee he'd wanted steaming and undrunk.

"Are you going to tell me what this visit is all about or not?" she said, following him into the living room.

"It's not about anything. I just wanted to see how you were."

"Bullshit," she said mildly. She was barren, not stupid. "You've been leaving since you got here. And since *I* didn't initiate this visit, it's got to be something with you. So what is it?"

"Catherine, it's . . . nothing."

"You don't come out into the rain for 'nothing,' Jonathan. You stay at home by the fire with your feet up and a copy of *The Wall Street Journal.*"

"You think you've got my number, don't you?"

"I *think* you're changing the subject. If you need a loan, you've come to the wrong place."

"I don't need a loan."

"But you do need something."

"No, Catherine . . . yes."

But whatever it was, he wasn't going to stay long enough to tell her.

"I have to go."

"So you said."

22

He bumped the table lamp in passing, knocking the lamp shade askew and sending the box with the gnomes onto the floor. They both stopped to retrieve it, the newspapers and the gnomes tumbling out on the rug.

"Let me have it," she said, trying to take the sculpture out of his hands.

"What are you up to, Catherine? Buying erotic art?"

The joke was feeble, and she made another grab for the gnomes. He held it away, pulling the newspaper aside so he could see. His face fell at the sight of the gnome mother and child, as if he'd uncovered some terrible secret she had, one he'd rather not know.

"Catherine, I'm sorry."

"Fine. Now, if you're not going to tell me what you're doing here, I'd like for you to just go."

"Catherine—" He put his hand on her arm and she jerked it away. She was flagrantly working with young women who didn't want to be pregnant; she had even bought a mother and child sculpture, but she did *not* deserve his pity.

He helped her to stand up, anyway. "I . . . just don't know what to do."

"About what?" she said.

He tried to put his hand on her shoulders, but she backed away from him, still clutching the gnomes tightly.

"About you!"

"You don't have to do anything about me. I'm fine."

His eyes went to the sculpture. "Sure you are. God!"

He crossed the room and opened the front door, turning back to her before he went out. "It's not my fault, Catherine. I can't help the way I am. There are certain things that are important to me. I'm sorry I hurt you, but I can't help the way I am! I'm . . . getting married again, Catherine."

"Pregnant, is she?" she shot back, because she needed to

think him cruel, needed to think he wouldn't let himself be burdened with another woman who couldn't reproduce.

"I don't deserve that!" he said, his face flushed. "You know how it was with us, even before—"

"Before what, Jonathan? Before you made my having a baby a condition of the marriage? You're not going to get out of it that easily, because you and I both know better. You know what I remember, Jonathan? Nothing bad—until I couldn't do what you wanted." Her eyes welled. She had thought she was through with recriminations, but she couldn't resist one last one. "I really thought you were my friend."

"The friendship's still there, Catherine. We can keep that."

"No we can't!"

"Catherine, I just want you to know that I'm . . . happy. I do love her. I wouldn't marry her if I didn't."

"Congratulations. Does she know what a hard job it is being somebody you *love?*"

He chose to ignore her sarcasm. "Her name is Ellen. Ellen Jessup. She's a widow. I think you'll like her. We've talked about it, and we want you to come to the wedding. It would help both of us if—"

"No, I don't think so, Jonathan."

Old friendships ran deep, if not old marriages, and she realized that he wanted desperately to believe that she would like his new wife, just as he wanted to believe that Ellen Jessup really wanted her at the wedding.

"No, really. We want you there. It's the fifteenth of next month—at her house in the Heights—"

She forced a smile, then lost it. "You are such a fool sometimes, Jon," she said, pushing him the rest of the way into the hall.

"Catherine—"

"I'm not coming to your wedding."

"Katie—"

"Don't call me Katie!"

She shut the door hard, catching sight of a man on the landing, then a little girl in a yellow poncho standing a few steps above him, both of whom must have heard everything.

2

"Now, what, Joe?"

Joseph D'Amaro looked down at his daughter's upturned face, at this determined, youngest child of his who never called him anything but Joe and who had pressed him into coming to the Holben woman's apartment in the first place.

He knew that Mrs. Webber at the curio shop had meant well, but he hadn't cared that the gnomes had been sold to a woman who understood that he might want to buy them back one day. That was the operative phrase here—*one day*. He had no money to do it now; it was his lack of funds that had precipitated selling the sculpture in the first place. He hadn't wanted to track the Holben woman down, regardless of Mrs. Webber's kindness or his daughter's enthusiasm, not when he couldn't possibly make her any kind of viable offer or even the promise of one.

And now he'd blundered into some kind of embarrassing personal situation on the Mayfair stairs that left him no recourse but to get the hell out of there. He had seen the woman's face as she closed the door. The last thing she needed was a strange man with a kid on her doorstep making some halfhearted speech about wanting to buy back a gnome.

"That's it. We're going," he said.

"Joe, I don't want to—"

"Fritz, you heard me!"

He started back down the stairs, feeling her disappointment and wishing that he hadn't spoken so sharply. It wasn't that Fritz expected him to indulge her whims. If anything, it was exactly the opposite. She never made demands. It was as if she thought her wants held no credence with him, and she tried to save herself any further heartbreak by not asking.

He had puzzled over Fritz for a long time, finally deciding in the middle of a particularly sleepless night that the reason for her behavior was because Lisa was dead and because Fritz was the child who reminded him of it—and she knew it. And yet physically she didn't remind him of Lisa at all. It was Della, his other daughter, who did. Della, who had Lisa's same Irish prettiness and the same devilish smile and volatile personality. Fritz was unlike anyone in either his or Lisa's family. She had no boisterous laugh, no noisy Italian or Irish temper. She was solemn and quiet and less than beautiful to any eye but his, so solemn and quiet that he hadn't realized how much the gnomes had meant to her until they'd checked the shop window today and found them gone.

They had had a family meeting about selling the sculpture—several, in fact. He'd never kept the realities of money or the lack of it from his children, and he had given them the full details of their current budget problems. There was only one solution he could suggest, and it had been unanimously decided that the gnomes would be sold. All three of his children had voted yes, but somehow he had neglected to look into Fritz's eyes.

Now she reluctantly followed him down the stairs. She said nothing, but she looked at him once in that way she had, which made him defensive and angry. At seven she was far too wise for her years. He doubted that Fritz would have been so world-weary if Lisa hadn't died when she was so young and she hadn't been cared for by people who were immersed in their own private grief and guilt. Lisa's mother. His mother. He, himself.

Fritz had been barely two when Lisa was killed, and it was

27

not to his credit that days—weeks—passed before he could force himself to deal with the fact that he even had this child. He left her to the care of others because, emotionally, he had died himself, and he had nothing left to give anyone. Della had been twelve and Charlie eleven, both old enough to understand what he managed to tell them about their mother's death. But Fritz had been too young, too dependent, too much in need of him in the wake of Lisa's dying. Sometimes he felt that even now Fritz was patiently waiting for him to come up with the fatherly concern and caring she'd been shortchanged.

Still, he thought that Fritz had come through it all with remarkable good sense. She was much more stable than the dramatically emotional Della; more logical than her intellectual but absentminded brother, Charlie. Joe didn't worry about her. For all her quietness, she wasn't a pushover. His being in the Mayfair stairwell at the worst possible moment was proof of that.

"That lady's got problems of her own," he said as they went out the French doors. "She's upset."

He pulled the hood on Fritz's poncho up over her head. Fritz hadn't asked for explanations, but he felt the need to give her one. He wasn't above the parental standard, *Because I said so,* but generally he tried to respect a child's need to know.

"Because Jonathan's getting married?" she asked, hurrying to keep up. "And Ellen Jessup's pregnant?"

Joe glanced at her as they walked to where he'd left the truck. The truck was parked at the end of the street, and the man, Jonathan, was just ahead of them, getting into a small white Mercedes-Benz.

"Is it?" Fritz asked again, and he tried not to smile. He hadn't sorted out the scene they'd just witnessed to that degree, but he wasn't surprised that Fritz had. Fritz didn't miss much. He had always tried to be truthful with his children, but it occurred to him suddenly that Fritz was the only one of the three who seemed to expect it.

"That would be my guess, yes," he said.

"Couldn't we just leave her your business card? I've got one in my pocket."

"No."

Joe unlocked the door for Fritz to get in, giving her his hand as she climbed into the battered pickup truck Della was ashamed to be seen in and which Charlie didn't seem to notice at all. Fritz, on the other hand, wanted it painted candy-apple red. If he ever got the money, maybe he *would* paint the damn thing candy-apple red.

"Why?" Fritz said, looking into his eyes.

"Why what?"

"Why can't I give her a business card?"

He didn't answer her until he'd gotten in on the other side. "Because you can't just hand her a card with 'D'Amaro Brothers Construction' on it and expect her to understand what it's for. You'd have to give her some kind of explanation, and believe me, Fritz, that woman doesn't want to hear any explanations now."

Because she's going to cry? Fritz almost said. She knew that grown-ups didn't like children around when they cried. Joe didn't. He didn't cry much anymore, or at least it had been a long time since she'd caught him at it. She hated it when he cried, when he sat in the dark, smelling like beer, and held Lisa's picture even if he couldn't see it. She never knew what to do, only that somebody should do *something*. She only knew enough to stay away and pretend that it wasn't happening.

She leaned forward on the seat a bit to count the number

of streets from the Mayfair to Second Street. She knew how to get from home to Market Street, and then from Market Street to Second Street, because Charlie had showed her when he took her with him to the library, and she was almost certain that Joe wouldn't go back to see the sad lady who had the gnomes again.

"Can we come back to see that lady tomorrow?" she asked as a test.

"Not tomorrow," Joe said.

"Sometime soon?"

"Maybe."

Maybe. She pressed her lips together and looked out the window, still counting streets, satisfied now that she'd have to handle this matter herself.

Joe pulled the truck in front of the house, but he didn't come in with her because Charlie's light was on and because Joe was running late.

"Tell Della I won't be home until ten or so," Joe said. "Tell her she doesn't have to worry about keeping dinner warm for me. And tell her I'll be working on the interiors at the Allen job if she needs to call me for anything. Fritz, are you listening to me?" he asked abruptly when she was about to slam the truck door. She had listened to every word; she just didn't want to agree to anything he asked her to do, so she wouldn't be lying to him by saying she would do it.

"I'm listening," she said, because that was the truth. "Bye, Joe."

He frowned for a moment, then grinned. "Go on. You'll get all wet."

She gave him a wave as she ran up the walk, taking great pains not to splash in the puddles. Sometimes she liked to do that—stomp the water out of the puddles—but she didn't do it today. Joe was watching, and he was a builder. He and

Uncle Michael were losing a lot of money because of the rain, and she didn't want him to think she enjoyed it.

She stood on the front porch at the door, pulling back the screen and waiting until Joe thought she was about to go inside and drove away. Then she waited a moment longer until his truck had gone around the corner. She stuck her hand into the pocket of her poncho. She had three dollars in nickels, dimes, and quarters—milk money she'd saved from school—and a package of dry-roasted peanuts; plenty of money for the bus fare to the Mayfair and plenty to eat until she got back for dinner.

She let the screen door close slowly. Charlie was probably doing something at his computer. There wasn't much of a chance that he'd hear her even if she came in the front door with a marching band, but she didn't want to risk it. She smiled a rare smile at the thought of her leading a whole big band in red marching suits right into the living room—and Charlie not even looking up.

She looked at her watch, an old white plastic digital one that Della didn't wear anymore because the painted flowers on the band had nearly worn off. Fritz didn't care about the flowers, she cared about the time—six o'clock. The bus came to the corner at six-fifteen, only she couldn't wait at this corner. One of the neighbors might see her and ask what she was doing and did Della or Charlie or Joe know she was out here in the rain? They were sure to ask if they saw her, because she was a motherless child and whatever she did seemed to be everyone else's business. It was her opinion that people naturally assumed that children with mothers had permission and children without mothers didn't—and were up to something.

She jumped off the porch into the wet grass, causing a splash of cold rainwater she felt on the backs of her legs and inside her running shoes. But she didn't linger. She ran as fast as she could around the house and through the backyard, taking all the shortcuts she knew between the neighbors' garbage cans and compost heaps to get to the next block ahead of the bus.

The bus was coming when she rounded the corner, and she had no time to reflect upon the advisability of this venture. She had never gone anyplace without Della or Charlie or Joe knowing, but she didn't hesitate. She got on and carefully dropped the correct change into the slot, smiling slightly at the driver, who clearly thought she was about to make his life miserable with a dollar bill. She sat in the back, knowing that the bus would stop at Market Street without her having to pull the cord. She would get on another bus then, one going in the direction of the Mayfair. She was a little worried about knowing when to signal the driver to stop. She had to ride for six streets. She'd count five, and in the middle of the fifth she'd pull the cord. Simple. She hoped.

The second bus was crowded with people, and she had a hard time getting to a window so she could count. She remained standing, letting a girl with a big stomach that meant she was going to get a baby sit down in her place. The girl was chewing bubble gum, and she blew a bubble, then popped it loudly. Fritz wished she had bubble gum instead of the peanuts. She was hungry, and peanuts were a lot of trouble. She couldn't count streets and eat them at the same time. She would have to pay attention to every mouthful to keep them from falling between her fingers, and it would be hard to do that and count too.

She squirmed to get down the aisle, trying to move around a fat boy carrying a big radio. He was very wide, as wide as the whole aisle almost, and he had on a red beret with buttons pinned all over it. She read the ones she could read: U-2 and

Sting and ZZ Top. He was wearing earphones, and Fritz was close enough to feel the bass notes from the music in the pit of her stomach. He didn't move when she pushed him in the back.

"Where you going, baby?" a black woman asked kindly, in spite of Fritz's squirming to get past. The woman smelled nice, like when Fritz took a bath, and Della let her open a new bar of soap.

"The Mayfair," Fritz told her, and the woman smiled.

"You all mashed in there where you can't see nothing, baby. You want me to pull the buzzer cord for you?"

"Yes, please," Fritz said politely, wondering if she should offer to pay the woman for doing it.

But the woman didn't seem to want any money. She pulled the buzzer cord when it was time and made the fat boy with the radio move so that Fritz could get off.

"Thank you very much," Fritz said, and the woman patted her head.

It was still raining, and Fritz stood at the corner for a moment before she crossed the street to the Mayfair. She took a deep breath. There was no sense in worrying now. She was here, and she wanted to see the woman who had bought the gnomes. She wanted to see Daisy and Eric, too, and she had to get back before someone missed her. She hadn't really thought about that part of the plan—how to get home before she was missed—and she didn't waste time with it now. She waited until a line of cars went by, then darted across the street. The Mayfair faced the side street rather than Second, and she walked along the sidewalk under one of the big trees to the front door. The rain sounded louder under the tree, and she decided that she liked the Mayfair's front doors. It had a sort of little porch over it that was held up with chains, so people coming out wouldn't get wet before they got their umbrellas up. And she liked the panes of glass in the doors. She could see inside easily, to where a lamp sat on a little table in the foyer. Someone had turned the lamp on, making the dark foyer look warm and dry. She had always liked looking into places from the outside and wondering what kind of people were in there, and if it smelled like chocolate-chip cookies baking, and if there were children with a mother.

She had some trouble with the doors because they had swollen from the rain, but she managed. If Charlie had been with her, he wouldn't have opened the doors for her. He'd have made her do it herself, to build her character. She was glad that Charlie did that, worried about her character. It made her feel a lot better about things, knowing that even if she didn't have a mother, with Charlie's help her character would be all right.

The first door by the stairs was open, and she glanced through the screen at the old woman inside. She could hear the television playing—the man on Channel 6 talking about all the rain. She expected the woman to call out to her as she passed, but she didn't. Fritz climbed the stairs quickly, the soles of her shoes making little squeaking noises on the wooden steps.

Three flights was a long way up, and she was panting by the time she reached the right door. She waited for a moment to catch her breath before she knocked. Her first knock was weak and timid, and no one answered. She tried again, knocking louder this time, and again she waited.

Nothing happened.

She looked around her, wondering if she should knock again. Maybe Ms. Holben had gone somewhere. No. No, she didn't think Ms. Holben would leave. Ms. Holben was going to cry, and when grown-ups cried, they sat in a dark room at home to do it. She took another deep breath. The door across the hall cracked open, and Fritz could see half a face wearing eyeglasses.

"Knock harder, honey. She's at home," the face said, and the door closed.

Fritz knocked again, hard this time. She tried to do it the way they did it on television—really hard—and her knuckles hurt. She could hear muffled noises on the other side, but it was a long time before the door opened.

"Yes?" the woman, Ms. Holben, said. She still had on the same clothes—a denim skirt and a white blouse and red shoes. Her voice was whispery soft, and the room was dark behind her.

Fritz pushed her hood off her head. She should have done that sooner. She shouldn't be standing inside with a dumb hood on her head. Ms. Holben didn't seem to notice, and Fritz searched her pocket for Joe's card. That was something else she should have done. She should have found the card before she knocked at the door.

It was in her jeans pocket, and it took her a moment to locate it. She kept glancing at Ms. Holben, expecting her to say something, but she didn't. She just waited, and Fritz liked her for that, for waiting and not asking a lot of questions, as if Fritz didn't know where she was or what she was doing there. She handed Ms. Holben the card, wishing that she'd put it in another pocket so it wouldn't be so bent now.

Ms. Holben stepped out into the hall to read it, holding it under the light in the ceiling. Fritz was relieved to see that while her face was still sad, she wasn't crying.

"D'Amaro Brothers Construction," Ms. Holben said, her voice puzzled. Joe had been right. Ms. Holben didn't understand, and Fritz had forgotten all about giving an explanation.

"My name is Mary Frances D'Amaro. You bought the

gnomes," Fritz said in a rush. "We want to buy them back. Sometime when it stops raining and we get the money," she added, because she felt she owed Ms. Holben the truth. She waited, and it seemed to Fritz that they *both* were waiting.

"You want to buy it back," Ms. Holben said finally, looking again at the wrinkled card. "You and the D'Amaro Brothers."

"Me and Joe," Fritz said. That wasn't exactly the truth. She wasn't sure whether Joe really wanted to buy back the gnomes or not. She was sure about Della and Charlie, though. Della liked money better than gnomes, and Charlie didn't care about either, only computers.

"You were here earlier, weren't you?"

Fritz didn't want to say. If she said yes, Ms. Holben would be reminded that she'd heard all about Jonathan and Ellen Jessup, the very thing Joe said had made her upset. "Yes," she said, anyway, because she was supposed to tell the truth, and she couldn't see any way out of it.

"Are you by yourself?"

Fritz nodded. "Could I . . . see Daisy and Eric?" she said before Ms. Holben asked any more questions.

Ms. Holben stood back. "Come in. What did you say your name was again?" She turned on a lamp behind her.

Fritz looked around the room. It was a nice room, she decided. Just big enough with not much furniture. She could dance in this room, turn a cartwheel and not break anything if she aimed herself just right. Her room at home was too small, too crowded, because she had to share with Della. She couldn't walk without bumping into things, and Della hated having her underfoot no matter how quiet and tiny she tried to be. She knew that Joe wanted a bigger place for them, but that was somewhere "down the road," down the same road as buying back the gnomes.

"Mary Frances," Fritz said. "But I like Fritz. Everybody calls me that. Except the sisters. They call me Mary Frances."

"Fritz," Ms. Holben repeated. "Is that because you couldn't say Mary Frances when you were little?"

She looked at Ms. Holben in surprise, wondering how she had guessed that. "Yes—Joe says all I did was spit, and Fritz is what it sounded like."

"I'm Catherine, but I guess the lady at the Purple Box already told you."

"No, she said Ms. Holben. But I heard Jonathan."

"Jonathan?"

"On the stairs. You don't like him to call you Katie," Fritz reminded her.

Ms. Holben smiled slightly. "Oh, yes. Jonathan."

Fritz looked at her gravely. Joe had been right about the card and the explanation; he was probably right about not bothering Ms. Holben too. She stood in the middle of the room, waiting for Ms. Holben to show her the gnomes and wondering if she really could call her by her first name. She'd never had the chance to call a grown-up woman by her first name before. Brenda, the girl from the construction-company office who went with Joe to the movies, had said to call her Brenda, but Joe had never brought her home with him again.

"Daisy and Eric are in that box," Ms. Holben said. "Let me take your raincoat."

Fritz gave up the poncho, but she was immediately cold without it. She couldn't keep from shivering.

"Why don't you sit over there," Ms. Holben said, pointing to the flowery couch.

Fritz hesitated, then went and sat down where Ms. Holben had pointed.

"Cover up with this until you get warm," she said, helping Fritz pull an afghan off the back of the couch. The afghan was white with pink crocheted flowers on it. She handed Fritz the box and went into another room—the kitchen, Fritz could tell when she leaned forward. She expected Ms. Holben to come right back but she didn't, and after a moment Fritz turned her attention to the box. She glanced again in the direction of the kitchen. It must be all right for her to look into the box. Ms. Holben wouldn't have given it to her otherwise. She waited a moment longer, then reached in and parted the newspapers. Daisy and Eric were in there. She lifted them out and put the box aside, letting them sit on the afghan on her lap. Daisy was still smiling, and Eric was still falling asleep.

She looked up to find Ms. Holben watching.

"Do you like hot chocolate, Fritz?"

"I like it a lot."

"I think I'll make us some, then. It's nice on a rainy day."

"I know how to help," Fritz offered.

"Are you still cold?"

"Not that cold."

"Good. Come on, if you're warm enough. And bring Daisy and Eric. You can tell me about them."

Fritz slid off the couch, taking the time to try to rearrange the afghan with one hand when she held on to the gnomes with the other. As she came into the kitchen Ms. Holben was taking down two cups from a china cabinet filled with blue dishes.

"I always use the Blue Willow mugs when I make chocolate," Ms. Holben said. She took down a Blue Willow plate as well. "Would you get the milk out of the refrigerator?"

Fritz carefully set Daisy and Eric in the middle of the kitchen table, then brought the milk. Together she and Ms. Holben worked to make the hot chocolate—Fritz handling the measuring and Ms. Holben heating the milk on the stove. Fritz watched her closely, comparing her, as she did all women, to the framed picture Joe had of Lisa in her wedding dress. Ms. Holben looked older than Lisa. Her hair was dark and short and curly, not long and blond like Lisa's. And she didn't have blue eyes. She wasn't like Lisa at all, but she was still nice.

"I almost forgot," Ms. Holben said as she poured the hot chocolate into the mugs. "We need one more thing." She went to the refrigerator and got out a container of vanilla ice cream, then put a big spoonful into each cup. "Do you ever put ice cream in your chocolate?"

"Just marshmallows sometimes."

"You'll like this, I think. When I was little girl and went shopping with my mother, we used to stop in this little drug-store by the bus stop. In the winter we had hot chocolate with ice cream in it. In the summer we had fresh limeade. I don't think you can get either one anymore, unless you make them at home." She sat down at the table. "Tell me about Daisy and Eric. . . . I forgot the cookies," she said, getting up again. She brought a tin of plain butter cookies and put some out on the Blue Willow plate. "Did you have Daisy and Eric long?"

"Joe got them when I was a little kid. He won them at the PTA. I like them because I like things with mothers." Fritz let the ice cream bump her upper lip as she sipped the chocolate. Ms. Holben was right. She did like it, and she liked Ms. Holben telling her about when she was a little girl.

"I like things with mothers too. Is Joe your brother?"

"No, he's my father. I call him Joe because I don't want him to die." She slurped her chocolate loudly, but Ms. Holben didn't seem to mind. "Lisa died," she added. She looked down at the mug of chocolate, losing herself for a moment in the Blue Willow pattern on the sides, imagining herself with Koong-Shee and Chang escaping over the little bridge as she braced herself for the questions she knew would follow.

"Lisa's your mother?"

She avoided Ms. Holben's eyes. "I don't have a mother. . . . Do you know the story of the Blue Willow on the mug and the plate?"

"No. Tell me."

Fritz glanced at her to see if she meant it. She shouldn't have said why she had to call Joe by his name. It was a secret, the kind of secret that made grown-ups upset, and she had never told anybody. She just couldn't be sure about grownups. Sometimes she sensed that they wanted her to talk because they felt sorry for her—because she was a motherless child, not because they wanted to listen. And sometimes they wanted her to talk so that they could really find out something else. Like Aunt Margaret asking her about school and Della and Charlie when she really wanted to know about Joe and Brenda. She had seen Aunt Margaret kiss Joe one time in the kitchen, kiss him hard while she hung on to him as if she thought he'd run away. And Joe did want to run away. He kept turning his face and trying to pull Aunt Margaret's arms from around his neck. And he kept saying, "For God's sake, Maggie, don't! Michael's my brother!"

But Ms. Holben *was* listening—even if she knew Fritz had just told her something she hadn't meant to tell.

Fritz moved the cookies off the plate and pointed to the people on the bridge. "This is Koong-Shee here in front with a staff. And this one in the middle is her true love, Chang," she recited solemnly.

"And who's this?" Ms. Holben said, pointing to the third figure. Her fingers were long and her fingernails short and polished with clear polish. Fritz liked fingernails like hers,

40

like a mother's when she wanted to be special and not every day, like the mothers who came to the Parents' Tea at the Catholic school. She didn't like fingernails long and painted shiny red like Aunt Margaret's. She liked shiny red just on cars and trucks.

"That's Koong-Shee's father. He's carrying a whip because he's mad."

"Why is he mad?"

"Because Koong-Shee is running away with Chang. Chang is her father's secretary. He's very poor, and her father wants her to marry another man—a *rich* man."

"Does she?"

"No, she escapes with Chang. They go and live in the little house there across the lake. And for a while they're very happy." Fritz hesitated, thinking of Lisa and Joe. They hadn't been happy for very long, either.

"Then what happened?" Ms. Holben asked quietly, as if she knew something bad was coming.

"The rich man was very angry when he couldn't marry Koong-Shee. He set fire to the little house across the lake. And they died." She gave a soft sigh. "The end." She looked at Ms. Holben. Ms. Holben was looking at the plate.

"No, I don't think that's the end," she said. "See here? These two birds flying high over the lake? I think those are Koong-Shee's and Chang's souls. I think they're changed now, but they're still happy and they're free."

Fritz looked at the birds. "That's not what the lady in the China Room at the museum said."

"Maybe she didn't know that part of it."

Fritz looked at the birds again. Maybe she didn't. And it made sense. Why else were those two big birds there?

"I'll have to think about it," Fritz said, and Ms. Holben smiled.

"While you're thinking, maybe you'd better tell me how much trouble you're in."

She looked at Ms. Holben guiltily, but she didn't answer.

"Does Joe know you're here?"

"No."

"Don't you think you ought to tell him?"

"He's working on the interiors at the Allen site. I can't bother him. It's been raining. He's got to do the inside work so he can get some money."

"If he thinks you're lost someplace, I doubt he's getting very much work done."

"I'm not lost."

"He doesn't know that, does he? Maybe all he knows is that you're not where you're supposed to be."

Fritz thought about this. "I can call Della and Charlie," she decided.

"Who are they?"

"My sister and my brother."

"I think you should do that."

Fritz looked at Ms. Holben closely. She wasn't angry; she was just using the kind of voice that meant Fritz had better do it.

"I know you just wanted to make sure Daisy and Eric were all right. But it's not good to worry people who love you if you can help it."

"I couldn't help it," Fritz said. "I wanted you to have a card with Joe's name on it."

"I know. Now finish your chocolate and go call them."

Fritz dutifully took a last swallow of her chocolate and stood up.

"The telephone's over there," Ms. Holben said.

"Maybe I can't reach it," Fritz suggested in desperation.

"Maybe you can stand on the stool right in front of it."

Fritz took a deep breath. She was going to have to call Della and Charlie. There was no way out of it. She climbed up on the stool and dialed the number. The line was busy.

"It's busy," she said, holding the receiver out in case Ms. Holben didn't believe her and wanted to listen. "Della has a lot of boyfriends."

"Try one more time," she said, but she didn't come to listen to the busy signal.

Fritz dialed again. "Still busy." She climbed down from the stool. "I can go get on the bus. That's how I got here."

"I'd rather you didn't do that. Let's don't give me nightmares about your riding on the bus by yourself at this time of night, all right?"

Fritz looked at the windows. It *was* dark, and it was still raining. "All right," she said agreeably. She didn't want to give Ms. Holben nightmares, and she liked it here.

Ms. Holben ran the sink full of hot water and squirted in some dish detergent so she could wash the mugs and the pan they'd used to make the hot chocolate. "Who looks after you when Joe's working?"

Fritz brought the spoons to the sink. "Della."

"Della," Ms. Holben repeated. "How old is Della?"

"Sixteen. She can drive a car. Charlie's fifteen. He likes computers."

"And what does Della like?"

"Being a cheerleader, and dancing classes and boys and parties. And new clothes that cost too much. What do you like?"

"What do I like?" Ms. Holben stopped washing. "Oh, old ghost movies with Abbott and Costello or Topper or the Dead End Kids . . . and popcorn . . . and gnomes."

"And hot chocolate," Fritz supplied.

"And hot chocolate," Ms. Holben agreed.

"And Blue Willow stuff."

"That too. Go call."

"I was hoping you'd forget."

"Not a chance. Go call."

Fritz dialed the number again, and this time Della answered. "This is Fritz," was all she managed. She had known Della would be mad—if she'd missed her yet—so she was prepared. She waited until Della wound down.

"The Mayfair with Ms. Holben," she said in answer to Della's yelling. "Apartment 3-A." She waited in case Della had more to say, then hung up the phone. "I'm supposed to wait here," she told Ms. Holben.

"I think that's a good idea."

"Ms. Holben?"

"What, Fritz?"

"Could I hold Daisy and Eric until she gets here?"

"Yes, Fritz. Take them into the living room."

Fritz carried them back to the couch, making herself comfortable and covering her legs with the afghan again. She wasn't cold now; she just liked the pink crocheted flowers. She held Daisy and Eric carefully, turning them around and around to see their faces from different angles, to touch the daisies and acorns, to find the coin. Ms. Holben stayed in the kitchen, coming out only when someone knocked on the door. Fritz sighed. From the sound of the knock Della must be really mad.

But it wasn't Della. It was Joe. And from the look of him he hadn't been working. Fritz wondered how grown-ups knew these things about each other, that Ms. Holben wouldn't understand about the business card, and that Joe wouldn't be working if he thought she was lost. He said a few words to Ms. Holben, then came into the living room. She put Daisy and Eric carefully into the newspaper and back into the box before she got up.

"Get your coat," Joe said, his voice making her want to shiver worse than being out in the rain ever had. He was tired and dirty and he smelled like sweat. She wished he smelled better here in Ms. Holben's apartment.

"I gave Catherine the card," she told him, using Ms. Holben's first name so he would know that her visit had gone well.

"I don't care about the card! Get your coat!"

Ms. Holben was holding the yellow poncho. Fritz walked across the room, and she let Ms. Holben help her put it on.

"Good-bye, Fritz," she said. "I enjoyed our visit."

"Good-bye, Catherine." Fritz knew she should say thank you for the hot chocolate, but she didn't trust herself to do it. She tried never to have Joe mad at her, and his anger was a lot harder to bear than she remembered.

"I'm going to put the card on the bulletin board by the telephone. Come and see me again—when you have permission."

"There's not much chance of that," Joe said.

"I really would like for her to visit again, Mr.—"

"What you would like doesn't count for shit," Joe said, and Fritz cringed. He jerked open the door and she went out ahead of him, looking back at Ms. Holben once when she reached the bottom of the first flight of stairs.

3

"Cherry, who's your baby's daddy?"

"I already told you. I told you *three* times. Maria, you don't listen to nothing."

"I listen. I know what you *said*. What I want to know is, how come I never heard of him?"

" 'Cause he ain't from around here, that's why you never heard of him. Who's *your* baby's daddy, you so smart?"

"Sweet Eddie, that's who."

"Girl! You lying! Ain't no way in this world Sweet Eddie Aikens is going to have anything to do with a ugly girl like you. 'Cause he's cool, and he can have any girl he wants. Tell her, Beatrice. Tell Maria about Sweet Eddie."

"There's no way Sweet Eddie Aikens would have anything to do with either one of you," Beatrice said, "so both of you can shut up. I'm tired of hearing it. Ms. Holben's tired of hearing it too."

Beatrice Delcambre was the recognized leader of the group, her authority secondary only to Catherine's, though Catherine hadn't quite decided why. Abby was the likely one, Catherine thought. She was the *A* student among them, the smart one, the "brain." But then, Maria was bigger and more quarrelsome, and she had the prestige of already having had one baby. Cherry—Cherry was feisty but new, and therefore at the bottom of the pecking order. And Sasha had the good sense to stay out of the way of all of them.

"Aren't you tired of hearing this, Ms. Holben?" Beatrice asked.

Catherine rolled her eyes upward and declined to comment. She had learned early on that there was no way she could dispel the mystique of having, or even pretending to have, a baby fathered by a young man the group held in high esteem.

"Ms. Holben?"

"What, Sasha?" Catherine responded to the pulling on her sleeve. Sasha was her "little one," the thirteen-year-old who still watched the Saturday morning cartoons. Unlike the others, she never mentioned the father of her baby, even in the most general of terms—or perhaps she was too young to be impressed by a Sweet Eddie-type status symbol. If Sasha was impressed by anything, it was a world championship wrestler with bleached blond hair. She was wearing her favorite wrestling T-shirt today, one that saluted the wrestlers of the past with a big picture of Mr. Moto and Gorgeous George. Sasha liked Gorgeous George—because she'd read that he used to throw gold bobby pins to his fans.

"Ms. Holben," Sasha said again, because Catherine's attention had already wandered. Catherine couldn't stop thinking about another child today, about Fritz D'Amaro.

I call him Joe so he won't die—

She kept thinking about the look that Fritz had given her at the bottom of the stairs, as if it were she, Catherine, who needed reassurance.

Don't worry. He's not like Koong-Shee's father—

"Are we eating outside today, Ms. Holben? It ain't raining."

She forced her attention back to Sasha. "Do you want to?"

"Yeah! It's like a picnic! Beatrice's got her radio—she won't play it loud and get all them office women upset, will you, Beatrice?"

"Who, me?" Beatrice said innocently.

47

Catherine smiled. Beatrice Delcambre's radio only had two alternatives: off and loud. She looked at her watch. "All right. We'll go outside. Sasha, you go down to the refrigerator and get the lunches."

"By myself?" she asked, alarmed. The building's only refrigerator was in the front office, and Sasha was afraid of the long, dark hallway she had to walk down to get there.

"Take Abby with you."

"Aw, Ms. Holben, don't send Abby," Maria said. "If she meets somebody saying they hungry between here and that refrigerator, she'll give away every bag she's got."

"No she won't," Beatrice said, "because Sasha won't let her. Will you, Sasha?"

"No, Beatrice," Sasha said, more than pleased at having Beatrice's trust.

"And don't you go eating anything out of those bags," Beatrice added.

"No, Beatrice," she said again.

Catherine waited until Sasha and Abby had come back with the lunches—all of them, she was happy to see—then walked with the group to the one picnic table out under the pine trees in the back school yard. She and her five students had been banished to a classroom in a recycled school building too old to be used for anything but administrative offices and projects like the one for pregnant students, and its dark and sagging interior hadn't been improved by the week of rain. Catherine was glad for the chance to get outside, glad to be in the sunshine again.

"Ms. Holben, this table's all wet! We can't eat out here!"

"Maria, here," Catherine said, bringing a large plastic drop cloth out of her tote bag. She'd found, too, that one couldn't function in a sixty-year-old building full of leaks and drafts and falling plaster without anticipating problems never considered by the better housed.

The weather was still cool, deceptively cool, because of yesterday's rain. But the mid-September heat would be back, and she and the group would soon swelter in their un-air-conditioned classroom on the west side of the building. She'd managed to get permission to have one of the closer school cafeterias send bag lunches every day, but she hadn't been able to get the class moved to the cooler, shadier side. Beggars, it seemed, couldn't be choosers.

Catherine sat amid the rattling sandwich papers and Beatrice's rock music, trying to keep her space on the drop cloth on top of the table, her mind again going to Fritz D'Amaro. She had a telephone number—a business number. She needed to talk to Joe D'Amaro, if he'd stand still long enough to listen. She thought that Fritz was a troubled little girl, and her father needed to know that.

"Ms. Holben, Sasha's eating candy," Maria informed her. Maria was partial to bib overalls—bib overalls with tank tops in warm weather, bib overalls with flannel shirts when it was cold—and she wasn't above keeping her own supply of junk food in the bib pocket.

"I am not! I ate all my other stuff! Ms. Holben don't care if sometimes you eat candy last, Maria. She just cares if you eat candy and nothing else, ain't that right, Ms. Holben?"

"That's right, Sasha."

"Ms. Holben?"

"What, Sasha?"

"This candy ain't bad for you, Ms. Holben. It's got peanuts, okay?"

"That's good, Sasha."

"Do you think Sweet Eddie's cute, Ms. Holben?"

"I've never seen the gentleman, Sasha," Catherine had to confess.

"Sweet Eddie ain't no gentleman, Ms. Holben," Cherry said. "He's a good-looking, sweet-talking son of a gun, but he ain't no—uh-oh, Ms. Holben!"

"Cherry, what?" Catherine said, somewhat alarmed by the look on Cherry's face.

"I forgot to tell you! You're supposed to call that sucker!"

"What sucker?"

"That sucker coming right there. Here," she said, thrusting a piece of paper with a phone number under her nose.

Catherine looked down at the paper.

"He came here this morning, Ms. Holben. I said you rode the bus and you didn't get here till it did. He said he wanted you to call him—as soon as you could. Is that your boyfriend, Ms. Holben?"

"No," Catherine said as she got off the table. She crossed the grass to head off Joe D'Amaro before he got any closer. She didn't know what kind of mood he was in, and if last night was any indication of his usual behavior, she didn't want the girls to hear him.

He looked the same as he had yesterday—like a construction worker who wasn't wearing his hard hat. It occurred to her as she walked toward him how little she'd thought of Jonathan today. She had been thinking only of this man's child.

"Ms. Holben," he said, holding up his hand as if he thought she might try to ignore him. He took long strides to close the distance between them, but if she was expecting an apology for his parting remark last night, she was mistaken.

"Ms. Holben, I wanted you to call me. I wanted to ask you about—" he glanced at the picnic table, then glanced at it again—"about . . . are all those girls pregnant?" he suddenly asked, as if what he had seen had only just registered.

"Yes, they are."

50

He frowned slightly. "Oh. What I want to know is what Fritz said to you. What do you do for a living, anyway?" he asked, looking back at the table. This time Beatrice and Maria waved.

"I work with the city school program for pregnant students."

"They're . . . awfully young, aren't they?"

"Yes."

"Just little kids," he said, more to himself than to her.

"What?"

"Nothing. It's kind of sad." He looked back at her. "About Fritz—when can you talk to me?" It seemed not to have occurred to him that after his rudeness last night she might not want to talk to him.

"I have some time now—"

"No, I can't now. I'm working. I can come by your place tonight. I'm not sure when—six or seven. Maybe later."

She hesitated, not wanting to commit herself to waiting an entire evening for someone who might not show up, and yet she needed to talk to him about Fritz.

"Look, Ms. Holben. I'll come by as soon as I can. That's the best I can tell you. If you're there, maybe you'll have time to talk to me. If you're not, you can call me when you do. It's important, Ms. Holben. I . . . know you've got your own troubles."

She ignored his allusion to the scene he'd witnessed with Jonathan.

"Fritz is all right, isn't she?" she asked.

For the first time he looked into Catherine's eyes. "I don't know."

She stared back at him, seeing more than she thought he'd want her to see—that he was worried, perhaps afraid, and that his minimal courtesy now was likely his way of distancing himself from it.

"I should be home this evening," she said. "I'm usually at home by six."

Relief flooded his face. "Good. I'll see you this evening, then." He turned and started toward the street.

"Mr. D'Amaro?"

He looked around at her.

"The little old lady who lives behind the screen door is Mrs. Donovan. If she asks to see your driver's license, you'll save yourself a lot of grief if you show it to her."

For a moment she thought he was going to smile, but he nodded curtly and walked back toward the street and a battered pickup truck with an upside-down wheelbarrow in the back.

Catherine realized suddenly that Abby was standing at her elbow. Abby was in her fifth month of pregnancy, a pregnancy that to Catherine seemed incredible. Abby was certainly attractive enough to have garnered her share of male attention. Her hair was long and curly and blond, and she had startling but somewhat dreamy blue eyes that belied her high academic standing in the junior class. But she was sometimes as childlike as she was beautiful, leaving Catherine often feeling as if she were explaining the harsher realities of unwed motherhood to a Walt Disney character come to life. Abby was seemingly without guile, suspecting no one and nothing, trusting to a fault. Catherine had never had anything that even resembled a meaningful conversation with Abby, and she waited, not willing to let an opportunity slip by.

"Is he your boyfriend, Ms. Holben?" Abby asked, repeating Maria's earlier question.

"No. He's not my boyfriend."

"Does he have a . . . pregnant daughter or something?"

"Why do you ask that?"

"I just thought he looked like he did."

"Upset, you mean?"

"Upset," she agreed. "When my baby gets here, I'm going to do what Maria did."

"And what's that?" Catherine asked. She wasn't at all certain that Maria was any kind of role model.

"Whenever her father started yelling at her about what she'd done, she'd give him the baby to hold."

Catherine didn't think that Maria had a father, but she didn't say so. "Maybe you'd better try to talk to your dad before your baby gets here. Maria's method might calm down an irate grandfather, but I'm not so sure it's good for the baby."

The rest of the girls were wandering toward them, and she stood with Abby and waited, firmly putting Fritz and Joe D'Amaro out of her mind.

"All right, we've got a few minutes before Mrs. Bauer comes for your math class. . . ." She paused for the collective groans, knowing that Patricia Bauer could give a few groans of her own. It wasn't easy teaching mathematics or anything else on as many different levels as this group represented. "I want you to tell me what names you've picked for your babies. Beatrice, cut the music and tell me yours."

Another simplistic approach to a major problem, Catherine thought. She had no delusions about the fact that these girls had *chosen* to have their babies. The truth was that most of them had hidden their condition until they had no alternative, and they would continue to deny their pregnancies if she didn't do something to make them think of their babies as real. She understood their denial; she didn't fault them for it. She, herself, had used that most basic means of coping in trying to deal with her infertility and with Jonathan, perhaps just as Joe D'Amaro was doing in trying to cope with sad little Fritz.

"Mark or Darlene," Beatrice said. "You going out with

that guy, Ms. Holben?"

"No, Beatrice. I am not going out with him. He is *not* my boyfriend. He is not going to *be* my boyfriend. I don't even know the man, all right? What about you, Abby? Have you picked out any names?"

"You ought to go out with him, Ms. Holben," Beatrice continued, undaunted. "He's a nice-looking guy. There aren't too many nice-looking guys your age around here. Times have changed, Ms. Holben. If you like his looks, you should call him up and ask him if he wants to go out."

"We seen him checking you out, Ms. Holben," Sasha said. "He's funny—acting like he's all business and looking you over, so you don't see him—"

"Sasha," Catherine said. "I asked Abby a question."

Abby shook her head and looked at the ground.

"Abby's going to call hers It," Maria said. "She's going to say, 'Don't you cry, *It*.' 'Come here, little *It*—' "

"No I won't," Abby said, her eyes brimming. "I just can't find a name I want."

"Maybe you can name him after his daddy—if you know who *that* is."

"That's enough, Maria," Catherine said.

"I got me a name for my little girl," Sasha said, absently patting Abby on the shoulder.

"Sasha, you don't know if you got a girl or not," Maria said. "You can get a boy just as easy, you silly thing. You're so dumb, you don't know nothing."

"No, I ain't going to get no boy, either. I'm getting me a girl. My grandmamma put her ring on a string and held it over my belly and it went back and forth just like it's sup-posed to for a baby girl."

"That was them wrestlers on that T-shirt making it do that," Cherry said.

"No, it wasn't! My grandmamma says it's a girl and that's what it is. And her name's going to be Treasure, because that's what she is to my grandmamma and me. Treasure Mary Higgins. And me and Treasure ain't listening to nothing you got to say about no *boys*. Especially you, Maria."

"Sasha, I'm going to smack you silly!" Maria said, grabbing Sasha by her shirtfront.

"Hold it!" Catherine said. "Maria, I told you that's enough. You stay after class today so we can talk."

"I ain't got nothing to talk about."

"Well, I do," Catherine said, staring her down. She looked at her watch. "That's all the time we've got. Mrs. Bauer will be waiting for you."

She got the chorus of groans again.

"I don't know why I got to do math, anyway," Sasha said.

"So when Treasure asks you for a dollar to go to the store, you won't give her two," Beatrice said.

"Maybe I'll give her two just because she's Treasure," Sasha countered.

"And maybe you'll end up broke too."

The afternoon wore on, tense and uneasy because of Maria's sullenness. The temperature in the classroom began to rise as the sun came around to the west side, and Catherine fought off the sweaty listlessness that threatened to envelop her, trying to help Pat Bauer with her presence if nothing else. Pat was small and frail-looking and unusually pale today. Her hair needed washing and her cotton summer dress was wrinkled and too small. There were gaps in the seamline along her midriff where the threads had given way, and her skin showed through. It was as if all her energy went into her job now and she had no strength left over for her personal appearance. She was keeping her train of thought on her lecture, but Catherine could feel how much she was having to struggle to

55

do it. It was Catherine's mind that kept wandering, kept registering the background sounds of subdued voices and closing doors and ringing telephones throughout the building, the very fact that they were none of her business making them irresistible. She hadn't changed from the time she was Sasha's age. Her mind preferred anything to the hot, droning monotony of postprandial mathematics.

I call him Joe so he won't die—

"What do you think, Ms. Holben?" Pat said, catching her completely off-guard.

"I think . . . I think I wasn't listening," Catherine confessed, making the group burst into laughter. "Further, I think that this class is going to perish right here if it doesn't get up and go get a drink of water. What do you think, Mrs. Bauer?"

Pat hesitated, then threw up her hands. "Go. *Go!* And come right back. I mean it! What did you do that for?" she said as soon as the last girl had filed out. "You don't have to make exceptions for me, Catherine. I can pull my own weight. And when I can't, you'll be the first to know."

"Pat, I did it for *me*. I'm falling asleep here."

"Thanks a lot, Catherine."

"That's not what I meant. It's hot in here. And they're all pregnant. They're supposed to be learning math, not physical endurance. I thought a short break would do us all good— even you."

"From now on you let me decide who's going to get up and walk out of *my* class, all right?"

"Fine," Catherine said. She reached for a clipboard on a nearby table, using it for a makeshift fan and finding it totally useless.

"I didn't mean to make you mad," Pat said after a moment.

"You didn't," Catherine said truthfully.

"I thought we decided I didn't have to pretend with you. I thought we decided I could say anything I wanted to."

"Yes, but we didn't decide whether I'd knock you over the head with a clipboard for it."

To Catherine's relief Pat laughed. "That's what I like about you, Holben. You don't care if I'm dying or not."

The truth of the matter was that Catherine cared a great deal. She had met Patricia Bauer in the same place she'd met Charlotte Duffy—in the doctor's office. In her futile quest for pregnancy Catherine had been in the waiting room often enough to take up permanent residence, and there had been nothing for women stranded by an impending birth or overbooked appointments to do but talk. She had liked Pat immediately. Pat was blunt and outspoken, and they'd both been abandoned—Catherine because of her inability to conceive, and Pat because of a tumor in her breast.

"That, and a two-breasted floozy half my age," Pat had once said.

"Jonathan's got a floozy too," Catherine said now. It was that kind of friendship. Neither of them worried particularly about making sense.

"I beg your pardon?" Pat said with appropriate confusion.

"Jonathan. He's got a floozy," Catherine repeated absently.

"Face it, Catherine. We both married men who can't hack trouble and heartache."

"Jonathan's marrying his. Next month. The fifteenth."

"So how do you feel about that?"

"I . . . think she's probably not a floozy. She's probably some nice woman who's crazy about him."

"A brood mare, you mean."

"*No*, that's not what I mean."

Their eyes met and they both laughed.

"All right. So that's what I mean."

"So are you okay?"

"I'm not surprised. I expected it. He wants children."

"Yes, but are you okay? You've got to be upset, Catherine."

Catherine got up to try to force a few more windows open, but it was useless. "Well, it does put a kink in my favorite fantasy."

Pat smiled. "What fantasy is that?"

"The one where I take a dozen lovers—all of whom are rich and famous. I have a baby by each of them and we all go to Jonathan's inevitable wedding and sit in the front row."

Pat laughed out loud. "You are crazy, you know that? But *your* fantasies are vengefully healthy, at least. When Don left, I never could get past my coffin being slowly lowered into my grave—and Don throwing himself on it in abject contrition."

"That's not funny, Pat."

"Not funny but true. I forgot that I'm supposed to ask you on behalf of the front office staff who the guy was who came by here looking for you this morning."

"He's not anybody. He wants to talk to me about his daughter."

"Now why do I believe that?" Pat said.

"Because you know I tell the truth—usually."

"Except to yourself. You just have the fantasies, you don't do anything about them, right? Or didn't you notice that he was a *very* nice-looking man? Okay, ladies," Pat said loudly because the girls were coming back, "listen up!"

Catherine sat frowning. She supposed that Joe D'Amaro was what most women would call handsome, and she supposed that she had relegated his now apparent good looks into the same category as the renovations of the old downtown buildings—as something she hadn't really noticed because she wasn't ready to participate in that particular aspect of her environment. Perhaps she was still more involved with Jonathan than she'd thought.

No. It wasn't her enchantment with Jonathan that kept her from noticing another man. It was her disenchantment with herself.

The class ended—finally. Pat was clearly exhausted, sitting down immediately behind the desk. Catherine hovered close by, watching out of the corner of her eye and knowing better than to approach her.

"You know what's wrong with me?" Pat said after a time.

"Tell me."

"I had to ask Don for money. I had to ask Don Bauer for goddamn money!"

"Pat—"

"Well, I couldn't ask you, could I? You're in worse financial shape than I am. I mean, it's not like I can guarantee that I'll pay you back."

"Pat—"

"Be careful, Catherine!" Pat warned. "You know the deal. I get to say whatever I want." She grabbed up her books and papers, not taking the time to shove them into her briefcase. She dropped her purse as she went through the doorway, but Catherine made no effort to help her pick it up. She knew the "deal" only too well, and she meant to keep her part of it. Pat had wanted someone, *someone,* with whom she didn't have to be optimistic and brave. And Catherine Holben was it. It was a very difficult job.

"Pat," Catherine called before she disappeared down the hallway, and she looked back over her shoulder. "I think you'd better work on your fantasies too."

She made no reply, and Catherine could hear the echoing

of her heels down the long hallway. She went back to the desk and began to sort through her papers.

"Ms. Holben?"

Catherine looked up. Maria was standing in the doorway.

"You said you wanted to talk to me."

Maria had her thumbs hooked in the bib of her overalls, and her tone of voice suggested fully the burden she considered this to be.

"Yes. I do."

"I said I ain't got nothing I want to talk about."

"You don't have to talk. What you do is listen. I want you to lay off Sasha and Abby. Cherry, too, while you're at it."

"They get on my nerves—"

"They do *not* get on your nerves, Maria. What gets on your nerves is that you got caught again. You took no responsibility for your behavior, and now you're pregnant and you're stuck with it and you want to take it out on somebody who'll let you do it."

"I can't help how my nerves are," she said sullenly.

"Then why don't you jump on Beatrice? Somehow she never gets on your nerves, does she? All of you have got a hard time ahead of you, and I don't want you making it any worse."

"What do you know, anyway? You ain't never had no baby!"

"Who delivered your last baby, Maria?" Catherine said sharply.

She didn't answer.

"Who? A man doctor or a woman?"

"A man."

"Did he know what he was doing?"

"Yeah, I guess so."

"How many babies had *he* had, Maria? Personally, I mean.

60

How many times has he lain on his back in labor and pushed out a baby? I know what I'm doing —just like he does. I don't do this for fun, and I don't do it for the money. You think I stand in this hot place every day for the salary? I do it for *you*. I *know* what you need, and by the time your baby's born, you're going to know what I know. Now go home."

Maria stood looking at her.

"Go!"

She flounced out of the room, and Catherine wiped her sweaty forehead with the back of her hand.

"God!" she said under her breath.

"What is going on in here?" one of the secretaries from the front office said from the doorway.

"Nothing—except I've been here too long."

"We were afraid you might need some help."

"No, everything's under control," Catherine said. She began to gather up her things. She had paperwork to do, but she left the papers on the desk. She'd dealt with enough aggravation in the last twenty-four hours, and she was going home.

She took a different route to the Mayfair, stopping long enough at an old-fashioned grocery in one of the downtown stores to buy a few things, but she didn't look into the front window of the Purple Box while she waited for the next bus. She arrived at her apartment building shortly after six, wilted from the heat and tired in body and spirit. She took her shoes off as soon as she was inside the French doors, walking quietly into the entry hall and savoring the coolness of the wood flooring on the bottoms of her bare feet. She checked her mail and found a heavy, cream-colored envelope inside—an invitation to Jonathan's wedding that was not addressed in Jonathan's hand. If she hadn't seen him yesterday, she supposed she would have found out about his impending marriage like

61

this. No wonder he'd come out into the rain. She tossed the invitation into the flowered wastepaper basket, then fished it out again. She wanted to read it a few more times before she burned it, and she wondered if that, too, were "vengefully healthy."

Poor Pat . . .

God. If she made up a list of people she was feeling sorry for today, it would be endless—and Catherine Holben would be right near the top.

She didn't see Mrs. Donovan as she passed her door. Still barefoot, she began to climb the three flights of stairs, juggling her shoes and her groceries and her purse. There was a strong, cool draft coming up the stairwell; perhaps there was something practical in Mrs. Donovan's screen door, after all.

On the second landing she spilled the apples she'd bought out of her grocery bag, and she had to empty the bag and put them in the bottom to keep them from spilling again. She climbed the rest of the stairs, already anticipating a long, cool shower and something equally long and cool to drink.

But—like Jonathan—Joe D'Amaro was sitting on the top step.

4

Joe D'Amaro said nothing, just stood up before she was halfway up the stairs. When she was near enough, he took the tilting bag of groceries out of her arms. Catherine perceived no sense of politeness in the gesture, simply his assessment that her arms were full and that she would need to open the door before they could address *his* reason for being here.

"What kind of day have you had, Mr. D'Amaro?" she asked as she put the key into the lock.

"It's been a bitch," he said without hesitation.

"So has mine," she said before she pushed open the door. "I think this will go a lot better if you remember that."

He looked at her thoughtfully, and once again she had the impression that he was about to smile.

But he didn't.

"I'm here to talk about Fritz."

"Exactly. So let's both keep the aggravations of the day out of it."

"Hey, fine with me," he said as he followed her inside. "Where do you want the bag?"

"I'll take it."

She took the grocery bag from him and carried it into the kitchen, and she was a bit perturbed that he followed her. It wasn't that she was afraid of him, or that she was worried that the kitchen might be in a mess—actually she rarely had clutter now that she lived alone. It was more that he presumed, seeming to expect her goodwill with little attendance to the social amenities on his part. It was as if he didn't want her help, but he realized that he perhaps needed it, and that possibility had brought him here—but to hell with the p's and q's.

Still, she had no quarrel with a man who cared about his children. She had been in her line of work too long not to know what a rarity that could be. She began to empty the bag, putting the milk away and glancing in his direction as she closed the refrigerator door. He was looking at the ceiling.

She made no effort at small talk: how long he had lived in Wilmington, because his accent wasn't North Carolinian; or how many children he had, because she already knew. She dumped the apples onto the kitchen table.

"Would you like an apple, Mr. D'Amaro?" she asked instead. This time he was looking at the cabinet of Blue Willow dishes.

"Yeah, it's a long time until dinner," he answered, again without hesitation. Clearly he was a man who also didn't vacillate.

She tossed him one of the largest. "Do you want a knife to peel it?"

"No," he said, walking to the sink and washing it off briefly under the tap. "This is a great place," he said, looking at the ceiling again. "Really built to last. Me—I'd rather restore a building like this than throw up a hundred of those condos on the beachfront." He took a bite of the apple. "It makes my brother crazy."

"I can imagine," Catherine said. "Money's money. And there can't be much of it in restorations." She got an apple of her own, and she was readjusting her thinking about Joseph D'Amaro. She still thought he was impatient and volatile, and she'd also thought he would deliberately keep himself distant from strangers like her. She was surprised at his revelation about his building preference and his brother's response to it. Strange, she thought, that he had such admiration for the building, a building Jonathan had such disgust for. She washed the apple at the sink as he had done, and when she turned around, she found Joe D'Amaro looking at her intently, making assessments of his own.

You don't give a damn about money, Joe almost said, and it occurred to him suddenly that he had no idea where that notion had come from. He didn't know this woman, even if his years in the PTA did tell him that she couldn't be doing whatever she was doing with that bunch of pregnant girls in tow for the salary. But then, maybe she couldn't find anything else, and she was just marking time until she could get a better job. She could be like Michael's wife, Margaret. She could have kept Jonathan hopping to get her everything she wanted until Jonathan decided to keep the Mercedes-Benz and dump her—if he'd dumped her.

No, he'd dumped her all right. Joe could see it when he looked into her eyes. There was a kind of lost and sad look there, something he recognized because he'd seen it in his own eyes after Lisa died. It must not matter *why* the other person left, he thought suddenly—only that they were gone.

He pulled out one of the kitchen chairs and sat down, watching while she jerked the cord on the ceiling fan over the table and put away the rest of her groceries. The air from the fan felt good, and he took another bite of the apple and waited, fighting down the urge to hurry her along. She moved to the double kitchen windows, opening both of them. He could hear the wind in the willow oaks outside and the traffic from the street below. He wanted to tell her that the room would stay cooler if she left the windows closed, but he kept it to himself. Some people wanted fresh air more than they wanted to stay cool.

"About Fritz," he said because he didn't want to wait any longer.

"Is Lisa your wife?" Catherine asked, to be certain she understood Fritz's remarks.

He frowned. "She was," he said carefully. It hadn't occurred to him that Catherine Holben might know anything about Lisa. Jesus, what had Fritz told this woman?

"She died," Catherine went on. "And she was Fritz's mother." It wasn't a question.

He stood up, looking for a place to throw the half-eaten apple. "Yes. And I don't talk about her. To anybody. Could we just get on with this? I want to know what Fritz said to you. That's all."

"Under the sink," she said because he was still holding the apple. "Do you know why Fritz calls you Joe?"

"What the hell has that got to do with anything?" he snapped. Earlier he'd come close to admiring the straightforwardness in this woman, but now it was beginning to get on his nerves. And with that question she'd stepped squarely on the thing that had nagged at him for the past two years, when he'd suddenly ceased to be Daddy and he'd become the somber Joe.

He was afraid suddenly. He hadn't loved Fritz the way he should have, and he didn't want to hear that she had suffered for it. Love begat love. Maybe Fritz didn't love him now. Maybe he'd ruined it, and that quiet, gentle little girl of his didn't give a damn about him. He tossed the apple into the garbage can under the sink.

"Do you know?" Catherine persisted.

"No. She just does. She started it when she was about five. Look, are you going to tell me what she said to you or am I wasting my time?"

"She said she calls you Joe so you won't die."

He gave her a stricken look, and Catherine was certain now. He was not nearly so unaffected by the problems in his life as he wanted her to think. His lips pursed, as if he were going to say something, but he didn't say it. He walked to the double windows, instead, looking down at the traffic below.

Catherine waited, watching him draw a deep breath.

"Before we moved here," he said finally, "Fritz's grand-mother—Lisa's mother—lived with us for a while. I . . . always thought Fritz did it because that's what she heard her grandmother call me all the time." He looked around at her. "But you don't think that, do you?"

"No."

"What are you, some kind of expert on kids?"

"I've worked with a lot of children and—"

"Worked with," he said, interrupting. "But you don't have any of your own."

He remembered her argument with Jonathan. What had she said? "Until you made my having a baby a condition of the marriage?" She must be one of those career women, then, who didn't give a damn about having children. She was crazy if she thought she was going to tell him what he should be doing with his.

They stared at each other across the room.

"No, Mr. D'Amaro," she said quietly. "I don't have chil-dren of my own. You know, this is the second time I've had this same conversation today, and I'm getting tired of it. I am not a mother, but I know a lot about children and I think Fritz—"

"Maybe I don't want to hear what you think, Ms. Holben. I don't need your criticism about the way I raise my kids. And just what makes you such a goddamn authority?"

"I'm not an authority. Nobody is. And this has gone far enough. I don't like to be jerked around, Mr. D'Amaro. Particularly in my own home. *You* came to *me*. You asked me about Fritz, and I'm trying to tell you. I don't know what it is about this situation that makes you so defensive. I really don't care. But whatever it is that's giving you all this guilt, you're not taking it out on me."

"You think *I'm* guilty? Great! It's not enough for you to psychoanalyze Fritz—you want to take a stab at me too. What is it with you? You don't even know me."

She looked him directly in the eye. "I know you're making a big effort to find out what's bothering your child—on the surface. But you don't really want to know. You're worried about her, but you want to hear me say all little girls go around calling their fathers by their first names so they won't die. You want the status quo, Mr. D'Amaro, because anything else is inconvenient."

"Shit!" he said loudly.

"Right!" she said. "That's what it is, because it doesn't suit *you*. Life is full of inconveniences, Mr. D'Amaro, and I'm sure Fritz would have gotten around to telling you she's scared you're going to die like her mother did—instead of telling a total stranger. Oh, but I forgot. You're not home much, and Della's only interested in parties and clothes, and Charlie stays glued to a computer."

"I don't have time for this," he said impatiently, heading toward the front door. "Don't think I don't appreciate it, Ms. Holben."

He caught a glimpse of the gnomes on the coffee table as he passed through the living room, and the great weight around his heart grew heavier still.

Jesus, Lisa! Why did you leave me with this?

He jerked the door open and let it slam after him, but he knew before he reached the bottom of the stairs what he was going to have to do. He stood in the foyer by the mailboxes, trying to put his anger aside. He was always angry these days. It was stupid and he knew it, but he still let it overwhelm him.

He started to go back up the stairs, but the old woman behind the screen door stood watching. He went out the front doors instead, leaving his handprint on the beveled glass.

Catherine watched him from the living-room window, looking down on him with a bird's-eye view as he walked across the street to that same battered truck with the wheelbarrow in the back she'd seen earlier.

Way to go, Holben, she thought. For someone who was supposed to be reasonably skilled in handling people, she'd done a remarkably poor job of it today. First Maria, and now Joe D'Amaro—when she knew better. In both instances she had reacted to their behavior and not looked for the cause of it.

"I'm too tired to look for causes," she said aloud. "I've got troubles of my own."

Joe D'Amaro looked up as he got into the truck, and she moved away from the window. Tired or not, she had been concerned about Fritz, and she hadn't been much help to her—except to put her father more on the defensive than he already was. She sighed heavily. This was exactly what she did *not* need—more guilt.

She went back into the kitchen, her still bare feet padding across the wooden floor. Perhaps Joe D'Amaro would have found her a little more credible if she'd put her shoes on. She stood for a moment in front of the sink, replaying in her mind what she should have said and done.

But it was too late. She had missed her chance because she was tired and because Joe D'Amaro was defensive—and little Fritz had wound up getting the short end of the stick.

She roamed around the apartment, gathering up dirty laundry to take down to the basement. She was somewhat ashamed of her need to hurry past Mrs. Donovan's screen door, but she didn't want to have to elaborate on the number of irate men seen leaving her apartment of late.

Mrs. Donovan was nowhere to be seen, though the now familiar scent of Lucky Strikes wafted out into the hall.

Strange, Catherine thought as she passed. There was a time when she could have imagined herself trying to conjure up Jonathan's memory, if she, like Mrs. Donovan, had been the one left behind. Of course, she *had* been left behind essentially, but by choice, not by chance, and unlike Mrs. Donovan, she had recovered from it. She must be recovered, or else she would have been grateful to have been asked to Jonathan's wedding. Any crumb of attention would have been better than no crumb at all. If she was still in love with him, she'd *want* to go. She'd want his new friends to see what a civilized and understanding woman he'd given up. She'd want to justify Jonathan's trust in her by her exemplary behavior toward his new wife—instead of wanting to give him a well-placed kick in the groin.

She suddenly smiled. Another fine example of the difference between her fantasies and Pat Bauer's.

The laundry room was poorly lit, but she wasn't afraid. She put her first load of clothes into a washing machine and went to sit by the door that led to the parking area underneath the building because the light was better. The parking area was mostly an empty expanse of concrete with oil spots, because very few of the tenants had cars anymore. They were either like her—financially unable to resurrect an old and dying vehicle from its terminal disrepair—or they'd become physically unable to drive, or they'd never learned in the first place.

She glanced out the glass-and-wire window in the door, squinting a bit at the shaft of sunlight that pierced the dark underpinnings of the Mayfair. Surrounded by the pleasant smell of hot, soapy water and the quiet rhythm of the washing machine, she reached into her pocket for Jonathan's wedding invitation.

She carefully studied the handwriting on the envelope—not Jonathan's but Ellen Jessup's, she supposed. The script was rounded and vertical, almost childlike with its small, carefully closed-up letters. She wondered how much Ellen had been pressured into believing that the two of them could be friends. Poor Ellen. She must have hated sending this, but Jonathan could be so persuasive and so dense.

She opened the envelope and reread the invitation, running her fingers over the lettering as she did so. Engraved, not printed. But then Jonathan could afford that. She wondered, too, what the Jessup woman had been told about the breakup of her fiancé's former marriage. Jonathan's behavior yesterday indicated that the reason was now clear in his mind at least, and that by some quirk of logic Catherine's infertility had had little to do with it. He wanted it to be something else—some other catchall phrase for discarded wives, such as "irreconcilable differences."

But there really hadn't been differences. Sadly he still wanted to be her friend, and he actually thought it was possible, not only to do that but also to have the friendship encompass his new wife.

People think whatever they need to think.

Jonathan. Pat Bauer. Sasha and Beatrice and the rest of them. Even Joe D'Amaro.

Even me.

Perhaps she hadn't recovered so well from losing Jonathan, after all. Perhaps there had been more wrong than she—

She jumped because someone pecked on the glass window. Joe D'Amaro stood on the other side of the door. He didn't look angry any longer, but she still hesitated before she opened it, staring at him gravely through the glass.

She took a deep breath and stuffed the invitation into her pocket, bracing herself for another confrontation. She did care about Fritz, and she opened the door.

"It's not you," he said immediately, and she perceived it as a kind of shorthand apology and likely the best she would get.

"No, I didn't think it was," she answered. "If I had, I wouldn't have opened the door."

"So can we try this again? I . . . thought it over. I figure you must know something, and I'd like to hear it."

She couldn't keep from smiling at this heavy-handed appraisal of her expertise.

"No, I didn't mean it like that. I mean you work with kids with problems. You've got to know . . ."

"Something," Catherine finished for him when he realized that his amendment wasn't going to be an improvement.

"Well, yeah."

The washing machine was going into the rinse cycle, and Catherine went to put in the fabric softener. "Did Mrs. Donovan send you down here?"

"The lady with the screen door? Yeah. She sent me in through the garage here so you could see me before you let me in—in case you wanted to tell me to take a hike. Nice old woman. Smart."

Catherine glanced at him. He was being serious, not sarcastic, and he was looking at the ceiling again—or rather the building supports.

"Have you changed your mind?" she asked.

"What?"

"The building. You still think it's built to last?"

"Oh, hell, yes. The only thing that'll bring this place down is some greedy developer with a wrecking ball. About Fritz. I guess you know I didn't like her talking to you the way she did. It . . . hurt my feelings more than anything. She doesn't know you."

"That's probably why she said it—because I'm a stranger. Children sometimes do that—pick a grown-up who they think might help but not one that might be hurt. My knowing she's worried couldn't hurt me the way it might hurt you."

"You mean you've got kids spilling their guts to you all the time."

Now he was being sarcastic.

"No, I mean Fritz isn't the first."

He was standing in the patch of light from the glass window, and he was on the verge of being angry again. She could feel the effort he was putting into staying civil.

Blue eyes, she thought suddenly. Not brown. Why had she thought his eyes were brown?

And he was still wary. "Suppose you tell me what it is you are, professionally speaking," he said, and she wasn't offended by the question. It was only prudent that he should want to know how credible her opinion might be.

"I have a degree in nursing. I have half a degree in education. Aside from that, I'm not entirely stupid, and I listen to what people tell me one way or the other—even if they're Fritz's age."

"One way or the other?"

"People don't always tell you things in words, Mr. D'Amaro."

"They don't," he said, the sarcasm still in his voice, and Catherine turned away from him. The conversation was deteriorating again, and she still had laundry to do.

He followed along in behind her as he had in the kitchen. "I think . . . running around thinking you know what people *don't* say is damn presumptive, Ms. Holben."

She began putting her wet clothes into the dryer. "No, actually, my thinking I know what people don't say is a damn nuisance." She looked up at him, staring directly into his eyes. "Like now."

He held her gaze for a moment, then looked away. He understood what she meant—that she was suffering his rudeness because of what he *hadn't* said. He looked back at her. She was waiting, probably with more patience than he deserved.

"See, the thing of it is, Ms. Holben, I was really ticked last night. I got off on the wrong foot with you, and maybe you think I want to stay that way. It's just that Fritz has never gone off by herself without telling anybody like she did when she came over here. She's a good kid."

"Yes," Catherine said as she started the dryer.

"Yes? What does that mean?"

"It means yes. She seems like what you would think of as a 'good kid.' She seems very old for her age. Very responsible."

"What *I* would think—but not what *you* would think, right?"

"What I think is that she seems like the kind of child who wouldn't want to cause you any problems if she could help it. That's usually labeled 'good.' "

He was frowning, as if something had just occurred to him, something not entirely to his liking.

"She voted to sell the gnomes," he said.

"I beg your pardon?"

"The gnomes, the gnomes. I didn't just sell the thing out from under her, Ms. Holben. We needed the money. We had a family meeting. She voted with the rest of them to sell it—" He broke off suddenly, as if he hadn't meant to tell her that. "You think that's what she did? You think she voted yes to keep from causing me any trouble?"

To Catherine it seemed more an accusation than a question.

"I couldn't say. The only thing I know is that she loves the gnomes enough to go off on her own to see them."

"Yeah, well, I didn't, okay? I didn't know she was so crazy about that sculpture. If I had—" He stopped, then sighed. "You're right about her being . . . old for her age. Even to me she seems that way, like she's my oldest kid. But I don't keep things from any of my children. This town's not exactly wide open for a small builder, particularly one that came here from someplace else. When the mortgage payment's due and you don't have the money—you think it's wrong, don't you?"

"Mr. D'Amaro, will you stop putting words into my mouth?"

"I'm asking you a question."

"Fine. Then I suppose it depends on what's happening and who the children are. But, as you pointed out, what do I know?"

He glanced at her sharply, then began to pace aimlessly around the basement. Catherine left him to his thoughts, trying not to intrude while he pitted his desire to help his daughter against the reality of what Catherine supposed was a faltering business with no ready cash.

"The thing is, Ms. Holben," he said abruptly, "I don't know what to do now."

She looked up at him. He was asking her for help, and it was killing him to do it.

"Well, for what it's worth, Mr. D'Amaro, this is what I've learned—and not just from books but from experience. Children are very . . . logical. They have reasons for thinking what they think and doing what they do. It may not make any sense at all to an adult, but it does to them. I think Fritz has some reason for thinking she has to protect you, and not calling you anything but Joe is the way she does it. It may have something to do with her mother's death, but whatever it is, I think she'll feel better when you know about it, even if she doesn't want to tell you. You know Fritz better than anyone, and you'll know when you talk to her how serious the problem is. If you'll come upstairs, I'll give you the name of a child psychologist in case you need it. She's very good, very kind, children like her—or you could talk to her by yourself if you'd rather." She stopped, feeling his resistance.

"I think you're making too much of this," he said finally. "But I—I want the name."

She led the way upstairs, and this time Mrs. Donovan was standing at her screen door.

"This is Mr. D'Amaro," she said to Mrs. Donovan in passing. "He likes the building."

"Don't have any empty apartments now," Mrs. Donovan called through the screen after them.

"No, he doesn't want to move in," Catherine said over her shoulder. "He's a builder. He likes the architecture."

"She already knows that," Joe D'Amaro said as they climbed the stairs.

"I'm not surprised," Catherine answered. She let them into her apartment, and this time he didn't follow her into the kitchen.

While she looked for the business card she wanted among the collection taped on the bulletin board, he looked at the gnomes, picking the sculpture up and turning it around in his hands. He set it down when she returned with the card, as if he thought she might object to his handling it now that it no longer belonged to him. She gave him the card.

"Do you know how expensive something like this is?" he asked as he read it.

"She has a sliding scale for her fees. You pay according to

your income and the number of dependents."

He gave a small sigh and looked upward into her eyes. "I . . . appreciate your help," he said.

She held his gaze, not looking away until he did. He didn't necessarily mean it, and they both knew it.

"About Fritz," she said, "I really wouldn't mind if she came to visit the gnomes sometime. Just call first."

"Yeah, well—I don't know about that. I think we've bothered you enough." He turned to go, pausing for a moment as he opened the door.

But he had nothing else to say. He had already said more about his personal business to this woman than he should have. He'd expected her to press him about Fritz's coming to see the gnomes, and it surprised him that she hadn't. She had done her good deed, he supposed, and she was now waiting for him to leave so she could get back to her laundry.

He gave her a curt nod and closed the door behind him, anxious now to be gone. He hurried down the stairs, catching glimpses of the faces behind the partially opened doors along the way. Bunch of old busybodies, he thought, but not unkindly, and his suspicions were confirmed as soon as he reached the ground-floor foyer.

"Mr. D'Amaro!" Mrs. Donovan called through the screen door. "Will you be coming back to see Catherine again?"

"No," he said a little curtly, because he wasn't sure how Mrs. Donovan perceived him, and he wasn't here on a social call.

"Do you have a business card with you?"

The question surprised him, and he took the time to hunt through his wallet for a card, trying to find one that was still halfway readable.

"Do you do good work, Mr. D'Amaro?"

"Yes, ma'am, we do."

77

"This building may need some work done. I'll give your card to my sister. She owns the building. She always gets estimates—you do do that, don't you? Give estimates?"

"Yes, ma'am," he said.

"Good. Thank you for the card, young man."

"My pleasure, Mrs. Donovan."

He hesitated, wanting to ask for specifics about the possibility of some work in the future, but clearly he had been dismissed. Maybe his time hadn't been completely wasted, after all, he thought as he went out the glass doors. At least he'd made a possible business contact. That the coastal property building boom was in a lull was putting it mildly, and D'Amaro Brothers could use all the business contacts they could get.

But he had enough to be concerned about at the moment without considering D'Amaro Brothers' possible bankruptcy, and he pushed that worry aside. When he was well out into the street, he couldn't resist looking upward at the windows of the Holben woman's apartment.

This time she wasn't there. He still wasn't quite sure what he thought of her, except in a superficial way. She worked with those pregnant kids, and she probably meant well. And she was attractive enough, more so than she realized, he thought. And he found that . . . interesting. Lately he'd had more than enough of women who knew what they had and used it. God, he hated going home. He was going to have to talk to Fritz and he didn't want to do it. Maybe the Holben woman was right. Maybe he did want the status quo.

But what he wanted generally had little to do with what he got. Something was the matter with Fritz, and he couldn't pretend otherwise. He should have known about the gnomes. He should have known how much she loved them. And he should have had an alternative to selling them. He was so tired of needing money, of doing everything he knew to do and working as hard as he could work and still coming up short. He wished that he had his brother Michael's optimism. Michael really believed that they were just around the corner from the big job that would make them solvent, the big job that would end all the troubles he was having with his wife. Poor, dumb Michael. He really believed that keeping Margaret faithful was merely a matter of giving her the diamond jewelry, the big car, the country-club membership she wanted.

And Margaret was yet another worry Joe had no time for. She had been coming to the house more and more often of late. Her visits seemed innocent enough—she wanted to take Della shopping or she'd brought over some paperwork or blueprints from Michael. But she was a beautiful woman, and she'd made it perfectly clear that it didn't matter to her in the least that she was married to his brother.

He was sure now that Catherine Holben wasn't anything like Margaret D'Amaro. Catherine Holben was smart, tough enough to tell him he had a problem with his kid whether he liked it or not, and real enough to share her apples with him and to walk around barefoot. And she was a nice-looking woman. And Fritz liked her. Fritz. God, he had no idea what he wanted to say to her, and he had no time to think of something. Fritz was sitting on the front porch steps as he pulled into the driveway, her head bent over a book so he wouldn't think she'd been waiting for him.

He hesitated for a moment, then got out of the truck, carrying his lunch box inside with him. Fritz stared intently at her book, turning a page now and then as he approached.

"Doing your homework out here?" he asked. He set his lunch box down and sat down on the steps beside her.

She looked at him furtively, then nodded and turned another page. "Della's listening to her *Infernal Majesty* tape."

He smiled. "Loud, huh?"

"You know Della," she said, her eyes carefully on the pages of her book.

He reached to move it so he could see the title. "*Dinosaurs and Other Ancient Reptiles*," he read aloud. "Pretty heavy for the second grade, isn't it?"

"I'm going to talk about Tyrannosaurus rex."

"Like show and tell?"

"I'm too old for show and tell. Besides, all the boys keep bringing their monster toys. Now Sister says we have to tell about something in science. She doesn't want to see anything that shoots or changes into something else. And no dolls."

He smiled, but he could feel her worrying, and her worry had nothing to do with making an oral science report.

"So what do you think?" he asked.

She looked up at him, the worry he could feel clearly visible in her eyes. How long had it been since he'd really taken the time to talk to her?

"About what?" she asked.

"About Tyrannosaurus rex," he said kindly.

"I'm glad he's extinct."

"Oh, I don't know—probably be a lot more building jobs with a big guy like that around."

The joke was feeble but she smiled, anyway. He put his arm around her shoulders. "Things going okay with you?"

"Yes," she said. One single word, dropping like a stone.

"Sometimes I get so busy, I forget to ask. You know, if things aren't okay, you can tell me, anyway—even if I look busy."

"You get mad," she said, cutting him to the quick.

"I get mad when I'm worried. Last night I was worried because I didn't know where you were."

"I was okay."

"Yes, I know that. Now. But I didn't when Della called me

to tell me you hadn't come home."

"I came home. You brought me home. I just didn't stay."

"Della didn't know that. She was upset, Fritz. She's responsible for you, you know."

"Is she?"

"You know she is."

"Why?"

"Because she's the oldest. That's her job."

"Do I have a job?"

"Yes, you do. Your job is to make sure you don't do anything like that ever again without permission."

"That's not much of a job," she said, and he tried not to smile.

"It is to me. And you do it so I don't worry."

Fritz leaned against him, her fingers restlessly picking at the edges of the pages in her book. She felt better now that they were having this talk, but then again, she didn't. "Catherine said I shouldn't," she said, bringing up the subject that would likely make Joe mad again.

"Shouldn't what?"

"Shouldn't worry people who love me if I can help it. Last night I couldn't help it," she said earnestly.

"Yes, you could, Fritz. You made a choice. A wrong choice—and that's *my* job. To tell you when it's wrong so you won't do it again."

She sat quietly, her head bowed. "Am I getting punished?" She was pretty certain that was likely, but it never hurt to ask.

"Yes. No television for two weeks."

"Saturday too?"

"Saturday too."

She gave a quiet sigh. That would be the hardest, no television on Saturday, but she had no doubt that she deserved it.

"Did you . . . see Catherine today?" she asked, getting to

the reason she'd been waiting on the porch. She hadn't been waiting to mend her fences but to find out if he'd had another run-in with the new owner of the gnomes.

"Yes, I saw her."

She gave another small sigh, as if that were the worst news he possibly could have given her. It *was* the worst news. Catherine hadn't done anything; she didn't want him to be mad at Catherine, and she was almost certain that he would have been. She loved Joe, but he wasn't nice to people sometimes and people didn't understand that it was because he was still sad about Lisa. Her Grandmother D'Amaro had told her that, that Joe's sadness was like a thorn in his heart, and sometimes he didn't feel anything else but that. He'd probably yelled at Catherine and said bad words like he had the night before—when Catherine didn't deserve it. She had made hot chocolate, and she'd acted like a real mother and told her about when she was a little girl and everything.

"Ms. Holben says you can come see the gnomes again sometime if—"

"With you?" she asked, interrupting.

"Yes, with me. I'd have to take you—"

Fritz abruptly stood up. "I couldn't do that," she said, because Joe didn't understand. He'd made Catherine feel bad—and he'd made her feel bad too. She couldn't go back there; Catherine wouldn't be like a mother *now*.

"Why not?" he said, putting his hands on her shoulders to make her look at him.

But she wouldn't look. "I couldn't do that," she repeated, her voice small and quavering.

"I thought you wanted to visit the gnomes. I thought you liked Ms. Holben . . . Catherine."

She kept her head down. "She's all right," he thought she said.

82

"Fritz," he said firmly, and she finally looked up at him, but her eyes barely grazed his.

"Please, can I go inside, Joe? Please?"

He gave her a small hug because she was miserable, and he didn't know what else to do. "Go on. Tell Della to cut that racket down before the neighbors call the police."

He sat on the steps, surprised by Fritz's reaction, hearing and not hearing *Infernal Majesty* blaring from Della's stereo when the door opened and closed. My God, he thought. *My God!* Fritz was only seven years old—and she was ashamed of him.

5

Catherine saw Joe D'Amaro before he saw her. He was coming up from the lower level of the Cotton Exchange, the cluster of old, turn-of-the-century buildings that had been converted into a shopping complex near the river. She was sitting in the sun on a bench in the inner courtyard, and he was coming directly toward her. She would have liked to avoid him, but she had no place to go, and she was the only person sitting on the bench at the moment. He couldn't help but see her—unless he deliberately chose not to, which, of course, was a distinct possibility. She was hardly the person whose company he would seek if left to his own devices. It had been nearly three weeks since he'd come to talk about Fritz, and Catherine had more than once toyed with the idea of telephoning him at the construction company to make inquiries about something that was none of her business.

Yet she suddenly wanted to avoid him now, which was logical only in light of the fact that he was such an exhausting person to be around. He was so intense, and she had been able to feel the anger and the worry he worked hard to control.

She looked up at him as he passed the bench, their eyes meeting briefly. She was certain he would walk on by.

"Ms. Holben," he said immediately, "you haven't seen Fritz, have you?"

"No, why?" she answered, startled both by his recognition and by the abrupt question. Surely Fritz hadn't wandered again.

"She's here somewhere with Della and Charlie. I'm looking for the whole brood, but I'm not having much luck." He wore his usual plaid shirt and blue jeans, and he stood with his hands on his hips, turning to scan a group of shoppers coming through the narrow courtyard on their way to another level of shops. He looked tired and a bit rough around the edges, but he was as Pat Bauer had pointed out, a nice-looking man.

"Sorry. I haven't seen her," Catherine said, and he looked back at her, letting his eyes slide nonchalantly over her in a way that would have certainly drawn further comment from Sasha about his "checking her out."

Blue eyes, Catherine noted again. And hair not as dark as she remembered. Brown but not dark brown. His looking at her that way was more surprising than offensive. She would have guessed that he found her more nuisance than woman. She also thought he would walk on, but he didn't. He sat down on the bench beside her instead.

"Nice day," he said after a moment, squinting up at the sun. "I should be working, but you can't always do what you ought to do when you have children." He glanced at her, as if he thought the comment might have offended her. "Della's filling out applications to work during the Christmas season," he went on. "I don't think there are any computer stores here, so it's hard telling what Charlie's doing."

"And Fritz?" Catherine couldn't keep from asking.

He looked at her for a long moment before he answered. "You know, I thought you might ask that."

"And you sat down, anyway?"

He folded his arms across his chest. "I didn't mean for you to think your interest in Fritz . . . offended me, Ms. Holben."

"Didn't you?" she asked. Their eyes met briefly, and he was the first to look away.

85

"No," he said. Then, "Yes."

He gave a quiet sigh. "Look. If you don't mind, I'll just sit here. They're bound to come by sooner or later." He looked back at her, and this time he let his eyes linger on hers, as if he'd decided not to work so hard at hiding, as if he wanted her to see whatever might be there.

How sad you are, Catherine thought immediately, but she forced the thought aside. She didn't want to know that about him. She didn't want to know anything about him.

"This is a public place, Mr. D'Amaro. You can sit anywhere you like."

She moved to gather up her purse and the paperback books she'd just bought at a half-price sale in the bookstore. Books were her other major indulgence—besides gnome sculptures.

"About Fritz," he said when she was about to stand up. "I think maybe you were right."

She stayed where she was. She tried to look into his eyes, but now he didn't want that. He stared off into the distance, clearly regretting having said anything.

"I'm sorry," she said. She was, both for the problem with Fritz and for his discomfiture at thinking he'd revealed too much to her. She was a stranger, after all.

"Hey, it's got nothing to do with you. I think maybe I—"

"Joe?"

He looked around at the sound of his name. Fritz stood on the other side of the potted evergreen at the end of the bench, looking worriedly from one adult to the other.

"I found a friend of yours," Joe said to her. "Aren't you going to say hello?"

She bit her lower lip. "Hello, Ms. Holben," she said, her voice unsure and wavering.

Catherine smiled and held out her hand. "Catherine," she

said, reminding her. "You were going to call me Catherine."

"Catherine," Fritz repeated. She gave an almost smile that to Catherine was very reminiscent of her father's.

"Come sit down beside me. I'm glad I ran into you. I want to ask you something."

"What," Fritz said, relieved that there was no sign of ill will between Catherine Holben and her father. She took Catherine's hand and sat down on the bench between them.

"I haven't decided where to put the gnomes yet. I was wondering what you think."

"On the little table beside the couch," Fritz said without hesitation, because that was where she imagined the gnomes to be when she thought about Ms. Holben's—Catherine's—apartment. She tried to picture them every night just before she fell asleep—the couch, the afghan with the pink flowers on it, and Daisy and Eric sitting close by on the little table. She glanced at Joe. He didn't seem to be minding this at all.

"You know, I think you're right. Almost anybody who comes to visit sits there, and when they do, they can see the gnomes up close."

"Joe said I could come visit," Fritz said, hoping as she said it that he hadn't changed his mind. He had been awfully quiet lately, as he was when he was thinking about Lisa. But she wasn't quite sure if that was what he was doing. She didn't think it was the business. D'Amaro Brothers had just gotten the job of building a new condo on the oceanfront at the far end of Wrightsville Beach. Things were looking up, he'd said. They were even going to have their big Labor Day cookout next Saturday—even if it was a few weeks late. She looked at him now. He was looking at Catherine but in a nice way, like he wasn't mad at all.

"I hope I can," she added, in case Joe wasn't paying attention.

"I hope you can too," Catherine said.

"Okay, Joe?" Fritz asked him.

"Okay," he responded.

"I spent the money you gave me," she decided to tell him.

"On gummy bears, right?"

She grinned. "Yeah," she confessed, and he ruffled her hair.

"When she comes to visit, Ms. Holben," he said to Catherine. "Hide your gummy bears."

When, Fritz thought. He'd said when, not if. That sounded pretty firm to her. She smiled happily to herself. Joe wasn't mad at Catherine anymore, and Catherine wasn't mad, either—and here she was sitting with both of them. It was nice. She looked at Catherine's hands. Catherine still had fingernails like a mother's when she wanted to look special—short with clear nail polish. Joe's hands were always hurt and banged up. He *always* had scraped knuckles, just like Fritz always had skinned knees. Occupational hazards, he'd told her once. His from being a builder and hers from being a kid.

"Where's Della?" Joe asked, and Fritz frowned. That was a question she hated being asked, particularly now, because Joe wouldn't like the answer.

"Fritz," Joe prompted when she didn't say anything.

"You know Della," she said with a little shrug, hoping that would take care of it. She glanced at Catherine.

"Yes, I know Della," Joe said. "That's why I'm asking. Where is she?"

Fritz sighed. There was just no way out of it. "Getting interviewed."

"Getting interviewed *where?*"

"At the pub."

"She's not old enough to work at the pub!"

"You know Della," Fritz repeated philosophically.

Joe stood up. "Excuse me," he said to Catherine. "Fritz, you stay here with Ms. Holben."

That suited Fritz. Anything was better than having to go along to get Della out of a bar.

"Would you like a gummy bear?" she asked Catherine. She was used to having Della do exactly what would make Joe mad, and she decided not to worry about it.

"Can you spare one?" Catherine asked.

"I can spare one."

"Then I'd like one. You pick it out."

Fritz picked a yellow one, her personal favorite. She liked Ms. Holben—Catherine—more and more. She couldn't help but like somebody who wouldn't take her last gummy bear. A mother would do that—not take the last one. Catherine really was just like a mother.

"Thank you," Catherine said as she popped it into her mouth.

"You're welcome. Here comes Joe."

"That didn't take long," Catherine said.

"Joe doesn't mess around," Fritz said, and Catherine laughed.

"No, I don't believe he does."

"Della could get a job in the baby-clothes store, but they don't give tips," Fritz said as her father approached with Della in tow.

Catherine saw immediately that this daughter was quite beautiful, strikingly so in spite of the petulance she took no pains to hide. She was blond and blue-eyed, her hair pulled into a huge clasp on the side of her head and cascading over one ear to her shoulder. She had long, spiky bangs and meticulously made-up eyes in shades of gray and pink and purple that made her look older than she probably was. Catherine

89

could tell immediately that Della D'Amaro was one of the lucky ones among her peers. She obviously had the knack of picking the right clothes, the right hairstyle, the right "look" to belong, an accomplishment that escaped some girls her age no matter how hard they tried.

"Daddy, you embarrassed me!" she said as they approached.

"I embarrassed you? I didn't say a word!"

"Yes, but you would have!"

"You're damn right I would have. Della, you know good and well I'm not going to let you go to work in a bar. And you can't go around not telling people how old you are. The man could have lost his liquor license. We'll talk about this later. Now I'd like you to settle down and meet Ms. Holben."

"Daddy, I just wanted to find out about it!"

"Excuse us, Ms. Holben. We don't always air our disagreements in public like this."

"Who is she?" Della said rudely.

"I'm a friend of Fritz's," Catherine said, cutting in ahead of Joe D'Amaro's sharp reply. "Catherine Holben. And I have to be going. Fritz, thank you for the gummy bear. Call me when you can come to visit."

"I will," Fritz said, holding on to Catherine's hand for a moment. Then she let go so Catherine could pick up her things.

"Ms. Holben," Joe said abruptly. "We're having the annual D'Amaro Brothers' Labor Day cookout next Saturday. I was wondering if you'd like to come?"

"It isn't Labor Day," Catherine said, because he'd caught her completely off-guard, the fact that she hadn't considered the possibility that he might extend a social invitation compounded by the fact that since her divorce she almost never went out.

"We never let a thing like that bother us. We have the cookout on Labor Day if we've got the money. If we don't, we have it when we do. One year it was January. We nearly froze our butts off. What do you say?"

The refusal was already on her lips, but Fritz caught her by the hand again.

"Please, Catherine!"

Catherine looked into Joe D'Amaro's eyes. His gaze held hers, then shifted ever so slightly to Fritz, who was still clinging to her hand.

Catherine understood him as if he'd spoken aloud.

"You said I could invite *my* friends, Daddy," Della said at his elbow.

"There'll be enough to go around, Della. I'm sure Fritz can keep Catherine from eating more than her share. So can you work us in? You already know Fritz and me. And Mrs. Webber from the Purple Box will be there. You won't be totally surrounded by strangers."

"All right. That will be fine," Catherine said. "I'll need the address."

"No, Fritz and I will come and get you so you don't have to take the bus. I'll call you later and let you know when."

"Oh . . . well, I'll see you next Saturday, then." She was growing more and more flustered by this sudden invitation, and she abruptly turned and walked away, giving one last wave to Fritz before she went inside to the wooden stairway that led to Front Street. But when she looked back at Fritz, she walked directly into a gangly teenage boy.

"Oh, I'm sorry!" she said, laughing. "I wasn't looking where I was going."

"That's okay," he said. "You know my little sister? The one down there with her hand flopping on the end of her arm?"

91

"Fritz. Yes. You must be Charlie." She would have guessed that, anyway, he looked so much like Joe D'Amaro.

"In person."

He paused, both hands raised, listening intently.

"What?" Catherine said, mystified.

"I'm waiting to see if you say it."

"Say what?"

"You *didn't*. Oh, thank you, thank you, thank you! Thank you, rare individual, who doesn't say, 'Charlie, you look just like your old man!' "

"Well, I figured you already knew that," Catherine said, teasing him.

"Exactly."

"Got to go. I'll miss my bus," she said, hurrying toward the stairs. "Nice meeting you," she called back over her shoulder.

Joe D'Amaro watched his son talking to Catherine Holben. He began to walk in that direction, but by the time he got there, she'd already gone.

"Who *is* that?" Charlie asked him.

"Catherine Holben. She bought the gnomes. Just what are you looking at?" he asked, because Charlie was standing transfixed, staring in the direction in which Catherine had just gone.

"Catherine Holben. Man, she does a lot for the back pockets on a pair of jeans." He gave his father a sheepish grin and punched him on the upper arm. "Or are you getting too old to notice those things, Pop?"

"Get out of here," Joe said, unable to keep from smiling at Charlie's teasing. He had a good son here—absentminded and irrepressible but good nevertheless. "And don't call me Pop!"

Charlie's grin broadened. "Right, Pop."

He loped off to join his sisters, and Joe gave one last look at Catherine going up the stairs.

I noticed, he thought.

She was nothing like Lisa, and until a few minutes ago he would have sworn that the only reason he'd asked her to come to the Labor Day cookout was because of Fritz, because he knew she liked Catherine Holben and because Fritz thought he'd been rude to her. He *had* been rude to her, and he regretted it. For days he'd been thinking about calling her or going by where she worked. But then, there she was, sitting on the bench with her hair blown by the wind and shining in the sunlight. And she'd looked at him with those calm eyes of hers and made him feel as if he could tell her anything and she'd listen.

But he didn't want to tell her anything. He didn't want to think anything. He didn't want to notice anything. Not the back pockets on her jeans, or the gentle way she had with Fritz, or her soft woman's voice and her soft woman's smell that still buzzed around in his head.

Jesus! He shouldn't have invited her. Michael was going to think he had something going with her, and he'd have *that* to put up with—Michael and his questions. And he couldn't take the invitation back. Not with Fritz already on cloud nine. Jesus!

He walked faster to catch up with his children. Charlie bombarded him with a description of some new software he wanted for his computer. Della ignored him. And Fritz— Fritz took him joyfully by the hand.

Catherine caught the bus on Second Street.

You've been living alone too long, she thought the third time she nearly said, "Why did you say you'd go?" aloud on the way home. She liked Fritz, was concerned about her, but she

93

had no business going to some family gathering where she didn't really know anyone. She did *not* want to do it. She didn't want to do it so much, she rode a block past her stop, but on the walk to the Mayfair she got herself in hand. Her panic had nothing to do with the cookout per se. It had to do with Joe D'Amaro. Her recovery from her recent emotional trauma was now no doubt complete. He was on her mind; she couldn't keep from wondering about him and his children and the dead wife of whom he did not speak. And it scared her to death.

She spent the rest of the weekend mentally making excuses not to go, only to have them all wiped out by the reassertion of the poignant image of Fritz D'Amaro's little face.

"I've done something stupid," she told Pat Bauer before her math class on Monday. She hadn't meant to say anything, because it was only a cookout and because she thought Pat wasn't feeling well.

"Oh, good," Pat said. "I was really getting tired of being the only one."

"No, I mean it."

"Well, let's see, Catherine. How stupid can it be? Don't tell me you're going to Jonathan's wedding."

"No," she said morosely. "I accepted another invitation."

Pat looked at her sharply. "And a happy little soul it's made you too. So what is it?"

"I can't get out of it, Pat."

"Yes, I can see that. What are we talking about?"

"Joe D'Amaro."

"Who the hell is Joe D'Amaro?"

"You know who Joe D'Amaro is. I bought his gnomes."

"His *gnomes?* What gnomes?"

"I told you."

"No, ma'am, you did not."

94

"He's a building contractor. He needed the money, so he sold a gnome sculpture. He didn't know his little girl was so crazy about it until she ran away to see them the other night."

"To your place."

"Right. And then he came here."

"Oh, yes. The semi-hunk who stirred up the office staff."

"Right. He's asked me to come to a family cookout."

"Why, the filthy beast."

"Pat, I'm being serious here!"

"I know that, Catherine. That's what makes it so funny. So what's wrong with going to a cookout? He either wants you there because of his little girl or he doesn't."

Catherine suddenly realized that that was precisely the problem.

"Oh, I get it," Pat said. "You're not sure which you'd rather it be, are you?"

"No, I'm not. And this is all *your* fault."

"*My* fault!"

"Yes, yours. I didn't even notice he was nice-looking until you said something."

"Well, forgive me. These things happen when you're heterosexual. Look on the bright side, Catherine. He's got a kid—"

"Three kids," Catherine said, correcting her.

"Even better. If he's interested, he's not going to care if you can't have a baby or not. He's got all his. All you have to worry about is whether he likes *you*."

"No, I don't have to worry about that. I hardly know the man. And from what I do know, he's got more emotional baggage than I want to deal with. Besides that, he flatly told me I butt into things that are none of my business."

"You do."

"Thanks a lot."

"Well, you *do*. And what's worse, the things that *are* your business are hopeless. Look at this bunch of girls. You think you're going to make them wake up one day and care about themselves and their babies. They don't *care,* Catherine."

"Some of them care."

"Oh, yeah? Who? Maria? Doesn't it get to you, Catherine? That somebody like her, who's never wanted a baby and never will, can reproduce at the drop of a zipper and a decent person like you can't?"

She looked at Pat a long moment before she answered. "Yes," she said quietly. "It gets to me." She got up to leave.

"Catherine . . . wait. I'm sorry. I don't know why I say things like that. I can't even blame it on the cancer—I was a bitch before I got it. Don't be mad at me, okay?"

"I'm not mad, Pat. You hurt my feelings."

"I know I did—now. I just can't tell I'm going to ahead of time. I never was any good at that with people. Whatever I think pops out of my mouth the minute it hits my brain. It's no wonder Don left me."

Catherine didn't answer.

"Aw, come on, Catherine. I'm *sorry*. Look, if you don't like me, who will? You like *everybody*. If you don't like me, I'll really know I'm a piece of—oh, hello, girls. Welcome to the Wonderful World of Mathematics."

Catherine took her usual seat in the back of the class. The day was cool and overcast; she had no difficulty staying awake. Her mind was too full of concerns about Joe D'Amaro and Fritz.

I like that little kid, she thought. But she didn't necessarily like her father. She thought he was exactly what Pat said—an attractive man. Not handsome. Not *not* handsome. Masculine—but not too masculine. She had the feeling that he liked women—even when they got on his nerves. And that he would like making love with a woman better than he'd like having sex with her.

She had no idea why she thought *that*. She'd caught him casting a covert glance at her breasts, which was hardly an indication of his sexual preferences. She thought that he probably had a "relationship" with someone. All that intensity of his, that determination to make things happen or to change things around to suit him, would appeal to a lot of women.

But it didn't appeal to her. Jonathan had been like that, refusing to accept the finality of a situation. Joe D'Amaro was simply too intense for her liking. It made her uncomfortable, wary, yet at the same time she was drawn to him. He was so sad. She always came back to the raw, personal sorrow she'd glimpsed when she looked into his eyes. Getting involved with the D'Amaro family was going to play absolute havoc with her newly won tranquillity. What peace of mind she'd managed to resurrect out of the ashes of her divorce was already shot to hell, and she hadn't even seen the man socially.

I call him Joe so he won't die.

Clearly his child thought he was worth the trouble.

She sighed—too loudly, because it drew a few giggles from the girls and a look from Pat. She struggled to keep her mind on matters at hand, concentrating hard on the numbers Pat was writing on the blackboard. One of the women from the office came and stood in the doorway, catching Catherine's eye with a *T* she made with her forefingers and the fist she put to her ear.

"It's a man," she said as soon as Catherine came out into the hall. "He's called a couple of times, trying to catch you between classes. I told him if he'd just hold on, I'd come get you. I was going to take a phone number so you could call him back, but he said he wouldn't be close to a phone for a while."

"Thanks," Catherine said.

Their footsteps echoed down the dim hallway, and she braced herself to talk to Joe D'Amaro, wondering why he'd call her at school.

The phone was off the hook, and she turned her back to the office staff as she picked up the receiver.

"Hello?"

"Katie?" the voice said, and her heart fell. She was flooded with disappointment, a fact she didn't fail to note with some dismay.

"What is it, Jonathan?"

"Hi! I . . . just want to remind you about the wedding Saturday. Will you be there?"

"No. I've made other plans."

"Can't you get out of it?"

"I don't want to get out of it." That wasn't precisely the truth, but Jonathan didn't have to know that.

"Oh. Well. Can . . . you wish me well at least?"

Catherine closed her eyes and took a small breath. "I do," she said, opening her eyes. That wasn't precisely the truth, either. Sasha was standing tentatively outside the office door. Catherine motioned for her to come in and sit down in the nearest chair.

"Jonathan," she said into the receiver, "I know you'll have a good life. Thanks for calling." She left him no time to comment, immediately hanging up the receiver.

"Sasha, what is it?"

"I don't feel good, Ms. Holben. You said to tell you if we don't feel good." She hung her head, and her voice was so low that Catherine barely heard her.

She walked closer. "What's the matter?"

"I don't know. I don't like it in here, Ms. Holben. Those women are always looking at my belly," she added in a whisper.

Catherine glanced behind her. They were indeed looking at the evidence of Sasha's pregnant state.

"Come on, then. Let's go."

They walked out into the hallway.

"Tell me how you feel," Catherine said when they were away from the doorway.

"Tired, Ms. Holben. Nothing hurts, but I just feel tired. I'm trying to listen to Mrs. Bauer, but I can't."

Catherine frowned. "You're not catching a cold, are you? Runny nose, sore throat—anything like that?" She reached out to touch Sasha's forehead and cheeks. She didn't feel feverish.

"No," Sasha said.

"And nothing hurts?"

She shook her head.

"You haven't seen any blood in your panties or when you go to the bathroom, have you?"

"No, I ain't got nothing that's on the list they gave me at the clinic." She gave a heavy sigh.

"And you've been eating the things you're supposed to eat—and taking your vitamins and iron?"

"Yes. Grandmamma'd skin me if I go and forget my pills."

Catherine smiled. She'd met Sasha's grandmamma just before school started. She was a stern little woman, who in the heat of summer wore a gray felt pillbox hat. Rumor had it that Grandmamma was the only real "root worker" left in Wilmington. She did a steady business in the housing projects where, for the right price, she would make a charm out of plant roots for whatever one needed—love, health, revenge. Unfortunately she had had no charm that would have kept her thirteen-year-old granddaughter from becoming pregnant.

"Are you going home on the bus today?"

99

"No, I'm going to ride home in Beatrice's car. She said I ain't got no business on a bus if I don't feel good."

"Well, let's see what your blood pressure is," Catherine said, and they walked back toward the classroom. "When's your next appointment at the clinic?"

"Wednesday."

Pat was just dismissing the class for the day.

"Ms. Holben, you falling for that sucker stuff?" Maria said as she came out into the hall. "She ain't doing nothing but trying to get attention. Sasha, you don't fool nobody."

"Good-bye, Maria," Catherine said firmly. "Go sit down while I get my blood-pressure stuff," she said to Sasha. She got the stethoscope and blood-pressure cuff out of her briefcase. Pat still sat at her desk.

She checked Sasha's blood pressure quickly. It was higher than usual but not significantly so.

"Sasha, are you worried about anything?"

"I'm worried about not feeling good."

"But nothing else? Everything's okay with your grand-mamma?"

"Yep. Me and her, we're good."

"When you get home, I want you to go to bed and rest. Don't come to school tomorrow if you don't feel like it, but you be sure to keep that clinic appointment. And if you feel any worse before then, call the number the clinic gave you, all right?"

"All right, Ms. Holben."

"Go on now. I see Beatrice waiting for you."

"Thank you, Ms. Holben."

"You're welcome, Sasha."

She's a sweet child, Catherine thought, glancing at Pat. Pat was still sitting at the desk, her head propped in her hands.

"You want your blood pressure checked?" Catherine asked.

"Only if you'll let me stay out of school tomorrow too," Pat said tiredly. She rubbed her eyes and took a deep breath.

"What's wrong?"

"I've got cancer. Haven't you heard?"

"One of these days I'm going to hit you over the head with the first thing I can pick up— deal or no deal! I asked you a question!"

"All right, all right! Jesus! I forgot I was already on your shit list! I'm getting a cold. Maybe my chest hurts a little bit."

Catherine came closer, reaching out to touch Pat's forehead the same way she had Sasha's.

"Maybe you've got a fever too," Catherine said sarcastically. "A high fever. You haven't talked to the doctor, either, have you?"

"I will," Pat said, getting up from the desk.

"I'd strongly advise it."

"Oh, well, if Ms. Holben says so. Ms. Holben's word is law around here, isn't it?"

"You're damn straight. What?" she said sharply to the same woman from the office who stood hovering in the doorway.

"Telephone call for you."

"I don't want to talk to him," Catherine said.

"It's not the same man. This one called right after you left the office. I told him one of your baby chicks was out of whack, and if he'd call back in about fifteen minutes, he could probably talk to you."

"Is it *him?* The filthy beast?" Pat asked archly.

"Oh, shut up," Catherine answered. "You go home and call your doctor. Do you feel like driving?" it suddenly occurred to her to ask.

"Yes, I feel like driving!"

"Then do it!"

"Why don't you go answer the telephone!"

Catherine grinned. "Think I will."

She hurried down the hallway well behind the woman from the office, who would likely advise her coworkers that Ms. Holben's telephone call was from *him*—among other things.

All eyes turned in her direction as she came into the office. She took a deep breath before she picked up the telephone, noting both her anticipation and a certain degree of nervousness, neither of which should have been there.

"Ms. Holben," she said, hoping to throw the office staff off the track.

"So how's your baby chick?" Joe D'Amaro responded.

6

He was on time. No, he was early. Nearly twenty minutes early, Catherine thought as she glanced at her watch. She was glad that he hadn't been twenty minutes late, that she hadn't had to wring her hands and pace back and forth in front of the windows wondering if she'd misunderstood or if it had suddenly occurred to him again that she had no business becoming involved in his problems with Fritz. She was by no means confident enough to return to this phase of single life—waiting for the arrival of some man—without a great deal of anxiety. Going out with Joe D'Amaro, even as a result of so meaningless an invitation as this, had made her a basket case.

She listened for him to come up the stairs. Fritz was with him, and when they knocked, she waited a moment before she opened the door, telling herself once and for all that she *was* going to do this.

She opened the door. Fritz was smiling shyly; Joe D'Amaro wasn't.

"Ms. Holben," Joe said without prelude, not Catherine, as he had on the phone. His face had that tight look she'd come to recognize as Joe D'Amaro in turmoil.

Second thoughts, she thought immediately. He was sorry he'd done this.

"She's not wearing hair curlers," Fritz said. "Joe said if we came too early, you might be wearing hair curlers."

Catherine laughed. "No, no hair curlers. Come in. You can visit the gnomes."

"Okay, Joe?" Fritz said to her father.

"Okay," he answered, but he was definitely not the almost relaxed man he'd been when Catherine had seen him at the Cotton Exchange.

Fritz ran happily to the couch. "You've got them on the little table," she called over her shoulder.

"You were right," Catherine said. "That's the best place."

"Can I hold them?"

"If you want to."

Fritz's smile widened as she picked up the gnomes. She sat down on the couch, pulling the flowered afghan over her knees before she put them on her lap as she had the other night.

Joe D'Amaro stood watching, his face immobile. His impulsive invitation to her wasn't the only thing he regretted, Catherine thought.

"Would you like to sit down?" she asked him.

"No," he answered. Period.

Fine, Catherine thought. You carry the conversation, Mr. D'Amaro.

She stood there. Waiting. There *was* no conversation.

"Look," Catherine said when she couldn't bear the awkwardness any longer. She kept her voice low so that Fritz wouldn't hear her. "We don't have to do this. You can tell Fritz whatever you like."

He glanced at her, but he wouldn't meet her eyes.

"Ms. Holben . . ."

"I don't want to intrude on a family gathering, Mr. D'Amaro."

"You wouldn't be intruding," he said, looking at her now for the first time since he'd arrived.

"Then what would I be doing that makes you so miserable?" She hadn't meant to ask that, but there it was.

"It's not—"

104

"I've been on the wrong end of your goodwill enough times now to recognize it when I see it, and I've told you before—"

"Ms. Holben!"

"What!"

"Do you think you could let me say something here? At least a whole sentence, if it's not too much trouble."

"Say it."

"This makes me nervous."

She was surprised at the revelation, but she tried not to show it.

"Why?"

He shrugged. "I . . . don't know what you think."

"What I think? I think you want your little girl to feel better, and you hope that inviting me to this cookout will do it."

He looked so relieved that she nearly laughed. She certainly didn't have to worry any longer that he might have an interest in her beyond her significance to his daughter.

"Okay, Mr. D'Amaro?" she asked pointedly.

A small smile worked at the corners of his mouth. "Okay," he said.

"Fine."

"You could call me Joe," he suggested.

"I could," she agreed. "But I don't want you to think I want us to be engaged."

He laughed—and an actual, genuine laugh. "You must think I'm an arrogant son of a—"

"Yes, I must," she assured him.

"You're probably right."

He was still grinning, and she saw the difference it made in his features. He really was a nice-looking man, she thought yet another time.

"Are you ready to go? That is, if you'll still go with us."

"I'm ready," she said. "And I'm still going—for Fritz."

He watched as she went to get her jacket, Fritz tagging along behind her into the other room without invitation. Catherine Holben didn't seem to mind, he thought, and he was still puzzled by Jonathan's remark. Why wouldn't she want children? She seemed to like them—she liked Fritz, anyway. He was certain about that.

She looks pretty today. The thought surfaced when he really wished it hadn't. There was no point in his standing around admiring her appearance. She'd looked pretty the other day too. Not beautiful like Lisa—or Margaret. But pretty in that soft, womanly way she had. She was wearing jeans again. He wondered if she had any idea what she did for the back pockets on a pair of jeans, as Charlie had so astutely put it.

He felt rather a fool at having implied that she might have designs on him. I just don't go out with women much, he'd almost said in his own defense when he realized that a relationship with him was the farthest thing from her mind. He'd forgotten that she wasn't over Jonathan. He'd seen her face when she'd found out that Jonathan was getting married.

"I'm the A-number-one helper," Fritz was telling her when they came back with Catherine's jacket. "Della won't help because she doesn't want to smell like smoke, and Charlie forgets what he's doing and everything."

"So what does an A-number-one helper do?"

"I remember stuff—like which one is medium and which one is rare."

"Well, that sounds like a good thing."

"Sometimes I get to turn over stuff. And if the meat catches on fire, I get out of the way."

Catherine laughed, glancing at Joe.

"And she finds the salt shaker when I lose it," he said,

opening the front door for both of them.

"Yeah, he's always doing that."

He caught a faint whiff of Catherine's perfume as she went by him. Oh, God, he thought, once again regretting his impulsiveness.

The weather was mild, the day sunny and beautiful—excellent for the Annual D'Amaro Family Cookout. He drove the distance to the house deep in thought, with Fritz sitting between them in the truck. He had nothing to complain about. Unlike most women, Catherine talked to Fritz; she didn't bother him with the kind of small talk that always made him impatient or with inane questions about where he came from and how long he'd been here. He wondered why that was. Probably she simply wasn't interested.

The house was in one of the quiet, older neighborhoods—vintage 1940, not one of the old Victorian ones that were so sought after in Wilmington now. The place was too small for the four of them—Della should have a bedroom of her own—but it had been all he could afford when he moved the family here, and certainly it was all he could afford now. He'd done a lot of work on the house; he still did when he had the time. In the three years they'd lived here, he'd managed to squeeze two bedrooms into the attic space, and a yellow paint job and new white shutters on the outside had given it a major facelift. Small and unfashionably old or not, he was proud of it.

"This is it," Fritz said as he pulled the truck into the driveway. "D'Amaro Estates."

Catherine smiled. "You did the restoration, didn't you?" she said to Joe. It was the first thing she'd said to him since they'd left, and he was beginning to wonder if she was one of those women who pouted when things didn't suit her—like Margaret.

"Yeah, why?"

"Why? Well, you said you liked to restore old buildings better than you liked to build new ones, and this house has been restored. It's lovely, so I thought you probably did it."

He frowned. She was already getting out of the truck, and he glanced at her, then at the house. She meant it. He looked at the house again. Yeah, well, hell, it *was* "lovely." He just hadn't expected her to say it.

"Take Ms. Holben in through the front door," he said to Fritz. "Show her the inside."

Fritz was clearly thrilled. "I'll show you my room, Catherine. It's Della's room, too, but half of it's mine. I've got a seashell collection and everything."

Catherine Holben didn't know what she was letting herself in for, he thought as he watched Fritz drag her away. The kid must have a thousand seashells. Della complained about them taking up space all the time. He walked toward the gate in a tangle of hedge that separated the backyard from the front. All the guests, invited and uninvited, were on and around the back patio. They were a noisy, exuberant crowd—practically everybody he knew was here, and it had already occurred to him that Catherine's arrival might prove interesting. He'd only told Michael that he was going to pick up a friend of Fritz's, and unless Della or Charlie had told him otherwise, he was going to be expecting another seven-year-old.

"The cook returneth!" Michael said in relief as Joe opened the gate. "Get your butt over here!"

Joe joined the gathering to a round of applause.

"Here, take this," Michael said, shoving a spatula into his hand. "I don't care if I never see raw meat again."

"How many did you burn?"

"Don't ask."

The group had grown since he'd left, Della's friends

108

mostly, complete with a sudden burst of loud music. Della flashed him a grin of apology at the volume, but she didn't turn it down.

"How long till we eat?" Charlie asked at his elbow.

"Ask your Uncle Michael," Joe said, giving Michael back the spatula.

"Where the hell are you going!" Michael said in alarm. It never ceased to amaze Joe that a man who could run around on a strut fifteen stories up could worry about turning over a hamburger.

"I'm going to wash my hands, Michael," he said pointedly. "Jeez!"

He went inside the house through the sliding glass doors on the patio. Mrs. Webber was busily heating baked beans in the kitchen.

"There you are," she said, smiling. "Michael will be so relieved. I just met 'Fritz's friend.' You didn't tell me Catherine Holben was coming."

"Didn't I?" he said innocently. "Imagine that."

"Oh, you," she said, taking a swipe at him with a paper towel.

"Where are they?"

"Still upstairs. Fritzie has a *lot* of seashells."

He smiled, because Mrs. Webber knew from experience. "Let me know when they come down, will you? I don't want Catherine to feel like she's been abandoned in a sea of strangers."

"I will do that," Mrs. Webber said, and he could read the small smile she gave him without difficulty.

"I'm just being polite," he said in answer to it.

"My dear Joseph, you are a lot of things, but you are never 'just polite.' "

The sliding doors opened, and Charlie poked his head in.

"Father," he said with mock formality, "I am urged to inform you that your cookout is on fire."

"Great!" Joe said. "Another gourmet success!"

Charlie looked over his shoulder. "Hurry, Father," he urged, his eyes a bit desperate.

Joe hurried, Catherine all but forgotten in the wake of saving the main course. He glanced up once to see her standing just at the edge of the patio. The sunlight was shining on her dark hair, and once again he noted the calm eyes, the serenity he found so intriguing.

Because they had both been hotheads, his disagreements with Lisa had always been loud and heated, filled with senseless recriminations from both sides. Even the exchange he'd witnessed when Jonathan had told Catherine he was remarrying had been tame by comparison. He'd had louder altercations with Lisa over who had left the cap off the toothpaste. He didn't know how to fight with a buttoned-up woman like Catherine Holben. Totally unimpressed, she had stood back and let him rant and rave all he liked. It annoyed the hell out of him. And it made him wonder.

What would it take, Catherine, to make you mad enough to throw things?

She looked in his direction, her eyes meeting his in that straightforward way she had. So pretty, he thought before his better judgment could censor it. He looked away, his growing awareness of her as a woman making him turn his attention back to not burning the hamburgers.

"Should I stand by to call the fire department?" she asked when the last of the flames had died down.

"No, I've got it now—I hope. I forgot to tell you that you'd have a choice of well done or well done."

She smiled and was about to walk away.

"Where's Fritz?" he asked to keep her there, because she

was a guest and he wanted her to feel at home, he told himself, not for any other reason.

"She's coming. She's getting a pencil and paper so she can count how many people are here for Mrs. Webber."

"Have you met everyone?"

"Just Mrs. Webber."

"Well, wait a minute, and I'll take you around."

Catherine wasn't certain she wanted to be taken around, but she stood and waited, idly listening to the background of rock music that reminded her of lunchtime on the picnic table at school. The backyard was full of people, laughing or talking or dancing. She could feel their eyes on her, and the speculation, particularly from a young woman who lay on a lounge chair in the sun nearby. Catherine thought it was a bit too cool for shorts, but the woman was wearing them, anyway. She kept crossing and uncrossing her shapely, tanned legs, as if they were an asset she wanted to display regardless of the temperature.

Fritz came out to begin her counting, and it suddenly occurred to Catherine that the man this woman was displaying her legs for was likely Joe D'Amaro—and he wasn't looking.

"Come here, Fritz," the woman said, motioning for Fritz to come closer. She had a number of diamond rings on her fingers, and long red fingernails that prohibited any kind of manual labor. Fritz hesitated, then walked closer to the lounge chair.

The woman didn't bother to lower her voice, and Catherine could hear her easily.

"Couldn't your little friend come?" the woman asked.

"What little friend?" Fritz said.

"I thought you and Joe were going to pick up your friend. It looks like you brought her mother."

Fritz looked puzzled for a moment. "Catherine's not anybody's mother," she said, clearly not understanding. "Can I go now? I have to count, and then Joe needs me."

"Oh, sure. You go help Joe, honey. He needs all the help he can get."

I must be getting better, Catherine thought. Fritz's innocent remark about her not being anyone's mother didn't quite cut her off at the knees. She glanced at Joe D'Amaro. He was wearing that look again, the one most familiar to her, the one that meant he had heard Fritz and the woman's conversation just as she had, and he was *not* pleased.

An old girlfriend? Catherine wondered, doing a little speculation of her own.

Fritz finished her head count, then came to stand at Catherine's side, not touching her, but very near. Catherine reached out to put her hand on Fritz's shoulder, and the child pressed herself against Catherine's side.

"That was some pretty fast counting," Catherine said.

"It was easy. I already did it once for Joe."

"Did you tell Mrs. Webber how many are here?" Joe looked up to ask.

"Yeah. She said 'Oh, pooh.' "

He grinned. " 'Oh, pooh'? I'm going to have to speak to Mrs. Webber about that language of hers. Are you hungry, Fritz?"

"Yeah, boy," Fritz answered, looking up at Catherine to smile.

"Michael!" Joe suddenly called to a man who was coming out of the kitchen with a bag of ice. "Come over here!"

"Aw, Joey, don't make me watch those things again. You know I ain't no damn cook."

"Come here, come here—I want you to meet somebody."

"Hi," Michael said to Catherine as he walked up.

"Catherine Holben, my brother, Michael, the other half of D'Amaro Brothers Construction. He's also a firebug."

Michael D'Amaro was an older, heavier version of the D'Amaro men, looking like both Charlie and Joe. He was a bit shorter than the two, and his darker hair was beginning to gray. He shifted the bag of ice to his other arm and offered Catherine his decidedly cold hand. "Welcome, Catherine," he said, shaking her hand vigorously. "Don't listen to him. He's been spreading rumors about me since he learned to talk."

"No, I haven't. The old man cured me of that when I was five. Spanked the both of us. Michael for doing whatever it was he was doing—and me for informing. I haven't told on him since."

"I don't do anything for you to tell," Michael said. "Do I, Sweetcakes?" he asked the woman on the lounge.

"I doubt it," she said. She was smiling, but Catherine could feel the sharp edge to her words. Michael D'Amaro didn't seem to mind, though.

"I got another case of soft drinks," he said to Joe. "That teenage mob of Della's is drinking us dry. Hope you don't want beer, Catherine. Joseph doesn't allow alcoholic beverages at this gathering."

"No, a soft drink is fine," Catherine said.

"This isn't your normal gathering," Joe said quietly. "We've got teenagers and a construction crew here. Some of the crew are alcoholics and some are out on parole. A few are both. Besides that, they're going to have to drive themselves home. The last thing we need here is free-flowing beer."

Michael came up and clasped Joe on the shoulder. "Hey, Joey, I didn't mean anything. I wasn't thinking—"

"It's okay," Joe said, cutting him short. "Here, turn these so I can introduce Catherine to everyone."

113

"I can do it, Joe," Fritz chimed in. "I can turn the burgers or I can help Catherine meet everybody."

"No, I need you to go tell Mrs. Webber to speed up the beans. Tell her it won't be long now—unless we have another fire."

"I heard that," Michael said. He took the loathed spatula out of Joe's hand. "Give me that and go on, before I use it on you."

So, Catherine thought. She was Catherine again. She stayed Catherine through all the introductions. It surprised her that Joe D'Amaro knew everyone there by name, even Della's numerous friends. Della was civil—barely—and Charlie was what Catherine suspected was his typical, insouciant self.

"Guess what, Pop?" he said to Joe.

"What? And don't call me Pop," the two of them added in unison.

"The kid thinks I'm Ozzie Nelson," Joe said to Catherine, and she smiled.

"No I don't. *You've* got a job," Charlie said. "But guess what? Go on. Guess."

"One hundred and fifty-six days until you get your driver's license," Joe said without hesitation.

"Aw, heck, Dad, you guessed. Have I mentioned this to you before or something?"

"Yeah. Every hour of my every waking moment."

"You're kidding! No wonder you can guess."

"No wonder," Joe said, catching him in a brief hammerlock around the neck. "Go play in traffic," he said, letting him go.

"Nah, I think I'll help Uncle Michael start another fire."

"You do and you'll go hungry," Joe called after him.

"Nice boy you've got there," Catherine said as they continued their tour among the guests.

"Yes, he is. I just wish he knew what planet he was on."

Joe saved the woman on the lounge until last.

"Catherine, this is Michael's wife, Margaret. Margaret, this is Catherine Holben."

"Margaret?" the woman said, one perfect eyebrow raised. "What happened to Maggie?"

Joe didn't answer that, and she turned her attention to Catherine. "Don't you just hate formal names? I'll bet everybody calls you Cathy or Kate. Anything but Catherine."

"No, actually they don't," Catherine said. "Not if they want me to answer. Catherine was my grandmother's name. She lived with us when I was growing up, and she always had a fit if anyone tried to shorten our names. Now I'm stuck with the whole thing."

"You don't look like a Catherine, though," Margaret said, her eyes flicking over Catherine as if she didn't look like much of anything else, either.

"Yes, but I feel like one," Catherine said, wondering how they had gotten into this conversation in the first place. Ah, yes, she thought. Because Joe D'Amaro wouldn't call her Maggie.

"So how long have you known Joe? I'd ask him, but he didn't say anything about you in the first place. We didn't even know you were coming."

"Next time I'll make sure you get the guest list, Margaret," Joe said. "Would you mind helping Mrs. Webber if she needs it?" he asked Catherine, his dismissal of Margaret D'Amaro bordering on rudeness.

Catherine looked from one of them to the other. She hated being caught in this kind of tension when she didn't know what had caused it.

"You didn't ask *me*," Margaret said, and Joe laughed.

"Margaret, you've never helped in a kitchen in your life. Do you mind, Catherine?"

"Not at all," she said, relieved to have something to do besides this verbal sparring with Margaret D'Amaro.

"Joey! Come over here!" Michael yelled.

Joe went to head off another fire, and Catherine walked away, leaving unanswered Margaret's second question about how long she'd known her brother-in-law. Odd, Catherine thought. Joe D'Amaro wanted to make sure she herself didn't have any false notions about there being anything but reciprocal politeness to his invitation to come here, but he seemed to want Margaret to think anything she liked.

She looked back over her shoulder as she went inside the house to help Mrs. Webber. Margaret was talking intensely with Della, their heads close. Catherine had never considered herself paranoid, yet she was certain that she was the topic of Margaret and Della's conversation.

Margaret suddenly got up from the lounge, casting a furtive look in her husband's direction.

"Catherine?" Mrs. Webber called from the kitchen. "There you are. Fritz and I could use some help here."

"What can I do?" Catherine asked, pushing aside her curiosity about the women in the D'Amaro family.

"Well, if you'd stir the beans so they don't stick while Fritz and I take the rest of these plates and things out . . ."

"I can handle that. And I think you'd better hurry before there's another fire."

"Oh, no," Fritz said, and Mrs. Webber laughed.

Catherine began to stir the huge pot of beans simmering on the kitchen stove. She was hungrier than she thought, and they smelled wonderful, their spicy aroma filling the small kitchen.

She looked up as the sliding doors to the patio opened

again, expecting to see Fritz and Mrs. Webber coming back for another load of plastic plates and eating utensils. Della and Margaret came in instead.

"You shouldn't be doing that," Margaret said sweetly. "You're a guest."

"I don't mind," Catherine assured her, and she didn't miss the look the two of them exchanged. "What is it?" she asked, because whatever it was, she didn't expect to like it, and she had no intention of being put on the defensive.

"Well, Catherine, Della had some questions. I said there was no reason why she couldn't just ask you."

"I was just wondering," Della spoke up. "Dad didn't tell us *anything* about you. You're Fritz's friend, right?"

"Right," Catherine said, still stirring beans. "I told you that last Saturday at the Cotton Exchange."

"Well, Fritz gets things mixed up sometimes." Della shot Margaret another look that said, See? I told you.

"Are you a teacher or something like that?"

"Something like that," Catherine said. "I work with pregnant teenagers so they can stay in school."

"Oh," Della said. "Are you . . . married?"

"No."

"Have you ever been married?"

"Yes," Catherine said pointedly.

"Oh," Della said again. "Have you got any children?"

"No children."

"Why not?"

Catherine smiled. "That, Della, is none of your business."

Della's face flushed, but her chin came up. "If you *had* some children and you had to give them up to your husband or something, it is. I mean, if you think you're going to marry my father—"

117

"Now why would I think that?"

"You came here—"

"I came here because I was invited, not because I want to marry your father."

"You know what I mean," Della said. She looked to Margaret for help and got none.

"No, Della," Catherine said, "actually I don't. And I doubt if your father would, either."

"I just want to know what *your* plans are—if you're after my father or what."

"My plans are to eat and leave. That's all."

"Are you going to tell him what I asked you?" she asked, her tone of voice suggesting that that possibility worried her more than she was willing to let on.

"What's it worth to you?" Catherine said. "If I don't?"

Della glanced at Margaret.

"Catherine doesn't mean—" Margaret began.

"Catherine does mean," Catherine said, interrupting. "You want to strike a deal or not?"

"Like what?" Della asked.

"Like I won't tell him about this very rude conversation if you go back out there with your friends and stay off my case. Go have a good time, Della. And don't worry about me. Believe me, I'm just passing through."

The sliding doors opened again, and Mrs. Webber came in.

Della stood for a moment, then turned on her heel and fled.

"Catherine, you really shouldn't have talked to her like that," Margaret said, following after her. "I'm sure Joe wouldn't understand *that*, either."

"Goodness," Mrs. Webber asked, "what's going on?"

"Nothing much," Catherine said. "Della thinks I'm after her father."

"Della thinks everyone is after her father—though I'm not so sure she'd be so concerned without a little encouragement from Margaret. Anyway, it looks as if you gave as good as you got. Della's a bit headstrong and spoiled, but I have to tell you, Catherine, it's Joe's other daughter I'm worried about. Poor little Fritz. Who knows what's going on in that child's mind. Of course, she's very taken with you. Anyone can see that."

"I have the gnomes."

"My dear Catherine. It's more than that."

Mrs. Webber stopped talking because Michael and Joe were coming in for the beans.

"Here you are, Michael," she said. "If you can't cook, you can carry."

He was about to protest, but Mrs. Webber headed him off. "Joseph, why don't you show Catherine your stained-glass work. I'm sure she'd love to see it. Michael and I will take out the beans—you carry, Michael. I'll open the door."

Michael suppressed a grin at Mrs. Webber's heavy-handed maneuvering. "You got it, you good-looking thing, you."

Catherine stood awkwardly as she was suddenly relieved of her kitchen job. She glanced at Joe, expecting to see that hard-pressed expression of his again, but it wasn't there.

"This way, Catherine," he said, pointing toward the living room.

The room was small and neat, like the kitchen and the rest of the house, the only decorations an array of framed photographs on the walls and mantel. She wondered idly if Della was responsible for this meticulous housekeeping. She doubted it.

The telephone rang, and Catherine wandered over to look at the photographs on the mantel while Joe answered it. The

D'Amaro family, she thought, smiling a bit at the baby pictures of Charlie and Fritz. She moved to see the photograph at the end, a large head-and-shoulders shot of a man and a woman—of Joe D'Amaro and a woman with long golden hair.

Lisa.

How beautiful she was. She stared dreamily into the camera, content and secure in Joe D'Amaro's arms. He looked into the camera as well, younger, but with that same intense, blue-eyed gaze. Even then he seemed to be on guard, as if he expected the worst and had to be ready for it.

"Okay," Joe said behind her. He frowned suddenly, his eyes going to the picture.

"She's very beautiful," Catherine said. "Della looks very much like her."

"That picture isn't supposed to be in here," he answered tersely. "Come on, I'll show you the stained glass."

She followed him into the small hallway to a door that led into the basement.

"Watch your step," he said as they went down the stairs.

The basement was a combination laundry room–workshop and he led her to a long table against the far wall.

"This is it," he said, snapping on another light. "This is what I'm working on." He pulled an open pattern book forward. "And this is what it will look like when it's finished." He showed her the picture of a lamp shade that would be nothing but teardrop shapes of blue and green and lavender glass when it was finished.

She stood with her arms behind her back, careful not to touch anything, and looked at the half-finished lamp shade closely. To his surprise she laughed.

"I'm sorry," she said immediately. "It's just—"

His anger flashed. He had wanted her to appreciate the

meticulous work that went into making a lamp shade like this, possibly even be impressed. He did *not* want her to laugh. "Just what?" he said.

"The incongruity."

"I beg your pardon?"

She looked at him, and she was smiling still. "To the casual observer, Mr. D'Amaro, you are not the sort of man who has the patience to sit and do an incredible piece of work like this."

"No?"

"No," she assured him.

"Why?"

"Why?" She smiled again. "We don't want to go into that, do we? I saw the other lamp shades you did in Mrs. Webber's shop. They were beautiful. This one is really . . . incredible."

He gave a small shrug, feeling his anger dissolving. "It . . . settles me down."

"It would put me in an institution."

He showed her some other things—a damaged window for a small church outside Wilmington, a door panel for a restaurant that was opening in one of the old downtown buildings.

"You should see someone at the Cotton Exchange," Catherine said. "They have some cracked stained glass in some of the transoms in the upper-level hallway." She looked up to find him staring at her. "What?"

"I . . . wanted to tell you I talked to that doctor you told me about."

"And?" Her eyes looked into his, straightforward and calm as always, indicative as always that she was listening, interested.

He glanced at the basement stairway because he didn't want Fritz to pop in and overhear. "I feel better. She told me to sit down with Fritz and ask her—talk to her as gently as I

121

can. I'm going to do that when I get a break in the job we're doing. I don't want to start something I don't have time to finish, and I don't want to do it when Della and Charlie are here."

"Joe!" Fritz called down the basement stairs. "Hurry! Charlie's going to eat *everything!*"

"He will too," Joe said to Catherine. "After you."

He rested his hand briefly in the middle of her back as they turned to leave. Once again he could smell the soft fragrance of her body, and he could feel the warmth of her skin through the silky blouse she was wearing. He didn't realize until that moment how much he'd wanted to touch her, and how much it worried him that she didn't seem to mind.

7

"What's the matter, Joey?"

He looked up sharply at Michael's question. He hadn't been aware that anyone had come into the room.

"Nothing."

"You sitting in the dark over nothing?"

Joe ignored the question. "Is everybody gone?"

Michael switched on the fluorescent light over the kitchen sink, causing them both to blink. "Yeah, they're gone. Mrs. Webber said for you to come by the shop next week. The kids have gone with Margaret to the mall for something or other. Look, Joey, you're not being disloyal to Lisa. . . ."

Joe took a deep breath in exasperation. Michael knew he didn't like to talk about Lisa, but he was doing it anyway.

"Listen to me, Joey! She's been dead five years. Catherine's a nice woman."

"This is none of your business, Michael. I don't want to talk about Lisa. Or Catherine Holben," he added pointedly.

"That's the trouble, isn't it? Catherine's . . . special. She's not some bimbo like Brenda down at the office. You're going to have to deal with her. If you want to know if there's anything there for you, you can't half-ass it like you usually do. It's going to take some effort on your part. She's not out looking for a good time."

"Michael, what are we talking about here? I don't even know the woman."

"Yeah, but you want to, Joey. Anybody can see that—even

123

your big brother who's known you all your life. So why don't you?"

"Why don't I what?"

"Get to know her, you dumb ass. This might be it."

"This is not *it,* Michael."

"How do you know? How do you know if you don't check it out?"

"Michael, don't you have something better to do? I can find my own woman if I want one."

"Sure you can. Somebody who wants to get laid by a good-looking bastard like you, not somebody who might care enough to take on a man with a struggling business and three kids—a man who can't or won't get over his dead wife."

Joe stood up abruptly from the kitchen table.

"I told you I don't want to talk about this."

"And since when has that stopped me from saying what I want to say? I'm telling you. It's time to get on with your life. *Your* life, Joey. I want you to be happy like I am."

"Okay! You've said what you wanted to say, and I heard you! Now leave it, will you?"

Michael grabbed him and hugged him, giving him a fatherly pat on the cheek whether he wanted him to or not.

"Jesus, Michael," he complained, but Michael only hugged him again.

"See you Monday morning, sport."

"Yeah, yeah."

"You pay attention to what I said."

"Good night, Michael!"

He switched the light off and sat down at the table again. The house was so quiet. Nothing in it but him. And his memories of Lisa. And Catherine Holben.

He had enjoyed himself. That was the problem. He had *enjoyed* himself. He had spent half the day in the company of a woman who didn't want anything from him and he'd liked it. He'd liked it enough not to take her straight home. He'd driven her and Fritz out to Wrightsville Beach instead, because he wanted to stay in her company a little longer, and because he wanted her to see the building site on the far end of the island. It was on the oceanfront, a blank space in a strand of new resort housing that faced the Atlantic. He'd taken her all over the empty sand, showing her imaginary walls and walkways, and then, in the last of the late-afternoon sun, she and Fritz had walked up and down the windy beach looking for washed-up pebbles. He'd watched them running from the waves, laughing, sharing their finds with each other, and he'd felt such a pang of longing that he'd nearly cried out with it, longing for Lisa and all they'd missed together, and also longing somehow for Catherine Holben and the possibilities she represented. He felt disloyal and filled with anticipation all at the same time. Now he could do nothing but sit in the dark.

I want you to be happy like me.

Poor Michael. Didn't he know what Margaret was like?

He put his face in his hands. He was so tired. Life was so simple to Michael. If one was faced with the possibility of some kind of relationship, all one had to do was "check it out." Michael didn't see the consequences of that simplistic approach any more than he'd seen the consequences of marrying a hungry woman like Margaret. Joe didn't want his life any more unsettled than it already was. Della had always rebelled against even the idea of someone taking her mother's place. He was sure that it was Della who had resurrected that old photograph of him and Lisa and put it back on the mantel, just as he was sure that it had been done for Catherine's benefit. God knows he had enough to worry about with Fritz. He didn't want to have to deal with Della, too, particularly when there was no real reason. Catherine Holben had given no indication that she was interested in anything other than Fritz, and unless he took the initiative, he'd never have to see her again. Even if he took Fritz to visit the gnomes, he could do it without seeing Catherine. It wasn't too late. He could hold back, and she would be out of his life. Then he could just go on as he had before.

He heard the front door open, and he braced himself for the return of his children, hoping that Margaret didn't decide to come in with them. Charlie went whistling up the stairs, and Della followed him. He listened for Fritz. She was in the living room, and she was being very quiet.

He got up from the table and walked to the kitchen door. "Fritz?"

She jumped. She had the picture of him and Lisa in her hand.

He snapped the kitchen light on. "Come in here," he said. "Bring the picture with you."

She looked so worried. My God, he thought. Had he been that bad, so bad that his little girl thought she had to protect him from his own grief?

He smiled and took the picture out of her hands, setting it on the kitchen table.

"Did you have a good time today?" he asked.

"It was good," she said.

"Did you get enough to eat? There are a few burgers left. I'll heat us up a couple if you're hungry."

"I had ice cream at the mall."

She was still worried, and he sat down at the table, pulling out a chair for her too.

"I . . . wanted to talk to you," he said.

"What about?"

"Just . . . things. I wanted to make sure you had a good day today. Things like that."

She sat down. "I had a good day," she said, glancing at the picture, then away. She gave a soft sigh and looked up at him. "I had the *best* day. The burgers were crisp, but Catherine didn't mind." She reached into her pockets and began to put on the table the beach pebbles she and Catherine had picked up. "Catherine and I traded," she said.

"Pebbles?"

"No, stories. I told her the Blue Willow story one time, and so today she told me about these." She dropped more pebbles on the table. "These are the moon goddess's tears," she said reverently.

"Tell me about them."

She looked at him doubtfully.

"I'd like to hear."

"Well," she said, giving him a pebble to hold, "this is what happened. Long, long ago there was a beautiful princess. She was *so beautiful.* On the outside but not in her heart. In her heart she was cruel—cruel to her mother, cruel to her father, cruel to her own true love. . . ."

"Go on," Joe said when she hesitated.

"Well, she was especially cruel to strangers. You know what happened then?"

"No, what?"

"She was cruel to just one stranger too many, Catherine said. She *really* picked the wrong one this time. He was a wizard, traveling the world disguised as an old, old man, looking for doers of good deeds. Well, she wasn't a doer of good deeds, and he saw that her heart was truly unkind. So he decided to teach her a lesson."

"What kind of lesson?"

"I'm getting to that," Fritz said, and he grinned.

"This is what happened. The princess knew she was up the

creek without a paddle—especially when he said he was going to take away her beauty and make her just as old and ugly as he was. She didn't like that one little bit, because her beauty was all she had, after all, so she thought real hard until she remembered something somebody told her." Fritz paused and took a deep breath. " 'Nobody destroys that which is useful.' She told him that, just as humbly as she could."

"And what did the wizard say?"

"He said, 'Well! Perhaps I was wrong about this beautiful but cruel princess.' But he wasn't taken in yet. '*You* are not useful,' he said, and scared the living daylights out of her—because she knew she wasn't. So she thought really fast and she said, 'But I will be.' And the wizard said, 'How?' And the princess thought, 'Oh, gosh, this man is so tiresome. How do I know *how?*' So she had to think again, and it was really giving her a headache because she didn't think very often. 'I know!' she cried. 'I am *very* beautiful. I shall stay up an hour past my bedtime every evening so people will have more time to see me. Of course, I shall have to sleep in an hour later each morning or else I shall have bags under my eyes.' "

Joe chuckled and Fritz frowned.

"That's not the end, Joe."

"Oh. Sorry. Go on."

"So the princess told the wizard about staying up later and everything, and the wizard said, 'That's it? That's your idea of being *useful?*' Well, the princess got hacked—"

"Hacked?"

"*Hacked.* P.O.'d," she added, using one of Charlie's phrases for clarification.

"I see. P.O.'d. Go on."

"Well, here she'd been doing *all* the thinking—she even had a headache. 'Do I have to do everything?' she said. '*You* think of something!' And the wizard said, 'Oh, my dear girl, you shouldn't have gone and said *that.*' So there was a big puff of smoke, and when it cleared, the princess was a prisoner in the moon. 'You wanted to be useful, and useful you shall be,' the wizard said. 'From now on, twice a day, every day, you will send out the ocean tides and bring them back again. Every single day! Forever!' The princess was upset. She fell on the floor of the moon and had a tantrum, then begged and begged, 'Not forever!' Well, the wizard had a soft heart, and the princess *was* beautiful, so he said, 'Well, maybe not forever.' 'No?' the princess said through her tears. 'If your own true love will do a good deed in your name, I will set you free.' That didn't sound good to the princess, so she began to cry again, and the wizard said, 'Look, lady, that's the best I can do—you have to learn your lesson. Except . . . well, maybe I could give you a promotion.' "

"A promotion?" Joe asked, thinking he hadn't heard right.

"Yes, a promotion. The wizard said, 'From now on, you will no longer be a princess.' 'This is a *promotion?*' the princess asked. 'Silence!' the wizard told her. 'From now on you shall be the goddess of the moon.' She's still there today, being useful. All the tears she cried when she had her tantrum fell into the oceans, and they still wash up today. And, see?" She gave him some more pebbles to hold. "They look like pieces of the moon." She glanced up at him. "The end."

"What happened to her own true love? Didn't he save her?"

"Catherine said the princess was such a pain in the you-know-where, he was still trying to make up his mind if he wanted to."

"I don't blame him."

"Yeah," Fritz said. "Me, either." She didn't tell him that she thought the princess must have been a lot like Margaret.

129

"Did you like the story?" She thought he did because he laughed, but she wanted to hear him say it.

"I liked it."

"Me too. I'm going to remember it forever. Catherine's mother told her that story when she was a little girl—they used to come to the beach in the summertime. Catherine doesn't have a little girl, so she told it to me. She says I have to save it so I can tell *my* little girl. It's like when a real mother—"

Fritz stopped. She hadn't meant to say that. She glanced at Joe and he reached for the picture again, holding it in his hands for a moment before he set it back down on the table. "You don't remember Li—your mother, do you?" He looked at her and she bowed her head. "It's all right if you answer, Fritz. It isn't going to make me mad or sad or anything like that."

She looked up at him. She didn't necessarily believe that, but she knew he wanted to hear what she had to say. "Sometimes I think I do . . . but then I think, not really. I think I just remember what people tell me about her. Joe?"

"What?"

"Is it all right if I like Catherine?" Her eyes searched his face, as if she wanted to find out the truth regardless of what he said.

"Yes, Fritz, it's all right."

"I like her a lot," she offered, giving away as much of her feelings as she dared. She didn't tell him that Catherine was more and more like a mother—like the *real* mother she'd always wanted. "I'm glad you didn't—" She broke off.

"Didn't what? You can tell me what's on your mind, Fritz."

"Didn't . . . yell at her or . . . anything," she finished lamely.

"I'm trying to do better about the yelling. Okay?"

"You can't help it," she said. "It's how you are."

"Oh, it is. And how do you know that?"

She shrugged. "Experience—and Grandmother D'Amaro. She said you get mad fast and get over it fast. Ever since you were a little boy. I'm used to it, but . . ."

"Catherine's not," he said, finishing it for her.

She looked up at him. "I want to keep seeing the gnomes," she said. "Della says it's just a phase, but I want to see them until I grow out of it."

"Fritz, I've told you you can—whenever it's all right with Catherine. We just don't want to bother her too much, though. What else does Della say?"

"She says . . . she doesn't like Catherine. That's why she put the picture out." She didn't tell him that she'd tried all day to get the picture and put it away, because she knew it would upset him to see it. But being the A-number-one helper *and* a motherless child, she never got the chance. "Am I going to get to go see Catherine and the gnomes if Della doesn't like her?"

"I don't think Della has anything to do with this, does she?"

Fritz looked at him in surprise. "You know Della," she said in case he needed reminding.

"I know you too. If you think Catherine's okay, then she is. Fritz, there's something I want to ask you—"

"Joe?" she said, interrupting.

"What?" He hadn't intended to talk to her now, but suddenly he didn't want to wait any longer. He'd worried too long, and he couldn't do anything about it if he let it stay hidden.

"Is this turning into a serious talk?"

"Yes, I think it is."

"Do we have to?"

"Yes, we do." He reached out to brush her hair out of her eyes, and she fiddled with the pebbles on the tabletop, pushing them around into a circle.

"I don't like serious talks much."

"Why not?"

"Because I always end up not getting to watch television."

He tried not to smile. He supposed that it must seem that way to her. "This isn't that kind of serious talk. This is something I need to ask you about. I was going to wait until later to work up to it, but I don't think that's the way to handle it. I'm just going to tell you what's on my mind, and then we'll talk about it. I've . . . been wondering about why you call me Joe."

She looked at him sharply, as if that were the last thing she'd expected, but she said nothing.

"You know how Charlie and I tease each other. He calls me Pop and I say I don't want him to. You don't call me Joe because of that."

It wasn't a question and she looked away.

"You used to call me Daddy and now you don't. Can you tell me why?"

Fritz sat looking at the pebbles, the silence between them growing.

Charlie came whistling down the stairs.

"So what's going on?" he asked as he came into the kitchen.

"Fritz and I are having a private talk," Joe said. "Get whatever it is you're after and go back upstairs."

Charlie looked from one of them to the other. "What have you done now, kid? You go over the wall again?"

"Charlie—"

"I'm going, I'm going. I got to get me a little something to eat before I die of starvation. I can see the headlines now: REMAINS OF TEENAGER FOUND SHRUNKEN AND SHRIVELED

IN FRONT OF COMPUTER. Hey, Pop, she's bawling."

Joe gave him a hard look to squelch any further remarks, but Charlie stood expectantly until the silent reproval finally registered.

"Oh!" he said. "You want me to go. Okay, well! Here I am . . . *going.*"

He retreated back upstairs, taking as much as he could carry out of the refrigerator with him. Fritz was indeed crying. She sat forlornly in her chair, her head bowed, tear after silent tear sliding down her cheeks.

"Fritz," Joe said. He moved out of his chair and knelt down beside her. "Fritz . . ."

She didn't say anything, but she suddenly reached for him, wrapping her arms around his neck. She was his youngest child, his baby, and she seemed so fragile to him. He held her, gently patting her back and letting her cry, because he knew from personal experience what a relief tears could be.

"What is it, Fritz?" he said after a moment. He tried to see her face. "You can tell me."

She wouldn't look at him. She said something that sounded to him like "motherless child," and his heart contracted.

Ah, Fritz, he thought. Fritz felt Lisa's loss as much as he did. He'd been wrong to think that she'd been too young to be as affected by it as he and Charlie and Della. To talk about this was to pour salt in both their wounds, but it had to be done no matter how painful it was. He took a deep breath.

Please. Please let me say the right thing.

"Is that what it's about? Your mother dying?"

She moved her head, but he couldn't tell if it was an affirmation or not. Her wet face pressed harder into his shoulder.

"Your mother died, Fritz. She didn't want to leave us— she couldn't help it. But I'm here. You're my little girl. Whatever it is, I'll fix it if I can. But I can't do anything if you won't tell me."

Her weeping intensified. He didn't know what else to say, what to do. How had she become so miserable, and how had he been so stupid as to not see it?

"Fritz . . . ?"

Suddenly she lifted her head. "I—did it, Joe."

"Did what, Fritz? What did you do?" he asked her gently, wiping her tears away with his fingers.

"I jinxed—her."

"Who?" he asked, not understanding at all.

"Lisa!" she wailed. "I—don't want—to—jinx you—too!"

She flung herself on his neck again.

"Fritz, honey, you can't jinx me."

"I—can, Joe!"

He picked her up and sat down in the chair with her on his lap. "Stop crying now. I want you to tell me—"

"I—can't—say it."

"Yes, you can. I want you to start at the beginning, and I want you to tell me just like you told me Catherine's story about the princess. You can do that. We're going to sit here, just you and me, and you tell me the story about the jinx."

She kept sniffing, and he reached for a stray napkin left over from the cookout that was still lying on the table.

"Here, wipe your nose."

Obediently she did so. "One more," she said, and he handed her another. She took a deep, wavering breath, and she kept the napkins crumpled tightly in her hand.

They sat for a while in silence while she struggled to stop crying.

"Are you ready?" Joe asked after a moment.

She nodded.

"Okay, then. Let's go with it."

For a moment he thought she wasn't going to say anything, but then she sighed again.

"I . . . saw it on television," she said, her voice hesitant. "About the jinx. On *The Andy Griffith Show*. And *G.I. Joe.* . . ."

He waited for her to go on. "I see," he said when she didn't. "And what does a jinx do?"

"They make bad things happen. They . . . don't mean to, but they do. It's how they are."

"But you don't make bad things happen, Fritz."

"Yes, I do. I make Della mess up her fingernails when I come in the room. And I make Charlie lose things on the computer."

"*They* do that, Fritz, not you. They may blame you because they're aggravated, but that doesn't mean you did it."

"But that's how I *do* it," she insisted. "I aggravate. That's what I did to Lisa." She was in danger of crying again, and he hugged her tightly.

"Fritz, don't cry. Tell me."

"I don't want to."

"I know. But I want you to trust me that it's the best thing to do.

"Are you *sure*, Joe?"

"I'm sure."

He could feel her gathering up her courage, and the admiration he already had for her intensified. She was such a brave little kid, and God, the burden she must be carrying. "Go on now. Tell me."

"I heard my grandmothers . . ." she began again.

"They didn't know you were around, you mean?"

"Yes. Everybody said all I used to do was follow Lisa around and say, 'Mama, Mama, Mama, Mama.' And then Grandmother D'Amaro—she had to come stay with me that day because Lisa wanted to get out. She said Lisa was aggravated because I wouldn't take my nap or anything."

"Fritz, you were two years old. All babies that age follow their mothers around like that. Della did it. And Charlie. And you."

"But nothing happened when Della and Charlie did it. I'm the jinx. I'm the one that made her go out and die."

"No! No, you didn't. Here. Sit up here and look at me. Look now." He made her look into his face. "Whenever you ask me anything, what do I always tell you? The truth or a lie?"

"The truth, but—"

"You've never known me to tell you anything that wasn't true, have you?"

Her eyes searched his face and she didn't say.

"Have you?" he insisted.

"No."

"That's because I don't lie to my children. I never have and I never will. And I'm telling you now, it wasn't anything you did. Your mother wasn't upset with you. You had some new teeth coming in and you weren't feeling good, that's all. We were in a car wreck, and your mother was killed. It was an accident. That had nothing to do with you. It was *not* your fault. Do you understand?"

"But if I *am* a jinx, I don't want to jinx you too!" She hid her face again.

"Fritz, if you're a jinx, you're not a very good one. You followed me around and called me Daddy for five years and nothing happened."

She grew quieter. He could feel her considering this piece of information.

"Five years?" she asked finally. "Joe, are you *sure?*"

He held up his hand, fingers spread wide. "Five. You started calling me Da when you were ten months old."

"You don't think I'm a jinx?"

"No."

"Are you sure?"

"I'm very sure. You are . . . Mary Frances D'Amaro, also known as Fritz—the good and brave daughter of Joseph and Lisa. You are a doer of good deeds and an A-number-one helper—and no wizard will ever need to lock you in the moon."

She clung to him again. "I'm scared, Joe."

"I know you are. But I want you to trust me. I'm your father, and it's my job to know these things. You are not a jinx."

She leaned back to look at him. "Does this mean I don't get to call you Joe anymore?"

"No. This means you don't call me Joe because you think you're a jinx. If you call me Joe, you do it because you're used to it, okay?"

"And you won't care?"

"I won't care. I'll answer to either."

"Are we through talking now?"

"If you're feeling better."

"I feel better. Do I . . . have to tell Della what we were talking about? She'll think I'm a nut."

"This is between us. You don't have to tell anybody if you don't want to."

"Charlie will tell her I was down here bawling."

"Charlie probably forgot it before he got upstairs. You know Charlie."

She gave him a wavering smile and slid down off his lap. "I have to wash my moon goddess tears," she said as she gathered up her beach pebbles.

"Fritz," he said when she reached the door, "thank you for worrying about me."

"You're welcome."

137

"But you don't have to any more."

"Okay . . ."

He thought she was about to say Daddy, but she didn't, and he didn't press it. She wasn't ready to take the chance yet.

He felt completely drained, emotionally and physically, and he continued to sit at the kitchen table. The image of Catherine Holben suddenly came to mind—Catherine standing on the windy beach, Catherine smiling in the sun. He wanted to talk to her. He wanted to tell her about Fritz. He wanted to look into her calm eyes.

But he stayed where he was. He picked up the picture on the table, feeling the same pain he always did when he looked at one of Lisa and him together.

God, Lisa, when is it going to stop hurting?

8

"So how'd it go?" Pat Bauer asked first thing on Monday.

"Are you feeling better?" Catherine said, posing a question of her own. While she was interested in how Pat was feeling, her primary concern at the moment was *not* talking about Joe D'Amaro. She wasn't quite sure why. Certainly she and Pat were close enough friends for her to ask anything she liked. It was more that Catherine simply didn't know what she was feeling, and she didn't want to enter into any discussions about it until she did. Unfortunately Pat wasn't going to be put off.

"Don't change the subject," she said.

"I'm not changing the subject. I want to know how you are."

"You know damn good and well that I don't like to be asked that. I've got cancer. What can I say? I'm just fine?"

"You can say whether or not you went to the doctor and what he's doing about your fever."

"Yes, I went to the doctor. I'm taking an antibiotic. Now, how did the thing with the semi-hunk go?"

"It wasn't a 'thing'—"

"Catherine! Tell me! I've been waiting all weekend. I almost called you yesterday, but I figured it would make you testy."

"You figured right."

"Read my lips, Catherine. *How did it go?*"

She shrugged. "It went all right."

"And?"

"There is no 'and.' "

"There has to be an 'and.' *And* you hated every minute. *And* you're going out with him again. *And*—"

"None of the above."

"You're not going out with him again?"

"No."

"Why not?"

"He didn't ask."

"You could ask *him,*" she suggested.

"You sound like Beatrice and Sasha."

"Well, you *could* ask him."

"I don't want to ask him, thank you."

"Then never mind that. Just tell me if it beat the hell out of going to Jonathan's wedding."

"It was . . . all right."

"Jesus, I hate talking to you!"

"What do you want me to say?"

"Tell me how you feel. I tell you how I feel often enough. It's your turn."

"I feel . . . relieved."

"Now that's interesting. 'Relieved.' What does 'relieved' mean?"

"It means that Joseph D'Amaro and I aren't interested in each other personally. It means that I don't need any complications in my life right now, and I'm glad to find out that we aren't about to start anything, so I don't have to deal with it. All right?"

Pat looked at her closely. "Are you sure you aren't interested in each other personally?"

"Positive."

"You sound a little disappointed to me—"

"I am *not* disappointed!"

"So what kind of complications would you have if this

mutual disinterest *weren't* the case? I mean, if he just had the hots for you and you just had the hots for him too. Nothing major. No lifetime commitments. Just a little unadulterated sex."

"Nobody has the hots for anybody—"

"Uh, Ms. Holben?" someone said tentatively in the doorway.

"What!" Catherine said in exasperation.

"Telephone call in the office."

"Man or woman?" Pat asked.

"Man," the woman from the office said, trying not to grin.

"Bet it's the filthy beast," Pat said.

"He said to tell you he was in a hurry," the woman said.

He's in a hurry, Catherine thought. She supposed it could be Jonathan stranded someplace on his honeymoon and wiring for money, but she strongly doubted it. Who else but Joe D'Amaro would give someone else *his* particulars and expect the rest of the world to adjust itself accordingly?

She should have been annoyed. She wasn't. She should have suddenly found herself too busy to talk to him. She didn't. The best she could do was to ignore Pat's grin as she followed the woman from the office back down the corridor.

"You know you don't have to take the call," Pat called after her.

No, she didn't—except that she wanted to know about Fritz. Joe D'Amaro wouldn't be calling for any other reason.

At first she thought there was no one on the line—he'd been in too much of a hurry to wait until she could walk from the classroom to the front office.

"Hello?" she said again.

She could hear background noise—voices, some kind of machine—and then, "Catherine?"

"Yes? Who is this?" She knew perfectly well who it was, but

141

she played the game, anyway.

"This is Joe . . . D'Amaro," he added, as if it suddenly occurred to him that she might know hundreds of Joes. "Are you doing anything after work today?"

"Why?" She wasn't about to say yes or no until she knew the reason he was asking.

"I . . . was wondering if we could talk. About Fritz. I have to work late tonight, but I thought we could get together for a little while when you're finished there—go get something to eat, maybe. I mean, we both have to eat and we could kill two birds with one stone."

Catherine listened to his voice. He sounded . . . nervous. Why would he be nervous?

I am not going to do this, she thought. *I'm not going to go sit with him and talk to him and feel what I've been feeling.*

"Catherine? Did you hear me?"

"Yes, I heard you." *Oh, God!* "All right. I usually leave here at four-thirty."

"Just wait for me there. I'll make it as close to four-thirty as I can."

"Joey!" someone—Michael—yelled in the background. "Get a move on!"

"I'm coming, I'm coming!" he yelled back without covering the phone. "Catherine, don't leave if I'm late."

"That depends on how late you are."

"Give me till sundown, okay?"

"Oh, sure," she said, and he laughed.

"See you, Catherine."

He's happy, she thought. *He's happy and he's nervous.*

She stood holding the receiver until she realized that she had the full attention of the office staff—again. No wonder Sasha didn't like coming in here. If there was nothing to see, they listened.

142

She walked back to the classroom, knowing Pat was waiting like the proverbial spider for the fly.

"I'm going out to eat with Joe D'Amaro," she said before Pat could ask her anything. "He wants to talk about his daughter. That's all there is to it."

"Are you talking to me or to you?" Pat said.

"I'm talking to you."

"Oh. Well. If you say that's all it is, then that's all it is. Of course, you do look a bit happier than you did a few minutes ago. Now why is that?"

"This is not happy, Pat."

"It's not mutual disinterest, either. Which reminds me, what kind of complications are you worried about with him? The worst that can happen is you'll care and he won't, right?"

Catherine was saved from having to answer that by the arrival of the class. She had noted of late that all their arrivals and departures were en masse. Even Maria came and went with the group. They must be car pooling, she thought. She was glad that they were growing close. A pregnant woman, particularly one that was unmarried and well below the age of twenty, needed all the support she could get.

The day dragged on, and she had to keep reminding herself that she wasn't seeing Joe D'Amaro socially. She didn't need to fuss with her hair or freshen her makeup. All she needed was to keep her mind on what she was doing *now,* which would have been no problem under normal circumstances. But circumstances weren't normal. She couldn't stop thinking about him, about their walk on the beach around the construction site. She had liked being with him. She'd liked hearing him talk about the place he was going to build in a way she'd never liked hearing Jonathan talk about his accounts.

Why was that? she thought in exasperation. She was

willing to admit that she was sexually attracted to the man, but that shouldn't make her want to hang on his every word. She had actually wanted to know about sand erosion and footings, just as she'd wanted to know about stained-glass lamp shades. *God help me, I'm interested,* she thought. *I'm really interested.*

Joe D'Amaro wasn't late coming to pick her up. He was an hour and a half early. He stood outside the door in plain view of all her students *and* Pat Bauer.

To say that their curiosity was piqued was putting it mildly. It didn't take Sasha five seconds to accost him after class was dismissed. Catherine dared to glance into the hallway. He was ringed by pregnant teenagers.

"Hey, what's your name, mister?" Catherine heard Sasha saying with the authority of someone whose business it was to ask.

"Joseph D'Amaro," he answered. "What's yours?"

"Sasha."

"Sasha what?"

"Sasha Higgins. Are you looking for Ms. Holben again?"

"Again," he conceded.

"Are you going to take her out?"

"Yeah, is that okay?"

"Depends on whether you're married or something like that."

"No, nothing like that."

"Well, that's good. 'Cause, Ms. Holben, she don't know nothing about taking out no man."

"She doesn't?"

"No, she don't. We told her the other day to call you and ask you out sometime. I bet she didn't do it. I bet *you* called *her.*"

"I called her," Joe confessed.

"She said you weren't her boyfriend."

"Well, she probably knows," he answered.

"Excuse me," Pat said, trying to get through. She extended her hand to Joe. "I'm Pat Bauer. I work with Catherine. You don't look like a filthy beast to me."

"Ah . . . thank you," Joe said, shaking her hand.

"All right!" Catherine said at the doorway. "You can all go home now."

"Aw, Ms. Holben," Sasha said, "we're just checking him out for you."

"Don't think I don't appreciate it, Sasha. Now go, *go*. See you tomorrow. Good-bye!"

"Bye, Ms. Holben," they sang in chorus. And then, "Bye, Joseph!"

He laughed and waved.

"You think I'm going to ask you about the 'filthy beast,' don't you?" he said, following Catherine into the classroom.

"I have no idea what that woman is talking about," she assured him, and he grinned.

"Does this bunch of yours always ask whatever they want like that?"

"Always. Or Sasha does, anyway. It was something I started to get them to ask things about their pregnancies. I've had many occasions to regret it."

He smiled again, and it struck her that she hadn't been wrong earlier. He *was* happy today, or at least happier than she'd ever seen him.

"I'm early," he said unnecessarily. "I thought I'd better head out before Michael found something else for me to do. How soon can you leave here? I know it's early to go eat, but it's the only chance I have."

"No, it's all right. I have to lock up. And I have to make sure Pat gets out of the parking lot."

"Something wrong with her car?"

"She's . . . not well. Sometimes she covers up how bad she's feeling. I've found her still sitting out there because—" She broke off, surprised that she was telling Joe D'Amaro a thing like that.

"You lock up, then," he said smoothly. "I'll watch for her. Don't worry," he added. "I'll be subtle."

He left the room, and she could hear him walking down the hallway to the end door on the parking-lot side of the building. She began straightening the desks in the room, wondering if *Joe D'Amaro* and *subtle* weren't a contradiction in terms. She picked up her briefcase and her purse, and she was ready to lock the door when he came back.

"She's all right," he said. "I think you're right about her hiding how she feels. She wasn't the same lady out there that she was in here. She was driving okay, though."

Catherine nodded and locked the door. "So . . . how's the family?"

"Good," he answered as they walked down the hall. "You got anyplace special you want to go?"

"No. I'll pay for my own meal, by the way."

"You don't have to do that. I'm taking up your time."

"I want to do that. I'm interested in Fritz, anyway. You don't have to feed me."

I want to feed you, he almost said. Which would have been an entirely dumb-ass thing for him to say. It was incredible to him how ill-at-ease he felt. One would have thought he was no older than Charlic.

"You don't mind riding in a truck, do you?" Somehow it hadn't mattered on Saturday, and today he needed to ask.

She smiled. "You're asking a person with no transportation at all if she minds riding?"

"You should get a car."

"Tell me about it."

"I'll let you know when one of the guys on the crew breaks parole again."

"I don't think I need a stolen car."

"No, Bobby's not the car thief—I've got a couple of others on the crew who do that. Bobby's not too good at keeping his appointments with his PO. Then he gets sent back and he's got a car he's got to sell. See?"

"Yes, I see. Did I meet him at the cookout?"

"Yeah. He was the big guy—balding, tattoos, one front tooth missing."

"Yes, I remember. What would I do if he got out and wanted the car back?"

"I'd give it to him," he said dryly, and she laughed. He walked on ahead of her to open the truck door, and it occurred to him that he was entirely on his own here. He didn't have Fritz to buffer any silences. He supposed that he wasn't doing too badly. At least she was still willing to get into the truck. If he were only here to talk about Fritz, it wouldn't matter, but he wasn't here just for Fritz, and he knew it. He was here for himself. He wanted to see once and for all if he really was attracted to her or if it was something else—though he wasn't quite sure what that something else might be. Gratitude, maybe, for helping Fritz.

But gratitude wouldn't make him intensely aware of her body the way he was now—just because she'd passed close enough to him so that he got a whiff of her perfume when she got into the truck. He recognized the scent; it was the same kind she'd worn before. But she'd been working all day, and now there was more of *her* in it. He could tell the difference, and it was more of a distraction than he cared to admit. He found himself wanting—needing—to touch her again, and he had no way, however casually, to do it. He was as thwarted as some teenage boy who wanted to put his arm around his girl in a dark movie—if teenage boys still worried about that kind of thing—and from the look of Catherine's class, they didn't.

He looked at her from time to time as they rode along the streets of Wilmington, but she said nothing. He kept driving, into the downtown area and past the riverfront and the *Northwind*, the Coast Guard vessel that was usually moored at the foot of Princess Street.

"Paddy's Hollow all right?" he asked as he pulled the truck into the parking lot behind the Cotton Exchange.

"Yes, that's fine. I like Paddy's."

"Okay, now, I want you to just sit here and don't move," he said as he stopped the truck.

"Why?"

"Because I'm going to get out and go around and open your door. I don't want you jumping out before I get there and leaving me standing there looking like a fool."

They stared at each other across the cab of the truck, and then she suddenly smiled.

"Fair enough," she said, and she waited for him to open the door.

"That was very good, Ms. Holben," he said as she got out.

"Thank you. I'm just not used to it."

"That's what I thought. Come on, it's going to rain."

They had to run the last few steps across the parking lot to stay ahead of the raindrops. She let him lead the way into the Cotton Exchange and up the wooden staircase, and she felt the same pang she always felt as they passed a small inner shop with an array of baby dresses and sleepers in the window.

"Where were the broken transoms?" he suddenly asked.

"Down that way," she answered, surprised that he had remembered.

"I want to look at them. I'm good at stained-glass repair, and I'll do it for a reasonable price. There's no reason why the job should go to someone else if they want it replaced."

She had no argument for that, and she showed him the cracks in the panels of glass over two of the doors in the corridors.

"It's probably too small a job for your time."

"At this point in my brilliant career there's no such thing as a 'too small job.' It won't take much to fix it," he said, making his inspection.

She was looking up at the cracks in the glass, and she suddenly realized that he was looking at her. They both smiled awkwardly and started back in the direction from which they'd come.

It was raining hard when they reached the inner courtyard that led to Paddy's Hollow. It amazed him that Catherine Holben, unlike other women he'd known, didn't seem to care if it was raining or not.

He took her elbow as they walked over the old brick cobbling to get to the pub. *Pretty good, D'Amaro,* he thought. He'd managed to touch her, after all.

This is the pub where Della had intended to apply for a job, Catherine thought, trying not to be distracted by Joe D'Amaro's warm hand on her arm. She was glad Della had voluntarily cut the interview short. If Joe had had to do it, he probably wouldn't have been allowed back on the premises.

The place was dark and uncrowded at this time of day and smelled of french fries and beer. They took a small table in the back, but it was too close to the piped-in music, and they moved to a booth across from the bar. Several men were playing a game of darts, and several others sat at the bar watching *Love Connection* on the television.

The waitress came promptly, and Joe offered Catherine

149

unsolicited advice on the menu selections—all of which she politely ignored. She wanted what she wanted.

"Have you seen the renovations they're doing on the courthouse?" he said when the waitress had left. "God, I wanted that contract so bad, I could taste it."

"You wanted to talk to me about Fritz," Catherine reminded him. She was somehow wary of small talk, as if knowing any more about him, however trivial, might cause her more difficulty in sitting here with him than she already had.

He was . . . handsome to her—when he wasn't handsome, really—and that's all there was to it. He was wearing beat-up work clothes and was scruffy-looking because he needed a haircut and a shave, and he still was the handsomest man she'd ever seen. She looked into his blue eyes. He didn't look away, and that unnerved her. She couldn't think of anything to say. She didn't want to say anything. She just wanted to stare at him. She was like a child with a new toy. She just wanted to *look* so she could decide if he was as interesting as she'd first thought or not, though she'd really long since given up expecting to find anything bad where he was concerned. The things he'd said and done in his ruder moments were entirely understandable, now that she was beginning to know him. She did have one question, but it was one she couldn't ask.

What kind of man are you that you should matter to me one way or the other?

"Catherine, I wanted to tell you again that I appreciate your help."

She gave a small shrug. "You're welcome."

"I think—hope—it's going to be better for Fritz now. I don't know if I said the right things."

"It doesn't matter what you said. I think Fritz will know."

"You sound so damn sure."

"I am sure. I told you before. It's not the words."

"What is it then?"

"It's . . . what comes out of the eyes. You have very kind eyes."

She looked sharply away, as if it had suddenly occurred to her that she shouldn't have made that observation, and it embarrassed her.

"I'd like to tell you about it," he said.

She looked back at him. "I'd like to hear."

"It was the damndest thing. She had the idea that she was a jinx. She'd heard some things her grandmother had said, and she put that with some things she'd seen on television, and somehow she thought she'd caused her mother's death."

"I don't understand."

"I'm not sure I do, either. Fritz was two when Lisa died, and she'd heard about how she used to follow right on Lisa's heels, calling 'Mama' all the time. She thought she was being an aggravation. I told her that all two-year-olds do that. Charlie did. And Della. But she said *they* weren't jinxes. She thought she'd driven Lisa into harm's way the day she died because *she* was a jinx. And—I don't know—she stopped calling me Daddy so the same thing wouldn't happen to me. It was like you said. It wasn't logical to me, but it was to her. She's still calling me Joe, but I think she feels better about things. I can't say I really understand why she thought everything was her fault."

"Children do that—especially at certain ages. Divorce or a death in the family can be very hard on them."

He looked at her across the table, letting his eyes linger on hers. He was still puzzled but not so much about Fritz as he was about Catherine Holben.

The waitress brought their beer and he took a long sip.

"I'd like to ask you a question. It isn't about Fritz."

"Go ahead."

He looked at her for a moment. "You . . . never ask me anything. Why is that?"

"I don't know what you mean."

"I mean, we've had several long conversations now, and you've never asked where I come from or what I'm doing here in Wilmington. Things like that. You're the first person I've met down here who didn't want to know what kind of accent I had or why I was living here."

"It could be because you told me to butt out of your business."

He smiled. "It could be," he agreed. "But I don't think it is." He had the feeling—no, he damn well knew she'd ask anything she wanted to ask. "So why haven't you? I get the feeling you're . . . holding back."

"Being so compulsively nosy, you mean," she said, but he didn't comment on that. She thought for a moment before she answered. "It's because you said you didn't talk about your wife, about Lisa. I thought your living here might have something to do with her death. So I didn't ask."

He was surprised. He had prepared himself for some flip answer that would put him in his place. He had been afraid that she would think he was being coy, that this was some kind of line, but she'd answered him truthfully.

He studied his beer, then took another swallow. "It does," he said, letting himself look into her eyes. "You know anything about Dorchester?"

"England?" Catherine guessed. She was being flippant because that familiar, intense expression of his had returned, and she was still wary of it.

"Boston, Ms. Holben. A neighborhood of Boston."

"No. I don't know anything about Dorchester."

"I grew up there. We were living there when Lisa was killed. Lisa and I had gone out to see some friends—a night out away from the kids, you know? On the way back a drunk driver crossed the centerline and hit us head-on. She was killed. I wasn't."

Yes, you were, Catherine thought. Her eyes held his. "Go on," she said quietly. For some reason he seemed to want to tell her this, and she intended to hear all of it.

"That's all."

It wasn't all, and they both knew it.

He suddenly avoided her eyes, but he'd run out of other places to look. He glanced back at her, knowing those calm eyes of hers would be waiting. He realized that he was going to say to her what he'd never said to anyone. "I'd . . . had a few beers. I wasn't drunk, but I always thought if I . . . hadn't had them, maybe I could have . . . done something."

He stared at her now, waiting for her reaction.

"Yes," she said, and for some reason it made him angry. He had just told her the darkest secret of his life, and she had no more to say than that.

"You keep saying that, Ms. Holben. In this particular case, what does *yes* mean?"

"It means," she said carefully, "that if I were in your place, I might think that too."

"You're not in my place."

"No. But I think I can understand why you didn't want to live where everything reminded you."

He didn't know what to say to that, so he said nothing. Somehow she always seemed to be able to disarm him by simply telling him the truth. Part of him resented her presumption that she could share his pain, and part of him was more than grateful for her empathy. He looked around the pub. More people were coming in, the happy-hour crowd

153

from the downtown businesses.

"I have another question," he said, looking back at her. He knew the beer was making him more bold than he would have been otherwise, but he didn't worry about it. He wanted to know. "There's something else about you I don't understand."

"What?"

"You seem to like children. I was wondering why you didn't want to have any of your own."

She frowned. "What makes you think that?"

"I heard the . . . argument you were having with Jonathan. Something about your having children being a condition of the marriage. I thought he was marrying somebody else because you wouldn't have his kids."

She stared at him across the table. He thought for a moment that she was going to get up and leave.

But she didn't. She looked at him, her eyes unwavering. "Not wouldn't," she said evenly. "Couldn't."

Couldn't, he thought. The word hung in the air between them.

"Catherine, I'm sorry," he said quickly. "This is none of my business."

"No, you asked, and I'll tell you. I'm barren. Jonathan came from a big, loving family. Going to his parents' house on Christmas Day or Thanksgiving Day was like going to the Waltons'. Going to Sunday dinner was like going to the Waltons'. He wanted a big family like that of his own. I couldn't give it to him, and now I try to compensate for it— my barrenness—by helping the teenage girls you met today have the best babies they can."

She made it sound very matter-of-fact, but it wasn't. The calm eyes weren't so calm now, and it was all he could do not to touch her. It hadn't occurred to him that Jonathan would

154

have left her for a reason like that. If it had, he wouldn't have asked. *Jesus!* No wonder she hadn't wanted to go to the son of a bitch's wedding.

"Are your parents living?" he suddenly asked, because it was somehow important for him to know that she had family—someone to look after her if, God forbid, she should ever admit to needing it.

"No," she said.

"Any brothers or sisters?"

"No," she said again. "I was a spoiled only child."

Damn, he thought. All she had was that son of a bitch, Jonathan. He didn't think she was spoiled. There was nothing about her that would make him think that.

The waitress brought their food.

"So how did you happen to pick Wilmington?" Catherine said to him. She was attempting to change the subject, and he didn't want to change it. He wanted to say something, do something, that would make her feel better.

"Catherine . . ."

She looked at him, her eyes still filled with pain. "I'm not comfortable talking about my barrenness, Joe. I probably won't ever be. Would you . . . humor me now? Let's talk about something else."

He could do that, at least. God knows he'd been in the same situation enough himself when someone had wanted to talk about Lisa. He knew all about "talking about something else," so he launched into the D'Amaro family history, starting with Michael's hitch in the Marines twenty-three years ago and his being stationed at Camp Lejeune and ending with their decision to take over their father's construction company and move it to the North Carolina coast, where there was a building boom.

"You were right. I didn't want to stay around Boston,

where everything reminded me of Lisa. I used to come down
on the bus to visit Michael when he was at Lejeune, and I
liked it down here. I still do. Are you going to eat that pickle?"

"Yes," she said pointedly.

He grinned. "I was only wondering."

"Well, you can forget it. This one's mine."

His grin broadened, she smiled in return, and a thousand
warning bells went off in his mind.

*You don't want to do this, D'Amaro. This is going to be
nothing but trouble from the word* go.

But he did want to do it. He wanted to sit and talk to her as
long as she'd let him. He wanted to tease her until she put
him in his place. He wanted to be close to her. He wanted to
know what it would be like to kiss her, to make love with her.

Good.

It would be good. Somehow he knew that. He let his eyes
follow the curve of her throat to her breasts. The sudden
mental image of Catherine, aroused and willing, made him
stir uneasily in his chair.

"So did your father come here with you?"

"What?" he said, because he definitely wasn't listening.

"Your father. Did he come down here with you?"

"No, he retired. He's still in Dorchester with my mother,
making things in his workshop and going to Red Sox ball
games. So . . . are you a Wilmington native?"

"No, I'm from a couple of hundred miles inland. We used
to come here to the beach every summer when I was growing
up—to Wrightsville or to Carolina Beach. You know, when
you travel a long way to get here and you catch that first
glimpse of the ocean between the hotels and the houses—it's
wonderful. I never did get over the thrill of it. I said I was
going to live here—and here I am."

"But you're not living on the beach."

"No, I still want to catch that first glimpse of the ocean. Only now I don't have to go as far."

The conversation dwindled, and they sat looking at each other. Two of the men playing darts began to argue about the regulation distance to the board on the wall.

"It's seven feet, nine and a half inches, Herb! That's the regulation, and that's where you're standing. Seven feet, nine and a half damn inches!"

Music still played in the background, the kind of music Della and her friends—or Beatrice and the girls—would like, and the participants on *Love Connection* still struggled to establish a meaningful relationship with a blind date.

"Catherine, I was wondering," Joe said abruptly. "Sunday afternoon there's a meeting for the building association. If you're not busy, I thought you might go with me." He shrugged. "Keep me company? Eat a steak? The meeting will be a pain, but the meal is always great."

She didn't answer immediately.

Here it is, she thought. The point where she would have to make a decision. He was asking her to go someplace with him—when he knew she was less than a woman—and he'd made no mention of Fritz. He was looking at her intently, and she suddenly realized that she had let the silence go on too long.

"What time?" she asked, because when everything was said and done, she'd never had trouble making up her mind.

"Three. I'd need to pick you up about two-thirty."

"All right," she said, and he smiled.

"All right. Good." He looked away, as if he were suddenly shy because he hadn't really expected her to say she'd go with him. "Well, I'd better get back to work before Michael realizes how long I've been gone." He stood up, and he didn't try to take both checks.

It was still raining when they went outside, and she walked through the rain with him to the truck instead of letting him bring it around. He didn't argue with her about that, either.

On the way back the conversation lagged again. He didn't mind. He was still patting himself on the back for getting her to agree to go out with him.

"Catherine . . ." he said when she was about to get out of the truck in front of her building. "Sunday—it's a suit-and-tie thing."

"I don't have a suit and tie," she said, teasing him.

"Borrow one," he advised her.

He chuckled to himself several times on the way home. He liked this woman. She'd been badly hurt, but she was still funny and sweet and tough. And kind. And pretty. No, she was beautiful. And sexy. Very sexy.

He *liked* this woman.

He liked her well enough not to say anything about their going out together to any of his children.

9

The telephone in the kitchen rang briefly at six A.M. on Sunday morning. Catherine was awake, but she was still lying in bed. She had been idly trying to decide what she should wear to a builders association dinner meeting in lieu of a suit and tie, a rather pleasant pastime in the early-morning quiet, one calculated to take her mind off a more pressing matter. Rightly or wrongly, she was looking forward to her afternoon with Joe D'Amaro, and yet she still needed to reassure herself that this so-called date didn't mean anything—to either of them.

No. Not reassure. Convince. If she let herself believe otherwise, then she let herself become defenseless against more hurt, more emotional pain, and she was afraid of that. By his own admission Joe only wanted her to keep him company. He was obviously still in love with his dead wife, and he had his three children to consider. Della had made it clear how she felt about the possibility of Catherine Holben becoming involved with her father. Catherine had problems of her own. She was fully aware of how recently she had been divorced, and she still cared about Jonathan, though she certainly couldn't be accused of thinking about him much of late. All the magazines warned divorced women to beware of behaving impulsively in the early stages of their return to single life, and her going out with Joe D'Amaro could definitely be described as impulsive. She'd agonized over the possibility of becoming more involved with him ever since the cookout, but when the time came to say yes or no, she'd said yes fast enough. She was still agonizing—and not very covertly, according to Pat.

"If you're not careful, you are going to fool around here and return to the living," Pat had said.

Catherine had forgotten how upsetting belonging to the living could be. She'd hidden in her safe cocoon of misery for a long time, and it was painful to be out again. She felt vulnerable and exposed, but she thought logically that Joe must be feeling the same way—unless, of course, he was used to starting relationships, however meaningless.

She lifted her head to hear if the telephone was ringing. For some reason the previous tenant had never felt the need to have a phone in the bedroom, and Catherine had never bothered to have it moved. Or, more truthfully, neither she nor the other tenant could afford it. The phone was quiet, and she gratefully closed her eyes. A wrong number, she decided, and not Joe calling with another acute attack of cold feet.

The telephone rang again when she was on the brink of going back to sleep, and this time it didn't stop. She fumbled her way through the still dark apartment, mentally bracing herself to hear Joe's voice when she answered it.

"Is this Sasha's teacher?" a woman said.

"Sasha Higgins?"

"Yes, Sasha," the woman said.

"Yes, I'm her teacher. Who is this?"

"You come over to the hospital now. Sasha's wanting you."

"What?" Catherine said. "What's wrong with her?"

"You come over to the hospital, Teacher."

"Which hospital?"

But the woman had hung up, and Catherine stood holding the receiver.

"What in the world?" she said under her breath. The

largest hospital, New Hanover Memorial, was her first guess, and she quickly looked up the number.

"Do you have a patient named Sasha Higgins?"

"Middle initial, please."

"I don't remember her middle initial."

"One moment, please."

Catherine waited. If she located Sasha, there was still the problem of how she'd get here. The buses didn't run on Sunday.

"Yes," the hospital receptionist said. "She is admitted to the obstetrical unit."

"Thank you," Catherine said.

The obstetrical unit. Sasha hadn't been feeling well for days, but she had exhibited no significant symptoms, nothing the doctors at the prenatal clinic could treat. There was no treatment for being thirteen years old.

Catherine had no alternative but to call a taxi. She dressed hurriedly, then went downstairs to the foyer to wait. She stood where she could see out the glass doors, wondering what Joe D'Amaro would be doing at this time of the morning. Sleeping in? Getting his children ready for church? Working? She sighed and pushed her thoughts of him aside. She had no reason to worry about canceling their plans yet, not until she knew what was wrong with Sasha.

"You're up early," Mrs. Donovan said as she came out to get her Sunday paper. She was wearing a red-flowered duster and red fuzzy slippers, and she had her hair wrapped in toilet tissue.

"Yes," Catherine said, watching a cab drive slowly by. She walked toward the front doors, but it kept going.

"Is something wrong?"

"I hope not," Catherine said vaguely, for once resenting Mrs. Donovan's curiosity. She had never gotten over the feeling that Mrs. Donovan saw her work with young girls who were pregnant and unmarried as morally offensive.

She knew that Mrs. Donovan was waiting to find out whether or not anything of interest was happening, but she didn't go on.

"Well, don't you worry about anything here," Mrs. Donovan said finally.

"No, I won't."

"If anyone comes to visit you today, I'll tell them where you are—just where *are* you going, Catherine?"

The cab returned, and the driver had no compunction about blowing the horn at this early hour. Catherine smiled and gave Mrs. Donovan a wave, hurrying out the door without answering.

She had the cabdriver let her out at the front door of the hospital. Whatever was happening with Sasha, she was certain that it wasn't good. Sasha's grandmother wouldn't have called her for anything trivial. She had a sudden mental image of little Sasha, alone and frightened in this place of shiny halls and intercom voices.

The obstetrical floor seemed quiet when she got off the elevator. She could smell coffee brewing somewhere, and no one slept in the waiting area. The nurses' station, too, was empty. She walked in that direction.

"Catherine!" someone called as she passed an open door, and she leaned back to look in.

"Hello, Clarkson," she said to the doctor sitting on the countertop next to the sink. "Been up all night?" He was the junior partner in the practice where she had had her infertility testing, and he looked a little ragged around the edges. He'd done some of her tests once, in her regular doctor's absence. He was as irreverent as they came, but endearing somehow, and she liked him.

162

"Oh, hell, yes," he said in disgust. "Who's on call for the strays this weekend? Good old Clarkson. There's nothing I like any better than an unregistered OB with no prenatal care."

"Those are the breaks," she said. "Maybe you should have been a dermatologist."

"And miss *this?*" he asked incredulously, encompassing his makeshift place of repose with a sweep of his hand. Unfortunately it was the hand holding the cup of coffee. "Ah, shit—you been to the office lately?"

"No, why?"

"I thought you might have met the new doctor in the practice—nice Hindu boy, one of Jackson's classmates at Duke. Man, I'm glad to get off the bottom of the totem pole. You realize we've now got all the holidays in three major religions to worry about? We're thinking of taking in an atheist just to cover for the rest of us."

Catherine tried to suppress a grin. "You know anything about Sasha Higgins?"

"I know *everything* about Sasha Higgins. Don't you see this furrowed brow? She's having contractions. She's borderline hysterical. Her blood pressure's way up, and her grandmother's driving me and everybody else nuts. We're trying to keep a lid on it, but she'll probably drop her load before the day's over—Sasha, not the grandmother."

"I'd better go find her, then."

"Hey!" he called after her. "How about doing me a favor?"

"What?"

"Do something with Grandmamma, will you? She keeps standing around with her arms folded like she's going to turn somebody into a frog."

Catherine smiled. "What do you want me to do, Clarkson?"

"I don't know—settle her down, take her for a walk, lock her in a closet. I don't want to have to deliver that baby with Grandmamma breathing down my neck. *Man,* she's a tough old broad."

"I'll see what I can do."

"Thanks, Catherine."

"No promises. I think Grandmamma does pretty much as she pleases."

"That's what I figured," he said morosely. "Hell, I *should* have been a dermatologist. Probably wouldn't do any good, though. Any weirdness that stumbles into this hospital has got my name on it. Why do you think that is, Catherine?"

"I have no idea," she said. "Probably something to do with the indifference of fate and the meaning of life."

He grinned, and she walked on toward the nurses' station. She caught a glimpse of an old woman standing off to the side. As she walked closer she recognized the gray felt hat and the big black pocketbook the woman had under her arm.

"You come down here, Teacher," the old woman called. "Treasure's coming. They can do all they want, but Treasure's coming."

"Where's Sasha?" Catherine asked, taking Sasha's grandmother by the hand.

"In that room down there. They doing something else to her. They won't let me in. You go down there, Teacher. My Sasha's scared in this place. You go down there and help Sasha." She held Catherine's hand for a moment, then let it go.

Catherine nodded. The door to the room Mrs. Higgins had indicated was slightly ajar, and she could hear Sasha crying inside. She pushed the door open. A very harassed nurse was trying to talk her into being hooked up to a fetal monitor.

"Come on, honey. It's so we can hear your baby's heart-beat—"

Sasha cried louder, still pushing at the equipment in the nurse's hands.

Catherine came closer to the bed. "Sasha," she said quietly.

"Ms. Holben!" Sasha wailed, reaching for her with both hands. Catherine put her arms around her, trying to keep her from coming out of the bed.

"What's all this, Sasha?" Catherine said, stroking her hair. Someone—Grandmamma, probably—had braided it for her, and the braids were coming all undone. "I'm surprised at you. You know what this equipment is for. I showed it to all of you. We put it on Beatrice—"

"Beatrice—ain't—*scared!*"

"Now what did I tell you about when you go to the hospital—"

Sasha cried louder.

"Sasha, are you listening to me? I said it was all right to be a little afraid because this is something you've never done before."

Sasha's voice went up a few octaves. "Maria said—"

"Are you going to listen to Maria or to me? If you think Maria knows more than I do, then you can just call her to come over here and I'll go back home." Catherine knew her psychology professor would hardly approve of such blatant emotional blackmail, but she wasn't above doing whatever it took to calm Sasha down.

"Don't—go—Ms. Holben!"

"Well, then stop crying so we can talk. Here. Let's wipe your face."

She disentangled herself from Sasha's grasp to reach a wet washcloth on the bedside table. "Look up here." She gently washed Sasha's face. "Take some tissues." She held the box so Sasha could reach it. "And wipe your nose."

Sasha sniffed loudly.

"Tell me how you feel."

"My—stomach—hurts, Ms. Holben!" She threw her arms around Catherine again, and Catherine held her tightly.

"All the time? Or does it come and go?"

"Comes and goes. Oh, Ms. Holben, it's hurting bad!"

"Don't hold your breath, Sasha. It makes the pain worse. Breathe like we practiced in class. That's it!"

Catherine waited until the contraction ended, her eyes meeting the eyes of the nurse, who stood waiting with the monitoring equipment in her hands. "Now, Sasha, didn't I tell you you had to be a good mama to your baby *before* it gets here?"

She said something into Catherine's shoulder that could have been yes.

"And didn't I tell you to help the nurses all you could when you went to the hospital?"

This time she nodded.

"I know you feel really bad, but it's time for you to be a good mama to Treasure. And it's time to help this nurse here. She needs to hook you up to the machine so she can hear Treasure's heartbeat, so she can take care of her—and you. Are you going to do it?"

"Don't go, Ms. Holben—"

"I won't, Sasha."

"Is it going to—hurt?"

"No. Beatrice didn't say anything about it hurting, did she? It's like wearing two belts. One up high and one over Treasure's heart."

"Are you sure?"

"I'm sure, Sasha. If it hurt, I'd tell you."

Catherine lived to regret those words almost immediately.

The monitor was hardly in place before someone came in from the lab to take a blood sample.

"Is it going to hurt?" Sasha asked again.

Catherine sighed. "Yes, Sasha," she answered, because Sasha was waiting to see if she would tell her the truth.

"How much?" she asked, her mouth trembling again.

Catherine held her thumb and forefinger apart about an inch. "That much," she said. "Not as much as when your stomach hurts."

Satisfied, Sasha took Catherine's hand and held out her arm.

Catherine lost all track of time. She soothed, cajoled, coerced, whatever it took to get Sasha to participate in the procedures to monitor the condition of her unborn child. The contractions intensified, and the same nurse came in to start an IV.

"Sasha," she said, "this is one stick, so we don't have to keep giving you shots like we've been doing. One instead of a lot. What do you say?"

Resigned, Sasha capitulated easily this time, and Grandmamma Higgins was allowed back into the room.

"They won't give my Sasha nothing to eat," she said to Catherine. "This child ain't been fed nothing. She needs something now."

"It's better if she doesn't eat," Catherine answered, holding the old woman's eyes with hers to try to make her understand what she didn't want to say in front of Sasha. "The IV fluids—the water that's running into her arm—has sugar in it and something to make her contractions stop. They're not starving her, Mrs. Higgins."

Dr. Clarkson came in. "I gotta do what I gotta do," he said to Catherine as he put on an examining glove.

"I don't like it!" Sasha wailed, but she didn't put up the same fight as she had over the monitor.

"Feet together, little one," Clarkson said to her. "Knees apart—great, Sasha! That is mighty fine! Let's see what's happening here."

He did the vaginal exam, and his glove came away bloody. He quickly peeled it off and turned it wrong side out so Sasha wouldn't see.

"Yutopar's not holding her," he said to Catherine.

"I told you Treasure's coming," Grandmamma said. "It don't matter what you do."

Clarkson rubbed his hand tiredly over his forehead. "You're right, Mrs. Higgins. We're going to have to take Sasha into the delivery room."

Sasha began to cry in earnest.

"Catherine, I want you to come into the delivery room."

"Clarkson, I haven't helped with a delivery in years—"

"Catherine, please! Don't give me your résumé. Just let me see your little bod in a scrub dress PDQ, okay?"

She still hesitated. She didn't mind going with Sasha, but she knew doctors. When one gave them an inch, they expected a mile, and the mere fact that she wasn't an employee of the hospital wouldn't matter at all. She was too rusty to get involved in a complicated delivery.

Clarkson motioned frantically toward Grandmamma Higgins with his eyes, his back turned so the old woman couldn't see him.

"*Okay?*" he repeated.

"Okay, but don't ask me where anything is."

"Deal!" he said, shaking her hand. "Get going."

"One more thing."

"What?"

Catherine lowered her voice. "I think Grandmamma had better come in the delivery room with us."

"Catherine—"

"She doesn't understand anything about medical things, Clarkson. It will be better if she's in there where she can see what's happening. Trust me on this."

"Ah, hell, Catherine!"

"I mean it."

He sighed. "All right, but keeping a leash on that old woman is *your* job. You want me to tell the kid or will you?"

"I'll do it."

"You aren't going to try to keep me *out*, are you, boy?" Grandmamma said.

"Who, me? No way. Catherine, I leave Grandmamma to you. And get rid of that hat," he added under his breath.

Clarkson went out, and Catherine moved back to the bedside. She reached to gently touch Sasha's face. "Sasha, it's time for Treasure to be born now. Your grandmamma and I both will be going into the delivery room with you, but we have to go change our clothes."

"Don't go, Ms. Holben!"

"Sasha, it'll be all right. I'll tell you what. Your grandmamma can stay with you while I go change clothes, and then when I come back, she can go."

"I'm scared, Ms. Holben!"

"I know. But you aren't going to be by yourself. Now take your grandmamma's hand. I'll be right back."

Catherine stepped into the hall. A nurse was motioning for her to come in her direction, a few doors down.

"Here you go," she said when Catherine walked in. "This scrub dress should fit you—and I'll leave Grandmamma's right here. And here's your cap. I'll put hers on top of the dress. You look tired, kiddo. You had anything to eat?"

"No," Catherine said, realizing suddenly how hungry she was. She hadn't even been out of the room since she'd arrived. She had no idea how long she'd been with Sasha.

"Here, take this," the nurse said, tossing her an apple from a nearby paper bag.

"I don't want to take your lunch—"

"Listen, you're keeping Grandmamma occupied. You can have anything I've got."

Catherine smiled and took a bite of the apple. "What time is it?"

"Twenty till one," the nurse said, looking at her watch.

"Oh, Lord! I need to make a telephone call. Is there a phone I can use?"

"Use the one at the desk. Punch nine to get an outside line."

"Thanks," Catherine said again. "I appreciate it."

"Hey, I told you, you handle Grandmamma, you get whatever you want."

The nurse left, and Catherine changed hurriedly, taking big bites of apple as she went. She had no idea it was so late. She walked to the nurses' station and borrowed the telephone book to look up Joe's number.

Maybe it was better this way, she thought. If she broke their date and he asked her again, she'd know whether or not he was serious.

The phone rang, but it was a long time before anyone answered.

"Charlie?" she said, because the voice wasn't deep enough to be Joe's.

"Yeah, who's this?"

"This is Catherine Holben. I need to talk to your dad." She could hear the sound effects of a computer game in the background.

"He's not . . . back from church . . . yet. He and Fritz . . . probably stopped at . . . McDonald's."

"Then can you tell him something for me?"

"Oh . . . sure."

"Tell him something's come up." She realized that Charlie was engrossed in whatever he was doing and she had better keep it simple. "Tell him I can't go with him to the builders association meeting this afternoon. Tell him I'll call him later."

"You got it, Catherine."

"Are you sure you know what to tell him?"

"Um . . . you're . . . no, uh . . . something's come up . . . and you can't go to the . . . builders association meeting. And . . . you'll call him."

"Right. You won't forget?"

"Me? I never, ever forget. I am—"

There was a big explosion from the computer game.

"Super Memory!"

"Thanks, Super."

"Anytime, Catherine."

She stood grinning and holding the receiver, and she tried to push aside the disappointment she was feeling at not being able to see Joe. For once she didn't agonize. She wanted to see him but she couldn't. It was as simple as that. God, how she wished she were walking with him and Fritz on the beach.

She took a deep breath. She had to return to the problem at hand. Clarkson was doing everything possible to stop Sasha's labor, and it wasn't working.

She walked back toward Sasha's room, trying to get in a few more bites of apple on the way. She could see several of the new mothers in their rooms as she passed, women primping for the arrival of their newborns. None of them was as young as Sasha.

Grandmamma was waiting at Sasha's bedside, and Catherine took her into the hall to show her the room where she could change.

"Your scrub dress and cap like mine are in there on a

chair. If it's not the right size, you can look on the shelves for another one—or come and get me and I'll see if I can find one for you."

"You're good to my Sasha," the old woman said, putting her hand on Catherine's arm.

"I like Sasha very much. I want everything to go all right for her."

"We're going to have to see about that, ain't we, Teacher?"

Catherine looked into the old woman's eyes for a moment, then nodded. Grandmamma may be ignorant of medical procedures, but she understood the situation perfectly.

"I'm going to work a root for you, Teacher. I'm going to work one for you that'll make the sun shine on your back door."

Catherine smiled. "I can always use a little sunshine, Grandmamma."

"Ms. Holben!" Sasha called, and Catherine went back inside to take her hand.

"It hurts *bad,* Ms. Holben," she said, punctuating it with a little mewing sound as another contraction came. "It's hurting me and it's hurting Treasure."

"It won't be much longer, Sasha. Now breathe like you're supposed to—pant like a dog pants."

Sasha gave a weak effort, and Clarkson came back in with a nurse Catherine hadn't seen before.

"One more time, Sasha," he said, but Sasha was past caring about another vaginal exam. Tears rolled out of the corners of her eyes and down her cheeks.

"Okay, boys," Clarkson said at the end of his examination. "We've got to go. Unhook our Sasha so we can roll. Where's Grandmamma?"

"She's changing her clothes," Catherine said.

"Well, she'd better get on the stick. We got to get this show on the road."

He helped pull the bed out into the hall. "There she is," he said as they moved the bed in a wide turn to go toward the delivery rooms. "Let's go, Grandmamma!" he called, but he didn't wait for her. He rolled the bed forward, leaving her to hustle along after them as best she could.

"Nice outfit," he said to her when she caught up.

"You too," Grandmamma said stonily, neither of them cracking a smile.

"Don't you think so, Catherine?" Clarkson asked innocently.

Catherine frowned because Grandmamma still had on her gray felt pillbox hat and her huge black purse was under her arm. She hadn't bothered at all with the cap to cover her hair.

Catherine gave him a hard look. "Yes," she said pointedly. "It's nice." She was worried about Sasha and her baby, and she had no time for his cuteness.

"When's Treasure going to get here, Ms. Holben?" Sasha asked as they rolled her down the hall.

"It won't be long now. She'll be here soon," Catherine said.

"What makes you two so sure we're having a baby girl?" the nurse asked as they pushed Sasha's bed in through the double doors that led to the suite of delivery rooms.

"Grandmamma said," Catherine answered.

The nurse rolled her eyes and mouthed a silent *oh,* as if that were a good enough reason for her too.

"Hold it, Clarkson! I need to talk to you!" another nurse yelled as they made the turn to take Sasha into the delivery room.

"Not now, Becky—"

"Now, Clarkson!"

"Becky, I am busy here—"

"Some of you are not properly attired, Clarkson!" the nurse said pointedly, clearly referring to a certain huge black purse and a gray felt hat.

"I know that, Becky," he sang back, and he didn't stop. "If you don't like it, *you* handle it."

"Jesus, Mary, and Joseph!" Becky said as he pulled Sasha's bed the rest of the way in.

"Don't forget, Buddha!" he called to her.

"I'll Buddha you!"

"Anytime you say, Becky!"

"You've got some explaining to do, Clarkson!"

"Right! Sasha, sweetie, move over here on the table—"

"I can't," Sasha wailed. The room was bright and cold, and she began to shiver.

"Yes, you can, because kindly old Dr. Clarkson's going to lift you. You ready?"

"Oh! I can't! I can't do that!"

"Come on, Sasha, just a little bit more. Atta girl! See there? You did it good. Now, Miss Catherine's going to stand right here so she can lift you up when I need her to. And Grandmamma's going to stand over here so she can help. Let's get the kid a blanket."

The nurse was already there with it, and Clarkson nodded his approval.

"Okay, ready, team? Where's my gown?"

"Where it always is," the nurse said.

"Well, damn, so it is!"

Clarkson began putting on the sterile gown and gloves. "Where's my pediatrician? You got my pediatrician coming?"

"He's on his way."

"Who is it?"

"Merchinson."

"You tell him about thirty-two or thirty-three weeks' gestation?"

"I told him everything you said—word for word."

"You tell him if I can't go sailing, he ain't going sailing, either?"

"That too."

Clarkson chuckled happily. "Okay, boys. Catherine, move those stirrups in a little, will you? Sasha, you're just about too little for this table. What's her BP?"

"Up," the nurse said, writing it down on Sasha's record for Clarkson to see.

"My stomach's *hurting* again, Ms. Holben! It's not stopping!" Sasha said, and Catherine took her hands. Grandmamma stroked Sasha's brow and began to hum a song, something Catherine recognized vaguely from her childhood.

Not a children's song, she suddenly realized, but an old hymn, one her own grandmother used to sing when one of her grandchildren needed soothing. For a moment Catherine was there again, back home, a child sitting on her grandmother's lap on a rocking chair on the back porch and listening to that song—"Rock of Ages."

Sasha closed her eyes, her contractions coming harder and closer together. She clung desperately to Catherine's hands. The pediatrician arrived. "How's it going?" he asked as he put on a gown.

"Won't be long now," Clarkson told him. "Let's have the lights down."

Catherine talked to Sasha quietly, and Grandmamma sang. Treasure Higgins was born at thirteen minutes after two.

"Baby girl, Sasha," Clarkson said. He cut the cord quickly and handed the baby to the pediatrician.

"I want to see," Sasha said, straining forward. "I want to see Treasure."

"In a minute," Clarkson said. He concentrated on delivering the placenta, his eyes meeting Catherine's once and shifting away.

"Yo, Merchinson!" he said after a few minutes of silence. "How's it going?"

Merchinson worked over the baby in the far corner, his back to everyone else, the attending nurse at his shoulder pulling a light around so he could see. Catherine kept listening for some sound besides suctioning. She could hear Merchinson talking to himself, checklisting out loud, the way some doctors did to calm themselves when the situation was out of hand.

"Move my light around a little, Catherine," Clarkson said, his eyes again grazing hers, worried eyes that belied his usual silliness. "Merch?" he prompted. "What's happening?"

"She's not picking up," Merchinson said.

10

It was raining when Catherine came out of the hospital, and it had been for some time. The taxi was slow in coming, and she stood forlornly just inside the front doors to wait, her mind on nothing but the rivulets of water that splattered on the glass doors from time to time when the wind changed. She was cold and tired, and she had no idea what time it was. Seven o'clock? Later? She looked behind her into the lobby, but she couldn't see a clock on the walls. She'd been lost all day without her watch, a stupid oversight on her part that surely must have some Freudian overtones. She hadn't really wanted to go out with Joe D'Amaro, and therefore she'd subconsciously hoped to miss the time. Or she *had* really wanted to go out with him, and therefore she didn't want to know when the hour she was supposed to see him came and went. Well, it didn't matter what time it was now, and she was being ridiculous. That was something else she knew about herself, that when she was emotionally exhausted, her head became filled with the absurd.

She's not picking up.

One more absurdity echoing inside her head. She closed her eyes for a moment to make it go away again. That one was the greatest absurdity of all—Treasure Higgins, wanted so desperately and dismissed so easily with a carefully neutral euphemism for death.

A taxi pulled up outside, the falling rain visible in the beams of the headlights. Catherine walked quickly to get to it, not because of the wet weather but because she wanted nothing but to be home. She smelled of hospital and sweat and sorrow, and she wanted to be clean again.

Thankfully the driver wasn't talkative. He let her sit in silence after the obligatory remark about the storm coming in off the ocean. She ignored the cigarette-stale air, the damp mustiness of the inside of the taxi, and she kept her mind fixed on the sounds around her instead—the windshield wipers, the occasional background noise of the two-way radio, the hiss of passing cars. Where had she learned that? Some credit course she'd taken somewhere along the way as she vacillated between careers. She remembered the axiom quite clearly: *"In order to keep the mind from racing, one should select some sound and listen."* It was good advice, but it wasn't working.

She sighed heavily, and she could feel the taxi driver looking at her in the rearview mirror, trying to assess her condition. Sick? Distraught? Drunk?

None of the above, she nearly said. *I'm quite fine. Really.* She was fine—because she had no alternative.

She paid the cabbie too much money. The lamp in the Mayfair foyer hadn't been turned on. She walked carefully into the dimness of the downstairs. She could immediately smell the aromas of evening meals in the building—coffee, onions frying somewhere, baking bread. Her stomach rumbled. She was hungry. And she was too tired to eat.

She didn't bother to turn the foyer lamp on, and she climbed the stairs slowly, quietly, because she didn't want to have to deal with any of Mrs. Donovan's questions. Halfway up the first flight she could smell the pungent sweetness of a newly lit Lucky Strike. Mrs. Donovan was too busy conjuring to bother with the foyer lamp.

She let herself into her apartment, turning lights on as she went because she didn't want to be in the dark. She sat down heavily on the couch, letting her head rest against the back, her eyes closed. Her throat ached and her eyes burned with the need to weep, and yet she had no tears. Sasha had cried enough for the both of them.

But she was too restless to sit. She didn't want to be home, after all. If she had a car, she'd go somewhere—to the beach, rain or no rain. She'd walk from Johnnie Mercer's pier north toward the D'Amaro Brothers building site, and she'd feel the wind and the rain and listen to the rough sea, and she'd be afraid all the way. But when she came back again, she'd feel better. She'd be glad she was alive and—

She abruptly got up from the couch and walked to the front windows to look down on the rain-wet street below. She could see her own reflection in the dark glass of the window, and she turned away from it. It made things worse somehow, seeing herself. Her eyes went to the gnome sculpture on the small table by the couch. She went to pick it up, holding it a moment, staring into Daisy's gently smiling face before she set it back down again.

Hold on to your baby, Daisy.

She went into the small bathroom, discarding clothes along the way. She showered and washed her hair to get rid of the hospital smell, and she got dressed again because she still wanted to go out somewhere—a walk around the block, anything, anything.

She looked around sharply at a knock on the door. Mrs. Donovan, probably, finished with her nostalgia rituals and ready for inquiries into things that were none of her business. Or if not her, one of the other tenants, who was equally as curious. It had done her no good to creep up the stairs like an errant child, after all, and the last thing she needed was an interrogation about her whereabouts today. She stood quietly, waiting for whoever it was to leave.

"Catherine?" someone called through the door.

Joe.

She crossed the room quickly. She was glad he was here.

179

She wanted to smile but she couldn't. Her eyes were burning again, and when she opened the door, she had to fight down yet another ridiculous notion—one to reach for him so that he could hold her and tell her everything was going to be all right.

But she didn't reach for him. No one could comfort her—not Joe D'Amaro, not even Jonathan. She knew what Jonathan would say, his words kind but still cutting like a knife. *Poor Katie. Burned out* again?

Joe was wearing that look of his—Joe D'Amaro, disgruntled—that was no better than Jonathan's flippant dismissal would have been.

I don't need this! she thought.

"Hi," she said, anyway, standing back so that he could come in.

He didn't move. He stood in the hall with his hands on his hips. He wasn't wearing a suit and a tie. He had on his usual jeans and plaid shirt. This shirt was blue and white and beige. She had the idea that because he was wearing this particular shirt, his eyes would look very blue—if she could have seen them in the dim hall light.

The door behind him cracked open slightly.

"That's it?" he asked. "Hi?"

She threw her hands up in exasperation. "I give up, Joe. What is it I'm *supposed* to say?"

"You could say where the hell you've been, for one thing. I think you at least owe me that. I have called you. I've been by here three times, and I can tell you right now, Catherine, I'm getting damn tired of showing the old lady downstairs my driver's license!"

"I don't—"

"Were we or weren't we supposed to go out this afternoon!" he interrupted loudly.

"Yes!"

"You're damn right we were! But you weren't here, were you? Okay, I thought, she's stood you up. Except I don't think you'd do that, and don't ask me why," he said, pointing his finger at her. "I don't know where you are. Nobody here knows where you are. I don't know if something's happened to you, so I get to worry all damn afternoon! And why the hell should I care, anyway? I've got better things to do!"

"Then go do them," she said, attempting to close the door. She wasn't in the mood for this, and she was *not* going to listen.

"Wait a minute," he said, catching the door so that she couldn't close it. "If you didn't want to go, you could have told me."

"I left you a message," she said.

"Where?" he asked, his tone of voice suggesting that he didn't believe it for a minute.

"With Charlie."

He started to say something else, then didn't. He stood staring at her, his eyes searching hers. "Charlie," he said finally. "My Charlie. The kid that lives at my house."

"That's the one."

He exhaled sharply, looking away from her and then back again. "I didn't get it."

"So I gathered."

"So can I come in?"

She shrugged. "Why not?" she said, standing back again to let him inside.

"What was it? The message?" he asked as she closed the door.

"That I couldn't make it this afternoon and I'd call you later."

"That's not much of a message, Catherine. So what happened? Did you get a better offer?"

Watch your mouth, D'Amaro, he thought immediately. He was pushing his luck here; the look she shot him told him that. Catherine Holben didn't yell and scream and throw things, but right now she wanted to. She wanted to *bad.*

"What's wrong?" he asked.

She shook her head, her lips tightly pressed together. He thought for a moment she was going to cry.

"What is it?" he persisted. "You got some trouble with Jonathan?" It was the only thing he could think of that might cause her to look the way she looked now.

"It's not Jonathan," she said, her voice husky. "Joe, I think you'd better go."

He came closer. There was a big difference in what she said and what he saw in her eyes. "I think I'd better not."

"I want you to go," she said again.

"No, you want to bawl your head off and you don't want me to see you do it. Look at you. You look like hell."

"Thanks a lot."

"Catherine . . ."

She looked up at him, her dark eyes huge and filled with pain.

He didn't know he was going to do it, so he gave her no chance to object. He suddenly put his arms around her and hugged her tightly. He could feel her resistance, but he didn't let go.

"Joe . . ."

"Yeah, yeah, I know," he said, his voice soft against her ear. "You're a tough guy, right? You don't need anything from anybody. Well, maybe *I* need this, Catherine. I was worried, okay? Maybe it makes *me* feel better."

She made a small sound and pressed her face against the front of his shirt. He wasn't angry anymore, and he knew perfectly well what he'd been doing all afternoon. He'd been looking. He'd kept coming here hoping to find a reason not to get involved with this woman. He'd been hoping to find some major flaw in her character, something to prove beyond a doubt that she was wrong for him, that she was a liar, that she was flighty and inconsiderate like Margaret, and he should run like hell.

But all the time he knew better, and now he wanted to hold her. It amazed him that he was willing to stand there and do it when he didn't even know what was the matter with her. He stroked her back, and she leaned into him, her arms sliding around his waist. He could feel the warm softness of her breasts against his chest. He thought that she was crying, but not because he could hear her. It was just that she was so damn miserable, she had to be.

"Catherine."

He didn't mean that she should stop crying; he didn't mean anything. He only meant to say her name because he thought it might help. He only meant to nuzzle the softness of her neck because she was soft and warm and clinging and because she felt and smelled so good to him.

So good.

"Catherine . . ." he said again, his arms tightening around her in a way that left no doubt in either of their minds as to what he was feeling. Her body stiffened, and she leaned back to look at him. When she did, her mouth grazed his. He was totally unprepared for the intensity of his desire, for the rush of feeling so white-hot that it made him catch his breath. He let his mouth lightly touch hers again, then again when she didn't resist. She was so sweet, and she wasn't doing anything to stop him.

Don't do this.

The thought came from far away, but he wasn't going to let himself get out of hand. His eyes searched hers. She wasn't crying, after all, but God, what sad, sad eyes. He wanted to tell her, he wanted to *say* that he wasn't Jonathan and that he didn't want to *be* Jonathan. He was Joe D'Amaro, who had missed her all day and who right now wanted very much to make love with her.

He didn't want whatever she felt for her ex-husband to have anything to do with it.

But he said nothing. He saw the sadness in her eyes and her need for someone—anyone?—and he didn't care. He just wanted to be close to her. Was he taking advantage of her? He didn't know.

She didn't look away. A single tear slid down her cheek; she was so beautiful.

God, don't cry, he thought. Slowly, tentatively, he lowered his mouth again toward hers.

Let me, Catherine. Let me . . .

Let me taste you. . . .

The kiss was not gentle, regardless of his good intentions. It was openmouthed and hungry, and she gave a soft moan. His hands slid low to press her into him. He wanted her to feel his hardness. He wanted her to know how much he wanted her.

Go easy, he thought. *Don't call her Katie.*

But he couldn't go easy. He put his hands into her hair to keep her mouth where he could reach it. He was so hungry for her, and incredibly, she returned touch for touch, kiss for kiss. Had it been like this with Lisa? He didn't remember. God, he didn't remember.

He needs a shave.

The thought came as the stubble of his beard rasped against the tender skin of her face. It hurt, burned. She didn't care. She tilted her head back, eyes closed, to experience whatever he wanted to do. Her fingers dug into his shoulders

184

because her knees had gone weak. She didn't want to think. She wanted only to feel. His fingers hooked into the front of her blouse, trembled as they strained to touch the tight buds of her nipples. Several of the buttons came undone. She felt the cool air of the room on her exposed breasts. She felt the warm moistness of his mouth, the delicate tasting of his tongue, and deep inside her, where she had thought of herself as irrevocably and perhaps conveniently dead, a welcome pinpoint of desire began to grow. And burn hot.

She gave a shuddering sigh.

"Catherine," he said, and she opened her eyes. He held her away from him when she would have kissed him again.

"I want to make love with you, but I'm not . . . prepared. I don't—" He broke off. Hell, he didn't carry a condom in his wallet the way he had when he was a randy kid, regardless of Michael's weekly safe-sex lectures. He hadn't *needed* a condom. He'd loved Lisa with all his heart. He'd had to work twelve hours a day to make ends meet, and he had three kids. How could he have a sex life? He'd only let Michael think he did so he'd tell Margaret. He'd been angry with Catherine this afternoon. He hadn't expected even to see her, much less progress to this point.

"I'm prepared," she said quietly.

"You're prepared," he repeated, because he wanted to make sure he'd heard right. He pursed his lips to say something, but the question didn't quite form. He was very aroused, and he wanted to stay that way. "Which way?" he said urgently, looking around at doorways. "In there?"

"Yes," she answered, her voice barely a whisper.

Catherine led the way, taking him by the hand. Her bed was still unmade, but she didn't care. Having him was all that mattered to her.

She began to undress, standing at the foot of the bed. She

felt no awkwardness, no false modesty. She wanted this man, and she forgot her inadequacies as a woman. She pulled at her clothing and at his until they were both naked, but there was no time to admire him, no time to touch him the way she had in the back of her mind for days. He held out his arms, and she went into them without hesitation. The room was dim, but she could just make out their reflections in the dresser mirror. She looked abandoned, wild. How could that woman be her? she wondered.

They tumbled into bed together.

He was impatient in his lovemaking, as he was in all things. He entered her immediately. It had been a long time since she'd made love with anyone—with Jonathan—and she sheathed him tightly. She reveled in the grunt of pleasure he gave. He was trembling, his breath warm against her face.

Joe.

He filled her mind as he filled her body. She loved his smell, his strength, his heavy weight on her. He wasn't Jonathan and she was glad. He wanted nothing from her. This was no test of her ability to reproduce. This was a man and woman eager for each other. They were both trying to escape, and for a little while they would elude their pain because she needed him. She needed *him.* And she didn't care if he knew it. She wrapped herself around him to return his thrusts, her need for him swelling to bursting. His mouth covered hers. She could taste the saltiness of her own tears, and, shameless in her passion, she could hear the sounds she was making, sounds that he drove from her in his exquisite taking of her body.

She wanted to make the pleasure last forever. How wonderful it was to feel something again, to feel wave after wave of bodily pleasure instead of relentless emotional pain. She could hear him say her name, a whisper lost in the low, guttural sounds of his release.

Catherine. Catherine!

She clung to him, her fingernails raking his back, because he took her with him, over the brink, and into that place where, for a small space in time, there was only oblivion.

He rolled away from her almost immediately, because he thought he was too heavy for her, and he lay sprawled beside her, his eyes closed. He could hear that it was still raining outside, and he could tell that she was still upset. He had never made love to a woman who wept before, yet he thought that her tears had little to do with him. He repressed the urge to smile. He felt so good, except for her crying. He felt so damn good! He'd made sweet, consuming love with her, this woman he'd thought was so buttoned-up and reserved. She'd wanted him and let him know it, and he felt wonderful.

Don't let me say anything stupid.

He reached down to take her hand, sliding his fingers between hers, caressing her palm with his thumb.

"Did I hurt you?" he asked. He hadn't gone off like that since he was a sixteen-year-old kid. Jesus, he'd wanted her. He still did. The way he felt at the moment he'd never get enough of her.

"No. No, you didn't hurt me."

He was surprised at how normal her voice sounded. They might have been sitting across the table from each other at the pub.

"Are you sorry we—"

"I'm not sorry."

She let go of his hand, and she would have gotten up if he'd let her.

"Don't run away, Catherine," he said, pulling her around so that she was lying against him, spoon fashion, his body curved around hers. "Please."

He pulled the sheet up over them both. She didn't resist, and he pressed his cheek against her shoulder. "Tell me what's wrong. Tell me what happened today. I want to know."

He waited. He could almost feel her trying to decide. She'd gone to bed with him, but did she want to *talk* to him? He thought that she wasn't going to, that she was going to be content with their lying silently in the dark, but then she gave a wavering sigh.

"It was Sasha," she said after a moment.

"Sasha . . . one of your pregnant kids? The little one with the mouth?"

"Yes."

Again he waited, but she didn't go on.

"What happened to her?" he asked.

"She went into labor. The baby died."

The words were spoken so quietly, belying the sadness he'd seen in her eyes. He tightened his arms around her because he needed to comfort her if he could, and she turned to him, moving so that she could lie with her head on his shoulder.

"In the class I . . . try to make them understand that it's not so easy to have a baby—especially when you're so young. I try to make them understand that they can do all the right things and still . . ."

Her voice trailed away. He reached up to touch the side of her face, to brush the tears away with his fingers.

"I was at the hospital all day," she went on in that same quiet voice. "They tried to stop her labor, but they couldn't. The baby was all right, but then it never . . . breathed on its own. Sasha didn't understand at first. Even when they took the baby out of the room, she didn't understand.

"Clarkson—the doctor who did the delivery—wanted me

to tell her. He thought it would be better somehow, coming from me. I don't know how I was supposed to do that—make it better. She really wanted her baby. She'd already decided it was going to be a little girl. She'd already named it. Treasure—because 'That's what this baby is to my grandmamma and me,' she said. A *treasure*. Treasure Higgins. . . .

"But I . . . told her, and she looked at me and said, 'Does Treasure look like she's sleeping, Ms. Holben?' That's all she asked. That's all she wanted to know. I wanted to say, 'Yes. Yes, just like that. Like she's sleeping.' Dead babies don't look like they're *asleep*, Joe!"

"Easy," he whispered, holding her tightly.

"And then she put her arms around me, and she whispered in my ear so nobody would hear. She said, 'Don't make it real yet, Ms. Holben. Don't make it real.' As if there were some bureaucratic *ritual* you have to go through when you find out your baby's died—something you're supposed to say and do to satisfy the hospital or the people in charge. But she wasn't ready for it, and she wanted me to know she wasn't—so I wouldn't keep after her—oh—"

"It's okay," he whispered, because he didn't know what else to say. She was trying so hard not to cry, and he wondered if it was because of him that she didn't want to let go, or if it was something left over from her marriage to Jonathan. Maybe Jonathan didn't put up with that kind of emotionalism. Maybe he had a rule, no crying, no matter how sad she felt.

He rubbed her back in long, gentle strokes.

"It's okay," he whispered again. "It's just you and me. You can feel as bad as you want to."

"Joe?"

"What?"

"I do feel bad. I feel so *bad*."

"I know."

"It's got nothing to do with you."

"I know that too."

"You don't have to stay—"

"Catherine, shut up, will you?"

"Yes, I think I will," she said, and she cried then, out loud, the way he thought she'd wanted to do ever since he'd come into the apartment. He held her, soothed her, let her cry all over him if that's what she needed. After what seemed a long time she grew quiet.

She had one of those clocks that projected the time on the ceiling, and he watched the minutes change. Once. Twice. Three times. Her body was warm against his, and her hand rested lightly on his chest.

"You okay?" he asked, covering her hand with his.

It took her a moment to answer.

"Yes," she said.

He kissed her forehead and gave her the edge of the sheet to wipe her eyes.

"You . . . know I have to go." It wasn't quite a question, and he didn't say that he had to get home because of his kids. It was the truth, but it sounded like a half-assed excuse somehow. And, anyway, she knew about his responsibilities.

"Yes," she said.

"There's something I need to tell you."

"Joe, I don't want anything from you. I understand—"

"Don't tell me you understand until I say it, okay? Okay?" he repeated when she didn't answer him.

She sniffed and wiped her eyes again. "Okay."

"I . . . took advantage of you tonight. I knew I was doing it, and I did it, anyway. I thought you needed somebody, and I wanted it to be me. I wanted to make love with you, Catherine, and I don't want you to think, because it happened so fast, that it didn't mean anything to me. I don't want you to think I didn't know you were upset or that I didn't care."

She tried to interrupt. "Joe—"

"Catherine, I want to say this. I'm afraid after I leave—in the cold light of day or whatever—you're going to think this was some kind of hit-and-run deal here, that I just wanted to get laid and I knew you were upset enough to give in to it. I didn't want you because you were convenient or willing or anything like that. I wanted you because I couldn't help it. I don't know what we've got here—maybe nothing. But whatever it is, I don't want it ruined because you don't know what's going on with me. That's all I've got to say, except—"

He abruptly sat up on the side of the bed and began looking for his clothes.

"Except what?"

"I . . . think I've said enough."

She watched him for a moment, suddenly feeling ill at ease. She had nothing with this man but a moment of ill-timed passion, and there was nothing to sustain their relationship now that the passion was spent. She wanted to get dressed, but there was no graceful way to do it, not when one's clothes had been so hastily discarded.

Her robe was lying over the foot of the bed. She put it on and left him alone, her mind on what he'd just said. He'd wanted her—and not just because she was willing and convenient. She supposed that he meant it; he wouldn't have had to say it otherwise, but as always, she was more concerned with what he *didn't* say, and she had no idea how she should respond to it. She had expected nothing, and yet, if she chose to believe him—intense, sad, hot-tempered Joe D'Amaro—on some level he seemed to care about her, and, for whatever reason, he wanted her to know it.

What reason? she kept asking herself as she paced around

the kitchen. Because he wanted a woman who had her own life and who wouldn't make demands on him? Because two thirds of his children liked her and he didn't have to worry about getting her pregnant?

She was standing at the kitchen sink filling the kettle with water when he came out. She didn't really want coffee. The sudden mental image of Jonathan's last visit came to mind. Apparently neither she nor Jonathan could face an awkward situation without some kind of prop in their hands.

"What else were you going to say?" she asked immediately. They might as well have it all out in the open.

He looked into her eyes so long that she blushed. It was a lover's look, intimate, knowing.

She was wrapped up in her robe as if she thought that covering herself would somehow take his mind off the fact that they had just made love. He thought she looked adorable, and he knew that the longer he stayed, the more difficult it would be to leave her.

He sat down in the closest chair. "I was going to say that I wouldn't mind if you said . . . something too." He gave a small, offhanded shrug.

She set the kettle on the burner, then turned to look at him. "Something . . ." she repeated, because she didn't understand.

"Personal."

"Personal?"

"Catherine, don't keep saying what I say. Say something original."

She smiled. That was something else about him. He made her smile. "How about . . . 'thank you'?"

"For what?"

"For making me feel better."

He gave a slight smile of his own. "I made you feel better?"

192

"I thought we were going to be original."

"I'm fishing."

"I know, and yes, you made me feel better."

"I'm . . . glad."

"There's one other thing."

"What?"

"It's personal."

"I can take it."

She looked into his eyes so he'd know she meant it. "I like you," she said simply.

"Why?" he asked immediately because he was Joseph D'Amaro, and Joseph D'Amaro would always want reasons.

"God only knows," she answered truthfully, and he laughed out loud, as if she had summarized their situation perfectly and he couldn't agree more.

"I like you, too, Catherine," he said, still smiling. "You're . . . okay."

Okay? She wanted to ask him in what context she was "okay." As a conversationalist in the middle of her kitchen or the Mayfair's basement? As a dinner companion at a family barbecue or a pub? As a lover in bed?

He stood up and reached for her without hesitation. She went into his arms willingly, the awkwardness she'd felt earlier somehow completely gone. She didn't want him to leave, and it was all she could do not to say so.

"I'll call you tomorrow," he said. "Maybe we can go someplace—if you don't mind having Fritz along. She's not going to let me get away with seeing you by myself again."

"I don't mind."

"Catherine?"

"What?"

The *what* was a kiss, one filled with intent and purpose, from a man who made her recognize that she wasn't going to be logical or sensible or detached about anything that had to do with him.

It was she who broke away. She hugged him tightly, her face pressed against his shirt. She didn't want him to leave!

"Go home, Joe," she whispered. "While you still can."

11

It took him ten minutes to get home. The lights were on all over the house when he arrived. Michael's car was parked in the driveway, and he had to leave the truck on the street out front. It was still raining, and he ran the distance from the truck to the back door.

Michael stood in the kitchen, opening the storm door for him before he could get to it. He could see Margaret just behind him, her arms folded across her breasts, her expression put-upon and annoyed.

"What's going on?" Joe said, looking at Michael.

"Where the hell have you been?" Michael said.

"None of your goddamn business! What's going on?" He wasn't a teenage kid coming in late from the prom. He didn't have to answer to anyone, least of all to his brother.

"Do you know what time it is?" Michael said.

Joe looked at his watch. "Ten-thirty. Why?"

"Your kids are scared to death, that's *why*."

He felt a cold fist in the pit of his stomach. "What's happened?"

"Nothing's happened, no thanks to you—"

"Then what's going on?"

"You left your kids here and they didn't know where you were—that's what's going on, Joey!"

"Look, Michael. I didn't just disappear. I told Della I had some things to take care of. I have been gone all of two hours. I'm out working later than this any night of the week you want to name. She knows what to do in an emergency. They all do!"

195

"She was scared, Joe!"

"Of what?"

"Do you hear him?" Michael said to Margaret. "Of what? She didn't know where you were!"

Della had come to stand in the kitchen doorway, her face tearstained and her mouth trembling. She wouldn't meet his eyes.

"Della," he said, but she still wouldn't look at him. "Della, what's wrong with you? Where's Charlie and Fritz?"

She crossed the room to Margaret, all but flinging herself into Margaret's arms.

"I don't think she wants to talk to you," Margaret said.

"Well, that's tough. I want to talk to her. I want to know what the hell is going on here!"

Della began to cry, flashing him a guilty look before she hid her face in Margaret's shoulder again. There was more noise than emotion in Della's weeping, and it suddenly occurred to him that she wasn't upset because she hadn't known where he was. She was upset because she did know. Charlie must have told her about Catherine's message.

He walked to the kitchen door. "Charlie!" he yelled. "Get down here!" He could hear running feet across the upstairs, clear evidence that Charlie had remembered he'd forgotten to tell him about Catherine's call, and he wasn't about to push his luck now. He came down the stairs three at a time, arriving at the kitchen door in a skid. He was wearing a pair of too big, red-polka-dot pajamas he'd dug up from somewhere.

"You look like Clarabell," Joe said.

"Nah. Clarabell wore stripes. You should know that, Pop." He gave a big grin that was all bravado, his eyes shifting to the others in the room.

"You want to tell me what the crisis is?" Joe said. "I can't get anything out of anybody else."

196

"Well . . ." He glanced at Della and Margaret. "Maybe it's . . . the weather?"

Joe stared at him and tried to control his temper. Charlie was proud of his beautiful older sister—even if she wouldn't give him the time of day. He wasn't about to get on her bad side, too, if he could help it.

"The weather," Joe repeated. "It's raining outside. It's not a damn hurricane! It's nothing any worse than you were used to in Dorchester!"

"Well, yeah, Pop, you're right about that—"

He jabbed the air in Charlie's direction. "Don't jerk me around, son. I don't like it. Was there a problem here tonight or wasn't there? Before you answer that, remember how many days it is until you get that driver's license."

"Ah, Pop, that's not fair—"

"Fair is for people who don't have children. Now answer me!"

He could feel Charlie making up his mind. Sibling loyalty was one thing; driving a car was something else again.

"Well, Pop . . . Della didn't know where you were. *I* thought we ought to just call Catherine—I mean, you were supposed to go out with her and everything. Did I tell you she called?"

"No," Joe said pointedly.

"No," Charlie repeated, confirming his fear that he hadn't told him. "Sorry, Pop. I must have forgot or something."

"Why didn't you?"

"Why didn't I what, Pop?" Charlie asked abruptly. Joe could feel him stalling for the time to anticipate the question and then to think up an acceptable, if not particularly truthful, answer. He had to admire the boy.

He was between a rock and a hard place here, and he was working every minute.

"Why didn't you call Catherine if you were looking for me?"

"Oh, is that where you were?" Charlie said, his voice rising to a higher pitch.

"Where else would I be, since you didn't give me the message! Damm it, Charlie!"

"Well, I thought we did call her, Pop. I mean, I thought Della did. I guess she thought calling Uncle Michael was a better idea or something . . ." he finished lamely.

"So Della wanted to know where I was." It wasn't quite a question. It was a technique Joe had learned from his own father to keep a recalcitrant child off-balance. The effect it had on Charlie was much the same as it had been to him when he was Charlie's age. Charlie looked at him now with probably the same expression Joe's own father had seen. Was this a question because his old man didn't know? Or was it a statement of fact because he did?

Charlie glanced in Della's direction. "I guess."

"You guess."

"Yeah."

"And *you* wanted to know where I was."

"Nah. I figured you'd turn up sooner or later. You always do, Pop."

Joe gave him a warning look. He was *not* in the mood for cute.

"You weren't exactly late or anything—" Charlie said before the significance of his father's look registered.

"Where was Fritz during all this?" Joe asked. "I suppose you had her thinking I'd disappeared too?"

"Oh, heck, no, Pop. She's asleep."

Joe stared at him, his look encompassing Della as well. "It's a good thing for the two of you she is. Michael," he said, turning to his brother, "I think what we have here is a foul-up in communications all the way around." He didn't owe his brother an explanation, and he wasn't going to give him one. "So you want to get out of here so I can talk to my kids?"

"Sure, Joey. Let's go, Margaret."

"I don't want to talk!" Della said, pushing herself out of Margaret's arms. "I'm going upstairs!" She ran out of the room, and Margaret started after her.

"Margaret!" Joe said sharply. "I'll handle this, you understand?"

"Joey, the kid's upset," Michael said, trying to intervene on Margaret's behalf.

"She's not the only one. I said I'll handle it. If I want Margaret's help, I'll ask for it."

"I don't think you understand the situation here, Joe," Margaret said. "Della doesn't like that Holben woman."

"Why do you suppose that is, Margaret? Della doesn't even know her."

"Why? Haven't you learned yet that you can't just bring strange women into your home? You should have heard what she said to Della the other day at the barbecue."

"What was that?"

"Oh, I'm sure she's given you *her* version."

"What did she say!"

"She told Della to mind her own business!"

For a moment he was torn between his loyalty to his daughter and his need to know what had really happened. He knew what Della was like—headstrong, impertinent—and he knew what Catherine Holben was like. It wasn't likely that Catherine would respond like that without provocation—a *lot* of provocation.

"What did Della say?"

"Nothing! She was stunned. When you're sixteen years old, you don't expect that kind of rudeness in your own house."

"I mean *before* Catherine told her that. You were there, I take it. Della must have said something."

"I really don't remember, but nothing to cause *that* kind of remark. She was only asking the things *you* should have told her before you brought that woman here. It was upsetting for Della, having her just appear out of nowhere—"

"She was here for Fritz!"

"Oh, please, Joe. She's not very hard to figure out. She's using Fritz to try to get to you."

"Why do you think that is, Margaret? You think she's after my money or my carefree life-style? Maybe she's got this thing for pickup trucks."

"I think, Joe, if you care about your daughter at all, you won't see Catherine Holben again."

"Oh, you do? Well, I'm glad to know how Della feels, Margaret—and *you,* of course. But you see, I like Catherine Holben. And she's not anybody's wife, you know what I mean?"

"Fine, Joe," she said sweetly. "But don't say I didn't warn you. Men really aren't very good judges of character—especially when they're thinking with the wrong head. You know what *I* mean? Come on, Michael."

But Michael didn't move. "What kind of remark was that, Joey? What did you mean, she's nobody's wife?"

"Nothing, Michael—"

"I want to know what you meant!"

"Nothing!"

They stared at each other. He knows, Joe suddenly thought. He knows how Margaret is.

He had said too much, too much even for Michael to ignore, but he didn't look away. He had nothing to feel guilty about. He hadn't given in to Margaret. He'd only wanted to.

"I didn't mean anything," Joe repeated, because he was

determined not to let his annoyance at Margaret hurt his brother. "I'm mad, okay? When I'm mad, I got a big mouth."

After a moment Michael shrugged. "Yeah," he said. "That you got."

Charlie kept clearing his throat in the background.

"Charlie, what?" Joe said in exasperation.

"I like her," he offered.

"What?"

"Catherine. *I* like her. I just thought you might want to know that. Aunt Margaret says Della doesn't like her. Well, I do—just in case anybody else's opinion matters around here—"

"Charlie, go to bed," Joe said.

"You mean it?" he asked, clearly relieved.

"Yes, I mean it! Go on. And tell Della I'll be up to talk to her in a minute so she can just get herself together."

"That's it? I'm off the hook?"

"Don't press your luck," Joe advised him.

"Oh, no, Pop. Luck pressing is not for me. Can I say one more thing?"

"What!"

"You got good taste—"

"Charlie—"

"Catherine," he said, elaborating. *"Nice*-looking woman, Pop. *Nice!"* He gave Joe the okay sign with both hands.

"Get out of here," Joe said.

"Right, Pop. Catherine got any younger sisters?"

"I don't know."

"How about older ones?"

"Beat it!"

"You got it, Pop."

Charlie trotted away, complete with sound effects—explosions and whining missiles all the way up the stairs. Joe turned his attention to his brother. "Michael, I appreciate your coming over—"

"I'm going to the car," Margaret interrupted, but for once Michael wasn't listening.

"Joey, when are you going to get your shit together?" he said. "I'm too old for this kind of stuff."

"Michael, I didn't do anything!"

"Yeah, yeah. You're off with some woman—"

"*Some* woman? A couple of days ago you were telling me to be off with her!"

"Yeah, well, I didn't tell you to forget you got kids."

"Michael, weren't you listening here? Charlie knew I was probably at Catherine's. I didn't get her message. I went by her place to see if she was at home. I didn't expect her to be, but she was. I wasn't gone that long—oh, what am I explaining this to you for!"

"Joey, you got to remember you got responsibilities—"

"Jesus Christ, Michael! If I didn't remember that, I wouldn't have come home!"

Michael suddenly broke into a broad grin. "Yeah?" he asked, punching him on the arm.

"Michael, quit! I'm not in the mood for this."

"Yeah?" he asked, punching him again.

"Now quit! I'm telling you . . ."

But he didn't quit. He kept after him until they were both laughing and behaving like schoolboys in a territorial scuffle.

"Okay, okay," Michael said when he'd had enough. He grabbed Joc around the neck and kissed him on the cheek, hard.

Joe strained to get away from him. "How many times I got to tell you? Don't do that!"

"You don't like it?"

"No, I don't like it!"

"Too bad. You're my baby brother and I love you. So sue me. And you pay attention to what I said. You get it together or I'm going to whip your butt."

Joe grinned. "Yeah, old man?"

"Yeah! Margaret, let's go."

But she was already halfway to the car.

Michael gave a sheepish grin. "Looks like I'll be sleeping cold tonight. See you, Joey."

Joe switched off the kitchen light and stood at the door, watching as Michael backed the big car Margaret had to have out of the drive. Joe had his sympathy. There was nothing pleasant about sleeping cold. He closed his eyes and gave a quiet sigh.

Catherine.

He missed her. Already. The feelings he had for her were sexual—strongly sexual—but he wanted to *be* with her too. He wanted to talk to her—about Della, about Margaret. No, he couldn't talk to her about that. Yes, he could. In his mind's eye he could see the quietly intent way she'd listen to him, and then she'd tell him what she thought—whether he liked it or not. He closed his eyes again, his mind now filled with other things, with the way she'd felt and smelled and tasted. God, it had been good with her.

"I wanted to stay with you tonight," he whispered, surprising himself that he'd spoken out loud. He had to get himself together. He had to deal with whatever this was with Della, and he certainly wasn't looking forward to that. He was just going to have to make her understand. He liked— maybe more than liked—Catherine Holben.

Maybe more than liked. There it was. The thing he'd been so afraid of all afternoon. Maybe he was on the verge of something here, something major that was going to upset his life and hers, and his children's.

What if it isn't worth it?

He still loved Lisa, and it was so much safer "sleeping cold."

And so lonely.

He switched on the fluorescent light over the sink. He stared at the telephone on the kitchen wall, then went to it and dialed Catherine's number. He'd called so many times today, he knew it by heart now.

She answered almost immediately.

"It's Joe," he said quietly, praying like a moonstruck teenager that she wouldn't say "Joe who?"

"What's the matter?" she asked.

"Nothing . . . why?"

"I just thought you sounded . . . I don't know. Like something was the matter."

"No. I was just thinking about you. I . . . wanted to see if you were okay."

"I'm okay."

He paused. "Good. Then I just wanted to tell you good night." He could feel her smile.

"Good night, Joe."

Good night, baby . . .

"Joe?"

He jumped. "Jesus, Fritz! Am I going to have to put a bell on you? What are you doing up? I thought you were asleep."

"It's not easy sleeping around here," she said, watching him listen to the receiver for a moment before he hung up the phone. Della had been throwing things, but he didn't like tattling, and she didn't tell him that.

"So what do you want? You want to get on my case too?"

"Nope. I want a glass of milk."

He smiled. "Milk, huh?"

"I wanted to see if you were mad or anything," she added,

because she wanted to tell him the truth about that at least. She'd been worrying ever since she'd heard about Catherine's message. She would have to tell her the next time she saw her not to give any messages to Charlie. "I wanted to see if you were mad at Catherine."

He was opening the refrigerator to get the milk out for her, and he stopped in the middle of it. "Why would you think that?"

"Charlie said she stood you up."

"She didn't stand me up. She left me a message. You aren't stood up if somebody leaves you a message."

"Even if you don't get it, like when Charlie didn't give it to you?"

"Even if you don't get it."

"Oh. Is Charlie in trouble?"

"About like usual," he said, pouring her some milk in her favorite *Star Wars* glass, which she'd gotten years ago at Burger King.

"Oh," she said, taking the glass from him. She set it down carefully and pulled out a chair at the kitchen table. "You know Charlie," she said as she sat down. She watched him pour a glass for himself. "I was surprised," she said when he sat down to join her.

"About what?"

"You let Catherine go to the dinner with you. You don't let *anybody* go to that."

"I don't let kids go to that. And I didn't *let* Catherine, I just asked her. She couldn't make it."

"Didn't she want to go?" Fritz asked, trying to find out why his plans had fallen through.

"Yes, I think she did, but something came up."

"What?" Fritz asked. She watched him closely. He'd either tell her or he'd say it was none of her business. She was hoping for the former, because she didn't understand the way "things came up" for grown-ups at all. A kid couldn't get by with that kind of reason in a million years. *Where's your home-work, Mary Frances? Oh, something came up.*

He was thinking about it. She could tell he was thinking about it.

"I'd like to know, so I don't worry," she said. That was the truth, but telling Joe that was like something Della would have done, trying to make him feel bad so he'd do what she wanted. She sighed. She really didn't like doing things that way, even if she did want to know about Catherine really badly. "You don't have to tell me," she decided.

"Have you been worrying?" he asked. He got up from the table and found the box of vanilla wafers, letting her reach in for a handful first.

"Yeah."

"Why?"

"I don't want you to be mad at her."

"Fritz, I'm not mad at her."

"You were mad when you came in."

"That was Della's doing."

"Della?" she asked, and she turned down the corners of her mouth for a moment to consider that. "What did Della do?"

"I have to talk about that with her."

"Oh," Fritz said. She didn't mind that he wouldn't tell her. She really liked the way Joe did those things. When you were in trouble, he didn't spread it around.

"Didn't Catherine want to go to the dinner?" she asked again.

"She was at the hospital with one of her students."

"Did one of them have a baby?"

He frowned. "What do you know about that?"

"Catherine told me she only had students that were having babies."

"She did? When?"

"When we were walking on the beach. I asked her what she did to get money. She said she helped students that were going to have a baby so they wouldn't have to leave school."

He smiled. "One of these days you're going to ask one question too many."

"I do that now," she said. "People just tell me to butt out. Can I go see the gnomes tomorrow?"

"I'm not sure about tomorrow."

"Why? Catherine said I just have to call first."

"She's . . . kind of sad, Fritz. It may not be a good time."

"Why?"

"Because she is."

It wasn't the usual kind of answer she got from him. She looked up at him for a moment, then decided to press her luck. "Why?" she said again.

"The baby died, Fritz," he said quietly, handing her another vanilla wafer.

She took the wafer. The baby died. Catherine probably liked babies. No wonder she'd be sad and couldn't go to the dinner with Joe. Fritz looked up at him again. He was sorry he'd told her, but she wasn't. When she *knew* things, even if they were bad, it was better than guessing.

"Sometimes those things happen," she said, hoping to make him feel better.

"Yes," he said.

"It's not anybody's fault or anything." She knew better than to say it was God's will. Joe didn't believe God wanted anything dead, and that kind of thing really made him mad. "Like when Lisa died," she added, because she thought it would be all right to say that.

"Yes," he said again.

She sat for a time in silence, thinking about Catherine and the little baby.

"Is there anything you want to ask me, Fritz?" Joe said.

"I just hope the baby had a name. Sister Mary John says babies who die are angels, but—" She broke off and sat drumming her fingers on the table.

"But what?"

"In the cemetery. On the little tombstones. Sometimes it just says 'baby son' or 'baby daughter.' That's not much of a name for an angel."

She waited for him to comment. "Is it?" she asked when he didn't.

"This baby had a name," he said. "Her name was Treasure."

She smiled. She liked the name a lot. She'd heard somebody say one time at a PTA meeting that life was strange. Maybe this was what they meant. Here was a mother without her baby, Treasure. And here *she* was, without a mother. Sometimes things just didn't match, no matter how hard you tried, and it made you miserable, wanting to sit in the dark, the way Joe used to do. She looked at him. He wasn't miserable now, but he *was* worrying.

"Catherine won't be sad for long," she said.

"We can't bother her tomorrow, Fritz," he said, and she realized that he still thought she wanted to visit, and that wasn't what she meant at all.

"Catherine won't be sad long," she said again. "She can't be."

"Fritz . . ."

She looked into her father's eyes, a little surprised that he didn't understand. "Because," she said earnestly, "Catherine has the gnomes."

12

They don't know, Catherine thought, looking at the group of pregnant girls who waited by the classroom door. They were as lively as ever, dancing to Beatrice's radio and horsing around.

"Good morning," she said as she walked up. "Kill the radio, Beatrice."

"I knew you were going to say that."

"All of you come inside. I want talk to you, and I don't want to do it out here."

"What's the matter?" Beatrice said. "The big shots downtown cut the funding?"

"No, Beatrice."

"Sasha's not here yet, Ms. Holben," Cherry said.

"I know. Everybody get your things situated and sit down."

"It ain't time for class, Ms. Holben. Don't we have to wait for Mrs. Bauer?"

"No," Catherine said. Pat was in the office hiding, because she had made it clear she didn't want to be present for this discussion.

Catherine waited for the girls to get settled, and when it was finally quiet, she took a deep breath and looked up at them.

"I have some sad news about Sasha. . . ."

Maria was sticking a pencil in and out of her hair, and she stopped immediately.

Catherine knew of no easy way to tell them. She had to just say it, and say it quickly.

"Sasha had her baby yesterday afternoon. The baby died."

There was a stunned silence until Abby began to cry.

"Ms. Holben," Maria said. "Did you see Sasha?"

"Yes, Maria. I saw her."

"Did you see her baby?"

"Yes. I was there when the baby was born."

"What was wrong with it?"

"I don't know. Nothing that anyone could see."

"It just died for no reason?"

"I'm sure there is a reason—I just don't know what it is."

"It don't make no sense to me," Cherry said. "Sasha *wanted* that baby."

It didn't make sense to Catherine, either, but she made no comment. She let them talk, fielding as best she could the questions for which there were no easy answers.

"Ms. Holben," Abby said, "you don't think it was that candy Sasha ate, do you?"

"No, I don't think it was the candy. Sasha ate the good things she was supposed to eat. Her grandmother saw to that."

"Yeah, and what good was it?" Maria said. "I knew it was all a bunch of crap."

"Sasha is very young, Maria. It's not easy having a baby when you're that young."

"It's not easy having a baby, period," she said sullenly. "If you want it, then that's it. You let yourself want it—boom! It dies. Or Welfare takes it."

"That's not true, Maria," Cherry said. "You always saying crazy things."

"Yeah, well, you ask Sasha if it ain't true. You ask Sasha!"

"Sasha is still in the hospital," Catherine said. "Mrs. Bauer and I are going by to see her after school. Any of you who want to come along are welcome to do so, with your parents' permission."

"Ms. Holben," Beatrice said. "Is Sasha having a funeral for Treasure?"

How strange, Catherine thought. She hadn't told them the baby was a girl, and yet they all seemed to take it for granted that it was.

"Yes. Her grandmother will let us know when. I assume it will be after they let Sasha come home."

"Ms. Holben?" Cherry said. "We got to have class today? I don't feel like having class today."

"Yes, we do. I want you to take the rest of the period to talk about Sasha and ask questions if you have them—and to call your parents about going to see her this afternoon. And then we're going to work hard the rest of the day. It helps to keep busy."

"Might help *you*," Maria said under her breath.

"Right," Catherine said to her. "I'm not going to be busy by myself."

Catherine was as good as her word, keeping them working until lunchtime. They were subdued, but the morning wasn't wasted, except that once again Catherine had a difficult time not thinking about Joe D'Amaro. She was going to have to talk to him as soon as possible. He'd been right—things were different in the cold light of day.

A fine mist of rain still fell, and they ate their lunches in the classroom with Beatrice's radio for solace.

"Uh-oh, Ms. Holben," Cherry said shortly after they'd started eating.

Catherine looked up in alarm, expecting that someone's water had broken, or, at the very least, a grimace of pain. Sasha's early labor had left her more than uneasy about the rest of them. "What?"

"He's back," she sang, cutting her eyes toward the door.

Catherine pursed her lips to respond to Cherry's heavy-handed subtlety, but Joe was pacing in the hallway. She was surprised that he'd come here—almost as surprised as she'd been when he'd called the night before. She got up from her desk, fully aware, too, of how glad she was to see him. Her gladness only served to underline her need to make sure he understood how things were going to have to be with them.

I like him, she reaffirmed as she walked toward him. She liked him; she liked the way he looked, scraggly though it might be. He wasn't like Jonathan. She didn't have to concern herself about being attracted to the same kind of man.

"Working hard, I see," she said by way of greeting.

He smiled. "You know what's a real kick in the you-know-where? Being all ready to start building—and it won't quit raining. So how are you doing?"

"I'm doing fine," she answered, not knowing why he was asking. Because of Sasha? Because they'd made love? She decided to ask. "Why?"

His eyes searched her face, lingering on her mouth, dropping to her breasts. It was very disconcerting. She knew exactly what he was thinking about—because so was she.

"I . . . thought maybe you had regrets," he said.

"No. No regrets. Not about last night. Joe . . . ?"

His eyes met hers again. "What, Catherine?"

"I . . . we have to talk."

"I thought so," he said, his voice resigned. "So talk."

"I can't here."

"You have to if it's important. I'm going to be at the building site, rain or not."

She looked down at the floor for a moment, then back up at him. "About last night . . ."

"You don't have any regrets," he reminded her. "Or weren't you telling me the truth?"

"I meant what I said, Joe. I don't have regrets. It's just . . ."

212

She glanced over her shoulder because she sensed some of the girls might be moving closer.

"Let's walk," he said, taking her by the arm. They walked slowly toward the front office. "Go on."

"I want you to understand how I'm feeling."

"Well, that sounds ominous."

"Joe . . ."

"Go on, Catherine. If you're going to tell me to take a hike, then do it."

"I don't want you to take a hike."

He looked so relieved that she instinctively put her hand up to touch his cheek, stopping in mid-reach because she remembered where she was.

"Then what do you want?" he asked.

"I want you to understand that I'm just not ready for anything so . . ."

"So what?" he prompted. "Don't leave me hanging here."

She gave a short exhalation of breath. "Intimate," she decided.

"Intimate. You mean, you hated going to bed with me and you don't want to do it again."

"No," she said with some alarm. That wasn't what she meant at all—exactly.

"You mean you *liked* going to bed with me," he amended.

"Yes," she said, looking in his eyes.

He looked at her thoughtfully. "And you don't want to do it again."

"Yes," she said again. She expected him to be angry.

He stopped walking and leaned against the wall. "Do you know how bad I want to touch you right this minute?"

"No," she said, but she was lying. She did know. "Joe, I'm not ready for a serious relationship—"

"Serious meaning sexual."

213

"Yes! I don't know how to be . . ." She trailed off again because one of the secretaries had come into the hall to stick something up on the bulletin board. Catherine watched her until she went back into the office.

"Go on," Joe said. "You don't know how to be what?"

"Casual."

"Casual? What the hell does that mean, *casual?*"

"It means I'm not ready for anything serious," she said again. "And you certainly aren't, either. I don't know how to do these no-strings-attached relationships where you hop into bed with somebody just because you need sexual release."

"Is that what we did?"

"Didn't we?"

"No, we didn't. *I* didn't."

She didn't, either, but she couldn't bring herself to tell him. They stood there in the hallway as the silence between them grew more awkward.

"Catherine—" he began, but she interrupted.

"Probably nothing would have happened if I hadn't been so upset about Sasha. I don't want to get hurt, Joe. I don't even know if I'm over Jonathan, and you're not over Lisa—"

"That's not the same thing."

"Yes, it is. I'm just starting to put my life together. It's just too complicated for us, without being . . ."

"Intimate," he finished for her.

"Yes."

"So how do we back up, Catherine? How do we pretend that we didn't make love and that it wasn't good between us?"

"Joe, I don't know. But I know I can't handle it. I can't be just a bed partner and nothing else—no matter how good it is. I don't even know if I *want* to be anything else. It's all too new, and I'll make you crazy worrying about you—you know how I am."

"You butt into things that are none of your business," he offered.

"Exactly. I don't want to be hurt," she said again.

"So you want me to take a hike?"

"No!"

"No? Catherine, you're right. You *are* making me crazy. What do you want?"

She didn't want to end their relationship, such as it was. She just wanted it modified. "Couldn't we just do what you said? See if we have anything? And if either of us decides we don't, then that's it, and no hard feelings."

He gave a slight smile. "And no s-e-x," he whispered.

She sighed. "No."

"How about kissing?"

"Joe, I'm being serious here!"

"I am too. I have to know what I'm agreeing to. This *is* where I agree or I don't, right? I mean, you're giving me a graceful way out if I want it?"

"Yes."

"So what about kissing?"

"Kissing is in," she said curtly.

"I can't kiss you and not—"

"Joe!"

He laughed. "Look, Catherine, you don't get off that easy. If you want some kind of platonic relationship, then I guess there's nothing I can do about it. It looks good on paper but . . ."

"But what?" she said when he didn't go on.

He gave her a long look, one she felt and one he knew she felt. "But I don't think it's going to work." His face suddenly grew grave. "So what do you want me to do, think it over and let you know?"

She pressed her lips together. How angry was he? For once she couldn't tell. Did he understand or didn't he?

"Yes," she said, her chin coming up a bit.

He gave a resigned sigh. "Then I'll call you later."

"I'm taking the class to see Sasha after school today," she said, trying to keep her voice matter-of-fact. If by some chance he called this evening, she wanted him to know ahead of time that she might not be there.

His response was a curt nod of acknowledgment and "I'll be seeing you around." He took a few steps down the hall, then turned back to her. "You know what gets me? I *knew* this was going to happen. I knew you'd panic. I even understand why—and it still pisses me off."

With that he walked away, leaving her in the middle of the hallway.

She stood for a moment, watching him until he went out the end doors. He let both of them bang shut, and he didn't look back.

"Well, kiddo," Pat said at her elbow, "you sure know how to rain on a man's parade."

But he called. He'd said he would, and he did. The conversation was neutral at best. He asked about Sasha and the rest of the girls. He talked about Fritz. Then he said good night.

Good night. Not good-bye. She had to keep reminding herself that the rest of the week when he didn't call again.

On Saturday she cleaned house, convinced that the graceful way out she'd given him, he'd taken. Shortly after noon she looked out the front windows. Joe was crossing the street below, carrying a big white bag from Burger King.

She waited nervously for him to climb the three flights of stairs, then impatiently, because once again Mrs. Donovan stopped him for one of her routine interrogations.

She could hear his footsteps on the stairs again. She looked at herself in the mirror, raked through her hair with her fingers, pinched her cheeks to give them some color, and despaired of the results. She looked like a little kid who'd just been greeted by an overzealous relative.

He knocked at the door and she waited. She didn't want to seem too eager. She took a deep breath to steady herself, then jerked open the door, anyway, because she thought he was leaving.

Oh, God, she thought when she looked at him. He was right. It wasn't going to work. It wasn't going to work at all.

"You had lunch?" he said cheerfully as he stepped inside the apartment, and then, when he saw the longing in her eyes, "Ah, Catherine, don't . . . *don't* let me see . . ."

But he reached for her, dragging her against him, letting the Burger King bag drop with a thud on the floor. His mouth came down hard on hers, hurting, hungry. She wrapped herself around him, her knee sliding between his thighs. He was overbalanced, and he fell against the door she'd barely had the time to close.

He pulled at her clothes, trying to get her shirttail out of her jeans so he could touch her bare skin, her breasts, and still he tried not to lose contact with her mouth. He'd missed her so, and she tasted so good. He was aware of the sound of heavy breathing—his—and soft moans—hers.

He half carried her across the living room and into the bedroom, lying down on the bed with her, both of them working feverishly to get their clothes off. Buttons. Zippers. Work-boot shoelaces. He hated every damn one of them.

"I told you," he said as his body finally covered hers. "I *told* you . . ."

Yes. He'd told her.

She reached up to touch his lips and he kissed her finger-tips, coming inside her in one deep thrust. She arched toward him, and he gave a deep grunt of pleasure. Her eyes were open, staring into his, fluttering closed as he began to move. He was trembling. He couldn't stop. Her hands, warm and light, skimmed over his body, and he reveled in her touch. He wanted to love her long and slow, but he couldn't. How could anything feel this good?

"Hold me. Hold me tight!" he whispered to her, because he was desperate to have her close to him. Close. Tight. She was so tight. And hot. He strained to take all she had to give, to give her everything of himself.

The telephone rang in the kitchen and he stiffened.

"No," she whispered against his ear, her voice urgent, pleading. "Don't stop! Oh, Joe!"

He buried himself in her, lost himself in her, and he never wanted to be found again.

The phone rang on, but she belonged to him. Nothing, *nothing,* could touch them.

They were both lying on their backs. He had his eyes closed. He turned his head to look at her. She was staring at the ceiling.

"Now what?" he asked simply.

She abruptly turned toward him, hiding her face in his neck. "Oh, Joe!" she said.

He put his arms around her, holding her fast. He knew exactly how she felt. Miserable. Bewildered. Good. He had deliberately stayed away from her, deliberately not called after that one time when he'd given his word that he would—just to see whether or not this thing he had for her was going to be worth all the trouble and heartache. Della was giving him hell; he was getting nowhere with her. She wouldn't talk to him about Catherine. He couldn't reason with her. She saw no similarity between his accepting the wild-haired, punk-looking boys she admired as possibly decent human beings and her accepting his judgment regarding Catherine Holben. He was trying to be fair—to Della and to himself. Given the incentive of Catherine's restrictions on their relationship, he had planned not to rush into anything, to be sensible, to give Della time to adjust to his having an interest in another woman besides Lisa, to give *himself* time to know what the hell was happening here. So much for his plans. He'd been thinking with the wrong head, all right. He hadn't even gotten past hello.

"I have to make a phone call," he said abruptly, disentangling himself from her arms and legs so he could get up.

"Now?"

"Yeah, now," he answered. He walked away into the kitchen.

Catherine lay back on the bed with her hand over her eyes. This is crazy! she thought. One minute she was vacuuming and cleaning the toilet, and the next minute she was lying naked in bed, completely sated, with an equally naked man roaming about.

She could hear him on the phone.

"Michael, I'm going to be late. This is the number where I'll be if my kids need me . . . I don't know *how* late—late! . . . No, just don't look for me. . . . None of your business what I'm doing. You can get along without me for a couple hours. Do I ask you what you do in the middle of the afternoon?" He laughed. "Trust me, Michael. It's worth it."

He gave Michael her telephone number and came back into the bedroom. She stared at him brazenly as he crossed to the bed. He had a beautiful body, and he didn't seem to mind her scrutiny. He lifted the sheet and slid in beside her.

"I've been thinking," he said as he gathered her to him.

"About what?"

He gave her a mischievous smile. "I've been thinking maybe this is something we ought to just get out of our systems."

They stayed in bed all afternoon. Making love. Talking. Eventually eating some reheated burgers and fries from Burger King.

"I meant to try," he said at one point. "I meant to do what you wanted. I meant to keep things platonic."

"So did I."

He turned so that they were lying face-to-face, their bodies close, touching. "You shouldn't have looked at me like that."

He was staring into her eyes. God, how he liked looking into her eyes, because when he did, he saw *himself* there.

"Like what?"

"Like now," his whispered, his mouth covering hers.

"So how old are you?"

She was lying on her back with her eyes closed. He was lying on his side, his head propped in his hand. His other hand lazily traced an imaginary line from her collarbone to the tip of her breast.

She opened her eyes. "Why?" she asked, moving her head so she could see him better.

"I want to know about you. I'm thirty-eight."

"I'm thirty-two."

"Thirty-two," he repeated. He repeated the line from shoulder to breast, causing her to take a small breath. "You like that?"

"No, I hate it," she murmured, closing her eyes as he did it again.

He chuckled. "Liar."

"The other day," he said when he'd been quiet long enough for her to think he'd fallen asleep.

"When?" She was sleepy herself, and she stretched and moved closer to him.

"At the school. When you told me you didn't want a sexual relationship . . ."

"Well, so much for that."

"No, listen to me. I want to tell you this. I wasn't mad at you. I was disappointed, you know? And I was jealous."

"Of what?"

"Of Jonathan."

"Why would you be jealous of Jonathan?"

"Because he was married to you. Because he did a really stupid thing leaving you. Because . . . one day he's going to re-alize it. I didn't want to think you were . . . leaving the door open." He brushed her hair back from her face, his touch gentle, loving. "You understand?"

"I . . . understand."

He gave her a brief, hard hug, then moved so that he could see her eyes again.

"Show me you understand, Catherine," he whispered. "Show me . . ."

"There's one other thing."

"What?" she asked, her head lying on his chest. She could hear the soft pounding of his heart as he gently stroked her hair.

"When we make love, when I'm inside you and it's so good"—he hooked his fingers beneath her chin so that she would look at him—"I'm not thinking about Lisa."

"Joe—"

"Shh," he whispered, putting his fingers to her lips to keep her from saying anything. "I just wanted you to know that."

"I'm not thinking about Jonathan, either," she said.

"Yeah?"

"Yeah."

No words of love. No words of commitment. Yet she felt both. Loved. Committed.

It's the way I am, she thought. She had no business in this kind of relationship. Already she was trying to take a pleasurable afternoon and turn it into something real. He didn't want anything long-term. He certainly didn't want anything permanent. Neither did she. She didn't want to care about him. She didn't want to care about anyone the way she had cared about Jonathan. Caring left you unsuspecting and vulnerable.

She wanted to ask him outright, *Joe, what do you want from me?*

But she didn't. Joe D'Amaro would tell her. He seemed not to feel any constraint about telling her anything.

She closed her eyes. He wasn't an easy lover. He was intense, demanding—not crude but specific. He talked to her. He talked to *her.* Before, during, after. What he felt, admired, needed, he wanted her to know. The pleasure he received, he gave back tenfold. Jonathan's lovemaking, by comparison, was almost pristine.

I am going to miss this, she thought, as if he'd already grown tired of her and gone.

"Could I bring Fritz by to see the gnomes tomorrow afternoon about two?" he asked, because he could feel that she was far away and he wanted her back with him.

"Fine," she said.

"You want me to call first?" He didn't want her to think he was presuming just because they'd spent this incredible afternoon together.

"Only if you can't come."

"Oh, we'll be here. She really wants to see the gnomes. Did I tell you she thinks they're going to keep you from being sad?"

"Why does she think I'm sad?"

"I told her about Sasha and Treasure. I don't think she wanted me to worry about you, so she said you wouldn't be sad long—because you had the gnomes."

Catherine smiled. "Sasha's grandmother is fixing me a root charm that will make the sun shine on my back door. Between the two I ought to be in good shape."

"You *are* in good shape," he said, growling into her neck and making her laugh.

She suddenly hugged him tightly, because he was going to have to leave and because she already missed him.

"What's the matter?" he said.

"Nothing."

"You want to break my ribs for *nothing?*"

She smiled and leaned back to look at him. He deserved as much of the truth as she could give. "I . . . just don't want you to go."

He smiled, the smile a little mischievous, a little sad. "Does that mean you still like me?"

"Still," she admitted.

"Well, that's a good thing . . . isn't it?"

"Is it?"

"I asked first," he said, and she laughed. He liked that about her, her laugh. Her smile. Her.

"Catherine?"

"Yes, Joe," she answered, and she was smiling still, teasing, looking into his eyes.

He didn't say it. Fritz wasn't the daughter he wanted to talk about. He wanted to talk about Della. He wanted to tell her that he was having a problem with Della and that he didn't know what to do about it. Della was his firstborn; he loved her and he didn't want her to be unhappy, but maybe he was more than halfway to loving Catherine too. If Catherine didn't feel the same, he didn't want to sacrifice Della for nothing.

You're not giving me the business, are you, Catherine? he wanted to say. *You're not here with me just because we're good in bed together, are you? Tell me what you're feeling. Tell me you want me the way I want you, so I'll know what to do.*

But he didn't say any of it. It was too soon. He wasn't sure and she wasn't sure, and he was scared, scared of finding out that Catherine didn't care about him, scared of finding out that she did. It surprised him how scared he was. Della was his problem, not hers. Catherine had problems of her own. He didn't want to complicate her life, not when everything between them was so fragile and new.

"What?" she said again.

He managed a smile he wasn't particularly feeling.

"Ah, nothing. I . . . don't want to go, either, and I've got to."

She nodded and looked away, afraid, for once, of trying to determine what he *didn't* say.

No words of love, she thought again. No words of commitment.

13

He brought Fritz by to see the gnomes on Sunday afternoon, but he didn't stay. He owed Michael the time he'd taken with Catherine the afternoon before, and he left Fritz there while he went to the building-site trailer to catch up. He made a point of telling Della that he would be seeing Catherine Holben that afternoon, albeit briefly, staring down her incredulous look until she had no alternative but to sulk in her room. He imagined that she would be immediately on the phone, pouring out her troubles to Margaret.

Fritz was very quiet after Della's indignant send-off, and Catherine was beautiful and worth the aggravation. She looked so pretty to him, and it was all he could do to keep his hands off her. He had to rely on inane conversation and furtive looks to get him through his arrival and almost immediate departure, because he couldn't do anything else with Fritz there. God, he wanted to stay, but he wanted to hit Michael for another free Saturday afternoon he could spend with Catherine more. Afternoons were good for him. Fewer distractions. No irate children, because they supposedly didn't know where he was, or perhaps because they did. He wondered if Catherine had any idea how much he wanted to make love with her again and what he was planning. He smiled to himself as he drove out to Wrightsville Beach. He thought he'd tell her if he got the chance and make her blush.

The smile faded. He hoped that Fritz wouldn't say anything about the scene he'd had with Della before they left home. He didn't think that she would. Fritz was always very careful of other people's feelings, and it didn't occur to him to tell her that there were things she shouldn't say.

He didn't have to work as long as he'd intended. Michael had nearly everything in order; they were ready to build from the paperwork standpoint, at any rate. Now, if they could just get the weather to cooperate.

He went back to Catherine's, expecting to let Fritz visit longer so that he could spend some time with Catherine. But he was greeted with the bane of the best-laid of parental plans—a child running a fever, and he had no alternative but to take his ailing Fritz home.

"How are you doing, Fritz?" he asked when they were nearly there, because she looked a little green.

She gave him a sigh and a thumbs-down. "Don't worry," she said. "I remember."

"Remember what?"

"No barfing in the truck."

She managed to spare the truck, but not much else. He was up most of the night holding Fritz's head and finding clean sheets and pajamas. Della had nothing but a cold shoulder for either of them.

"Wait a minute," he said, finally losing his temper at one of her long-suffering sighs. "Your little sister is sick. You can be mad at me, but don't you take it out on her, you understand me? Do you understand me!" he yelled when he got no answer.

"Yes, Daddy! I'm just *trying* to get some sleep."

"You try much harder and you're going to get a lot more than that."

"Go ahead and ground me, Daddy. I don't care."

"Della, I have just about had it with you—" He stopped because Fritz was pulling at his sleeve. "Again?" he asked her more kindly than he felt.

"Again," she told him.

★ ★ ★ ★ ★

Fritz was still running a fever in the morning, and Della was stonily silent.

"I want to talk to you. Come by the building site when you get out of school."

She gave him a surprised look. "We don't have anything to talk about, Daddy," she said, as if he were too dense to have realized that.

"I said *I* want to talk. What you do is be there."

She pressed her lips together, and he could feel her trying to decide how far she wanted to push this. "Oh, all right!" she said, apparently making up her mind.

"Good. And don't be late. I'm going to have to take Fritz to work with me, so you can bring her back home later after *I* talk."

He could tell that prospect hardly thrilled her, but it couldn't be helped. The family had to work together or it didn't survive. "You got some problem with that?" he asked.

She smiled. "No, Daddy. No problem."

He stared back at her, wondering why he felt like the spider's first-choice fly. "Don't leave for school without Charlie," he warned her. He didn't have time for any crap this morning.

"Daddy, give me some credit!"

"I give you what you deserve," he said.

Fritz came downstairs, looking as pale and wan as she probably felt.

"Am I going to school?" she asked, apparently game to try whatever would cause the least trouble.

"Nope. You're going to the building site with me."

Charlie came through on the run. "She didn't leave me, did she?"

"No, Charlie, I'm right here!" Della snapped.

"In that case, let's go! Let's go!"

"Della!" Joe called as she went out the door behind Charlie. She heaved a great sigh and turned back to him.

"What!"

"Have a good day."

"Oh, I *will*, Daddy. I will." She smiled that smile again, the one that made him so uneasy. "Fritz," she said to her sister, "feel better, okay?"

"Why would she want me to do that?" Fritz wondered aloud after she'd gone.

"She's your sister," Joe said.

Fritz shot him a look: *Oh, please!* Fortunately, for his frazzled temper, she didn't say it.

He called the pediatrician's office, to find that the doctor could see Fritz immediately, except that when they got there, they had to wait. And wait. He arrived at the work-site trailer shortly before eleven—with a folding lounge chair, a quilt, three pillows, a box of Popsicles, a box of crackers, a bottle of ginger ale, a bag of ice, and Fritz.

"What the hell is all *this?*" Michael said when he came in with the first load.

"Walking wounded," Joe said absently, looking for a place to unfold the lounge chair.

"Joey, who?"

"Fritz. Michael, get out of the way, will you? She's got the works—ear infection, sore throat, upset stomach. I couldn't send her to school."

"She's going to stay *here?*"

"I can't board her at the vet's, Michael."

"Oh, that's cute, Joey. Real cute. Where is she?"

"In the truck."

"I'll go get her. Don't put that there! Move it down at that end where she'll stay warm."

"Don't say anything in front of her about her causing a problem. She takes everything seriously."

"I'm not going to say anything. What do you think, I'm stupid? Jeez!"

"Come on, Cleopatra," Michael said as he carried Fritz in. "Your barge awaits." He made great ceremony of helping her off with her coat and placing her on the lounge and arranging her pillows, making her smile in spite of her misery. "Up or down?" he asked her about the back of the chair.

"Down," she said. "I'm awful sleepy."

"Best thing for you," Michael assured her, covering her with the quilt. "What are you doing?" he asked, because Joe was taking all his beer out of the small refrigerator.

"Making room," Joe said, stuffing in ice and Popsicles.

"Making room," Michael repeated. He slid the trash can closer to the lounge, rearranging the plastic liner and taking out the bits of paper that had been thrown into it. "Here, Fritz. *Don't* use this, but if you do, *do*. Got it?"

"I got it," she assured him.

"Smart cookie," Michael said, and she grinned.

"You want anything, Fritz?" Joe asked her.

"Nope."

"Okay, I've got to go get Fritz's prescription filled—" he said to Michael.

"You got a phone call," Michael said, interrupting. "Something about some stained glass at the Cotton Exchange. You might as well see about that, too, while you're at it."

"Yeah, I think I will. Fritz, I'll be back in a little while." But she was nearly asleep. He bent down and put his hand on her forehead. It was still hot. "You're going to feel better before you know it," he told her.

She nodded, snuggling deeper into the pillows. "I like it

here," she told him. "I can hear the ocean. Tell Uncle Michael I'll try not to throw up while you're gone."

"She'll try not to throw up," Joe said, passing it on.

"Thank you, thank you, thank you," Michael said, making Fritz smile again. "Hey, Joey," he said as Joe started out the door. He came closer and lowered his voice. "You got another phone call—Catherine."

Joe couldn't keep from smiling. "Yeah? What did she say?"

"Nothing. She just wanted to talk to you, and she said tell you she called."

"If she calls back, tell her I'll call her first chance I get."

"Hey," Michael said when he was about to go out the door again. "Is this . . . serious with you and her, or what?"

I might as well say it, Joe thought. He certainly felt it. In admitting it to Michael he was finally admitting it to himself. "It's . . . serious."

"Yeah?"

"Yeah."

"*How* serious?"

Joe grinned. "More serious than I've got time to stand here and explain. I'll see you later."

He left the prescription at the drugstore and went on to the Cotton Exchange. He negotiated his fee for the repair work that needed to be done on the stained glass faster than he ordinarily would have, because he had to get back to Fritz. He decided to go ahead and take one of the transoms with him, borrowing a ladder from the janitor.

The Cotton Exchange wasn't crowded, but he still had to watch for shoppers as he worked to get the transom down from one of the passageway doors. Three young girls kept milling around and giggling just beyond where he was working. He had to stop and start because he couldn't see them through the stained glass, and he thought they intended to pass by the ladder. The last thing he needed was to drop a transom on some kid's head. When he had to stop for the third time, he came down a few steps on the ladder to tell them they could come on through.

But he could only see their legs, and he had to come down another rung to see their faces. When he bent down to speak to them, all three of them looked at him in what could only be described as abject horror.

"Little girl," he said, pointing to the one farthest away, "this is *not* your lucky day."

"Della sick too?" Michael asked as they came into the trailer.

"No, she's not sick. She cut school. I caught her at the Cotton Exchange."

"What the hell did she do a thing like that for?"

"How should I know? I'm only her father."

"I don't know what you're so upset about, Daddy!" Della put in, folding her arms in a way that reminded Joe of Margaret.

"Sit down and be quiet!" he snapped at her.

"There's no place to sit."

"You can sit here," Fritz said, offering her the lower part of the lounge.

"I don't want to catch what *you've* got," she said, and she continued to stand.

Michael was trying not to grin. "So what do you think the other one's up to?"

"With my luck," Joe said, "he ran off on his lunch break and got married." He picked up the telephone and looked up two numbers.

"Daddy, what are you doing!" Della cried when he started to dial. "You're not going to tell on Sharon and Tessa—"

"You watch me, kid."

"Daddy, you *can't!* Everybody does it!"

"Yes, I can. It's part of the parents' cooperative, Della— sort of like a neighborhood watch. We stick together so our kids can't jerk us around. I know both their parents, and I can tell you right now, everybody is about to get their butts busted."

"It's no big deal. If it was Charlie, you wouldn't say anything!"

"I'd say plenty, and you know it. The *deal* here is you weren't where you were supposed to be. I didn't give you permission to hang out instead of going to school. While we're at it, Charlie's an *A* student. He can afford to miss a day's classes a lot more than you can. Now sit down!"

"Daddy, don't! I've never done it before!"

He stopped dialing. "And if you haven't, we both know why you're doing it now, don't we?"

She flushed and looked away.

"Well, you wanted my attention, so now you've got it. Let's hear it."

"I don't know what you mean—"

"I *mean,* Della, that I know you're doing this because you don't want me to see Catherine. The thing I don't know is why. What have you got against her? You know, I could understand it if she was some kind of bimbo I'd picked up in a bar someplace. But she isn't. She's a nice woman."

"I don't like her—"

"You don't even know her! You don't know anything about her—"

"I know I don't want her to be my mother!"

"She doesn't want to be your mother, for God's sake!"

"Have you *asked* her?"

"No, I haven't asked her."

"Then how do you know? How do you know what a woman like that wants?"

Margaret, he thought suddenly. He wasn't talking to Della. He was talking to Margaret. Della was parroting *her* words.

He worked hard to hang on to his temper. "Well, you're just going to have to get used to it. I like Catherine. I don't intend to stop seeing her."

He glanced in Fritz's direction. Poor, worried little Fritz.

"Michael, I'm going to go on home," he said to his brother. "I'm even going to take my kids with me."

"Joey, Joey," he said, coming to help him pack Fritz up again. "Hey," he said quietly as they walked to the truck. "Don't look so grim. It'll all work out."

"Yeah? You think any woman is going to want to take on *this?*"

"Nah, not any woman. Catherine, maybe." He patted Joe on the back. "Don't worry about the business. I can handle it. You get Della straightened out."

I could if it wasn't for your wife, he almost said. God, his head was killing him.

He sent Della ahead in her own car, instructing her to pick up Charlie at school and then get the both of them back to the house without delay. He intended to have a family meeting and settle things once and for all. When he arrived home, he put Fritz to bed on the couch, took some aspirin for his headache, called Catherine and got no answer, and ran into Charlie in the kitchen.

"What the hell are you doing here?" Joe said.

"I live here?" he suggested.

"Don't be cute! How did you get home!"

233

"Well, I heard about Della going over the wall . . . See what you started, Fritz?" he called into the living room. "So I figured she'd be 'delayed,' as we say in truant teenage circles. So I got a ride with Chip and the guys."

"So where is Della?"

"Don't know, Pop," Charlie said.

"Charlie, are you sure you don't know where she is?" Joe asked him nearly an hour later.

"Pop, honest. I don't know."

He didn't know. Nobody knew. She didn't come home.

14

"You just missed him," Pat said.

"Who?"

"Joe D'Amaro. You know, the Filthy Beast?"

Catherine stood there, trying not to acknowledge her acute disappointment so she wouldn't have to deal with it. Since Sunday she'd had to make do with two hurried telephone calls—the first one to let her know that Fritz was better and the second one after Treasure Higgins's funeral, when she had been emotionally exhausted because of the terrible sadness that surrounded the baby's death and because Sasha had suddenly decided that she wanted the "memory envelope" with the lock of Treasure's hair and the identification bracelet and the copy of her footprints the hospital had offered her before she had gone home.

Knowing that they were kept on file in the likely event that a mother changed her mind, Catherine had gone to the hospital to get it, only to find that Treasure Higgins's envelope had been misfiled. No one could locate it, and Catherine had had to return to Sasha empty-handed when she'd wanted nothing more than to be able to give her this small comfort.

At best, Joe, too, had seemed distracted, lapsing into a silence that Catherine could neither fill nor bring herself to ask about. Now, on Friday, he'd finally come by to see her.

She'd missed him.

"Did he say anything?" she asked a lot more casually than she felt.

"Only that he couldn't wait. He looked pretty harassed."

"Harassed?" Catherine repeated, because that was precisely the way he'd sounded on the phone.

"Yeah, you know. The way you'd look if the hem of your dress was caught in a paper shredder."

"He didn't say *anything?*"

"Just where were you. I said you were in a meeting. He said he couldn't wait. End of conversation."

She could feel Pat looking at her.

"So," Pat said, "what's this with your face? I thought you were seeing him."

"I am—or I was."

"Is there trouble in paradise or what?"

"I don't know."

"Hadn't you ought to find out?"

"How am I supposed to do that? I can't catch up with him long enough," she said irritably, because of how badly she wanted to know why she hadn't seen him.

"Ever hear of *the phone?*"

"I can't tell anything on the phone—"

"So write him a letter."

Pat was being cute, but Catherine was nearly desperate enough to do that. Or to go see him at the construction site. If Fritz was all right, it must be something else, something with the business or some part of his life she didn't know anything about. She *hated* trying to second-guess his behavior, particularly when it always led her to the same conclusion—that their brief interlude was over. She wished he'd extend the same courtesy he'd asked of her—if he wanted her to take a hike, she wished he'd just *say* it.

"So how are you feeling?" she asked Pat abruptly, because Pat was more unkempt than usual. Her clothes were wrinkled and her hair needed to be washed.

"Who, me? I feel like hell is full and the dead are walking

the earth, Ms. Holben." She gave a sarcastic smile. "You know, I still think it's got something to do with trying to kill the cancer and not killing me in the process. But . . . onward and upward, as they say."

"That's not what I mean, and you know it. We haven't talked lately—"

"You mean *I* haven't talked. All you do is listen." She sighed. "No, we haven't 'talked'—since you fell in *love.*"

Catherine pursed her lips to say that she wasn't in love, but she didn't say it. Perhaps she was. She was at least in like. She was most assuredly in lust. She was familiar with Pat's moods by now. She waited for her to get her sarcasm out of the way.

"It's Don," Pat said after a moment.

"What about him?"

"You'll laugh."

"I won't laugh. What about him?"

"He . . . thinks maybe he wants to put the bimbo on hold and come back to me." Pat looked into Catherine's eyes, then looked away. "You're not laughing."

"You're not, either," Catherine countered.

"That's because I know why he's doing it. Do you know why?"

"No," Catherine said truthfully.

"You want to know?"

"Yes."

Pat laughed. "Yes? Now you've done it. I'm not prepared for anything so direct as *yes.* I thought you'd play Twenty Questions out of your Psychology 101 book with me. You know, I say, 'Do you want to know?' and you say, 'Do you want to tell me?' Until I get tired of trying to spill my guts here and forget about the whole thing, or if I don't, you won't have to take the responsibility for prying it out of me."

"Pat—" Catherine began, but Pat held up both hands to stop her.

"I'll cut the bull. It's this. If Don goes through with the divorce, the house goes to me. He wants to be sure he gets it when I die—he doesn't want the divorce final before then—or if it is, he wants to make sure I don't leave it to somebody else," she said in a rush, as if she didn't hurry and say it, she wouldn't be able to.

"Why do you think that?"

"Aha! There it is. The Psych 101 question. I knew you had one someplace. I think it, Catherine, because it's true. I've even run a little test—he's not very bright, you know. He can't see through womanly wiles at all—even mine. It goes like this. Every time I make him think I can get along without him, he starts making coming-home noises. I know what he wants. Oh, I've shocked you, Catherine."

"You don't *know* what he wants, Pat," Catherine said, but she was shocked. Pat was seriously ill. She shouldn't have to play these mind games with a greedy, errant husband.

"Oh yes I do. I've known him since he was a nineteen-year-old boy and a soldier in Vietnam. He doesn't want *me*—he just wants everything I've got. For *her*. The man is vile. The worst kind of—" She broke off then gave a sad smile. "If you're going to play psychologist, Catherine, you're going to have to learn to do something about your face."

"I'm not playing psychologist. I'm listening to you."

"Yeah, but I know what you're thinking. You're thinking, *how* could a woman like me get herself all tangled up with a son of a bitch like Don Bauer? Now that's where life will screw you, Catherine. You really have to be careful. See, he wasn't *always* a son of a bitch. When I first met him, he wasn't the way he is now—I swear," she said, holding up her right hand. "I'm a smart woman, educated, not too ugly.

You think I could love a jerk like he is now? He just . . . changed somehow. Maybe it was his war experiences. Maybe it's the bimbo"—she gave a short laugh—"or maybe it's me. I took a good man and turned him into a piece of shit."

"Don't, Pat. It's not true and you know it."

"Don't? You're right! Don't! The trouble is, Catherine, I remember. I remember what he was like in his snappy little military uniform—when he was young and decent—before he started hating me." She sighed. "God," she said in a whisper, her eyes welling up. She looked away, and Catherine stood up to leave.

"Catherine," Pat said, "I can't wash my hair."

"What?"

Pat looked at her. "I said I can't wash my hair. If I do, it'll all come out."

"Yes," Catherine said, because at this stage of Pat's treatment that was very likely.

"You want to go with me this afternoon to buy a wig? If I've got to deal with Don, I don't want to do it bald."

Catherine smiled. "Sure."

"Catherine?"

"What, Pat?"

"I think you ought to call Joe. Even if life screws you, the good times can be worth it. Will you call him?"

"Maybe. I don't know. He knows where I am."

"You're not so easy to catch up with, either, you know."

"I am if he wants to."

"Catherine, the days of playing hard to get are long since past."

"I'm not playing hard to get. I just said he can find me if he wants to."

Apparently he didn't want to, at least not badly enough

to wait ten minutes until she got out of a meeting or to pick up the telephone.

But she didn't have time to think about that now. The class was waiting—or should have been. She'd left them things to do while she was in the budget meeting, and they were all still practicing giving an infant a bath—except for Maria. Maria was sitting in the classroom alone when Catherine came in.

"Where is everybody?" Catherine asked.

Maria had been very quiet of late, and she was quiet now. Quiet and seemingly bored. "Across the hall washing a doll, she said."

"Why aren't you with them?"

"Because I already know how to do that."

"Maybe you could go watch and give them some hints," Catherine suggested.

Maria looked up at her. "Maybe *you* could—" She didn't finish the sentence, getting up noisily from her desk.

"Maria," Catherine said when she'd reached the door. "What's wrong?"

"Nothing, Ms. Holben. Everything's just great."

"Is there anything you want to talk about?"

"Not with you."

Catherine ignored the sarcasm. Her friendship with Pat Bauer had made her very adept at doing that. "I'm here, if you change your mind. I know you're upset about Sasha—"

"It's not Sasha!" she said vehemently.

"All right! It's not Sasha. I just want you to know that I have been known to help on occasion. If you want to talk, I'll listen."

"You get *paid* to do it," Maria accused her.

"Right. And since I have to eat, you can be sure my heart's in it. It's not just a whim. I meant what I said. If you need help with something, I'll try to help you. If I can't, then I'll try to find somebody who can—paid or not."

"I don't need any help."

They stared at each other, and for a moment Catherine thought Maria was about to relent. She did want to talk, so much so that she couldn't hide it, not when she dared to look Catherine in the eye.

"Maria . . ."

But the others returned and the moment passed. Cherry was carrying a very clean, very nude, plastic infant-size doll.

"Ms. Holben! We're going to have to get a life jacket for this baby if you're going to let Abby wash it," she said, holding the doll up for her to see.

"My hands were slippery," Abby said in her own defense.

"Yeah, and the baby's head was under the water."

The others laughed, and Abby gave a sheepish grin.

"I guess I just won't wash my baby."

"Lucky baby," Cherry assured her.

"Okay," Catherine intervened. "Let's review . . ."

The day ended. She tried to catch some of the Friday afternoon, weekend enthusiasm her class had, but she couldn't do it. She didn't feel enthusiastic about anything, and she was annoyed with herself for it.

She went with Pat to purchase a wig, and they found one in the third place they looked that was both affordable and becoming. The day had accomplished something; Pat was in better spirits, at least.

Catherine heard nothing else from Joe. All that evening, after she'd gotten home, she toyed with the idea of calling him, but she still believed that either he was too busy to take the time to talk to her or he didn't want to, and the latter was becoming more and more likely. He'd said that he didn't know whether they had anything together or not. Apparently he'd decided they hadn't.

She stayed up late, anyway, just in case, finally giving up around midnight. She slept reasonably well for her state of mind, and she woke up early, dreaming she'd heard the telephone.

"You have got to get yourself together, lady," she said aloud.

She tried to stay busy with her usual Saturday morning cleaning chores. She had a life of her own—such as it was—and she was going to live it. She went out early to do her grocery shopping, then out again for a late lunch with Pat in her new wig, both of them deciding on the German restaurant in the Cotton Exchange neither of them could afford.

"Where else would someone named Bauer want to go?" Pat said lightly, in a better mood regardless of the fact that Don Bauer had given her that name in matrimony, and now he wanted it back again.

Pat looked so much better today. She was wearing makeup and a new-looking peach-colored dress that warmed her sallow skin. They had kraut dumplings and onion tarts and topped them off with chocolate-covered *Baumkuchen*, laughing as they ate, neither of them mentioning the men in their lives.

The day was bright and cold but not unbearably so, and afterward they strolled around the shops and through the inner courtyard in the Exchange. Catherine was enjoying herself—until she saw the missing stained-glass transom over one of the passageway doors.

Ah, Joe!

She felt the way she had when she was a teenager—unsure of herself, miserable, abandoned. But she was supposedly a big girl now. She knew the ways of the world; she certainly knew about the fickleness of men. She even made her living trying to help pick up the pieces of relationships gone awry. She just didn't know what Joe D'Amaro wanted from her. Perhaps he hadn't wanted anything but sex. Perhaps she was no different from Beatrice or Abby or any of them, regardless of her so-called experience. Like them, she'd given in to that terrible need women had to be close to someone, and like them, she believed that *her* experience had meant something, that she and Joe had been as close physically and emotionally as it was possible for a man and woman to be. In the face of his seeming indifference now, it was impossible not to have regrets. She simply didn't know how to care about someone and still be unattached; she'd told him that. She didn't want to learn. Whatever was happening with him now, she was determined not to let it get her down. Probably *nothing* was happening with him. She could imagine him happily going about his business with no thought of making the effort to nurture a relationship that was so fragile and new. Why should he? She had certainly proved willing enough. He had no reason to concern himself about their brief affair.

That was exactly what it was. For all her foreknowledge she'd behaved no more wisely than her students. She'd participated in a short-lived affair between two people who needed to relieve their sexual tensions. Nothing more, nothing less—except that she had the growing realization that she was indeed getting over Jonathan. Her involvement with Joe wasn't a complete loss if she could come away with that. She hardly thought about Jonathan at all, unless it was in some comparison to Joe D'Amaro. She wondered idly how Jonathan's new marriage was going. She still believed that his new wife was already pregnant.

"There goes the face again," Pat said. "Stop brooding. I'm the one dying of cancer."

"I wish you wouldn't say things like that!"

"I know you do. That's why I say them. So what's on your mind?"

"Nothing worth the effort."

"Aha! Joe D'Amaro."

"I was not thinking about Joe D'Amaro."

"Bullshit. So tell me. Is he a good lover or not?"

Pat's question was loud enough for two elderly women who were sitting on one of the inner-court benches to turn around and stare.

"Pat, will you hush?"

"No. I don't have a sex life, so I have to share yours. I want to know if he's a good lover or not. They do too," she said, gesturing to the old ladies. Both of them giggled.

"Is he?" she persisted.

"Yes!" Catherine said to the three of them. "He is!"

"I knew it! It's something about those buns of his, Catherine. I mean, the man has got *great* buns . . . You should see them," she added to the little old ladies. She cupped her hands, fingers spread wide, and demonstrated vividly in the air her approximation of that particular part of Joe's anatomy.

"Let's go!" Catherine said, laughing. "Honestly! You're worse than Sasha and Cherry."

But it felt good to laugh. She hated having her sense of well-being depend so much on someone else's whims. On Joe D'Amaro's whims. He had wanted her when he wanted her. When he didn't, he didn't know she was alive.

Her telephone was ringing. She climbed the last flight of stairs on the run, but it had stopped by the time she got the door unlocked.

It rang again almost immediately.

"Hello?" she said, still breathless from the climb.

"Catherine?" Joe said, and she closed her eyes, ashamed of

the rush of feeling the sound of his voice gave her. She was in over her head with this, way over her head.

"It's Joe."

"Yes, I recognized the voice," she said, smiling.

"You sound like you've been running."

"I was downstairs when the phone rang."

"So are you busy this evening?"

Yes, she thought. She wasn't at his beck and call. Tell him yes.

But she didn't want to lie because her feelings were hurt. "No. I'm not busy."

"I was wondering if I could bring Fritz by to see the gnomes."

"What time?"

"Well, now, if you can do it."

"Yes, that's all right."

"Catherine, I can't . . ." He trailed off into silence in much the same way he had the last time they'd talked. She waited for him to go on.

"Catherine," he said again. Something was the matter. She could hear it in his voice. Her hand tightened on the receiver. She didn't have the nerve to ask him what it was.

He gave a soft sigh. "I'll bring Fritz by in a little while."

"I'll be here."

He didn't say good-bye. There was only the click of his hanging up the phone.

"A little while" was nearly an hour. She had almost given up by the time she heard footsteps coming up the stairs. Onc set of footsteps. She waited for the knock, and when she opened the door, Fritz stood in the hallway alone.

"Hello, Fritz," Catherine said. "Come in. Are you feeling better?"

Fritz didn't answer her question. She didn't want to say—

245

unless Catherine just meant the ear infection and the sore throat and the upset stomach. That must be what she meant, Fritz decided. Catherine didn't know about anything else.

She looked up at her briefly, then away, and she continued to stand in the doorway.

"I'm . . . okay," she said finally. "I'm still taking medicine. It doesn't taste very good."

"Well, it's working, at least. You look a lot better than you did last Sunday. Come in and sit down. That's a long climb when you've been sick."

Fritz nodded. She *was* tired, but she was more worried about what to tell Catherine when she asked about Joe. She didn't know what she should say. Joe wouldn't tell her *anything,* not even when she asked. He just kept having arguments on the telephone with Della; he'd had one with her right before they'd left to come here. When they got here, he'd just said "I'm not coming in with you" when he'd pulled up out front—and that didn't seem the right thing to tell Catherine. She thought that Catherine would ask why, and there was no *why* as far as Fritz could see. He just wouldn't come in. She really thought that he'd only promised to let her come see the gnomes because she'd been sick last Sunday, and if he hadn't promised, she wouldn't be here at all.

"What's the weather like outside?" Catherine said, helping her off with her coat.

"Cold. It's going to rain again."

"Hot-chocolate weather, do you think?"

Fritz looked up at her. Maybe Catherine wouldn't ask. "It's *especially* hot-chocolate weather."

"Well, then, you go make yourself comfortable and I'll make it."

Fritz didn't offer to help. Catherine was wondering where Joe was, she could tell. Her eyes were all disappointed, and she'd looked twice down the stairs before she closed the door. Right now she was like Brenda from the office or Aunt Margaret when they expected Joe to be around and he wasn't, only so far Catherine hadn't said anything.

Fritz thought she had better say what she was supposed to say now. "Catherine, Mrs. Webber is going to pick me up when she closes her store."

There was a pause before Catherine called to her from the kitchen. "All right," she said, but something about the way the words came out made Fritz think it wasn't "all right" at all.

She gave a soft sigh and pulled the afghan with the pink flowers down off the back of the couch so she could arrange it over her legs when she sat down. She reached for the gnomes, and she picked out just the place where she wanted to sit. She thought that she was going to feel better here, that the feeling she'd had ever since Della had run away would be gone. It felt like *she'd* done something wrong, and she was sorry for it, only she didn't know what it was. She knew that it had something to do with this business with Della; she just didn't know how to fix it.

She got comfortable, the way Catherine had said to do. She had the afghan spread over her legs and she was holding Daisy and Eric close. But it wasn't enough. It just wasn't enough.

Fritz sat very still, waiting for Catherine to come in. When she finally did, she had the two Blue Willow mugs of hot chocolate on a silver tray, just the way they did it on television. They *always* took things to eat and drink into the living room on a silver tray.

"I thought we'd be special," Catherine told her. "These napkins I embroidered when I was a little girl. My grandmother and I used to work on them on summer afternoons. We'd sit on the porch in the shade, and she'd try to show me how not to make such a mess with my stitches. I wasn't very good, but I liked for my grandmother to teach me the things her grandmother had taught her. It always made me feel as if I knew all those long-ago women in my family, because they'd learned to do it just like I was learning."

Fritz took one of the cloth napkins. Catherine was telling her things again, special things about when she was a little girl. She loved to hear about that, and she wanted to tell her so, but somehow no words came.

The napkin was stiff and crisp, and it had pale blue and pink flowers embroidered on it. The thread was shiny and thick, and she touched a flower gently with her fingertip. She could feel Catherine looking at her, and she bowed her head. She spread the napkin on top of her lap, and she kept her eyes on the gnomes. She was feeling so sad again, and she didn't know what she might do if she looked up.

Catherine set the tray aside. "Fritz," she said, her voice soft and quiet.

Fritz kept her head down, and she clutched the gnomes tightly. But they still weren't helping. Daisy and Eric weren't helping at all.

She looked up at Catherine. "Catherine?" she said, surprised at how her voice sounded. She didn't sound like herself at all. She sounded like she had on Monday, when her throat was so sore. Her throat hurt now, but it wasn't the same kind of hurting. Her throat *hurt* and her eyes burned.

"What is it, Fritz?"

"Can you—" she looked down at the gnomes "—be like a mother?"

She was afraid to look at Catherine. She was afraid that Catherine wouldn't understand, that she'd have to explain it, and if she had to do that she'd cry like a little kid. Only she *was* crying—and it must be because Catherine *did* understand—because Catherine sat down on the couch with her

248

and held her arms out, just like mothers were supposed to do. She let Fritz crawl into her lap—afghan, gnomes, and all. She didn't try to make her say what was wrong or anything like that. They just sat together for a long, long time, until Fritz grew quiet.

"This is where Joe always says I need to go wash my face," Fritz offered when she knew she had cried enough. She sat up and sniffed loudly. It surprised her to see that Catherine had been crying too. "I guess we felt bad, didn't we?"

Catherine smiled. "I guess we did. Well. Let's go wash our faces. I think that's the best thing we can do."

Catherine's bathroom was small and had plants growing everywhere, and she gave Fritz a special washcloth and towel, thick blue ones with bands of white, flowery lace across the ends.

"Are you going to tell Joe I cried?" she asked when they both had their faces clean.

Catherine led the way back into the living room. She picked up the tray to carry it back into the kitchen, and Fritz followed after her.

"Well, I think if he knew it, he could help you with whatever the problem is," Catherine said as she poured the hot chocolate back into a saucepan to reheat.

Fritz thought about this. "It would just worry him," she decided. "He's worried enough about Della."

Catherine looked around at her. "What's wrong with Della?"

It was all right to say. Fritz knew it was. Catherine was really and truly just like a mother. It would be all right for her to know.

"She ran away on Monday. She left school, and then Joe found her hanging out at the Cotton Exchange. But then she really ran away, and Joe couldn't find her. He says it was a pretend running away. He thinks Aunt Margaret sent her someplace so he wouldn't know where she was. He was really mad."

"Is she . . . at home now?"

"No, she's at Uncle Michael and Aunt Margaret's house. She won't come home. Joe's trying to get her to, but she won't as long as he—" Fritz stopped. She didn't want to say that part of it.

"As long as he what, Fritz?"

Fritz shrugged instead of answering. "Is the hot chocolate ready?"

Catherine lifted the pan off the stove. "As long as he what, Fritz?"

Fritz looked up at her. This must be like a real mother, too, she thought. Catherine wasn't being like Brenda or Margaret now. She wasn't asking one thing so she could find out something else. Catherine wanted an answer, and she meant for Fritz to tell her.

"Tell me, Fritz. As long as he what?"

"Likes you," she said, because she couldn't see a way out of it. She watched Catherine's face. It didn't change much, just enough to make her feel worried again.

Catherine poured the hot chocolate back into the cups and set them on the kitchen table.

"I don't have any ice cream," she said, and Fritz nodded.

"That's okay, Catherine. It's still good."

But Catherine wasn't listening to her; Fritz could tell that she wasn't listening. Catherine sat down at the table and took a sip of the hot chocolate.

"Fritz, I'm sorry to cause you all this trouble," she said after what seemed a long time.

"It's Della," Fritz said, because that was the one thing she was sure about. "You can't help it."

Catherine looked at her and smiled. "Yes, honey, I can."

15

Joe looked out of the trailer window when a car pulled up not far from the work site. He didn't recognize it, but he recognized the woman who got out of it.

Catherine.

She stood looking at the ocean for a moment before she came toward the trailer. The wind was blowing her hair, and she was wearing a navy-blue suit and red high-heeled shoes. She looked all-business and she looked lovely.

He could smell the sea air when he opened the trailer door. He waited, smiling when she looked up at him and gave him a slight smile in return. A chorus of appreciative whistles went up from the crew as she made her way toward him across the sand. She ignored them with the ease of a woman used to being admired.

The step into the trailer was high, and he offered her his hand. Her fingers were cold in his, and the skirt she was wearing rode up. He could see a good expanse of stockinged thigh as she stepped up beside him. Beautiful, he thought. Legs that looked beautiful, felt beautiful wrapped around him.

He hardly gave her time to get inside before he pushed the door closed and reached for her. He should have gone in to see her the night before when he took Fritz by to visit the gnomes. He should have sat down with her and told her the kind of trouble he was having with Della. He realized that now. Just having her here made him feel better.

"I'm so glad to see you," he whispered, pressing as much

of her body as he could against his.

"Are you?" she said, but he wasn't listening.

"God, you feel good. . . ."

He meant to kiss her, but she held him away.

"Joe, wait—"

"I don't want to wait, Catherine. I've got maybe thirty seconds before somebody finds an excuse to come in here."

"Joe, I want to talk to you!"

He stopped trying to kiss her and leaned back, his eyes searching hers. He was annoyed. He knew that it showed and he couldn't help it. She'd come all the way out here so they could *talk?* He needed her, and somehow she didn't see it. Or she didn't care.

"So talk," he said, stepping away from her.

She didn't say anything. She looked around the makeshift trailer office instead.

"New car?" he asked, showing her he could make conversation if that was what she wanted.

"No, it's Pat Bauer's. Joe . . . ?"

"What, Catherine?" She was standing just close enough for him to smell her perfume. Or was it *her* scent? Whatever it was, it was making him crazy. He fiddled with some papers on the worktable so he could keep his hands off her. "What?"

The trailer door suddenly opened and Michael came in. He looked from one of them to the other, and he gave Catherine the barest of nods. But he said nothing to either of them. He pulled out the top drawer in the only filing cabinet D'Amaro Brothers had and began searching through some of the folders.

"I want to talk to Catherine," Joe said to him.

"I'm looking for something Brenda needs at the main office," Michael replied, clearly making no effort to take the hint and leave them alone.

"Catherine hasn't done anything, Michael," Joe said.

Catherine put her hand on his arm and said, "Don't. This wasn't a good idea. I'll see you some other time—"

"No, you won't. We're going to talk now." To hell with Michael, he thought. Apparently he was as malleable as Della when it came to having his opinion shaped. Thanks to Margaret, his brother had somehow forgotten that a few days ago he'd liked the idea of little Joey and Catherine Holben being together.

Joe opened the trailer door for her and followed her outside. Catherine intended to leave, but he took her by the hand, making her walk along with him toward the beach. The wind was strong, flattening the sea oats and whipping the water rough and gray. He could taste the salt on his lips, and a few gulls hung motionless overhead, held aloft by the strong air currents that came in off the sea. He slowed his pace because Catherine was having difficulty walking in the sand in high heels, and he led her down the dune onto the beach. The dune was long and sloping and offered little shelter from the wind. He kept thinking about the day he'd brought her and Fritz here. In his mind's eye he could see the two of them, laughing, running along the beach together.

"It's too cold out here," he decided, looking at her now, his eyes searching her face. Once again he was taken by the irrevocable fact that what he felt for her was more than sexual attraction. He liked this woman. He liked the way she looked. He liked the person she was. It was the liking that made his need of her so intense. He kept her hand in his, as if he were afraid she'd run away if he didn't.

"No, it's all right," she said. "It's better out here." She pulled her hand from his.

"I'm sorry about Michael."

He reached up to brush away a strand of hair that had

whipped across her face, and she didn't move away from him. He let his fingers linger for a moment on the softness of her cheek, and he felt like crying. He hadn't slept well for days, and his trying to talk to Della last night had accomplished exactly nothing. She wouldn't discuss her feelings with him, and she wouldn't agree to a family meeting. He wasn't about to be dictated to by a sixteen-year-old kid, and yet he didn't know what to do about it.

"Why didn't you tell me about Della?" Catherine asked.

"So you wouldn't come out here looking like you're looking now," he answered.

"I don't know what that means, Joe."

"I don't know what it means, either. Suppose *you* tell *me*. Why did you come out here?"

But she wasn't answering his questions. She looked down the beach for a moment, then back at him. "You should have told me about Della."

"Della is my problem, not yours. I'll handle it."

"It's mine if I'm the reason she's behaving the way she is. You should have told me."

He hadn't *wanted* to tell her. If he'd told her, he'd have had to say that a good part of the reason for Della's behavior was that he'd rebuffed his sister-in-law, and his loyalty to Michael made him not want to say it. Michael *loved* his wife, untrustworthy woman that she was. "It's not you . . . entirely. There are other things."

"Your daughter ran away from home because she doesn't want you to have anything to do with *me*, Joe."

"I told you. It's not your problem."

"What about Fritz and Charlie?"

"What about them?"

"Joe, you have a close, loving family. They care about each other. I don't want it torn apart because of me. Look at

Michael. People are already choosing sides. Fritz cried last night for nearly an hour—and she doesn't cry very often, does she?"

Ah, God, he thought. He had been so frantic about Della that he'd only been marginally aware of Fritz's distress. Again. He was some damn poor excuse for a father. He loved *all* his children, but the casual observer would never know it. It had become the pattern of his life that he could only deal with one crisis at a time.

"What did Fritz say?"

"She didn't want me to tell you she'd cried. She didn't want you to worry about it."

He looked out to sea, trying to stay calm, trying to keep her here on this windy, cold beach as long as he could, because he suddenly thought that he wasn't going to be able to be with her if he didn't. "Well, you're the expert in dealing with children. What do you think I should do?"

Her chin came up, and he realized immediately that he'd hurt her with that remark. He reached out to touch her, taking her by the hand again—surely she'd let him do that much. "Catherine, I'm sorry. I didn't mean that."

Again she pulled her hand away. "That's the difference between you and me, Joe. I don't say things I don't mean. I have to be very careful when I'm angry, because if I say it, I mean it. I can't ever take it back. I'd better go."

"Catherine, I don't know what to do! Can you understand that?"

"Of course I understand it."

"I . . . care about you." *I love you,* he'd almost said. It was too soon to tell her that, and from the determined look on her face now he was never going to be able to say it. "You're important to me, and this whole thing is making me crazy. I wanted to talk to you—to see you. But I had to find Della."

"Joe, this isn't about your not seeing me. It's about your not *telling* me you were having a real problem with Della because of me."

He looked into her eyes. "I didn't want to deal with it, okay? I had enough problems. I couldn't take on another one."

"I don't want to be a problem for you."

"You aren't."

"Joe, we're going to have to do something."

"Like what, for God's sake? Like what!"

His eyes were still holding hers, and he knew what she was going to say. He braced himself to hear it.

"I think . . . we ought to stop seeing each other for a while."

"And how long is 'a while'?" he asked.

"Until things are better between you and Della."

"Della is sixteen years old. For all I know, this is some teenage thing she's going through—something that's not going to get a damn bit better whether I stop seeing you or not."

"But you won't know if you don't try it. Things aren't going to get any better until you can sit down and talk to her. I don't think you're going to be able to do that as long as she knows you're still seeing me."

He knew that she was right, but damn it all, they were just beginning something here. It worried him that she was so willing to let it go.

"Tell me this one thing," he said. "Is there somebody else?"

She looked at him blankly. "Someone else?"

"Someone else! Some other guy—without pain-in-the-butt kids—you want to see?"

"Why are you asking me that?"

Because I love you.

"Because I want to know. Because you keep offering me a way out. I told you before if you wanted me to take a hike, you could just say so."

She gave a heavy sigh. He could tell she was now doing what she'd said earlier—being careful of what she said when she was mad because she'd never take it back.

"I don't know why you've asked me that. The only thing I can think of is that *you're* the one who wants to end it—"

"Don't put words in my mouth, Catherine."

"Do you or don't you!"

"No, damn it!"

"Then why did you ask me something like that? You know about Jonathan. . . ."

He looked away from her. He wasn't sure himself why he'd asked. Yes he was. He was going to say it. "I don't know how much you care about me. I don't know *if* you care about me. If you do, I want to know it's going to be worth what it might cost me."

"With Della, you mean."

"Yes."

"There's no way to know that, is there?" she said quietly.

"I guess not. So, is that it, then? We just forget the whole thing?"

"For now, yes."

He stood staring at her. God, she was so damn calm! Well, he wasn't and he had to get away. He turned abruptly and walked back toward the building site, leaving her there. He didn't make it halfway up the bank.

Tell her!

He wanted to tell her so bad. He'd lied when he'd said he didn't know if she cared about him. He did know. He could feel it. She cared, and she cared a lot, and it was crazy that neither of them could *say* anything.

257

She stood looking at him, her arms folded over her breasts. She took a step toward him, and he slid back down the bank. His arms went around her, and he didn't care that the entire crew of D'Amaro Brothers Construction could see them. She clung to him, and he couldn't hold her tight enough. This was it, the end, and they both knew it.

"We're going to have to do it, aren't we?" he said, his voice bitter, resigned. "We're going to have to let go of everything."

She leaned back to look at him. "It'll be . . . easier."

He nearly laughed. "There is no 'easier' in this, Catherine. Whatever we do is going to be bad for somebody."

"You know I'm right."

"Yeah. I know you're right. My obligation is to my kid. Yours is to yourself, so you don't get dragged around again like you did with Jonathan. But knowing doesn't help me one bit." *What if I love you? What if I love you, Catherine?*

"Joe—"

"No. The hell with it, Catherine. When you're right, you're right. God knows I'm worn out with being caught in the middle. I'll walk you back to your car."

He didn't try to take her by the hand again. He let her struggle up the dune in her red shoes, because he knew he couldn't touch her. He'd lose it if he touched her.

"I guess this ends Fritz's visits to the gnomes," he said when they reached her car.

"No. She can still come."

"How do you think I'm going to stand that!" he exploded.

"You stood it well enough last night," she said, and he gave a sharp exhalation of breath.

So he had. Only last night they were technically still seeing each other, still together. Last night he'd wanted to spare her feelings and his extremely taxed ability to cope. Now he'd have her on the fringes of his life, and he'd have to pretend to

himself and everybody else that she wasn't there. He didn't
know if he could do it—even for Della.

He opened the car door for her, and he said nothing. Not
good-bye, good luck, I'll call you. Nothing. She looked into
his eyes for a brief moment that was nearly his undoing. He
wanted to tell her that there was some other way—there had
to be. But he stood and watched her leave, until she was ready
to pull the car onto the street. Then he gave a loud, two-
fingered whistle to make her stop. She did, rolling down the
window and waiting for him to get there.

"One more thing," he said, and he leaned down, his hands
resting on the edge of the window so he could see her face.
"Don't . . . give up on us yet. If we've got something worth all
this aggravation, I don't want you to give up—" He stopped,
looking down at the ground and then back at her. "Because I
won't. I want you to take care of yourself, okay?"

She gave him a sad smile. "Okay."

"Promise me. I'm not going to see you for a while. I'm not
going to sneak around so my kid won't catch me with you.
I'm going to work on this like you said—but I need you to
promise."

She hesitated, and he thought she wasn't going to say it.

"I promise," she said finally, looking into his eyes.

He nodded, then gave her a quick kiss on her forehead and
walked away.

Michael was no longer looking for missing folders when he
went back into the trailer. He was waiting.

"You set her straight?" he asked immediately.

"What the hell does that mean?"

"It means, did you set her straight? Did you tell her she
can't be coming between you and your children?"

"She hasn't been doing that, Michael."

"Yeah, yeah. That's why Della's at *my* house."

"Della is at your house because—"

He bit down on it. He wasn't going to cause more trouble for the family than he already had—even if it killed him.

"Catherine didn't know anything about Della's leaving until last night," he said, making a supreme effort to be reasonable. Somebody had to understand what was going on. Somebody had to be on his side. "She came here to set *me* straight. She said that I couldn't settle things with Della until I could sit down and talk with her—and I couldn't do that as long as Della thought I was seeing her. Catherine called it off, Michael. Not me."

Michael shrugged. "So maybe it's for the best, Joey."

"That's it? Maybe it's *for the best?* I'm trying to talk to you here, Michael. I'm trying to tell you it's not *for the best.* I'm trying to tell you I love Della—and maybe I love Catherine too. She makes me happy. Being with her makes me happy, Michael. I'm trying to tell you that I think I'm going to have to choose between my daughter and a chance at having a new life with somebody I really care about—and it scares me to death. I'm trying to tell you that maybe I won't even get the chance to choose, because Catherine won't come between me and my kid. I'd like a little something more from you than that maybe-it's-for-the-best crap!"

"Joey, hey," Michael said, "take it easy. It'll work out—"

"Sure. Catherine won't see me anymore, and Della won't come home. So we're all going to live happily ever after, right?"

Michael grinned and poked him on the arm with his fist. "Hey, did I say it was going to be easy?"

Joe smiled in spite of himself, but the smile faded. *Not easy* was one thing; *impossible* was something else again.

16

Catherine sat in the empty classroom for a long time after Pat and the others had gone. She could hear the sounds associated with the end of the day throughout the building—the rattle of the radiators because the heat had been cut back, the secretarial staff slamming doors as they left for home, the cleaning crew chatting as they moved from room to room, emptying the trash.

She sat at her desk and stared at a stack of papers that needed grading, but she saw nothing. She felt so empty. It had been hard for her to go to Joe today, but she knew she'd done the right thing in ending their relationship. They were both doing the right thing, but, perversely, she still wished he'd protested more. Even knowing there was no alternative, she wished he'd come up with some other solution for the problem with Della. She understood that he loved his children very much—she'd always known that—but some part of her still would have liked to hear him say that they would continue being together no matter what, that Della would just have to learn to adjust.

She gave a long sigh, and she realized that she wasn't alone.

"Come in," Catherine said to the girl who stood tentatively in the dark outer hallway. She remained seated at her desk, not sure who the girl was or if she was going to comply. "I'm . . . glad you came," she added. She was used to frightened students who thought they might be pregnant seeking her out here, and she wanted to put the girl at ease.

This one, however, was not frightened.

"Do you remember me?" she asked, her features determined and a bit self-righteous.

"I remember you, Della," Catherine said easily. "As I said, I'm glad you came."

"Why would you be glad?"

"So we can talk. We don't know each other very well. Or is this meeting just for you and I don't get to say anything?"

"I want you to leave my father alone."

Catherine looked at her steadily, and it struck her again what a pretty young woman Della D'Amaro was, and how fashionably correct she was in her choice of hairstyle and clothes. Everything was just right—on the outside, at least. The inside, perhaps, was something else again. She seemed unlike the others in the D'Amaro family, and Catherine was faced with the fact that as much as she cared about Joe, she really didn't like this daughter of his very much. Whether she was prejudging or not, she thought Della had none of Fritz's gentleness, none of her father's caring nature, nor Charlie's insouciance. Della seemed an entity unto herself, her concerns both selfish and finite. She knew exactly what she wanted and didn't want, what she liked, and what she wouldn't tolerate under any circumstances.

"I see," Catherine said. "Why do you want me to do that?"

"You know why," Della answered obscurely. She came farther into the room, casting glances around her, as if she wanted to make sure they were alone.

"Not really. Suppose you tell me."

"Well, that's easy. I don't want you to be my mother. My mother's dead. She was beautiful, and my father loved her so much, he wanted to die too. Somebody like you can't take her place."

Somebody like me, Catherine thought. Apparently she wasn't the only one adept at prejudging; Della was quite good at it herself. She wondered how Della would respond if she told her that she had no intention of taking her mother's place —because she wanted a place of her own.

"You're right, Della. No one can take Lisa's place. She was beautiful—you look very much like her. And I already know she was your father's life. He told me how difficult it was for him after she died—how difficult it still is. But, Della, since we're being blunt here, let me tell you this. This is only the third time we've met. The first time was at the Cotton Exchange. You were having a tantrum because your father didn't want you to work in a bar. The second time was at the barbecue, where I was your *sister's* guest. Both times you were more than a little rude. Now, given these two occasions, why on earth do you think that *I* would want to be a mother of *yours?*"

Della flushed. "I know what you're up to. You lied before. You're after my father—"

"I didn't lie. I believed what I said to you at the barbecue. But you're right. Now that I know Joe better, I like him very much. If by 'after him' you mean that I want to be with him all I can, then the answer is yes, I'm after him. We enjoy each other's company, and I can understand why that scares you. But my being with your father now doesn't mean that he loves Lisa any less or—"

"You won't win," Della said, interrupting.

"Neither will you," Catherine said quietly.

"What do you mean by that?"

"I assume that you care about your father. . . ."

"I wouldn't be here if I didn't."

"Well, when you care about somebody, sometimes you make sacrifices—do things you may not want to do just because it will make that person happy. You understand what I mean?"

"No," she said rudely.

Cheryl Reavis

"No? Well, it's this, Della. If *I* cared about Joe, then I might be willing to do something that would make life easier for him, even if I hated doing it—like not seeing him because it upsets you, and you, in turn, make life hell for him and for everybody he cares about. Or if *you* cared about him, you might be willing to get to know *me* better—just because you knew that I made him happy when he's been sad for such a long time. And that, all by itself, would be reason enough for you to make the effort. You see?"

"I see. I know what you're doing, and I'm *not* going to make the effort."

"No. I didn't think for a moment that you would. You're too young to understand the subtleties here. And you're too concerned with what *you* want. So I've already told Joe that I don't think we should see each other. But I didn't do it for you—I really don't care how many tantrums you have or how many times you cut school or pretend to run away. I'm doing this for Joe, and for Fritz and Charlie, because I can't stand seeing any of them worried and upset. You do win, Della. So now you can move back home and enjoy your victory such as it is."

Della stood there, seemingly uncertain as to what to do next. Apparently she'd expected to execute some kind of dramatic confrontation, complete with tearful exit, and Catherine was determined not to give it to her. She had no intention of handling an irate Della any differently than she would anyone else.

"I don't have to like you," Della said, "just because *he* does!"

"Exactly," Catherine answered. "And that goes both ways. You don't have to like me—and I don't have to like you. I've certainly seen no reason to. But who knows? If we'd worked at it, we might have become friends. Not good

264

friends, perhaps, but friends. We certainly have one major thing in common—we both love Joe.

"So good-bye, Della. I'd ask you to say good-bye to Fritz and Charlie for me, but I'd rather handle that myself. Is there anything else?" she added because Della was standing with her fists clenched.

"You just stay away from my father," she said in her determination to have the last word.

Catherine made no comment, and Della turned abruptly and left. Catherine could hear her footsteps echoing down the long length of the hallway, picking up speed as she neared the end, then the banging of the outside door. She got up from the desk and walked to the window so she could see the parking lot. There was only one car there, something new and expensive. Margaret D'Amaro sat in the driver's seat.

Catherine made it through the rest of the week. And the next, her life reverting to the previously comforting and now relentlessly dull routine she'd known before she met Joe D'Amaro. Once or twice she thought she caught a glimpse of his truck passing the school, but it had been too far away for her to be sure. He didn't call—not that she expected him to, unless it was about Fritz coming to see the gnomes, but it seemed that she'd lost even that. It was as if the D'Amaros never existed, except for the great emptiness she was feeling. She missed them. She missed Joe more than she'd dreamed possible. It was incredible how tame the "right thing" could seem in theory and how painful it was in actuality. Joe was on her mind all the time, no matter what she was doing, no matter how busy she kept.

She was finding it difficult not to be short-tempered with both Pat and her class—particularly Maria, who still had something on her mind but who wouldn't say what it was.

265

She was annoyed with herself for going into debt. Impulsively she took out a bank loan and bought a used car, one she drove early some mornings to Johnnie Mercer's pier at Wrightsville Beach, where she was well away from the D'Amaro Brothers construction site and where she could walk along the beach for a while in some degree of solitude and think. Occasionally she went to the Cotton Exchange, and she was appalled at how seeing the repaired stained-glass transom back in its place came so close to making her cry.

She was being ridiculous, and she knew it. But the harder she tried, the worse she felt. She visited Sasha and Grandmamma, accepting the root charm wrapped in brown paper and tied with string Grandmamma insisted she have and keep so the sun would shine on her back door. Technically she didn't even *have* a back door, so there wasn't much chance of that happening.

She worked late at school one afternoon the second week in December, and when she started to get up from her desk, her legs wouldn't hold her.

She'd been sitting too long, or she had some kind of virus, she thought. Beatrice and Cherry had been sick briefly with one, and Pat had been dragging the last few days as well.

She sat back down. She felt so peculiar, and she rested her head in her hands. In a moment the weakness and queasiness passed, and she was able to pack up her things and leave for home.

But by the time she arrived at the apartment house, the sick feeling had returned, growing worse as she climbed the smoke-filled Mayfair stairwell. She let herself into her apartment and lay down on the couch immediately, trying to think of something that might make her feel better. Nothing came to mind.

The telephone rang, and she jumped.

"Oh, God," she murmured, making her way into the kitchen the answer it.

A woman on the phone identified herself as Dr. Vrie's nurse. "I'm calling for Pat Bauer," she said. "We've had to admit her to the hospital and she's worried about her car. She wants us to bring it to you, if that's all right."

"Yes, of course," Catherine said. "Do you know the address?"

"The Mayfair, right? I'll just park it out front—somebody from here is going to pick me up. I've got Pat's house keys, too, so if you could just watch for me, I'll be there in about ten minutes."

"Yes, fine," Catherine said. But it was the spirit that was fine, she realized: the flesh was definitely weak. She felt terrible. She drank some water—and lost it immediately—then she spent the next ten minutes bathing her face with a cold cloth and trying to feel well enough to get downstairs to get Pat's keys.

She managed not to leave the nurse standing on the street, but just barely. She looked at Catherine curiously as she approached.

"Are you all right?" she asked as she handed over the keys.

"Just a virus," Catherine said, pulling her jacket around her more tightly. She was cold suddenly, and it wasn't just from the brisk December wind.

"Better not go see Pat, then," the woman advised, and Catherine nodded. She really didn't feel able to make it to the hospital to see her, the fact that she shouldn't expose Pat to anything she might be getting notwithstanding.

"Pat's got pneumonia again—she told me to tell you that so you wouldn't think she was dying."

"Pneumonia's bad enough," Catherine said.

"She wants you to call her the first chance you get."

"Thanks for bringing her car."

"We didn't mind. We all like Pat. She's a gutsy lady—she participates in her treatment one hundred percent. But she still needs all the help she can get."

Catherine's eyes met hers for a moment in shared sympathy for Pat Bauer.

"Well, here comes my ride. You'd better get your virus back inside."

Catherine smiled and went back into the Mayfair. She heard Mrs. Donovan call her when she was on the second landing but she didn't stop. She had to get to a place where she could lie down. She left her jacket on for a long while, lying on the couch again in an effort to feel up to calling Pat.

She finally got up and took her temperature, sitting on the side of her bed to read the thermometer. She had no fever, regardless of how bad she felt.

The telephone rang again, and she made herself go into the kitchen to answer it.

"Did you . . . get my . . . car?" Pat said, her voice straining with the lack of breath she was obviously experiencing from the pneumonia. She sounded so much worse than she had earlier in the day, and typically she'd said nothing about how she was feeling physically. It was as if the emotions Don Bauer precipitated in her was the only thing that mattered. Catherine could understand that. She had been preoccupied by her own emotional roller coaster.

"I've got it," Catherine said, sitting down on the floor in the kitchen to talk, because the cord wouldn't reach as far as the kitchen chairs. "I've also got your house keys and the virus Beatrice and Cherry had."

"You're sick?"

"Feels like it."

"Who's going to . . . tame the . . . lions tomorrow?"

"I'll feel better by then. All I have to do is be there so they don't run wild. I can let Beatrice handle showing some films or something."

"Catherine? Will you do something for me?"

"Sure," Catherine said, expecting Pat to ask her to bring some nightgowns and things to the hospital.

"If this is it . . . you know, *it.*"

"I thought you didn't want me to think you were dying."

"Well, I'm not dying now . . . but if I was . . . or if I get worse and do start dying or something . . . I don't care how many times I tell you that I want to see Don . . . I don't want you to go out and find him for me. I'm in my right mind now, and I'm telling you I want to die in peace. I *don't* . . . want him at my bedside. Even if I cry and beg for him, okay?"

Catherine said nothing. She sat on the floor with her head bowed. She had no energy for this.

"Okay?" Pat said again. "Catherine?"

"Pat, no, it's not okay. Whatever you ask me, if I can do it, you'll get it. I'm not going to put myself in the position of having to second-guess whether or not you mean it."

Pat laughed, then began to cough. "Great," she said when she could. "I knew . . . I could count . . . on you. Good night, Catherine."

Catherine felt better in the morning. She had no fever, and she managed to keep a few saltine crackers down. Whatever this illness was, it was passing, except for her feeling of tiredness. She went on to the school. The pregnant students' program had no funds for substitute teachers, and Catherine certainly couldn't afford to pay one out of her own pocket.

She had crackers again at lunchtime. And some tomato juice.

So far, so good, she thought—prematurely. She barely

made it to the restroom in time, and she spent most of her lunch hour waiting for the nausea to recede. Maria was in the hallway when she came out, watching her curiously.

But she felt better after a while, and she tried some crackers again. Those stayed down, and by the end of school she felt well enough to call Pat about bringing whatever she needed in the way of clothes to the hospital. She still didn't want to chance giving Pat whatever errant virus she had, so she left the small bag of gowns and clean underwear she'd packed for her at the nurses' station, all the while thinking of Sasha and the last occasion she'd had to come here.

She still hadn't been able to get Sasha's "memory envelope" for her. Grandmamma was going to have to come out here, Catherine thought as she left the building. Grandmamma had nothing if not a commanding presence, and people were a lot more likely to find the unfindable for her.

She sighed and suddenly thought about Joe, about being with him later on the same evening that little Treasure had died. When she closed her eyes, she could remember everything about Joe. The way he looked and felt and smelled and tasted. Everything. She could hear his soft whisper: *It's all right, Catherine. It's all right.*

He had been kind to her—too kind, too accommodating. She'd been foolish enough to let herself need him physically and emotionally, and now she could think of nothing else.

Joe.

She was still feeling all right by the time she got home— except that she was so tired. She went to bed early and slept soundly, expecting to feel fully recovered by the time she awoke. She did, for a while. But the queasiness came back again, persisted, waxed and waned, no matter what she did to make it better. She managed to get through the school day, and the next one, and the next. In the front office on Friday morning she picked up a pen to sign for some videos she'd ordered about prenatal care. The UPS man handed her the clipboard and showed her the block where she was to write her name, and the next thing she knew, she had woken up on the floor in a circle of concerned faces, a cotton ball soaked in ammonia being waved under her nose.

Something was the matter. She'd never fainted in her life. She ran through all the things it could be. She'd been worrying about Joe and Della and about Pat. She hadn't been eating very well. Sometimes she slept all night; sometimes she didn't. She decided that it was just that she was so tired from the emotional strain, and perhaps the virus was more persistent in her case than it had been in the others.

It's nothing, she kept thinking, but in the face of her general lack of improvement as the day wore on, she made an appointment for a checkup, anyway. She had no doctor other than the gynecologist who'd done her infertility studies and her regular Pap smears, and she felt no qualms about using whatever professional clout she had to get in to see him as soon as she could.

She called the doctor's office, asking for one of the nurses she knew personally. She hated having to telephone from the office at school, but she had no choice about it. She didn't feel well enough to go someplace else.

"Mary Beth," she said when the nurse came on the line, "this is Catherine Holben. I'm having some problems. Can you move heaven and earth for me so I can be seen today?"

"You're having a gynecological problem, Catherine?"

"I'm . . . not sure. I just know I feel like the devil."

"Hold on. Let me look at the appointment book."

Catherine waited, trying to ignore the collective interest in the women supposedly working at their desks behind her had in this telephone call. She had heard quite clearly one of their remarks when she'd scared the UPS man out of his wits: "Somebody in this place is always throwing up or passing out."

"Good news and bad news," Mary Beth said when she came back on the line. "We've got a three-thirty cancellation, but it's with Clarkson. You know Clarkson? He's a good doctor, but he's kind of raw—doesn't care what he says. I have to resuscitate about three scandalized little old ladies a week."

"I've seen him before," Catherine said. She could hear the click of computer keys in the background.

"Is that a no?"

Catherine laughed. "No. Clarkson's fine. I feel too bad not to take whatever I can get."

"Okay. The computer says it's past time for your regular checkup. You want the works, or do you just want me to put you down as a problem?"

"I want the works, Mary Beth."

"You *are* feeling bad, aren't you? Okay, kiddo. We'll see you at three-thirty."

Catherine felt reasonably well for the rest of the day, and she was tempted to call back and cancel her appointment—except that "reasonably well" in this case was a far cry from "good."

She rushed to get from the school to the doctor's office on time, only to find that Clarkson was running behind schedule, because, she was advised privately, he was *always* running behind schedule. It took a long time for her to be called back to an examining room, and an even longer time for him to come in to see her.

"What's this with the fainting and the nausea?" he said as he opened the door, apparently feeling that they were beyond small talk and the social amenities.

"I don't know," Catherine said. "That's why I'm here."

"So how many times have you fainted?"

"Once . . . today."

"That's where you got the goose egg, I guess." He looked back at her chart, and Catherine reached up to touch her forehead. She did have a knot there.

"How long with the nausea?"

"About a week."

"You haven't been exposed to anything unusual, have you?"

"Just a peeled willow-tree root with chicken feathers stuck in it."

"That's not it," he said absently, as if patients reported similar exposures every day. He looked up at her. "Come again?"

"A willow-tree root from Grandmamma," Catherine said. "It's a charm."

"Well, it can't be that. She *likes* you. If she gave me a charm, I'd call the bomb squad." He frowned and flipped some pages in her chart. "Lot of winter viruses going around. You look like hell, by the way. You are definitely not your usual self. Mary Beth! Get your buns in here!"

"Dr. Clarkson, you do know that's no way to summon a fellow health professional, don't you?" Mary Beth said as she came in. She rolled her eyes at Catherine, and Clarkson grinned.

Catherine took a deep breath and gave herself up to the ordeal of being examined. There was a clock on the wall, apparently put there to take the patients' minds off their troubles—Mickey Mouse, whose eyes clicked back and forth to mark the seconds. It wasn't helping.

"Okay," Clarkson said at the end of his poking and prodding. He helped her get to a sitting position. "You been exposed to pregnancy?"

Catherine looked at him blankly.

"You know, Catherine. The Big Trick? Okay, read my lips. Have you had sexual intercourse with someone of the male persuasion within the last six or eight weeks?"

"Yes."

"Did you use an effective birth-control method?"

"Condoms."

"Then you could be pregnant."

"No I couldn't."

"Catherine, women have been saying that since the Virgin Mary—"

"I'm supposed to be barren."

He shrugged. "Famous last words, Catherine. The fertility of infertile people is what keeps us ob-gyn men humble. Besides that, there was no physiological reason for your not conceiving that I can see here in your record. Your husband is going to be one more happy—"

"You didn't read far enough," Catherine said. "I don't have a husband."

"No husband? Why do I get the feeling that you're leaving out all the good parts here? Okay, this is what we got. You throw up easy. You faint easy. You've got extreme fatigue. Your uterus is enlarged. Your breasts are tender and you haven't had your period. All of those things could be associated with a screwed-up menstrual cycle, particularly if we throw in one of these viruses that's been going around. But I don't think so, because you've got Chadwick's sign. Now, some doctors don't put too much stock in Chadwick's sign, but I'm not one of them. I'm going to have Mary Beth draw some blood for a beta sub blood test so we can be sure. Go ahead and get dressed and I'll send her in here." He paused. "What's the matter? You're not going to fall out again, are you?"

"I can't be pregnant," she repeated. Her heart was pounding and there was a roaring in her ears.

"Catherine, here, lie back." He made her lie down again. "Take some deep breaths." He fanned her solicitously with her chart while she tried not to retch.

"Clarkson?" she said after a moment.

"What, Catherine? You're not going to throw up on me, are you?"

"No . . . no, it's better." She sat up again, feeling Clarkson watching her closely, but she was all right now.

"You . . . really think I might be pregnant?"

"Didn't I say that? At the risk of having you keel over again—yes. I think you might be pregnant. This is how things work, Catherine. You lay down on the interstate, sooner or later you get run over by a car. You lay down with a man, sooner or later you get pregnant—particularly if you're in your prime and you're using a birth-control method that's only ninety percent effective. Now get your drawers back on. You can call us Monday morning and somebody will tell you what the blood test says and we'll go from there."

"Can't you get the results before Monday?"

"Nope. It's the weekend. The lab'll run a pregnancy test that's matter of life and death, but not yours."

"You could say it was a matter of life and death."

"Catherine, I thought I just heard you say you didn't have a husband. It's only until Monday morning. I think you need that long to get used to the possibility. Mary Beth will be in, in a minute."

Get used to the possibility. The phrase kept repeating in her mind. How could she get used to the possibility? She couldn't bear to think about it. It was as if her brain had completely shut down, the same way it had when Jonathan had moved out.

She left the doctor's office in a complete daze, driving the few miles into Wrightsville Beach and parking as she usually did near Johnnie Mercer's pier. She sat in the car for a moment, then got out and walked past the gazebo to the steep bank that led down to the beach. She stood there in the pale winter sunlight, staring out to sea until she could stand the thought of going home again. Alone.

17

She felt no happiness, no joy. Even a sense of anticipation was beyond her. What she felt was utter dismay. Pregnancy was the last thing she would have considered. She had been more prepared to hear that there was some shift in her blood counts, that her iron level was too low or her white count too high, and that she, like Pat, had some serious disease. One had only to pick up a magazine to read about how a troubled mind could make the body ill—and she'd certainly been troubled. She'd even seen enough diseases follow a sustained emotional trauma to believe in the likelihood of the mind-body link.

But she wasn't sick. She was "possibly" pregnant. "Likely" pregnant—if she could trust Clarkson's diagnostic skills.

She didn't dare trust them.

I can't be pregnant.

She stood naked and looked at herself in the mirror. Nothing was any different. Her abdomen was flat and smooth. Her breasts looked the same.

But her breasts hurt. When her nipples contracted from the cold, when she went outside or got out of the shower, they *hurt*. She'd never experienced that before. Never.

How could I be pregnant?

If she was, then it was more than just the fact that she'd had sexual intercourse. It was that she'd made tender love with a man, with Joe D'Amaro instead of Jonathan. Was she more compatible with him? Had she needed him more, responded to him more, opened herself to him like some hot-

277

house flower brought to bloom? Making a baby hadn't crossed her mind. It was Joe she'd wanted, just him and nothing more.

"I can't be pregnant," she said out loud.

Be careful what you want—because you might get it.

The thought came unbidden and in her grandmother's voice. How many times had she heard that when she was a little girl? She'd wanted a baby so badly. And to possibly have one *now* was one of life's little jokes, she supposed, the kind that Pat had talked about, the kind she'd experienced in her relationship with Don. A little cosmic sleight of hand to keep human beings from growing too arrogant, too secure in their existence.

My God, what would Jonathan say? Catherine—his barren, cast-aside wife—pregnant by her first and only lover?

She didn't think about what Joe might say, because she couldn't see herself telling him. He already had his family, his beloved Lisa's children. Given his troubles with Della, the last thing he needed was a bastard love child.

Then there was the matter of her job. She was supposed to help these pregnant girls. Being unmarried and pregnant herself was hardly setting any kind of example. Unfortunately, she had no difficulty seeing herself alone and unemployed.

God. She was getting used to the possibility, all right. She was behaving as if her pregnancy were a fact when she had two days to wait for the results of her blood test. More than two days.

She sighed. In the event that she was pregnant, she might as well practice what she preached.

She rummaged through her briefcase for a copy of a "dry" diet for the nausea of pregnancy—nothing fried, nothing spicy, no liquids until two hours *after* she'd eaten, then every hour or so until the next "dry" meal. If she really was pregnant, the diet would make the nausea better. If she *wasn't* pregnant, the diet also would make the nausea better. She wasn't going to prove anything by following it, except that she was somewhat in control of the situation. She had to do *something* to feel less like a victim and more in charge.

But, God, the waiting. How was she going to last until Monday morning? She didn't feel well enough to keep busy. She looked into the mirror again, not for signs of pregnancy this time but for signs that she was still a reasonably attractive woman. She didn't see any of those, either. No wonder Clarkson had said she'd looked like hell. She did.

She took a shower and washed her hair. She put on her best flannel nightgown and languished on the couch, spreading the pink-flowered afghan over her knees in much the same way Fritz would have done.

She watched television. She read. She didn't call Pat. If she called her, she wouldn't be able to keep from telling her about the possible pregnancy. She knew it would be easier in the long run if she went through the waiting alone. She was daring to hope, and she didn't want anyone to see her disappointment if Clarkson was wrong.

She picked up the gnomes. Gently smiling Daisy and almost sleeping Eric. She turned them around and around, looking at the daisies and the coin. She was in debt for gnomes and in debt for a car. But she didn't regret buying the gnomes.

"Are you responsible for this?" she whispered, gently touching Daisy's cheek with her fingertip, "or is it my peeled willow root with the chicken feathers?"

She wanted it, this "possibility." There was no need to pretend otherwise. She wanted it so much that she could only let her mind skirt the prospect in bits and pieces—a consequence here, a potentiality there. This time she couldn't fantasize her heart's desire the way she had in her early quest to become pregnant when she was still married to Jonathan. She didn't *dare* fantasize. She didn't dare hope that if life had ruled out the possibility of having Joe, she might somehow still be compensated by having his child.

She closed her eyes. She wanted this baby. Alone or not, employed or not, she wanted it.

She slept. When she awoke, it was well past midnight. She lay for a moment trying to think what had awakened her. The nausea was still there but not intensely so. Slowly she became aware of the dull ache in her lower abdomen, an ache that had always signaled the onset of her period. She carefully shifted her position. The ache didn't go away. She pulled a pillow around her and clutched it tight. The pain wasn't bad; it was just that perhaps it was significant. She lay very still, as if she could hide in the dark from yet another "possibility."

She awoke with the sun streaming into the room. The nausea was still there. And the ache. Both lasted through the day as she lived gingerly around them, expecting the worst.

But nothing happened—nothing new, at any rate. She seemed firmly entrenched in the status quo. All she had to do was wait.

On Sunday morning, she made her supreme breakfast effort: lightly buttered toast, crisp bacon, a hard-boiled egg, nothing to drink.

It stayed down. She was actually feeling better. Much better, except for a driving need to sleep. All day long she fought it off. She still had Sunday night to get through, and she didn't want to sleep all day and be awake all night.

In the afternoon she drove out to Wrightsville Beach, over

the Route 76 channel bridge and through the deserted downtown. She should have turned at Salisbury Street, parking as
she always did in front of the Silver Gull Motel close to
Johnnie Mercer's pier. But she didn't. It was too cold to walk
on the beach today. She continued north, all the way to the
dead end at Mason inlet, a route that took her past the
D'Amaro Brothers construction site. She drove by it slowly.
It, too, was windswept and deserted, as desolate-looking as
she felt.

She turned the car around at the end of the road, but she
didn't go home. She took the Masonboro Loop to Carolina
Beach Road, driving all the way into Carolina Beach. She
hardly recognized it anymore. A few of the older houses from
the fifties were still there, but the big, three-story wooden
apartment house that had sat in the middle of everything was
gone. She'd loved that place, and now she couldn't remember the name of it. It had porches on every story—with
an ocean view from the top one if she stood on tiptoe. An outside wooden staircase had zigzagged up the side of the
building, through the porches, and right past the double bedroom windows, so that if she went down them in the early
morning, she could see the guests sleeping in their beds. Old
men who'd been fishing all night. Soldiers on leave who'd
partied too long. Lovers all entwined.

She remembered the wonderful breakfast smells that came
from the apartments that housed the more energetic of the
early risers—coffee, country ham and bacon, and biscuits.
She'd been so happy then, in her halcyon days when time had
seemed to stretch without end in this wonderful place of sun
and ocean and overpriced souvenir shops. She'd loved the
seashell souvenirs, the ashtrays, the wind chimes, and what
she supposed now had been the world's tackiest table-size
night-lights. She had been in inlander's heaven, and all she'd

had to do was enjoy every second of it.

Now the place was filled with condos, the kind Joe hated building but built anyway.

Another memory surfaced. She'd been fourteen, letting herself bake in the sun while she listened to WAPE, out of Florida, on a transistor radio. At least once an hour they'd played "A Summer Place," and she'd lain on a gritty Army blanket, smelling of cocoa butter and baby oil, amusing herself, as she did even now, by watching the people around her. She'd turned on her side in her search from some small respite from the heat, and she saw a man and a woman sitting very close to each other on the sand. The woman wore a blue cotton dress and a big straw hat, and from time to time the man reached out to touch her. It wasn't the hungry, privileged touch of the other couples on the beach who were flagrantly "in love." It was something else, something special. She'd watched them for a long time, and when the woman finally stood up, she'd been quite obviously pregnant.

Catherine had never forgotten them, though the memory now made her wince. It was what she had wanted for herself—tenderness and loving support as she carried the child of the man she loved. The ultimate cruelty was that that kind of caring, in that special circumstance, existed, but that she'd never have it.

She drove back to Wilmington, shutting herself up in her apartment again. Whether or not she was better because of her afternoon drive, she couldn't say. By early evening it began to rain, a steady, gray drizzle that sent her already low spirits plummeting. She went to bed early. Perhaps the drive had been a good thing, after all, because she immediately fell asleep.

Her hands shook when she dialed the number. She took a

deep breath so her voice wouldn't shake as well. She waited while someone found Mary Beth and got her to the phone.

Her heart contracted at the sound of Mary Beth's cheerful voice.

"Catherine? Sit down, honey. The rabbit died," she said, using the old euphemism for a positive pregnancy test.

"It . . . died?" Catherine repeated, her voice nearly a whisper. She cleared her throat. "It died, Mary Beth?"

"Dead as a door nail. Says right here 'between six and eight weeks.' Congratulations."

Catherine closed her eyes, squeezing the telephone receiver tight. She knew the women in the office were looking at her and she had to get hold of herself. "Mary Beth, you're sure? There's no mistake?"

"Catherine, I'm holding the report in my hand."

"I want to hold it in *my* hand, Mary Beth. I'm coming over there right now."

Mary Beth laughed. "Catherine—"

"I'm coming, Mary Beth. I want to see it."

"Okay. Drive carefully, little mother."

She knew her request to see the lab report herself was a bit bizarre, but she couldn't help it. The receptionist was waiting for her when she arrived, and immediately sent her back to Mary Beth. The entire staff knew that she was a former infertility patient, and when she appeared at the nurses' station outside the examining rooms, they all stopped and gave her a slow round of applause. Catherine smiled, her eyes on Mary Beth and the blue-and-white computer form she had in her hands.

"Ta-da!" Mary Beth said, presenting Catherine with the form.

Catherine read her name. Her age. The date. The name of

the test. And finally the results.

She looked up at the group of women around her. "I'm pregnant," she told them quietly. *"I'm pregnant!"*

She threw back her head and laughed, accepting all the hugs and back-patting they wanted to give her.

And then she cried.

18

I miss her.

The thought kept repeating in his head, catching him unaware no matter what he was doing. For the first time in his life he wasn't thinking about Lisa.

I can't stand this.

It was seven in the morning, and he could waste time rationalizing the fact that he wanted to call Catherine, anyway, or he could just do it. Besides, the best time to catch her would be before she went to work.

He waited until Michael left the trailer before he dialed her number, but Michael came back too soon, and he hung up before she had a chance to answer. He picked up the phone again, annoyed with himself for behaving like a guilty schoolboy. He wanted to talk to Catherine, and he was going to do it.

This time she answered immediately.

"This is Joe," he said. "That was me just now. I'm sorry I hung up. I guess I . . . lost my nerve."

He waited, but she didn't say anything.

"Are you . . . all right?" he asked, glancing in Michael's direction. Michael was shaking his head.

"Yes, I'm all right," she said. "And you?"

"I'm . . ." he started, but he didn't go on with it. He didn't want tell her how he was. He shifted the receiver to his other hand and turned his back on Michael. "Look, can we go out someplace? I'll buy you dinner at the pub, how's that? Or it doesn't have to be there," he added quickly. "We can go wherever you—"

"No," she said.

She didn't even let him finish. Just "No."

"Catherine, I—"

"It's not a good idea, Joe. I can't go out with you."

"Can't?"

"Won't, then," she said.

She was so distant, almost cold. Except for the slight quiver in her voice, he would have believed she meant it.

"What's wrong, Catherine?"

"Nothing. I have to go now. I have to get to work."

"I could come by your place after work—"

"No. It'll be late when I get home. Thanks for calling."

She hung up.

He sat staring at the receiver. Thanks for calling? What the hell was "Thanks for calling"?

He looked up. Michael was watching.

"Don't start with me, Michael," he said, pointing in his brother's direction with the receiver. "You start with me and it's all over for you."

"Did I say anything? Jeez, I didn't open my mouth. Here, hang up the phone. This is a business, you know."

"Yeah, yeah." Joe dropped the receiver back in the cradle.

"So as long as you brought it up—" Michael began.

"I didn't bring up anything!"

"Sure you did. So, did Catherine—like they used to say in the old days—give you the air? I love that expression, 'give you the air.' "

"No, she didn't give me the air," Joe said irritably.

"Uh-*huh*. No air. What, then?"

"Michael, did it ever occur to you that this is none of your business?"

"Not with your kid coming to live at my house every

time I turn around, no."

"Once, Michael. Once."

"So what are you going to do?"

"What do you think? I'm going to go see Catherine. At lunchtime I'm going to go see her."

"Joey, you do that and Della's going to move out again."

"I told Della I still felt the same about Catherine. I told her that before she came back home. And I'm going to go see Catherine."

"I just hope you know what the hell you're doing," Michael said.

Joe hoped he knew what the hell he was doing too. He certainly felt better, having made the decision to see Catherine again. But the construction business didn't lend itself well to making plans. It was nearly one o'clock by the time he got to the school. Catherine was probably ready to start her afternoon class.

He took a chance, anyway, hoping that he could at least call her out for a minute. He walked down the long hallway to the classroom. Schools all smelled the same to him, regardless of what they were used for. This one. His old grammar school and the schools his children went to now. One he'd stopped at on a secondary road outside Wilmington that was being used as a furniture store.

He kept looking at the building structure as he walked along. It was well built, strong, solid. And it was probably filled with asbestos. He was going to have to say something to Catherine about that. Surely the building had been checked.

He stood outside her classroom door. He could see Catherine's desk, but it was empty. He moved so that he could see farther into the room. One of her students was fiddling with a television and putting a video into a VCR.

287

Catherine wasn't there. She hadn't been in the front office when he came in. Maybe she'd gone to the toilet. He leaned against the wall and waited, glancing at his watch. If he didn't get back soon, Michael was going to be fit to be tied.

"Hey, Joe!"

He looked up to find four pregnant girls gathered in the doorway, and it surprised him that they remembered his name

"Yeah," he said, grinning. "I'm looking for Ms. Holben."

"We know *that*," one of them told him. "She's not here."

"Where is she?"

"She went home sick. She's been sick a lot lately."

"Sick? I just talked to her."

"Yeah, well, maybe she don't tell you everything," another one said.

"What's *your* name?" he asked her.

"Maria," she answered, and her tone of voice dared him to make something of it.

He smiled. "Yeah, well, Maria, maybe you're right. If any of you see her before I do, tell her I was here."

"Hey," Maria called after him as he walked back down the hall. "You Ms. Holben's boyfriend?"

He turned around but he kept walking. "Yeah!" he called back. "I'm her boyfriend!"

At least he was, if he had anything to say about it. What was it with Catherine? The crazy way she'd hung up on him this morning, and now she'd gone home sick? Maybe she'd been sick then.

Catherine, what am I going to do with you?

Couldn't she tell him anything?

He made it into the Mayfair without having to show his driver's license. Mrs. Donovan was at home; he could hear

288

her television. But apparently she wasn't monitoring the front foyer today.

He climbed the stairs quickly, making a lot of noise in his work shoes on the bare steps. He had to pause briefly on the third landing. Catherine ought to be in good shape, making this climb a couple times every day.

He smiled to himself. She was in good shape, all right; he knew that personally. And, God, all he had to do was think about her and she got to him—sexually, emotionally. Every way a woman could get to a man. He hadn't seen her in weeks, and she was more a part of him than ever. So much for the out-of-sight, out-of-mind crap.

But Michael was probably right. Seeing Catherine was going to set Della off again. As far as he was concerned, it couldn't be helped. He missed Catherine, damn it all, and he wanted to know what was going on with her.

He knocked on her door, then waited. Nothing happened. He knocked again. She still didn't answer. He listened at the door. He couldn't hear anything. No movement, no music. Nothing.

He knocked louder, and the door across the hall opened.

"She's not *there*. She left a few minutes ago," a woman said testily.

"Thanks," he said.

He went back down the stairs, hesitating a moment before he knocked on Mrs. Donovan's screen door. The inner one opened immediately. Mrs. Donovan looked as if she had just had her hair done. It was all neatly waved, and she still had the hair clips in.

"You remember me, Mrs. Donovan? I'm looking for Catherine Holben. Her students told me she was sick."

"Yes, she came home sick, Mr. D'Amaro. But then she got

289

a call from the hospital. That sick friend of hers was asking for her."

"She went to the hospital?"

"That's what she said."

"You know which one?"

"She didn't say. I'd guess New Hanover, though. Catherine's going to ruin herself running around like she's been doing. Working at that school late and then off to that hospital all the time. Going to see sick people will wear you out, Mr. D'Amaro. There's nothing any worse than having somebody in the hospital. I've tried to tell her. Catherine, I said, you've got to look after your good health now if you want to have it when you're my age—"

"Mrs. Donovan, thanks," Joe said, interrupting, and he left the old woman still talking.

What sick friend? he wondered as he got back into the truck. Pat? It has to be Pat. Damn it all! He didn't have time to go to the hospital now.

Catherine sat in a straight chair by Pat's bed. She had come because Pat had asked for her, but now that she was here, Pat was sleeping. She was running a high fever and had been given something to make her rest. She slipped in and out of awareness, recognizing Catherine when she saw her and worrying about her whereabouts when she didn't. Several of the staff had suggested that Catherine move to the recliner in the room where she would be more comfortable, but she hadn't. She'd tried it earlier, but Pat couldn't see her as easily, and it squeaked every time she shifted her position, disturbing what little rest Pat was getting.

Catherine hadn't told Pat about the pregnancy; she hadn't told anyone. Another of life's incongruities: to have such special news and no one to tell.

"Catherine?" Pat said weakly.

"I'm here. Can I do something for you?"

"Some water."

Catherine picked up the Styrofoam cup with water in it and helped Pat drink from the straw.

"What time is it?" she asked after a moment.

"Oh . . . about five, I think."

"Morning or afternoon?"

"Afternoon."

"Oh. You came, didn't you?"

"Yes, I came."

"I've got an abscess in my lung. Did you know that?"

"Yes, someone told me."

"Better an abscess than the Big C, right? I think they're going to do something about it tomorrow. Something big-time . . ." She drifted off to sleep again, and Catherine stared out the window. It was nearly dark already. She was so tired, but she didn't want to leave until someone else came. People stayed with Pat all the time now, taking turns, women from her church and Catherine.

Catherine idly noted the hospital sounds around her. The big carts with the supper trays being dragged off the elevators. The chatter at the nurses' station. She wondered what Joe was doing. As it turned out, she'd told him the truth this morning, after all. She would be coming home late. She'd been so caught off-guard hearing his voice on the phone this morning; she'd thought the call would be something about Pat. She'd been so glad to hear from him—until the realization came that she absolutely could not see him. She wouldn't be able to stand it. It had been all she could do to keep from crying just talking to him on the phone.

"Catherine, I want to tell you something," Pat said abruptly.

I want to tell you something, too, Pat.

"What is it?"

But Pat closed her eyes again without answering.

Catherine waited, dreading the inevitable question about Don. Pat had indeed wanted him to come see her, but as yet no one had been able to locate him.

"Catherine . . ."

"I'm here."

"You know . . . I'm glad I didn't have children. I'm *glad* . . . do you understand?"

"No, Pat."

"You have to understand. You don't have children, either." Her hands twisted the covers. "Oh, I . . . forgot. You wanted . . . them." There was a long pause. "I . . . used to want them. You remember? I told you that."

"I remember."

"But now . . ."

Catherine waited, but Pat didn't say any more, sleeping again for a few moments.

Then she opened her eyes. "They wouldn't remember me," she said.

"Who, Pat?"

She frowned. "My children. My *children*. Don wouldn't let them remember me. He wouldn't let them come to me because I was dying. He wouldn't take them to the cemetery or anything like that after I was dead, would he?"

Catherine wanted to reassure Pat that she wasn't dying, but she didn't. Pat was very ill, and it wasn't a part of their deal to try to give false hope. "I don't know," she said instead. She didn't know. She understood next to nothing about Pat's relationship with her husband.

"Yes, you do. I told you what he's like. He wouldn't *let* them remember me. He'd let the waters of forgetfulness close over me. Isn't that poetic? The waters of forgetfulness? Hell, he'd hold my head under. Joe didn't do that with his wife, did he? His children remember her, don't they?"

"Yes," Catherine said.

"He made sure they'd never forget. What's the girl's name?"

"Fritz."

"No, the pain in the butt."

"Della."

"That's it. Della. I saw her name in the paper. Did I tell you that?"

"No, Pat."

"Did you see it?"

"No, I didn't see it."

"She was . . . something. Some kind of homecoming queen or something like that. Joe didn't tell you? No, I forgot. You can't see Joe, can you? But it was in the paper. Did you see it?"

"No," Catherine said again.

"Well, it said 'daughter of Joseph D'Amaro and . . . the late Mrs. D'Amaro,' or something like that. Don wouldn't do that. He wouldn't let them print 'daughter of the late Mrs. Bauer.' He'd have 'daughter of Donald and *Bimbo* Bauer'— period."

Catherine couldn't keep from laughing, and Pat laughed with her.

"No. It's true, Catherine. He wouldn't give me . . . credit for having anything to do with the children. So it's better we didn't have any. How could I rest for all . . . eternity knowing the bastard was doing something like that? I mean, I don't feel *well* enough to haunt the son of a bitch. Did I ask for him?" she asked abruptly.

"Any number of times."

"Oh, shit! I knew I would. Is he coming?"

"They . . . couldn't find him."

"Ah, well. He wouldn't come if they had. Catherine . . ."

"Don't you think you ought to rest?"

"No, I don't. I think I ought to . . . talk. That's what I had them call you for. So I can talk. I can't talk to those church women. I *like* them and all that, but I don't want to talk about cookies."

"Cookies?"

"Cookies, cookies," she said, gesturing with her hand and then letting it fall limply back on the bed. "First . . . they tell me I'm brave—and you and I know the truth about *that*— then they . . . tell me their cookie recipes. I have to spend half my time pretending I'm . . . in a coma."

Catherine looked away. She didn't know if this was more of Pat's black humor or if she knew how close her "comas" were to being an actual fact. They were trying a new antibiotic, and Catherine prayed that this one would help.

"Catherine," Pat said again. "I lied."

"So what," Catherine said. She pulled her feet up in the chair and propped her head in her hand on the edge of the bed.

"No, now don't stonewall me, Catherine."

"I'm not stonewalling you. I just said 'so what.' " But she was stonewalling. She didn't want to hear any dark confessions, not with her mind already so filled with problems of her own.

"I'm trying to tell you this," Pat said impatiently.

"Okay. Tell me."

"It's about the bimbo. She's not really a bimbo. She's very smart. Educated. Like me."

Catherine smiled. "Like you, huh?"

"Yes, like me. I don't have time for false modesty. She's

294

smart and I'm smart. You know why?"

"Why?"

"Because that's the way Don is. He wants a woman he can feel inferior to."

"I see."

"I doubt it," Pat said, chuckling. "But it's true. He likes a woman who's smarter than he is—some unresolved something with his . . . mother, don't you think?"

Catherine didn't answer and Pat drifted off to sleep again. Several young women from the dietary staff rolled a huge cart near the door and began to unload trays. Pat jumped as one of them dropped a glass.

"What is that?" she asked worriedly.

"Just your supper coming."

"I don't want any supper. You tell them."

"I will—after you see what it is. Maybe taste a little something."

"Catherine, you are a pain."

"I know."

"I keep forgetting you're a damn nurse."

"I know."

"Damn nuisance . . ."

"I know," she and Pat said together, and they laughed. Pat's laughter abruptly faded.

"I wish I were like you," she said. "You don't know what you're like, do you?"

"Tell me."

"You're like . . . Nietzsche."

"Nietzsche? Oh, great. Nietzsche went insane, Pat."

"Not at first he didn't. At first he was . . . informed."

"Informed," Catherine said, thinking that perhaps Pat's mind really was wandering.

"He knew about life. He said to consider every day lost on

which we have not danced. That's you, Catherine. Always dancing on the day. Now me, I dance, too . . . but the music's . . . wrong. I'm always . . . dancing to yesterday's waltz. You know who else does that? Joe D'Amaro. And it's the wrong thing to do. You have to look at where you *are* instead of looking back. Your dance and your music have got to fit *today*. You made Joe hear a different song, Catherine. Don't let that kid of his . . . run you to ground now. Joe needs you. It's scary out there on the ballroom floor when you don't know what you're supposed to do. . . ."

The girl from the kitchen came in with the supper tray, and the smell of the food made Catherine's stomach lurch. She turned away for a moment, fighting down the nausea that threatened to overwhelm her.

"I don't want anything," Pat said. "Really I don't."

"Just look," Catherine said, forcing herself to lift the lid. Liver and bacon. Rice. And greens. Oh, God.

"No," Pat said.

"There's a fruit salad."

"I'll . . . try that."

Catherine fed her the fruit, moving the plate with the liver to the food cart out in the hall. Afterward Pat slept again, worn out by their long conversation and the effort to do some justice to her evening meal. Catherine still sat by the bed, listening to Pat's breathing, watching her sleep and wondering how much of her observations about Nietzsche and the dancing had been hers and how much had been the fever and the sedative.

Don't dance to yesterday's waltz. Catherine thought it made sense in a wacky sort of way. But she wasn't as good at dancing on the day as Pat thought. It hadn't been easy to relegate Jonathan to the past where he belonged. Now she was going to have to do the same thing with Joe.

One of the women from the church came to take Catherine's place shortly before seven. Catherine wanted to tell her to forgo the cookie recipes, but she didn't.

Pat roused enough for Catherine to say good-bye, but not enough for her to be tempted to tell her about her pregnancy.

"Don't forget what I said," Pat whispered.

"I won't."

"You have to do something about Joe."

I think I've already done it, she thought, but she didn't say anything else, hesitating until she was sure that Pat had drifted back to sleep. She quietly left the room, taking a deep breath once she was in the hallway. God, she was tired. Her head hurt and she felt like throwing it back and bawling. For Pat. For herself.

She put on her coat and took the elevator down. Joe was standing by the receptionist's desk in the lobby. There was no chance at all that he hadn't seen her.

"Catherine, wait. Wait!" he called to her when she turned to get back on the elevator. He caught up with her before the doors closed.

"We have to talk," he said. "I'm not leaving until we do." He had her cornered, and she couldn't get away from him. He looked so good to her. He'd come straight from work, and he needed a haircut, and he looked so good.

Her eyes met his. She had to force herself not to look away. "Not now, Joe. I really don't feel up to it."

She could feel him assessing whether or not she was telling the truth.

Apparently he decided that she wasn't.

"Come on," he said, making her walk with him across the lobby to a small alcove among some plants. "Sit down."

She wouldn't sit, and he reached up to stroke her face.

"You're going to have to talk to me, Catherine. That's all there is to it."

"We can't see each other anymore," she said, trying to move out from under his touch. "Ever." She was trembling, and she prayed he wouldn't see it.

"Why can't we?"

"Della—"

"Leave Della out of it. Why can't we?"

"Because we can't!"

"Why!"

"I don't—" She was going to say that she didn't care anything about him, but he was looking into her eyes and she couldn't do it. She tried to walk away from him but he caught her arm.

"Tell me now. Tell me to my face."

She could feel her eyes welling. She opened her mouth to say something, but, oh, God, she was going to cry instead.

"Catherine . . ."

He pulled her roughly into his arms and she sagged against him. She'd been alone so long, worrying so long! Her arms went around him, and she clung to him as if she were a frightened, lost child.

"What is it? Are you sick?" he whispered urgently. "Tell me!"

"Oh, God, Joe," she said, every bit of the misery she was feeling evident in her voice.

"Catherine, tell me!"

"I'm pregnant, Joe. I'm pregnant!"

Pregnant! Pregnant!

He understood her. He understood perfectly. A rash of questions flooded his brain and every damn one of them wrong.

Are you sure?

Of course she's *sure,* dumb-ass! Would she be crying like this if she wasn't sure?

How can you be pregnant!

Oh, hell, he knew *how.* He'd enjoyed every second of the *how.* Even a dumb-ass like him could figure that out.

Is it mine?

No—God, no, don't say that!

Please, don't let me say the wrong thing!

She leaned back to look at him, hitting him once in the chest with her fist. "*Say* something!" she whispered fiercely.

She wasn't being fair about this, and he thought she knew it. Sudden, impending fatherhood wasn't the kind of news a man could take all at once, especially in the middle of a hospital lobby.

He said the only thing left in his mind. "I love you, Catherine."

But apparently that was the wrong thing too. She covered her eyes with her hand and cried harder.

He realized that people were looking at them. "Come on, let's get out of here," he said, putting his arm around her and walking her outside. She held her head down and was still crying. Other people were coming into the hospital, and they stared at both of them curiously. "My truck's down here. How were you going to get home? Did you call a cab?"

She shook her head. "I . . . bought . . . a car."

A car? he thought. Damn, she was full of news tonight.

He stopped walking and put his arms around her, holding her, just holding her and not caring that they were clearly visible under the lights in the parking lot. "Don't cry," he said. "We're going to work this out." The night was cold, and the words came out in white clouds.

"I don't want to work it out," he thought she said.

He kissed her cheek, her neck. *Don't cry, baby. Don't—*

"I don't want to work it out," she said quite clearly.

He held her away from him so he could see her face. "What do you mean you don't want to work it out?" For a split second he thought she meant an abortion or something crazy like that.

"I don't want anything from you."

"Well, that's tough, Catherine. This is my baby too. You can't expect me just to do nothing." *My baby too.* He realized as he said it how quickly he'd come from total disbelief to total acceptance. He loved her—and she was having his kid.

"That's exactly what I expect you to do," she said, finding that calm voice he hated. "Nothing."

"I love you," he told her again. "Did you hear me say that? I love you!"

"Well, I love you too," she said, as if that had absolutely nothing to do with what they were talking about.

"Catherine, this is making me crazy here—"

"Me, too, Joe! Don't you understand? I'm so . . . tired. I'm upset! I just can't take any more. This baby is important to me. I don't want anything to happen to it. I can't take any more!" She was crying again.

"Come on," he said. "You're coming with me."

"I've got . . . a car here."

"I'm not letting you drive yourself home, damn it! You just said you were upset! We'll get your car later."

"Joe—"

"Catherine, please. You're pregnant. Don't make me have to pick you up and carry you."

He hurried her along the rest of the way, and he opened the door for her to get into the truck, breathing a sigh of relief when she did.

"Did you mean what you said?" he asked when he got in on the other side. She sat forlornly on the seat—as far away from him as she could get.

"What?" she asked, sniffing loudly.

"You love me or don't you?" He started the truck and pulled out into the street. He could feel her looking at him, and he was thankful that he had something to do while he waited for her to answer.

"You . . . represent a lot of problems," she said vaguely.

"Do you or don't you!"

"Yes! But I can't cope with all the problems you represent, Joe. I told you. I don't want anything to happen to this baby."

"Is that why you're running yourself to death going to the hospital to see Pat? Mrs. Donovan said you weren't taking care of yourself."

"Pat asked for me, Joe. I had to go."

"Yeah, you had to go. And look at you—"

"Don't tell me I look like hell!"

"You don't look like hell," he said gently. "You look beautiful. You also look worn-out. Catherine—"

"Joe, I know how important your children are to you. Your first responsibility is to the ones you already have. You're going to have to trust me with this one. I'll love this child—I already do. And I'll take care of it. By myself. Do you understand? By myself!"

19

Joe made himself keep quiet. He understood. She was exhausted and she was pregnant. He still wanted to shake her. But he understood.

"I'm going to take you home," he said, and she nodded. It was several blocks before she realized that it was *his* home he meant.

"Joe—" she began.

"Catherine, you're going to have to humor me with this. I'm worried about you. You had to go home sick today."

"I went home pregnant today," she said. "There's a difference."

He reached out to take her hand. "I want you to eat something, and then I want you to lie down for a while. And when you feel better, we'll talk."

"There's nothing to talk about."

"I think there is. If you don't have anything to say, then you can listen. I have enough to talk about for the both of us."

"Joe—"

"Catherine, don't fight me on this. Just come home with me. Fritz is there. She's missed you. If you won't do it for me, do it for her—and for the baby you're carrying. Let me look after you for just a little while. Please."

"What about Della?" she asked.

"Della's spending the night with some girlfriends—a birthday slumber party."

She looked over at him and then back at the passing

scenery, and he had the feeling that he hadn't answered her question.

"Catherine, Della knows how I feel about you. She knows I haven't changed just because she left home. You said just now I had to trust you to take care of the baby that's coming. Well, you have to trust me to know what to do about Della."

She was silent for a long time. "All right," she said finally. He barely heard her, but he didn't ask her to repeat it on the off chance that he'd misunderstood.

He kept glancing at her as he drove. She looked so . . . defeated, as if she'd given in simply because she didn't have the strength to resist anymore. He hadn't meant to bully her, but he wasn't about to dump her at the Mayfair and just go home. They had a problem, and they were going to work on it together.

"I forgot it was so close to Christmas," she said when he turned down his street. Nearly every house had Christmas lights burning outside.

"Wait until you see the D'Amaros'," he said. "Fritz went wild." He squeezed her cold fingers, feeling her tenseness. He didn't want her to be so upset and worried. Everything would be all right. It had to be.

"They're nice," she said of the lights when he pulled into the driveway.

"Anything that doesn't move, Fritz wants lights on it, so don't stand in one place too long, especially if you're in the yard."

She smiled, not the best attempt he'd ever seen but not too bad.

"Wait," he said when she started to get out of the truck. "Come here just for a minute." He put his arms around her, pulling her closer to him. He didn't hold her tightly; she could get away from him if she wanted. But, thank God, she didn't seem to want to.

"You're not going to forget what you promised me, are you?"

"Joe—"

"No, now you promised me you wouldn't give up. I'm holding you to it." He gave her a gentle hug. "Let's go. I see Fritz peeking out the window."

He walked with her across the yard, guiding her in the dark on the safest route to the back door. Fritz opened the door for them, her eyes lighting up at the sight of Catherine. She stood in the doorway, unsure of what she should do.

"Hey," Joe said kindly. "You going to let us in or are you going to be like Mrs. Donovan and make us show you our driver's licenses?"

She giggled and stepped back. "I'm surprised, Joe!"

He grinned and ruffled her hair. "Yeah, I can tell. Where's your brother?"

"Computering," Fritz said. She still couldn't believe her eyes. Joe had brought Catherine. It wasn't even Christmas, and this was the best Christmas present ever!

"Give me your coat," Joe said to Catherine.

"I can hang it up," Fritz offered, taking Catherine's coat and hanging it on a hanger in the hall closet. She had a little trouble getting the hanger hooked, but she managed. When she came back into the kitchen, Catherine was still standing in the same place. Fritz looked at her closely, her stomach getting a sinking kind of feeling she recognized at once. It was the very worst kind of feeling, the kind for no reason, only there *was* a reason somewhere, and that reason was going to make everybody feel bad.

"Well," Joe said brightly, "Catherine, you sit down here and Fritz and I will fix you something to eat."

"I'm not really hungry," Catherine said.

"Just a little something. You'll feel better."

Fritz looked from one adult to the other. Something was wrong, all right. Catherine looked like she wanted to cry, and Joe wasn't acting like himself at all.

"I can make toast," she offered, and they both looked at her in relief.

"That's sounds like a good idea, Fritz. Catherine, what do you think?" Joe looked into Catherine's eyes, and Fritz could see what else he wanted to tell her but didn't. *Please.*

She thought that Catherine saw it too.

"Yes," Catherine said, reaching out to rest her hand on Fritz's shoulder. "That would be just the thing."

"Sit down, Catherine," Joe said again. This time he pulled out a chair.

Catherine sat down, but Fritz didn't think she wanted to very much.

Fritz went to the sink and carefully washed her hands the way Joe had taught her, and then she got out the bread for the toaster. She kept casting furtive glances at Joe and Catherine. Joe reached out once to touch Catherine's face, and Fritz thought that Catherine was going to cry for sure.

She didn't want Catherine to cry. She made the very best toast she knew how to make, cutting it carefully from one corner to the other and putting the butter on just right—not too juicy, not too dry.

"Thank you, Fritz," Catherine said, giving her a small hug when she put the plate with the toast on the table in front of her. "This is just what I need."

Fritz gave a small sigh and stepped back, looking at Joe for some kind of explanation for this worried feeling she was having. It was getting worse and worse. She had felt Cathcrine trembling when she'd given her the hug, trembling like the new gerbil they'd gotten in her class at school, trembling like she was cold or scared.

"Catherine has a friend who's very sick," Joe said. "She's in the hospital. Catherine's been staying with her this evening, and she's tired."

"Oh," Fritz said, wondering why knowing this didn't make her feel any less worried.

"What do you want to drink?" Joe asked Catherine. "Milk?" he asked when she didn't say.

"Nothing right now," she said. "Just the toast. Maybe later."

Joe and Catherine were talking with their eyes again, but this time Fritz couldn't tell what they said.

Catherine ate her toast, and Fritz sat down at the table with her.

"So what have you been doing?" Catherine asked her after a while.

"Oh, nothing much," Fritz said. She looked at Joe. He was watching Catherine.

"I'm in the Christmas pageant," Fritz said, remembering Catherine might like to hear about that.

Catherine smiled. "What are you going to be? I was a *T* one time—the *T* in Christmas."

"I have to be a wise person," Fritz said.

"A wise person?"

"Yeah, we didn't have enough boys in the class to be Joseph—and the shepherds, and the innkeeper, and *all* the wise men, too—so I have to be one. Only Charlie says I'm not a wise *man*, because I'm a girl. Charlie says it's a very bad case of miscasting and I should fire my agent. We had to cut Caesar Augustus out."

"Ah, well," Catherine said, "I'll bet it'll still be nice."

"Can you come and see me? It's on Christmas Eve."

"I don't know about that, Fritz."

Her heart sank. "It's all right if you can't," Fritz said quickly, trying to keep her disappointment from showing. The church was so beautiful at Christmastime—with the tree and the candles and the holly and evergreen branches. She could close her eyes and see it, smell it. All her life she'd wanted to peek out from behind the curtains and see a mother among all those smiling faces in the audience at the Christmas pageant. Catherine was as close to a mother as she would ever get. Catherine was almost one. She knew in her heart of hearts that Catherine was almost one. And she knew what that kind of answer meant. It meant no, only Catherine didn't want to come out and say it.

Joe and Catherine were looking at each other again. He reached out and took her hand.

"Come on," he said. "I'll show you where you can lie down."

"Joe, this really isn't such a good idea—"

"Catherine, let's don't beat a dead horse, okay? Come on."

She got up reluctantly from the table, but she stopped trying to say no. Joe thumped Fritz lightly on top of her head, the way he did sometimes when he was close enough and he wanted to get her attention.

"Fritz, if there's anything on my bed, run and clear it off, will you? We're going to let Catherine rest here with us for a while. Maybe take a nap if she can."

Fritz looked up at him. She couldn't believe it! Catherine was going to stay! Maybe it wouldn't be for long and maybe she wouldn't be awake, but it was still great.

She hurried on ahead of them to check Joe's bed, knowing what she would find—blueprints, blueprints, and more blueprints. He was always studying blueprints after he went to bed. He had more homework than she and Charlie and Della put together.

Fritz suddenly had an idea, a really good idea, but she gathered up the blueprints carefully in spite of her need to implement it. She'd learned before she could walk not to be reckless around her father's blueprints.

"That's good, Fritz," Joe said in the doorway. Then he smiled at Catherine. "Don't worry. Just sleep for a little while."

"I don't think I can," Catherine said. She sat down on the edge of the bed, as if she didn't know if she was in the right place or not and someone might come and tell her to move.

"Just try," Joe said. "Hand me the quilt, Fritz."

Fritz got the quilt from the back of the rocking chair in the corner of the room, and Joe carefully spread it over Catherine as she kicked off her shoes and lay down. Then he arranged her pillows for her, as if she were a little girl like Fritz instead of a grown-up woman.

"Catherine—" Joe began, and though Fritz knew better than to interrupt, she couldn't help it.

"Joe!" she whispered into his ear. "Can I do something for Catherine?"

"What, Fritz?"

"It's a surprise."

"Catherine needs to rest, Fritz."

"I'll hurry, Joe. Please!"

Fritz could see the no forming on his lips, but for some reason he changed his mind. "How long will it take?"

"That long," she said, trying to snap her fingers the way he did when he wanted to show her how quickly something would happen—Santa Claus coming, the duration of the shot she might have had to have for her sore throat the other day. It wasn't much of a snap but he understood.

"Okay," he said.

"You have to come and help me."

"*I* have to help? I thought this was *your* surprise."

"I don't want to push my luck."

He grinned. "Very wise, small daughter. Catherine, excuse us for just a minute—maybe not even that long."

"Don't go to sleep yet, Catherine," Fritz said. "I'm going to hurry!"

"We're going to hurry," Joe told her, too, as Fritz dragged him off to the kitchen.

Catherine closed her eyes, trying not to cry again. He was being so good to her. She hadn't planned to tell him about the baby and certainly not to do it in some fit of hysterics in the middle of a hospital lobby.

"*I love you, Catherine*"—that was the best thing he could have said to her, and the worst. She had thought him impetuous at best, hotheaded, yelling first and regretting it later. But he wasn't doing that now. He was giving her what she needed, a little time to relinquish her responsibilities to herself and everyone else—except their baby. It felt so good being here.

What kind of man are you, Joe? How many times had she asked herself that?

She opened her eyes, looking around the room as if she might locate some clue, but this neat room, save the stacks of blueprints, told her nothing. The blueprints were the only things in it that might be described as personal. There were no collectibles, no trophies, no pictures of Lisa.

She looked around at a small sound. Joe was standing at the foot of the bed. She moved over so that he could sit down beside her, and he looked so resigned. It was if he presumed nothing, expected nothing from her except pain, the same kind of pain he'd gotten from Lisa.

She wanted to cry again. She didn't want to hurt him, and there was nothing she could do about it. She looked into his eyes, probing for the truth in all this. Did he love her? Yes, she thought, perhaps he did.

"You know," he said quietly, "I think I'm getting the hang if it."

"Of what?"

"Knowing what people mean instead of listening to what they say."

His hair was mashed down over his ears from wearing a hard hat all day, and she wanted to reach up and run her fingers through it, for no other reason than to have some excuse to touch him. She wanted to put her arms around him so badly; she wanted to hold him and hold him until they both felt better.

"Like now," he added.

"I meant what I said."

"I know you did, but when you look at me—" He stopped, taking her hand and sliding his warm, rough fingers between hers instead of saying whatever was on his mind. He sat there, looking at her with all the desperation she herself felt.

"What?" she asked.

"When you look at me, I think you . . . care about me. I see it. I feel it. You care and that's what's behind the things you say. It makes all the difference in the world in whether or not I can stand it."

"Joe—"

"I hear Fritz coming," he said, interrupting her. "I hope you're up to this. She has her heart set on doing something special for you."

"What is it?"

"You'll see."

Fritz was coming into the bedroom. She carried a red metal lap tray with brass-colored folding legs. The tray had a picture of children riding a merry-go-round on it, and in the center of it sat a thick white mug filled with hot chocolate with a big scoop of vanilla ice cream.

"Just like when you were a little girl," Fritz said, carrying the tray carefully. "With the ice cream and everything." Joe helped her put it over Catherine's knees.

"Fritz, thank you," Catherine said. "It is just like when I was a little girl. The mug is the very same."

Fritz beamed under Catherine's approval. "Wait!" she said, taking a carefully folded paper towel off the tray and putting it on Catherine's chest. "We're out of napkins."

"This is fine," Catherine assured her.

"Are you sure you're up to this?" Joe asked as she took a sip.

She nodded and drank some more. "Fritz, you did a good job. It's wonderful."

"Joe helped me cook the milk in the microwave, so we could do it fast."

Catherine drank the rest of her hot chocolate with both of them looking on. Fritz to make sure that she drank all of it, and Joe, she supposed, to make a grab for the wastepaper basket in case her nausea asserted itself.

But she managed without incident.

"Take the tray away, Fritz," Joe said, handing it to her.

"Wait," Catherine said. "Let me give you a hug." She hugged Fritz tightly, savoring her warmth and her little-girl smell. She loved this child. Joe's child.

"Me too," Joe said when Fritz had left with the tray.

Catherine hesitated a moment then wrapped her arms around him the way she'd wanted to do earlier. He gave a soft moan, and she closed her eyes, afraid suddenly that she might never have the opportunity to do this again. He felt so good to her!

"Don't forget your promise," he reminded her again.

311

"You're not going to give up on us." He leaned back to look at her. "Now try to sleep, just for a little while. Is the hot chocolate going to stay put or not?"

"So far so good," she said. She was a bit surprised at the question—until she remembered that he'd been through three other pregnancies. Apparently he was used to these things. Irrationally she felt a stab of jealousy that what was entirely a new experience for her was for him merely routine.

"Well, thank God for that. I'll be around out here if you want anything. Catherine?"

She looked into his eyes, waiting for him to go on, but he didn't.

"Ah, nothing," he said. "It'll keep."

He kissed her lightly and gave her one last hug before he stood up. She could feel that he was lingering, that he wanted to talk now rather than later. But he turned off the lamp and went out, leaving the door slightly ajar. Catherine stretched out on the bed and closed her eyes, lying quietly in the soft darkness of the bedroom. She wished she'd made him lie down with her and hold her while she tried to sleep. She was so tired. And though her mind and her body felt numb, he mattered to her, he was the only thing in all this that seemed real. He was the reason she was here.

She let herself drift on the edge of sleep, rousing once at some outside sound—the wind, she decided. And she fell asleep, wondering if—no, knowing—that if she called out to him, he would come.

She woke up at the sound of voices, muffled voices that grew louder and louder. She sat up, not knowing at first where she was. Then she realized it was Joe's voice she was hearing. She rubbed her eyes in an effort to wake up.

". . . *you* are the child here. I don't have to give any kind of account for my behavior to you," he was saying.

She couldn't hear the response.

". . . if I'd done anything," he said next. "If I was hiding anything, I wouldn't have told you Catherine was here."

"You've got that woman in your bed!" Catherine heard quite clearly.

Oh, God, she thought, trying to get her shoes on. Della. The last thing in this world she needed was Della.

She hurried toward the kitchen, looking for Fritz along the way, hoping that Joe had banished her upstairs.

Only Joe and Della were in the kitchen. Della still had her coat on. The tray with the merry-go-round sat on the kitchen table.

"You!" Della cried, turning on Catherine immediately. "What kind of woman are you? You don't care! You don't even *care* that Fritz is here!"

"Della, that's enough!" Joe said. "I told you why Catherine is—"

"I don't believe you, Daddy!"

"Then that's *your* problem! I don't lie to my children. I never have!"

"That was before, Daddy. *Before* you got hooked up with a bitch like her!"

Catherine thought Joe was going to hit her. He had Della by both shoulders, but then he suddenly let go.

"I want you to sit down here! I'm going to tell you this one time—"

"I don't want to hear what you say!" Della yelled at him. "It's not you talking! It's her! You'll say what she tells you to. I know what she's told you about me—"

"Catherine hasn't told me anything about you. As far as I know, you haven't seen her since the barbecue, and it was Mrs. Webber who filled me in on *that* piece of work. Have you

313

and Margaret had another one of your little talks with Catherine that I don't know about?"

Della chose not to answer him.

"Catherine, have you talked to Della since the barbecue?" Joe abruptly asked her.

She looked into his eyes, hating this situation, and hating even more that she was the reason for it. "Yes."

"When, for God's sake!"

"It doesn't matter, Joe—"

"It matters to me! What happened here? Did you two get together and decide how things were going to be and just leave me the hell out of it? Don't I have anything to say about anything?"

"Everything was all right until she started hanging around!" Della put in, as if to keep her grievance in the spotlight.

"Catherine has nothing to do with the way you're behaving now!"

"Please!" Catherine said loudly, and both of them turned to look at her. She was feeling light-headed, and she grasped the back of one of the kitchen chairs to steady herself. "Joe, I want to go. Now. I can't . . ." She didn't finish the sentence, losing her train of thought in a wave of dizziness.

"Catherine, we have to talk. Della, where are you going!"

Della was already out the back door, Joe right behind her.

Catherine could hear him calling her as he ran down the drive, and then she heard the sputter of gravel and a car being driven fast.

She tried to walk to the window to see, but her legs wouldn't hold her. She had to sit down at the kitchen table instead.

I can't stand this, she thought, putting her head in her hands. *I can't.*

She started at a sudden hand on her shoulder—Fritz, with tears streaming down her face, worried little Fritz locking her arms around her neck and holding on tight.

20

Fritz waited at the top of the stairs. She heard Joe come back—alone—but the light didn't come on in the kitchen, and she couldn't hear him anymore. She knew that things were bad; maybe they were bad enough for him to start sitting in the dark again. She felt so worried!

She went down a step, trying to decide what to do, sighing heavily as she strained to hear something, *anything*, that would tell her what Joe was doing.

Nothing. That's what he was doing. *Nothing*. She was just going to have to go down there. Joe had told her to go upstairs when Della was there. Della was gone now, so it could be that it was all right for her to come down again.

"Fritz!" Charlie whispered from the top of the stairs, making her jump.

"Shh!" she said to him, putting her finger over her lips to show him there should be no talking, the way she'd had to do when she was in the first grade.

"What's going on?" he whispered, anyway.

"I don't know. I'm going to go see."

"Fritz!" Charlie whispered again, but she kept going. She couldn't stand this not knowing. It was just how she was.

She walked as quietly as she could—in case she could tell how mad Joe was by looking at him, and she decided not to disturb him. Of course, he'd said she could disturb him anytime she needed to, and that was some comfort. She certainly needed to. She wasn't crying now, but she still felt like it, and she wanted to know what was happening. Mostly she wanted

Catherine to come back, and she was afraid that Catherine would never come here again. She really couldn't blame her. All the D'Amaros ever did was make Catherine feel bad. First it was Joe, until he learned to like her better. Then it was Della, and who knew what would happen with Della? As far as Fritz knew, only she and Charlie had liked Catherine right from the first and still did.

It was so confusing! She was just going to have to ask, and that was all there was to it.

She stood in the kitchen doorway. The outside Christmas lights were still on, and they helped her see that Joe was sitting at the kitchen table.

But his back was to her. She didn't want to barge right in—what if he was crying like he used to when he felt sad about Lisa? She didn't want to sneak up on him. If he *wasn't* mad, that would just about do it.

He suddenly turned around and saw her standing in the doorway.

"Fritz, it's late. What are you still doing up?"

He didn't sound mad exactly, but she wasn't getting a warm welcome, either. She was just going to have to tell him what was on her mind.

"Is Catherine like Brenda?" she asked point-blank, because that was what she wanted to know and there was no use beating around the bush about it.

"What?"

Joe was frowning. She couldn't see it, but she could hear it in his voice.

"Is Catherine like Brenda?" she repeated.

"Fritz, I don't know what you mean."

She used the same expression Charlie used when there was cake enough for everybody on Sunday and she couldn't find a crumb of it on Monday. "Here today and gone tomorrow."

He didn't answer her.

"Joe—" she said, and to her dismay her voice locked up on her the way it had that night at Catherine's house. She was going to cry again, and she just hated it.

"Come here, Fritz," he said, and she didn't hesitate, running the short distance to get to him.

"Fritz . . ." he began as he took her on his lap, but she didn't want him to make her stop crying. She wanted an answer to her question.

"Don't you like Catherine anymore? I didn't think Catherine was like Brenda, but now I can't tell."

"Don't cry."

"I—can't—help it—"

"Listen to me. . . . Are you listening?"

"Trying—" she managed.

"I want to tell you this. Not many people know it."

"What?"

"I still like Catherine, Fritz. But I don't just like her. I love her. You understand? I guess nobody knows it except Catherine. And maybe Uncle Michael."

Fritz sniffed heavily. "And Della?"

"Yes. I've told Della. But I don't think she believes it."

"I believe it," she said.

"Yeah, I thought you would."

"I love Catherine too." Just like a mother, she'd almost said, but she was afraid that Joe wouldn't want to hear that. "Can't Catherine come stay with us?" *We could be like a family.*

"Not the way things are now, Fritz."

"Why not?"

She didn't get an answer to that question because a car turned into the driveway. Joe set her down and went to open the door and turn on the outside and kitchen lights. She knew that he was hoping it was Della, but it wasn't. It was Uncle Michael. She could see him when he came under the carport light on his way to the back door.

Joe looked at her, giving her a signal with his thumb that she was to get herself back upstairs.

She sighed heavily. She didn't want to go!

"Beat it," Joe told her, not in his mad voice but in a voice that let her know that she had no choice.

She lingered as long as she dared, hoping to hear something she could discuss with Charlie when she got upstairs. For once Charlie was more interested in what was happening in the family than what was happening on his computer.

Uncle Michael came in the back door, making enough noise for two or three people. He wasn't in a good mood, either.

"I want to know one goddamn thing!" he yelled. "What the hell is going on *now!*"

Fritz scooted up the stairs, surprised, because she'd wanted to know that very thing herself.

Your wife is two thirds of what is going on. Your persistent, jealous wife, who can't stand it because I won't . . .

Joe wanted to say it. He wanted to say all of it, but he didn't.

Ah, Catherine.

It was for her that he worked so hard to hang on to his temper. He was going to deal with his frustration straight on, the way she did. He had already been through what was turning out to be one of the worst nights of his life, and he wasn't going to make it any worse.

If he could help it.

He moved past Michael to sit back down at the kitchen table.

"You want something to drink?" he asked him, stalling to

give himself time to get some kind of grasp on his emotions.

"No, I don't want anything to drink! I want—"

"Is Della at your place?" he said, cutting in. He thought she was. Prayed she was.

"Yeah, yeah—where else would she be?"

Where indeed? Joe thought.

"So what happened?" Michael said. "Did she catch you doing it?"

"Is that what she told you?"

"Look, Joey. All's I know is Della is at my house in hysterics. Something about a woman in your bed?"

"That was Catherine," he said mildly.

"She still here?"

"No, I took her home. I wanted her to stay, but she wouldn't do it. This is all too much for her."

"Too much for *her*?"

"It wasn't what you think, Michael. Or what Della thinks." Or what Margaret *wants* her to think.

He got up from the table because he suddenly knew what he needed to do. He'd given all the explanation he intended to give.

"Joey, where are you going!"

"I'm going to get my daughter, Michael. Tell Fritz and Charlie I'll be back in a little while."

He didn't expect Margaret to open the door for him, but she did. She was dressed in a tight, short skirt. She stood with her hands on her hips, her carefully cultivated bright red fingernails very evident against the black fabric of the skirt.

"Well," she said lightly, "I didn't expect to see you."

"Where's Della?" he asked, and though she stood back to give him room to come inside, he didn't. He wasn't taking any chances with Margaret until he knew that someone else was on the premises—not with Michael likely on his way.

She looked at him thoughtfully, and it occurred to him how much she must be enjoying this. He'd told her to get lost, and now she had him by the balls—or so she thought. It amazed him now that he'd once thought her attractive. He nearly smiled. If he'd gotten involved with her, he would have been doing exactly what she had accused him of doing— thinking wrongheadedly where Catherine was concerned.

"Joe, I really don't think it's such a good idea for you to see Della—"

"Before you say anything else, Margaret, let me tell you this. I know what you're doing with Della. I know you keep her stirred up all the time about Catherine."

"Oh, Catherine does an excellent job of that all by herself."

"Because you *want* to get back at me. I know you think I won't tell Michael. But the truth is, Margaret—Maggie I think he already knows. I'm damn sure he suspects it. So this is how it's going to be: You get Della out here or I'm going to make sure Michael doesn't just suspect. I'm going to tell him why I can't come to this house or anywhere else you're going to be without at least one of my children along."

"Don't be silly, Joe. Michael wouldn't believe you."

"He'd believe Fritz."

Joe wasn't positive that Fritz had seen anything that time in the kitchen—except that after the incident Fritz had stayed well away from Margaret if she could. Fritz suddenly stopped wanting to go along with Della and her on their shopping sprees, stopped mentioning her flashy Aunt Margaret at all except in passing. He'd learned one thing for certain about Fritz. She didn't do anything without a reason.

"So what's it going to be, Maggie? Are you going to get Della out here, or do you want to go back to working for a living like you did before you latched onto Michael?"

Margaret stared at him coldly, then smiled. "You really are a jerk, aren't you, Joe?"

"You keep interfering with me and my children and you're going to find out just how much of a jerk I am. I want to see my daughter. Now."

It surprised him that Della came so quickly. He had underestimated Margaret's influence; one look at Della's face told him she was only here under duress. A sudden image filled his mind, one of Lisa at that age. How much she reminded him of her—in looks, at any rate. But then, Lisa, too, had been rebellious, particularly when her family had said no to her accepting the attentions of one Joseph D'Amaro.

"You remind me of your mother," he said, and her look softened for a brief moment.

"Not enough," she said.

He let the remark slide. "In one of our recent discussions you accused me of treating you like a child. I have been doing that—mostly because you've been acting like one—like a spoiled, vindictive brat. You've wanted to hurt me and in the process you've hurt your brother and sister as well. For the first time in my life I'm ashamed of you—"

"*You've* been ashamed of *me!* Really, Daddy—"

"Yes! I've been ashamed of you. But I don't blame you . . . entirely."

"I'm not going back home."

"I understand that you feel that way. But our differences—whatever they are—aren't just ours, Della. What happens between you and me affects the rest of the family—Charlie and especially Fritz. That's why I'm here. I want you to come home with me now so we can have a family meeting. I want to get all this out in the open. I want the younger kids to understand what's going on—why you feel the way you do and what's happening with me." He believed that he would carry her out bodily if he had to, but he still wanted to offer her a chance to behave better than she'd been behaving. "That's all I have to say. Will you do that? Will you come home?"

He stood there, trying not to say the things he needed to say. He was an impatient man, always had been; and Della had already pushed him to the limit. He'd never taken from another human being the kind of grief he'd taken from her.

"I don't see what good it's going to do," she said finally.

"Maybe none. You'll just have to decide whether or not the possibility that it might help everyone involved is worth your time and trouble." He decided not to stand over her for an answer. "If you're coming, I'd like for you to do that right away. I don't want to keep Fritz up any later than I have to."

He turned and left, not lingering, not looking back. Michael was just turning into the driveway.

He decided not to avoid Michael, and when the car stopped he opened the door and got in.

"I want to talk to you," he said.

"Won't Della go home with you?"

"I don't—"

"Hell, Joey, you can't blame the kid! If you're going to let her catch you and Catherine in bed together—"

"Michael, Fritz, and Charlie were in the house. Do you think I'd take Catherine to bed with my children there?"

"You said you had a woman in your bed—"

"I wasn't there, too, Michael. Just Catherine."

Michael shook his head in exasperation. "You're not making any damn sense at all, Joey. You know that, don't you?"

"Well, that's why I want to talk to you. Catherine is pregnant."

"Oh, fine! She got that way from *not* going to bed with you, I guess."

"That's cute, Michael. No, she got that way exactly—"

"For God's sake, don't give me the details. You know I expected to hear this kind of thing from you when you were a kid. I expected to hear it with Lisa. But goddamn it, Joey, you're thirty-eight years old! Thirty-eight years old, three kids, and you've gotten some woman in trouble!"

"Not some woman . . . Catherine. But I don't think she considers it trouble."

"So what is it? Some kind of blessing in disguise?"

"Catherine thought she couldn't have children. That's why her husband divorced her. He wanted children and she couldn't have them."

"So here you come along and fix that right up," Michael said.

"Yes."

"And now you're thinking you're pretty hot damn stuff, I guess."

"Well, yeah, Michael, I sort . . . of *do,*" Joe said, trying not to smile.

"Jesus, Mary, and Joseph! So now what are you going to do?"

"If there's any way on Earth to do it, I'm going to marry her."

"And what about Della? You're not going to explain tonight to Della?"

"Michael, I wasn't doing anything—"

"No, you never do anything, do you? You got some woman pregnant and you got this whole family torn up, but somehow you never do anything!"

"Catherine is not *some woman!* I love her, Michael. I *love* her. I didn't find out about the baby until tonight. Catherine was sitting with a friend of hers at the hospital and I went there. I don't think she meant to tell me she was pregnant, but she was so upset and I wouldn't leave without knowing what was wrong with her. She was in rough shape, Michael—exhausted. I wasn't just going to walk off and leave her like that. So I brought her home with me. Fritz fixed her toast and hot chocolate and she lay down on my bed to rest for a while. When Della came in, Fritz told her to be quiet because Catherine was sleeping in my bed. Della jumped to the wrong conclusion. That's it."

"That's it," Michael repeated. "That's not *it*, Joey. Do you know how much trouble you've got? How in the hell do you *get* in this kind of trouble just minding your own damn business!"

"Michael, I don't know. I just know I want to marry Catherine, and I need your help, man. You're my brother. I need your help." Absurdly he felt tears welling, but he fought them back.

"I should have been telling you to keep that thing in your pants, that's how I should have helped. Jesus!"

"Well, it's too late now," Joe offered.

"Yeah, yeah, it's too late. Joey—"

"Don't lecture me anymore, Michael. I've got to go. If my daughter decides to stay here and not come to the house tonight, just try to be on my side a little bit, will you?"

But Della came, in typical Della fashion, arriving just when he'd given up hope. He sat with Charlie and Fritz at the kitchen table, and he said nothing to her when she came in, letting her take the time she needed to save face by having done exactly what he asked. When she finally sat down, he took his time as well. They were his family. He looked at each of them, his children, his very fine children. He loved them collectively and independently, without reservation. They had been through a hard time after Lisa died, but they had come through it together. It was this meeting that might tear them apart. It occurred to him that the last time they'd met like this had been to decide to sell the gnomes.

He cleared his throat. "I'm not going to beat around the bush. The first thing I want to tell you is that I . . . loved your mother. It was very hard for me when she died. Very . . . hard. Della, you and Charlie will know that probably more than Fritz."

"I know it," Fritz put in, and he realized that she did, because she was his solemn and wise little Fritz, and somehow she managed to know these things. He smiled at her before he went on.

"Anyway, I don't think I would have made it if it hadn't been for the three of you. I want to tell you that I still love your mother very much. I didn't stop loving her because she died. I will always love her. No one—*no one*—can take her place. But I want to tell you that I love Catherine too. It isn't the same as what I felt for your mother, but it's just as strong. She's important to me and I want to marry her. And I want to know what you feel about that."

Fritz was the first with a question. "If you married Catherine, would she live with us?"

"Fritz," Charlie said, "what kind of dumb question is that? Of course she'd live with us."

"I just wanted to make *sure*," Fritz said.

"Does she want to marry you?" Charlie asked.

"No," Joe said, answering him truthfully.

"No? Well—if she—how can—*why* doesn't she?"

"She doesn't want to be bothered with us," Della cut in.

"She doesn't want to be bothered with *you*," Charlie retaliated.

"She doesn't want to cause a problem between me and my children," Joe said, ignoring Della as she rolled her eyes upward. "I don't know if she'll marry me or not."

"Does she love you back?" Fritz asked.

"Yes, I believe so."

"Well, if she loves you back, she'll marry you, won't she?"

"That's what I hope, Fritz."

"Would she be like a mother?"

"I think Catherine would be whatever you wanted her to be. Like a mother or like a friend—or maybe both."

"Or maybe neither," Della said.

"I want to know how you'd feel about my marrying Catherine," Joe said, looking at her sharply.

"Go for it, Pop," Charlie said.

"Yeah, go for it," Fritz assured him.

Joe was a bit taken aback. He'd been so concerned about Della, he hadn't anticipated such ready acceptance from the other two. "That's it? That's all you have to say about it?"

"How about 'good luck'?" Charlie added.

"I can't believe I'm hearing this!" Della said incredulously.

"Did you hear Pop say he loved her?" Charlie said. "Read my lips. *He loves her.* Get real, Della."

"Listen, Charlie, you're nothing but a kid! You don't know anything—"

"I know I like Catherine. I know she puts a spring in our old man's step—"

"All right!" Joe said interrupting. "Fritz, do you or Charlie have anything else you want to say—to me, not to Della."

They looked at each other and shook their heads.

"Then I want to talk to Della alone."

"Why can't we hear it?" Fritz wanted to know.

"Because I want to talk to Della alone," he repeated. "Go."

They stood up reluctantly, but they went without further comment.

Joe stared at Della across the table. How different she was now from the little girl he'd known. Charlie was basically the same—maybe all men were like that, just taller versions of themselves as boys. But not Della. She had become an entirely different person somehow.

"You're not going to talk me into this craziness of yours, Daddy," she said.

"I don't want to talk you into anything, Della. I want to know why you feel the way you do. Catherine isn't your mother, but you can't blame her for that."

"You don't see anything, Daddy!"

"Then tell me. What is it I'm supposed to see?"

She didn't answer him.

"I told you before that I could understand your feeling the way you do if Catherine was something besides what she is. But she's kind, Della. She's loving and she's gentle—"

"Catherine is not all that wonderful, Daddy! She's teaching pregnant girls, and she's no better than they are. She's pregnant, too, and she's not married."

"Who told you that?"

"Everybody knows it."

"Who told you that!"

"A girl in that pregnant class! Maria something! Catherine Holben is some kind of cheap tramp. She was pregnant and you didn't even know it!"

"I know, Della," he said quietly. He felt so sorry for her. She was still more child than woman. She wanted to prove Catherine's unworthiness to him so badly, she hadn't recognized the significance of what she was saying—or his response to it. He saw on her face the instant she understood what he meant.

"No," she said, getting up from the table. "No! If that's true, I'll leave here, Daddy! I'll go live with Uncle Michael and Aunt Margaret."

He looked into his daughter's eyes. He offered her no apology; nothing could be changed by her threats.

"You're my first child," he said as gently as he knew how. He was going to hurt her, but he knew of no other way. "I love you dearly. Everything about you is important to me. But you're not my entire life, Della. If I've made you feel that, if I've made you think that the world revolves around just you and that the rest of the family doesn't matter, then I've been wrong. The baby Catherine is having is mine."

21

The scene replayed itself over and over in her mind.

"I can't be the cause of all this trouble, Joe! Don't you understand? Della is never going to accept me—much less our baby. We'll all suffer for it—all of us. I won't do it."

She had looked into his eyes and seen what he didn't say: *If you loved me. If you loved me . . .*

She did love him. She could imagine herself with him so easily, living in his house, going with him to the Christmas pageant to see Fritz be a "wise person," having his baby. She wanted to be a part of his life—but not at the risk of ruining it. Some things never worked out, no matter how much one wanted them to.

And so she rested her body, if not her mind. She ate, slept—albeit fitfully. She took Pat Bauer a small Christmas tree her class had decorated with paper chains and snowflakes. Pat was getting better, but Catherine still didn't tell her about the baby.

On Sunday she decided to get a Christmas tree of her own, a tall, skinny red cedar that would fill the apartment with its wonderful evergreen smell and fill her with rampant nostalgia. Red cedars had been the traditional Christmas tree in the community where she had grown up—and practically no other place she'd ever been since. Most people wanted spruce or white pine, but she'd had a standing order with a local farmer who grew red cedar for fence posts for years, and this year she'd almost forgotten it. Almost. Some traditions mere unhappiness couldn't break, she supposed.

Wilmington was cold for December. She went to get the tree in the late afternoon when the sun had nearly set. The western horizon was orange and bleak, and she tramped the brittle broom-straw field with the farmer, her nose running, her toes and fingers aching, until she found the right tree for him to cut. She brought it back to the apartment house, never more mindful of her conflicting feelings than she was at that moment—so happily pregnant, so miserably alone.

After parking on the street in front she stood for a moment on the sidewalk looking at the Mayfair windows before she untied the tree from the luggage rack.

Very nice, she thought. There were decorations in every living room window except hers, and she was about to remedy that. No one could accuse the Mayfair tenants of lacking Christmas spirit.

She began untying the tree.

"I'll do that."

She looked around. Jonathan took the end of the rope she'd already freed out of her hand. She stood back and let him do it, because her fingers were cold and because she couldn't think of any reason not to. He was wearing a three-piece suit and tie. He must have just come from work.

"Still the same old ugly tree, I see," he said.

"Still," she agreed.

"But you like it," he added, replaying the conversation they'd had every year they'd been married.

"Exactly," Catherine answered. "So, Jonathan. What do you want?"

He laughed. "Catherine, why don't you quit beating around the bush and *really* cut through the social amenities?"

"I thought I was," she said lightly. She helped get the tree off the roof of the car, but he insisted on carrying it—a first for him. He'd never done it when they were married.

331

"I just wanted to see how you were doing," he said as they went into the Mayfair.

"Again? I thought you were going to tell me you'd made a terrible mistake and you wanted to get remarried." She glanced over her shoulder at him. He looked so odd—a pained expression that was gone almost as quickly as it appeared.

"So how *are* you doing?" he asked, following her up the first flight of stairs with the tree.

I'm finally pregnant, Jonathan. Pregnant and alone. "I'm fine," she said.

"You look tired."

"Ah, well. I've been working hard lately."

"So how's Pat?"

"She's in the hospital again with pneumonia, but she's been doing better the last day or so. She might even get home for Christmas."

"She still separated from Don?"

"Yes. Jonathan, what is it with the questions?"

"I . . . never heard from you."

"Did you expect to?"

"Catherine?" Her name echoed in the stairway, and she thought at first it was Jonathan who had spoken. She looked up. Joe was standing on the third-floor landing.

He came down the steps. "I need to talk to you, Catherine. It's important."

She stared at him, her eyes searching his. If anyone looked tired, it was Joe.

"It's important," he said again.

"All right," she answered, because she believed him. "Just put the tree down there," she said to dismiss Jonathan. "I'll get it later."

But Jonathan was going to be obstinate. He looked from

one of them to the other, and it was apparent to Catherine that he didn't like what he saw. For once the logic that had served him so well as a successful accountant failed him. He'd once been Catherine's husband, and yet he was clearly baffled that she would defer to someone else. "You can't leave it on the stairs, Catherine. One of these little old ladies might fall and break her neck."

"I'll take it, then," Joe offered.

"*I'll* take it," Jonathan insisted. "What are you trying to do, Catherine, get rid of me?"

"Yes," she said truthfully.

He stood and stared at her, because apparently he had thought he was making a joke.

"You really want me to go so you can talk to this guy?"

"Yes," she assured him. "I do."

"Who is he?" he asked, as if Joe weren't standing three steps away.

"None of your business, Jonathan. Thank you for carrying the tree and for your kind inquiries. If there's nothing else you want, then Merry Christmas and good-bye."

She attempted to drag the tree the rest of the way up the stairs.

"Catherine, I'll call you," Jonathan called after her, and she gave him an incredulous look. There must be some trouble with Ellen, she thought. She was sorry about that, but she was not acting as a low-budget marriage counselor.

"Jonathan doesn't approve," Joe said, taking the tree from her.

"He's never liked my taste in Christmas trees," Catherine said, choosing to be obtuse.

"That's not what I meant." He held up the tree. "Where did you get this, Charlie Brown Tree Sales?"

"You too?" she said as she unlocked the door.

He smiled. "Hey, I'm a builder. I like cedar. It lasts forever and it smells good."

She returned his smile. She'd forgotten that about him, that he liked things that lasted forever. But then she remembered that she couldn't stand here and talk with him like this. It was too hard, too hard not to reach for him, too hard not to tell him how much she needed him.

His smile faded and his eyes probed hers. "Are you . . . okay?"

She looked away and pushed open the door. "I'm okay. What did you want to talk about?"

He followed her inside, setting the tree in a corner. "I know a little girl who would love to help you decorate this thing."

"Joe, don't. Please. Just tell me whatever it is you need to tell me."

He reached out as if he were going to touch her, but he let his hand drop. "I had a talk with Della. She says your class knows you're pregnant."

Catherine looked at him sharply. "How could they know that?"

"I don't know. She says Maria told her."

Maria.

Maria, who always seemed to be around when she'd felt nauseous or faint. Maria, who had been pregnant twice herself. It couldn't have been too hard for her to figure out.

"Catherine, I'm sorry. I just thought you ought to know."

"What's happening with Della?" she asked abruptly.

"I told her the truth. I told her the baby is mine."

"Oh, Joe—"

"Catherine, she's going to know sooner or later. She might as well hear it from me."

"Then I don't have to ask you how things are at home, do I?"

He gave a small shrug. "She's . . . staying at Michael's again. It was hard for her to find out her old man is . . . human. Well, I have to go pick up Charlie, he's at a computer-club meeting. Is there anything I can do for you?"

She shook her head.

He came closer. "You'll tell me if there is, won't you? I'll do anything I can for you."

"I don't need anything, Joe." *Except you.*

He gave her an abrupt, awkward hug, because he couldn't stand not touching her any longer and because *he* needed it.

"I love you, Catherine," he said against her ear, his voice cracking as he said it. "Don't you forget it."

He didn't give her time to say anything. He let her go and quickly turned and left, pulling the door closed behind him. He paused once as he hurried down the stairs, half hoping the door would open and Catherine would call him back.

She didn't, but he had no time to feel disappointment. Jonathan was standing on the first landing.

Shit, he thought. As if he didn't have enough problems. Now he was going to have to stand here and pass some kind of inspection from Catherine's ex-husband.

"I'm Jonathan Rusk," he said. "I used to be married to Catherine. For some reason she didn't bother to introduce us."

"Joseph D'Amaro," he said, trying to get by. "I'm in a hurry."

"Look, D'Amaro. I'm not going to hedge here. I want to know what your business is with Catherine."

"I thought she already explained that it's none of your business. If Catherine wants you to know, she'll tell you." He tried to get past again, but Jonathan caught him by the arm.

"What is it with you?" Joe asked, jerking his arm free. "I'm not talking to you about Catherine. Now get out of my way."

"I want to know what you're doing here! I want to know what you're doing with Catherine! You're not the kind of man she'd have anything to do with!"

"I'm not? Well, if you say so, Jonathan." He tried to get by again, but the son of a bitch wasn't going to let him do it. Joe suddenly smiled. "Rusk? Your name is Rusk? Catherine wouldn't take anything from you, would she? Not even your name."

"Just what is that supposed to mean!"

"It means she's a Holben. It means you're the one driving the big Mercedes and she was the one walking." *And my baby's not going to be a goddamn Rusk.*

"Listen, you!" Jonathan said, grabbing Joe by his shirtfront. "I know Catherine! I was married to her for a long time. She's afraid of you."

"What, are you crazy! Catherine is not afraid of me!"

"I want to know what you're doing here!"

Joe's temper flared. He had had enough of this crap, and he tried to pry Jonathan's fingers loose. "If you don't get your hands off me, Jonathan, one of the things I'm doing here will be to kick your ass out into the street!"

But he had no chance to carry out his threat. Catherine came running down the stairs. She was barefoot, a sprig from the red cedar tree in her hand.

"My God, what are you two doing!" she cried, putting herself bodily between them. "Do you know Mrs. Donovan is ready to call the police? I live here! Are both of you crazy! How much do you think I can take, Joe! You want me to have to spend the evening at the police station, too—get my name in the papers for disturbing the peace?"

"Catherine, there's only *one* crazy person here and it's not—" Joe tried to put in. But she wasn't listening.

"Jonathan, what is the matter with you!" she said, letting him have it too.

"I want to know why he's here!" Jonathan shouted.

"He's the father of my baby!" Catherine shouted back. "That's why he's here! Now, I have had it. You get out of here and you leave me alone! Both of you!"

"Catherine!" Joe called as she started back up the stairs. He couldn't believe she'd told Jonathan about the baby and he tried to follow her, but Jonathan had his arm again.

"Goddammit!" he cried, shoving Jonathan hard. "Catherine!"

She turned on him. "I mean it, Joe! Stay away!"

"All right! You want me to go, I'll go! But by God, you're not the only one who's had enough here! Between Della and you—and this nut case ex-husband of yours, I've had about all I can stand too! If that's what you want, that's what you'll get. You want to see me again, *you* call *me*, Catherine!"

Catherine didn't wait for the end of his tirade, and the only response he got was her door slamming—hard. He stood on the stairs for a moment. His shirt was all crumpled up from Jonathan's handling, and one of the buttons was missing.

Jonathan was sitting in the corner on the landing where Joe had shoved him.

"She's pregnant?" he asked. "Catherine's pregnant?"

Joe didn't answer him. He still couldn't believe Catherine had told him like that—just out with it. For once he thought she'd said what she didn't mean to say. He was glad she'd told him; he wanted the bastard to know he'd dumped her too soon. He was going to do for her now the only thing he could— make sure her pregnancy remained none of Jonathan's business.

He stepped over Jonathan's legs and left.

337

22

Yes, Catherine thought as she looked around the group, they knew. Abby and Cherry and Beatrice and Maria. She put the papers she was about to hand out aside. She might as well get it over with.

She got up from the desk and came around to stand in front of it.

"Listen up," she said, and they all looked in her direction, none of them meeting her eyes. "I have two things I want to tell you. The first is about Mrs. Bauer. She'll be getting out of the hospital in a day or two. She's not well, but she has improved enough to go home. She asked me to tell you that she'd like for you all to visit her sometime before Christmas—something about Santa Claus having already visited her house and leaving some packages with your names on them."

They all smiled at that news, and Catherine smiled with them. She went on before she lost her nerve.

"The other thing I want to tell you is about me. Not too long ago we had a group discussion about being pregnant. I told you that I didn't think any of you *should* be pregnant. Do you remember that?"

There was a low rumble of acknowledgment.

"What else did I say?" she asked them.

"You said since we were pregnant, we had to forget about the things that shouldn't be and the things we couldn't change and set our goals," Abby offered.

"Right. And what were the goals?"

"A good healthy baby," Cherry said.

"What else?"

"Learning how to be a good parent," she added.

"Right. The first thing is for you to do everything you can to have a healthy baby. The second thing is for you to learn everything you can so you can be a good and loving parent. What I want to tell you is that the goals I set for you are also the goals I set for myself. I am . . . pregnant, and I want *my* baby to be healthy. And *I* want to be a good parent. I intend to do the same things that I've been teaching you—"

She stopped. They were all looking at the floor. Now came the hard part, and Cherry's hand went up immediately.

"Are you still going to be our teacher, Ms. Holben?"

"I don't know, Cherry. I'll have to wait and see."

"You going to get married?"

"I have no plans to get married."

"You going to take care of your baby all by yourself?"

"Yes."

"You said a baby needed a mother *and* a father."

"Yes, I did. I also said when that isn't possible, the baby's mother has to work extra hard to make their life together the best it can be. I have some advantages that all of you don't—I have a career, I have the means to support my baby and myself. That's why I think it's so important for you to get as much education as you can."

"How come you're not going to marry Joe?" Cherry persisted. "He told us he was your boyfriend."

Catherine was a bit taken aback at that information, but she didn't let herself be sidetracked. "I don't want to get into that. I just want you to know about me for sure"—she looked at Maria   "so you don't have to wonder about it anymore and we can get on with what we're supposed to be doing."

"But who's going to be your support system?"

"No more questions. Now, the central office is sending someone over to review the information for your math and English exams this afternoon. . . ."

She'd done it. She'd made the announcement but she was having some difficulty assessing the effect. She'd piqued their curiosity and she'd given Maria a certain credibility she'd been lacking with the group thus far, but whether or not she'd damaged her own credibility, she couldn't tell. And this was only the first hurdle. She still had to advise the school superintendent of her condition.

The weather was too damp and cold for any outside activities, so she sent the girls to the large empty room down the hall that had once been a library to eat their lunches and to dance and rehash Ms. Holben's announcement. She sat alone in the classroom, worrying about Joe. She'd been so angry with him—and for no real reason. God only knew what Jonathan had said to him. She supposed that she, with her battling ex-husband and ex-lover, had given the Mayfair tenants enough to keep them titillated for the next year. She could hear them all now. "Catherine seemed so nice and quiet . . ."

"Ms. Holben?"

Catherine looked up. Maria stood in the doorway, frowning, her arms folded over her chest.

"Beatrice says I got to talk to you," she said. Her tone of voice suggested that she was doing both Beatrice and Catherine an immense favor.

"Go ahead."

"How come you don't know if you're going to be our teacher?"

"Because I haven't talked to the superintendent of schools yet. It may be that they'd rather not have me continue this class."

"He don't have to know anything, does he?"

"Yes, Maria, he does. Pregnancy isn't the kind of thing you can keep a secret. Too many people already know about it. You should know that."

Maria looked away, and when she looked back, Catherine thought she was about to cry.

"Come sit down, Maria," Catherine said, but Maria stood stubbornly in the middle of the room.

"I didn't mean to go telling, Ms. Holben. All of us were at the mall looking at the Christmas stuff—me and Beatrice and Abby and Cherry—and we went and got Sasha so she could see it too. This preppy girl came around talking to Abby because she knew her in regular school. Then she started talking about *our* class—if you was a good teacher and stuff like that. That's when I said it, Ms. Holben. I *hate* those preppy girls like that—running around thinking they're so good. I thought she was a friend of yours, so I said you didn't have no business teaching us because you were just as pregnant and not married, as we were—" She stopped. "Beatrice says if you don't teach us anymore, it's my fault because I told that preppy girl. They're all mad at me, Ms. Holben."

"Well, they shouldn't be. I've told you before. We have a choice about our own behavior, but we don't have a choice about the consequences. I don't blame you for anything that might happen because of what *I've* done."

Maria continued to stand there. She didn't say anything else, but she sighed.

"Tell me," Catherine said. "How is Sasha?"

"Sasha says her milk don't come in anymore. Used to, every time she heard a baby cry, she got milk, and that made her cry, too, because she didn't have Treasure to drink it. It scares you, Ms. Holben, when that happens. It's like your mind knows you ain't got your baby anymore, but your body don't and you can't tell it—" She broke off and looked at the

341

floor. Surprisingly she sat down in the desk closest to her.

"Is that what happened with you? With your first baby?"

Maria wiped her eyes. "Yeah. The Welfare took it. They're going to take this one too."

"Is that what you want? You want them to take this baby?"

"It don't matter what I want. I used to drink a lot—everything I could get—"

"Are you drinking now?"

"No."

"Why not?"

"Because you make everybody feel so damn guilty! Ain't nobody can make a person feel guilty like you do!"

"I don't want you to hurt that baby, Maria, but I couldn't make you feel guilty unless you cared about your child."

"I do care about it, Ms. Holben! The others—they think they're better than me." Her mouth quivered and her eyes welled up with tears.

"Are they?"

She gave an exasperated sigh. "No, they ain't! Abby got her baby from some sucker she met last summer on the beach—some college dude—and she don't even know his name. Abby thought she was living in a movie, only it was real and there ain't no happy endings when it's real. And Beatrice, *her* baby's daddy's married and he's a teacher. She ain't got no more sense than to fool around with a *teacher*. She's dumb, Ms. Holben! She's still thinking he's going to marry her, and he ain't marrying nobody.

"I *love* my baby's daddy. We were going to get out of here—go someplace new where don't nobody know us. He had the money saved so we could get married, but somebody stole it. And now I got to go on living with my mama. My mama don't do nothing but wear one of those little robes with the snaps up the front so she can get it off quick when the men come. I have to keep my door locked all the time so her men don't come looking for *me*. She don't care if I'm pregnant. She don't even know if I'm alive, and I'm right in the same house with her." Suddenly Maria grinned, but the grin didn't reach her eyes. "How come you do that, Ms. Holben? How come I can tell you something like that and you sit there like it's *nothing?*"

"Because you're giving me the business," Catherine said.

"I ain't giving you nothing but the truth!"

"Oh, I know it's the truth, but it's not the truth you want to tell me. You want to give me an excuse for not keeping your baby—when I think you want that baby more than anything in this world. Let me tell *you* the truth. If you want your baby, you can do something about it. You've got a social worker, talk to her. Tell her what you want and let her help you get it. Get into AA. Tell your social worker you want to move out of your mother's place, and tell her why. Show them you'll do whatever it takes."

"Yeah, and they *still* might not let me keep it."

"Exactly. But they certainly won't if everything is just the same as it was the last time. If you want your baby, you have to try, Maria. You have to quit looking for somebody to blame and work on this yourself. Even if you lose, you'll know it wasn't because you rolled over and just let it happen. You know what you have to do. If you want a chance, do it."

"I *hate* talking to you," Maria said, sniffing loudly. "You *always* telling people what to do."

Catherine smiled. "I know. And that's mostly why you came in here."

Incredibly Maria smiled back. The smile was weak at best, but it was genuine. She stood up to go.

"Hey," Catherine said when she reached the door. "Tell the rest of them I said to stay off your case."

343

★ ★ ★ ★ ★

The phone was ringing when Catherine got home from work—Fritz asking to come and see the gnomes. For the first time Catherine hesitated. She didn't want to end up in another argument with Joe.

"Mrs. Webber will bring me," Fritz said, as if she'd been coached to give Catherine that reassurance.

"That'll be fine," Catherine decided. "You can help me decorate my tree."

She had the tree in a stand but hadn't decorated it. She passed the time waiting for Fritz to arrive by trying to locate her Christmas decorations. If Fritz found the tree in any way odd, she was polite enough not to say.

They had hot chocolate—Catherine's mostly milk—and Catherine told Fritz another of her childhood stories, this one about the grove of red cedars that used to grow near her house, where she would go in the heat of summer and stand in the middle of it—not for the shade but for the cedar smell—and she would close her eyes and pretend it was Christmas.

While they were decorating the tree Catherine noticed that Fritz had a small tablet with her and that she kept writing in it.

"What are you doing, Fritz?" Catherine asked, completely puzzled.

Fritz frowned. "Do I have to say?"

"No, you don't have to say. I was just wondering."

Fritz looked so relieved, Catherine didn't press it. Later, when the tree was done, Fritz sat quietly on the couch, holding the gnomes and watching Catherine closely, the notepad close at hand.

"Fritz, let's put on our coats and go downstairs and see what the tree looks like from the outside."

"Okay," she said, but she picked up the notepad again and began writing.

"How do you spell 'outside'?" she asked after a moment.

"O-u-t-s-i-d-e."

"Oh, I see. Like 'out' and 'side' only it's one word."

"That's right," Catherine told her.

"I didn't know if they did that thing they do," she said, still laboring with the pencil.

"What thing?"

"You know. Sometimes they sneak extra letters or straight marks or stuff like that in on you."

Catherine smiled. "Not this time. So, are you ready to go?"

"Yes. But don't say anything while we're out there, okay?"

"Why not?"

"Because I can't see to write in the dark."

"Well, Fritz, you don't have to write, do you?"

"Yes, Catherine," she said, as if that should have been obvious by now.

"Is this something for school? 'How I Spent My Afternoon' or something like that?"

Fritz sighed. "It's not for school. It's for . . . Joe."

"For Joe?"

"Well, he said he shot off his big mouth and now he can't talk to you. But he's worrying and worrying. So I'm trying to write down stuff about you for him, but you do things so fast." She sighed again. "I don't want him to worry, Catherine."

"Well, neither do I. From now on I'll do things slow."

"Can you help me spell? I can spell, but you don't do things in the words I know."

"Yes, that too. Now run get your coat."

She watched Fritz put her coat on and carefully button each button. She waited, surrounded by the scent of cedar and the ghosts of all her other Christmases.

Oh, Joe . . .

23

What the hell is this? Joe thought, moving to where he could see better. He had been checking the struts on the building framework with Michael when a red Volkswagen pulled onto the building site. He expected it just to turn around and head back into Wrightsville Beach proper, but it didn't. It kept circling and circling around the site, slinging sand as it went, and from his vantage point it looked like some runaway, windup toy.

"Bunch of damn kids fooling around," Michael said, and he agreed, moving along the steel girder to the platform so he could get down if he had to.

The car abruptly stopped, and the window rolled down on the driver's side.

"Hey!" somebody yelled up. "We're looking for Joe!"

The Volkswagen began to unload its passengers—four of whom were obviously pregnant, one who was obviously not, and one old lady with a gray felt hat and a big black pocketbook.

"Hey, Joe!" one of them yelled at the top of her lungs. "Where are you?"

He looked around at Michael and frowned.

"Don't look at me," Michael said. "My name ain't Joe."

What the hell is this? Joe thought again as he began to work his way down. He could feel every pair of eyes on the crew following him. He knew of only one pregnant group that might travel around en masse, and as he got closer, he recognized Maria and Sasha. He had no idea who the little old lady might be. The only thing he could think of was that there

346

might be something wrong with Catherine.

He quickly crossed the sand to where they were all standing.

"Sasha . . . Maria," he said, nodding to the only two whose names he remembered. "Is Cath—Ms. Holben all right?"

He looked from one of them to the other, but he couldn't tell a thing.

"If she is, it ain't no thanks to you, sucker," Maria said.

"Hmmpf," the little old lady said. The corners of her mouth were turned down, and she looked him up and down as if she'd expected the worst and had gotten it.

Who *is* this person? he thought.

"Joseph D'Amaro," he said to her, offering her his hand. She stiffened, and he thought for a moment she was going to hit it with the big black pocketbook she was carrying.

He took his hand back. "Okay," he said to the group at large. "Okay, what is it? What's going on?"

"How come you get our Ms. Holben pregnant and then you don't stand by her?" Sasha wanted to know, and Joe prayed that the wind wasn't carrying the sound up.

"Yeah!" the group said in unison, except for the little old lady, who still looked as if she wanted to hit him with something.

"Sasha, I don't—"

"We expect this kind of crap from Sweet Eddie Aikens," Sasha said, interrupting. "But we thought you were a *gentleman*. Ms. Holben's going around thinking she's like us, but she ain't like us. We all got somebody to help us. I got my grandmamma . . ."

Joe glanced at the little old lady. Grandmamma, he decided.

". . . we *all* got somebody to stand by us, but Ms. Holben, she don't. She got herself all tangled up with a sweet-talking devil like you—and we know you're sweet-talking, 'cause Ms. Holben wouldn't be in this fix unless you were smart enough to fool her. I told you myself, she don't know nothing about men, and you went right out and took advantage of it."

"Sasha—" Joe said in exasperation. *He* wasn't the one who wouldn't talk marriage.

"We want to know what you're going to do about it, sucker," Maria put in.

"Yeah!" the group said again.

"Could I say one thing here?" Joe asked.

"You make it good, boy," Grandmamma said, and Joe tried not to grin. He'd heard of irate fathers and brothers coming to see an errant father-to-be but never a pregnant class and a grandmother.

"Look," he said. "I appreciate your concern. But I'm doing the best I can here."

"What does that mean?" Sasha demanded.

"It means I'm working on it. I am. If there's any way to get Ms. Holben to the altar, I'm trying to find it. And if I make it, you're all invited to the wedding. Okay?" He frowned. "Who the devil is Sweet Eddie Aikens?"

"You just never mind," Grandmamma said. "We're going now, and I got one piece of advice for you, boy."

"What?" Joe said, not at all sure he wanted to know.

"You do right—or you live hard, you got that?"

"Yes, ma'am," he said politely. "I got it."

"Good. You can get back to work."

"Oh, thank you."

He stood and watched as Catherine's supporters fitted themselves back into the Volkswagen. They must do that a lot, he thought, because they got themselves repacked without a hitch.

He didn't dare look up, but it didn't do him any good. Michael was coming down.

"What the hell was that all about?" he wanted to know.

"Shotgun committee," Joe said as he walked away. "They want me to make an honest woman out of Catherine."

"Well, if I was you, I'd do it!" Michael called after him. "I wouldn't want to tangle with the one in the hat!"

"You look good," Fritz said. "Really good."

He grinned down at her and straightened his tie. "Thanks."

"How come you look so good?"

"I'm going to see Catherine."

"You want to look good to see Catherine?" she said incredulously.

"Yes, I want to look good to see Catherine," he said, mimicking her tone, and she giggled.

"Can I go?"

"No way."

"Why not?"

"Because I'm going courting, and you don't take your kids with you when you go courting. See?"

"No."

"Well, ask Mrs. Webber when she comes. She'll explain it to you. She's been married three times and she knows all about it."

"She doesn't have a husband now. What happened to all Mrs. Webber's husbands?"

He hesitated. He didn't want to get Fritz started thinking everything was her fault again—he was worried now that she might think she was the reason things weren't working out with Catherine. But he didn't want to shield her from things, either. "They . . . died," he said, but that news didn't particularly seem to concern her.

"Oh, yeah. I remember. She said if God kept on sending her husbands, she guessed she could bury them."

Joe laughed. "When did she say that?"

"At the barbecue. She told Catherine. Joe, how come we have to have Mrs. Webber come tonight?"

"Because Della isn't here and I might be late."

"How late?"

"Fritz, I don't know . . . late. I don't want to have to worry about you and Charlie."

"Charlie and me can look after ourselves. Della wasn't that much help, you know."

"Humor me on this, will you?"

"I don't know what that means."

"It means don't bug me."

"Oh . . . did you use your after-shave I gave you for Father's Day? Catherine'll like that. You know how I know?"

"No, how?"

"I told her I bought that for you for Father's Day and she said that was her very favoritest kind."

"Good. I need all the help I can get."

"Yeah, because you shot off your big mouth and Catherine might not talk to you."

"Exactly," Joe admitted. "So you think I look good?"

"*Real* good, Joe."

"Great! I hear Mrs. Webber at the back door. Run let her in—wait, give me a good-luck kiss."

He got out with a few more good-luck kisses—one from Mrs. Webber—and a good-luck handshake from Charlie.

"You remember, Pop," Charlie said. "The reputations of all us D'Amaro men are at stake here."

"I'll remember," he said. Armed with all those good wishes *and* his killer after-shave, he was definitely going to give it his best shot.

He rode past some of Wilmington's restored Victorian houses on his way to Catherine's, looking at the Christmas decorations as he went down the tree-lined street. God, he'd wanted to make enough money to move the family into one of these fine old houses, but there was no way he'd ever do it. Della would soon be ready for college.

Della. She just would *not* listen. And God, it hurt, this estrangement from his child. He'd been so tempted to tell her about Margaret, to try to make her understand that Margaret had motives of her own, motives other than saving him from a supposedly unsuitable woman like Catherine. But telling Della would have left her totally alone, with no support at all. Della was wrong, and he thought she knew it, and that made both their pain so much worse.

He parked in front of the Mayfair, looking up at the third floor as he crossed the street. Catherine's windows were dark, but he went inside, anyway, half expecting Mrs. Donovan to ask him to leave. He wondered how many times Jonathan had been back since their shoving match on the landing. He could feel sorry for Jonathan—if he didn't feel so sorry for himself.

Mrs. Donovan wasn't patrolling the foyer when he went in. He knew there was no point in his being here if Catherine had gone out someplace, but he didn't want to be anywhere else. He needed her, and when there was no answer to his knocking, he sat down on the top step and waited.

It was after nine—well after—when he heard Catherine coming up the stairs. He sat there, uneasy that she might be with Jonathan—or someone else, for that maker. But she was alone. She had a paper bag in her arms and he was reminded of the first time he'd done this—waited on the stairs outside her door for her to come home. She had looked so pretty to him that day, a soft, barefoot woman with an easy smile. She looked pretty to him now—beautiful—and sweet and pregnant with his child. He saw that she was surprised to see him, but she didn't back away. She came on up the stairs, her eyes holding his, and he took the bag from her, just as he had the other time.

"I lied," he said quietly.

"About what?"

He gave an offhanded shrug. "When I said I wouldn't come back unless you asked me—stuff like that."

"Oh. So . . . do you want to tell me why you're here?"

Because I love you with all my heart, he wanted to say, but he didn't.

"Because I need your company. Because I need a friend. I've checked all my friends, and it looks like you're the best one I've got."

She looked at him for a long moment. "Well," she said finally, "I guess you'd better come in, then."

She unlocked the door and he followed her inside, standing in the dark holding the paper bag while she went around turning on lamps and the lights on her odd little Christmas tree. She took off her coat and hung it in the foyer closet. She was dressed up, a pretty, dark red dress he'd never seen before.

"You look nice," he offered. He wanted to ask her where she'd been but he didn't. If she'd been somewhere with Jonathan, he didn't want to know.

"So do you. *Very* nice," she added as she took the bag from his arms.

He grinned, feeling himself blush. He was too damn old to blush. He knew exactly why he was wearing the suit. He'd wanted her to see that he cleaned up good, that she could take him anyplace, anyplace at all—if she wanted.

"Feels like you've been buying apples again," he said of the paper bag.

"No, this is my Christmas bag. Did you have Christmas bags when you were little in Dorchester?"

"No," he said, looking into her eyes.

"You had a deprived childhood, then. When I was little, they gave these out at church . . . see?" She opened the bag so he could look inside. "Apples, oranges, tangerines, walnuts and pecans in the shell, chewing gum, one Hershey's chocolate bar, one Snickers, one Three Musketeers, two pencils, and a box of raisins." She laughed up at him. "Absolute heaven! I told Pat about them once, and she gave me this one for Christmas—you can pick whatever you want."

"Well, that's pretty easy," he said. "I want you."

Her smile faded. "Joe, I . . ."

Wrong, he thought immediately. *You've said the wrong thing, D'Amaro.*

He looked into her eyes. *Catherine. Don't look at me like that!* No wonder Jonathan thought she was afraid of him.

"Catherine, you don't think I'd . . . hurt you or anything like that, do you? You're not afraid of me, are you? I don't want you to be afraid of me."

He wasn't quite sure how it came about—he didn't care—but she was in his arms suddenly, the Christmas bag mashed between them. He put it aside, setting it on the floor, so he could feel her against him. She hugged him tightly. She felt so good. He put his face into her neck. She smelled so good.

She leaned back to look at him. "I'm not afraid of you, Joe. Why would you think that?"

"Jonathan said—"

"Jonathan doesn't know anything about this," she said, interrupting. "If I'm afraid of anything, it's myself. I don't want to make everything worse for you because I—" Abruptly she turned away, picking up the Christmas bag and taking it into the kitchen. He followed after her.

"Because you what?" he asked.

She shook her head. She was still clutching the bag. No. She wasn't going to answer that.

"There's one thing I'm afraid of," he said, and she looked around at him. "I'm afraid you'll go to Jonathan for help."

She was about to protest, but he held up his hand.

"I don't think you would for yourself, but you would for the baby, if you thought you had to. I don't want you to do that, Catherine. I want you to come to me. I love you, and I want you to come to *me*. I want us to get married, Catherine. We aren't going to solve any of our problems apart. You know that."

She set the bag down on the table. "I don't want to make you unhappy."

"Well, what the hell do you think I am now, Catherine! I'm telling you, our being apart is making everything worse. The only way we can work things out is together. That way we can take care of the new baby, and Fritz and Charlie, and each other."

"And Della?"

"I won't lie to you. Della's leaving breaks my heart. She's my daughter, I love her. But she's left the family by her own choice. I've talked to her. I've tried everything I know. But I haven't done anything to make her leave but love you, and I'll be damned if she'll make me feel guilty for that."

"Joe, I don't want to break up your family!"

"Catherine, it's too late to worry about that. Della's already gone. She won't come back now because she's painted herself into a corner and she's too proud to admit it. I can't help her with that except to tell her that I care about her and I want her to be part of the family again."

"How can it work, Joe? Everything's wrong."

"Not everything. We had a family meeting. Fritz and

Charlie are on our side. And I love you." He smiled at her and reached out, lightly touching her cheek. "I didn't intend to, Ms. Holben. All I wanted to do was sell a couple of gnomes. I know, I know—you weren't exactly looking for me, either. You bought the damn things, and now look at you—you've got me and three and a fifth kids ready to shake up your life. But that's the way it goes, I guess. I can't give you much but aggravation. And love. A whole lot of love. The business is doing all right now. We wouldn't be rich, though. I don't know that we'd ever be rich, but we'd be happy. And you love me too," he assured her, but looking into her eyes, his self-assurance faded. "Don't you?" he asked quietly.

It scared him that she wasn't answering. "Don't you?" he said again.

"Joe, yes, I love you. But I don't know what to do. When I look at you, you're so sad. It's my fault—"

"Catherine, it's not your fault. It's *not.*" He reached out to take her hands, leaning forward to give her a quick, reassuring kiss on the mouth. But he needed her. He couldn't be this close to her and not . . .

He looked into her eyes. He never had been good with words.

Can you see, Catherine? Can you see how much I need you?

"Joe," she murmured. She reached up to touch his face, her forehead resting against his.

He nuzzled her cheek, his eyes closing. He was here and she didn't seem to mind. His mouth brushed over hers and she leaned into him. Then he kissed her, the way he'd wanted to for days and days. Her lips parted under his, letting him probe the soft recesses of her mouth, letting him taste her and taste her. . . .

He loved her so!

She gave a soft moan, one he felt as if it had been his. It

took his breath away. He'd been apart from her so long and she was so close to him now, so close and loving. He slid his hand upward to cup the softness of her breast, to press her body into his so she could feel how much he wanted her. *Catherine, my sweet Catherine, ah, God! Hold me tight. Hold me so I can stand it.*

He suddenly let her go and stepped away. His knees were weak and his hands were trembling. He wanted her so bad! But he wanted to take her to bed for the rest of his life, not just *now,* and they had to get this settled.

"I'm sorry," he said. "I didn't mean to do that."

She looked at him doubtfully.

He managed the barest of smiles as he tried to calm his labored breathing. "Well, I *did* mean to do it, because I want to make love with you. I *always* want to make love with you, but now I want you to answer me. Will you marry me?"

She looked at him, her arms folded across her breasts, as if she had no one in the world to comfort her but herself.

"I'm glad you're pregnant, Catherine," he said quietly, and her eyes probed his for the truth. He wasn't afraid of what she'd see, because he wasn't lying to her. He would never lie to her, and for once he thought he just might have said the right thing, because her look softened and her eyes slid away. He could see and feel it—her sense of relief. "Marry me," he said. "I want you to marry me."

"Are you . . . sure, Joe? Are you sure you want to?"

"Yes, Catherine! That's the only thing I *am* sure about. Now say you're going to do it. It's the best thing for all of us—even Della."

She drew a long breath and looked into his eyes. "All right."

"All right? You mean yes?"

"Yes."

Yes. It was a little tremulous but it was definitely *yes*.

He laughed out loud and grabbed her up off the floor, hugging her to him and making her squeal. "Hot damn!" he cried. "Wait till the shotgun committee hears this!"

24

Catherine stood with Joe at the vestibule doors because they were going to enter the church together and because Joe wanted them to greet the wedding guests as they arrived.

And because he was praying for some sign of Della. He didn't want to worry her with how badly he wanted his daughter there or how much he was still hoping. Her heart ached for him when he caught a glimpse of a teenage girl coming from behind the cars across the street.

But it was Abby, still pregnant Abby, with Maria and Beatrice and Cherry and Sasha in tow. And Grandmamma. Catherine watched the expectation on his face die into disappointment, and she could have cried, except that it was her wedding day.

She squeezed Joe's fingers and smiled up at him. *Joe.* Gentle, loving, passionate, exasperating Joe. He'd invited Jonathan to come today. And he'd horrified her by telling Father Hammond precisely why he couldn't dawdle over her religious instruction before the wedding.

"We're pregnant, Father Bob," he'd said at their first meeting, "so don't let's drag our feet on this. What?" he'd asked, apparently because of the look on Catherine's face. "I consider Father Bob my friend, Catherine," he'd explained patiently. "And even if he wasn't, you can't keep a thing like this under your hat—or wherever—for long. You've agreed to get married in my faith, but I don't want the Reverend Father here thinking he can just take his time. He's a nice man but he's slow. Right?" he'd blatantly asked the priest.

"Right," Father Hammond confessed, chuckling.

But even without the dawdling, March ninth had been the soonest they could arrange to get married. She would have liked to be married later in the spring—when the azaleas were blooming—but as Joe had pointed out, some things couldn't be kept under one's hat—or wherever. She looked down at the "wherever." She was definitely showing, and she didn't care.

Jonathan hadn't arrived. She thought Joe's invitation had done wonders for Jonathan's understanding of why she'd let *his* wedding pass her by. But even without Jonathan the church was filling nicely. Mrs. Webber had come. And most of the Mayfair tenants. Catherine smiled, thinking of Mrs. Webber and her announcement that it was *she* who had brought all this about. Perhaps she had, she and the gnomes.

"Here comes your crew," Joe said, and she smiled at the group of girls coming up the church steps. His "crew" would be coming, too, and she'd been both surprised and pleased at Joe's insistence that her class be invited—even before she could mention it herself.

"Maria and Beatrice have brought their babies," she said unnecessarily, delighted that they had. They both had baby girls, and they both, with Sasha's permission, had named their daughters Treasure, in honor of Sasha's lost child.

"Let me see," she said to Maria, who approached first. She reached out to touch the tiny baby girl Maria held protectively in her arms. "She's beautiful, Maria." She looked into Maria's eyes. "How's it going?"

"Okay, Ms. Holben. I got a social worker popping in on me every time I turn around, but it's okay. Ms. Holben, you look pretty."

"Thank you, Maria. I'm glad you came."

She greeted Beatrice and her Treasure, and then Abby and

Cherry, who were both very close to their delivery dates. And Sasha, who poked Joe on the arm and gave him a hug. And Grandmamma, whose hat was white in honor of the occasion.

Catherine was about to introduce her to Joe but he took the matter out of her hands.

"Hello, Grandmamma," he said solemnly.

"Joe," she responded with equal seriousness.

"I'm glad you came."

"Yes, you are," she assured him, and he grinned.

Catherine had her lips pursed to ask how they knew each other, but she didn't get the chance, because Grandmamma hugged her.

"How do you like it?" Grandmamma asked her. "The sun shining on your back door?" She rolled her eyes toward Joe.

"I like it," Catherine said, smiling. "I like it just fine."

Grandmamma reached up to pat her on the cheek. She nodded toward Abby and Cherry. "You say your vows fast, sweet thing. You don't want to spend this day delivering babies."

"I will," Catherine promised. "I'm going to leave that to you and Dr. Clarkson."

She waited until Grandmamma had moved on. "Where in the world did you meet Sasha's grandmother?" she asked Joe.

"Oh," he said airily, "around."

"Around where?"

"You know, I knew you were going to ask me that."

"Joe, where?"

"She sort of . . . came out to the building site to see me."

"Grandmamma Higgins?" Catherine said incredulously.

"That's the one," Joe assured her. "And the rest of them."

"The rest of whom?"

"The rest of your baby chicks. The whole brood." He grinned. "They came out packed tighter than sardines in a red Volkswagen. The crew's still talking about it."

Catherine looked away, then back at him. "I'm not going to ask what they said," she decided, and he grinned. Whatever it had been, he didn't seem to hold it against her.

"Here's somebody you'll be glad to see," he said, and she looked around. Pat was making her way slowly up the steps, looking better than she had in weeks.

Catherine hurried to take her by the hand. "I didn't think you were coming!"

"Well, the blood count was a lot better yesterday and the groom sent somebody to pick me up. So, here I am." She grinned at Joe. "For a filthy beast you are one hunk," she said, and he laughed.

"Thanks, Pat," he said. "What can I do but try?" he added philosophically.

Catherine smiled, wondering when Pat had upgraded Joe from a semi-hunk to the real thing.

"I want to sit down close," Pat said. "I don't want to miss a thing."

"You want to sit beside Cherry and Abby? Grandmamma thinks they might go into labor today."

"Hell, no," Pat whispered with some alarm, and Catherine laughed.

"Charlie!" she called, motioning for her favorite usher to come closer.

He came on the run, a big grin from ear to ear.

"Pat, this is my almost stepson, Charlie. Charlie, will you seat Mrs. Bauer down close to the front?"

Charlie held out his arm for Pat to take. "You got it, almost Mom."

Catherine stood there smiling. She really thought he was going to do it—call her Mom. He had approached her privately to ask if she'd mind, explaining that he knew that maybe she was a little too young to have a son his age but that he had a solution for that. When and if people asked how old he was, she could tell them he was nine.

"Won't they wonder why you're driving a car?" she'd asked.

"Yeah," he'd answered mischievously. He was full of himself. Exactly like Joe.

"What?" Joe asked, because she was still smiling to herself.

"I love your son," she said. She loved Fritz too. She was prepared to love Della, if only she got the chance.

Michael was coming up the church steps—alone.

"It's okay," Joe said quietly to her. "I didn't expect anything."

He didn't expect it, but it was so painfully apparent that he'd wanted it. Catherine watched as he stepped forward to greet his brother with open arms.

"Thanks for coming, Michael."

"Thanks for coming? Joey! You think you can get married without me?" He gave Joe one of his infamous bear hugs. "Catherine?" he said, reaching for her next. "I tried," he whispered in her ear. "I told Della what she does now can affect the rest of her life. But . . ." He shrugged to show her how futile it had been.

"Michael, I just—"

"Don't worry, Catherine. You make Joey happy. That's what matters." He kissed her soundly on each cheek and went inside to sit down.

At least *he'd* come, she thought. She supposed that Della was somewhere being comforted by Margaret.

It was nearly time for the ceremony to begin, and Father Hammond came into the vestibule.

"You may kiss the bride," he said to Joe.

"Now? Aren't you jumping the gun here?"

"I am, but you look like you need it."

Catherine thought he looked like he needed it too. She put her arms around him and gave him a lingering kiss on the mouth.

"One more," he whispered, and she kissed him again.

"I love you, Joe."

"I love *you*—with all my heart. If I ever do anything, say anything about Lisa or anything like that that hurts you, I want you to tell me. Will you?"

She smiled up at him. "I'm not worried about that, Joe."

"I know, but sometimes I shoot off my big mouth."

She chuckled. She couldn't argue with him there.

She kissed him one more time, then wiped the lipstick off his mouth with her fingertips. "Pat's right," she said, giving him a mischievous grin.

"About what?"

"About you. You *are* a hunk," she whispered. "And I'm going to keep you naked and in my bed for at least a week."

"Yeah?" he asked, returning her grin.

"Yeah," she assured him.

Father Hammond cleared his throat. "I thought we weren't dawdling. Let's get this ceremony on the road, children."

Catherine had wanted to make the wedding as personal as possible, so Fritz and Charlie stood with them at the altar. She had wanted Joe's son and daughter to know that she was marrying all of them, and having them as attendants had seemed the best way to express that.

But Della was so conspicuously absent.

"You may kiss the bride," Father Hammond said for the second time that day, and Catherine got more kisses than she'd bargained for—from Joe and from Charlie and from Fritz.

Laughing, the four of them moved together down the aisle to leave the church.

Fritz saw her first, stopping abruptly on the church steps so that Catherine bumped into her. She put her hands on Fritz's shoulders and smiled down at her, wondering a bit at the expression on Fritz's face.

"It's Della," Fritz said worriedly. "Della's here."

Catherine looked across the street. Della stood between two parked cars. She was wearing jeans and a short leather jacket, and she had her hands jammed in her pockets.

Joe had seen her as well, and he moved forward.

"Let me," Catherine said to him. "Let me go to her, Joe."

He hesitated, then nodded, taking Fritz by the hand. People were pouring out of the church, and Catherine left him standing in the middle of it.

She crossed the street, half expecting Della to run away from her. But she didn't. She stood there in the sharp March wind between the parked cars. When Catherine got closer, she could see that Della had been crying. Catherine's eyes searched that petulant, tearstained face, and she prayed for something to say, because now that Della had come, Catherine found that there was nothing she wanted to tell this child. If anything, she wanted to shake her until her teeth rattled.

Della looked at her warily, her eyes filled with contempt. How much of it was real and how much of it was bravado, Catherine couldn't tell.

"It's no use, is it?" Catherine said, and she could feel the tears welling in her own eyes. "I came over here to ask you one more time. I came to ask you to just *try*—to beg you if I had to—for Joe. But it's no use! I don't know what to do, Della! I don't! I *love* him. Are you going to punish him for that? Please . . . please don't hurt him anymore. He misses you so much. They all do." She stopped because she had to, because Joe was coming across the street and because she couldn't keep from crying. She knew that all the wedding guests were watching, and there wasn't a thing she could do about it. "Della!" she whispered fiercely, intending to make one last plea before he got there.

But she didn't have the time. Joe came and stood next to her and then Fritz and Charlie, all of them waiting, because it was up to Della to decide. The silence lengthened, and Della stood and stared back at the four of them, unrelenting and immovable.

"Come home," Joe said quietly. "I want—*we* want—you to come home."

She shook her head. No. *No.* But then her bottom lip began to tremble and the tears spilled down her face.

"I—" she began, but she suddenly stopped and bowed her head.

"Della—" Joe said, his own voice breaking with emotion.

Della looked up at him; Catherine could see the effort she was making. Her mouth still trembled and she wiped furiously at her eyes. She swallowed hard.

"I'm . . . late for your . . . wedding, Daddy," she whispered, and she flung herself into his arms. Joe rocked her back and forth, his eyes finding Catherine's. "Come here," he said, holding out his hand to her. "Come here, all of you."

They stood in the street, hugging, kissing, stopping traffic, but trying to mend the breach that had nearly torn them apart. They would have their work cut out for them, Catherine knew that, but they had made a start.

She leaned back so that she could look into Joe's eyes again. He smiled and she saw nothing but love there.

Three and a fifth children *and* him, she thought, except that it was more like three and *three*-fifths children now.

"I love you," she whispered, standing on tiptoe so he could hear.

The sun was indeed shining on her back door, and somewhere, not far away, a gnome mother named Daisy held her sleeping child and smiled.